Praise for Elmer Kelton

"Elmer Kelton is a splendid writer."
>—*The Dallas Morning News*

"One of the best of a new breed of Western writers who have driven the genre into new territory."
>—*The New York Times*

"Kelton is a master storyteller who offers more than just blood and gunsmoke. . . . The right blend of action, drama, romance, humor, and suspense."
>—*Publishers Weekly* on *Ranger's Trail*

"Wonderfully satisfying, sophisticated, unsentimental, superbly crafted, and full of a whopping good humor out of Twain. Hard to beat."
>—*Kirkus Reviews* on *The Buckskin Line*

"Kelton gives his characters flesh, bone, and body heat; puts them in believable situations; and tells their story with clarity and economy. If he isn't 'the best Western writer of all time,' he's awfully close."
>—*Booklist* on *The Buckskin Line*

Forge Books by Elmer Kelton

AFTER THE BUGLES

AND

LLANO RIVER

Elmer Kelton

FORGE®

A TOM DOHERTY ASSOCIATES BOOK | NEW YORK

This is a work of fiction. All of the characters, organizations, and events portrayed in these novels are either products of the author's imagination or are used fictitiously.

AFTER THE BUGLES AND LLANO RIVER

After the Bugles copyright © 1967, 1995 by the Estate of Elmer Kelton

Llano River copyright © 1966, 1991 by the Estate of Elmer Kelton

A Forge Book
Published by Tom Doherty Associates
175 Fifth Avenue
New York, NY 10010

www.tor-forge.com

Forge® is a registered trademark of Macmillan Publishing Group, LLC.

ISBN 978-0-7653-9339-5

Our books may be purchased in bulk for promotional, educational, or business use. Please contact your local bookseller or the Macmillan Corporate and Premium Sales Department at 1-800-221-7945, extension 5442, or by e-mail at MacmillanSpecialMarkets@macmillan.com.

First Edition: March 2017

Printed in the United States of America

0 9 8 7 6 5 4 3 2 1

CONTENTS

AFTER THE BUGLES

1

The bodies would lie there till they went to dust, for Santa Anna had lost the battle. And with the battle, he had lost the war.

His saber-cut arm resting in a loose sling, Joshua Buckalew silently waited while his horse was being saddled. His sober gaze drifted across the still and somber San Jacinto battlefield, where score upon score of lifeless Mexican soldiers lay crumpled on the ground or bogged in black mud or floating in the reedy marshes of Buffalo Bayou. Two days ago a swaggering Santa Anna had gone into his tent for siesta, confident that he held victory in his hands, for he had a ragged rabble of hungry Texans backed against the bayou. He awakened in panic to find the sodden plain slashed by musket and rifle and cannonfire, his red flag trampled by desperate men whose voices clamored in fury above the thunder of the guns: "Remember the Alamo! Remember Goliad!"

Now it was over. The war was won. A victorious army had repaired to its camp at the edge of the plain, shouting for the blood of the captured Napoleon of the West. Big Sam Houston, nursing a shattered ankle, grimly refused to let them have him. Dead men write no treaties, he declared. And Texas would have her treaty of independence.

Home. The exultation had faded now in the barren stillness of the battlefield, and the Texans thought of home. A bitter taste lay sharp in Joshua Buckalew's mouth, for he knew his home lay in ashes. What the retreating Texans hadn't burned, the Mexican army had. He gazed westward, his mind reaching far beyond what his pain-pinched eyes could see. He knew the desolation that waited there: the gutted homes, the burned-out towns, the unmarked graves scattered from here to the Rio Bravo. The land itself still lay there, neglected but otherwise unchanged by the war, still possessed of the elusive promise that had drawn Americans by the thousands into Mexican-owned Texas to colonize under the laws of Mexico. Yes, the land remained, but everything else would have to be built back again with sweat and blood and determination. After all those hard years of work and privation and gradual accomplishment—years that had drifted away in smoke—Joshua Buckalew wondered if he still had it in him.

Times, winning the war is only the beginning of the battle. After the bugles fall silent, there is always the long road back.

Short, shaggy-haired Muley Dodd finished saddling Buckalew's horse and looked worriedly at the sling. "Josh, you reckon maybe we ain't rushin' a mite? You'd travel better if that arm wasn't so angry-lookin'."

Joshua Buckalew had been standing hunched in unconscious deference to the throbbing arm. Now he drew himself to his full five-feet-eleven. "It'll heal as good on horseback as here in this cursed swamp. I've seen enough of San Jacinto to last me a lifetime."

There was another reason to be moving on. He looked

gravely at Ramón Hernandez, who finished lashing a blanket-wrapped bundle across the back of a captured Mexican packhorse. Beneath that blanket lay the body of Antonio Hernandez. "Ramón wants to bury his brother at home. If the weather turns warm, we got no time to waste."

In the early 1830s, Joshua Buckalew and his older brother Thomas had come to Texas from Tennessee to try to build a home in Stephen F. Austin's new land. They had drifted west and west and west, until at last they found what they wanted far beyond San Felipe de Austin, beyond even the Colorado River, near the Mexican colony where the Hernandez family squeezed a living out of the raw frontier by plowing their fields and raising cattle and catching wild horses. The Buckalews, copying the pattern, farmed some and branded wild cattle and broke mustangs to trade for supplies and now and again a handful of hard money in the eastern settlements. It had been a primitive life, in the main. But the Buckalews by their nature had been west-moving men, ever since Grandpa had frozen his feet that winter with George Washington.

Then had come Santa Anna, bringing cannon and sword to impose a terrible will upon his own people, finally crossing the Rio Grande to lay the same lash across the shoulders of the *Americano* colonists. He had slaughtered his way up by the Alamo and La Bahia. At Goliad, Thomas had fallen, cut down with more than three hundred other helpless prisoners in the shadow of that grim stone fortress. Joshua Buckalew had been among the fortunate few who escaped in the confusion of smoke and fire and dying men.

Now, suddenly, he still didn't completely comprehend it—the war was over. From Houston's camp the prisoner *presidente* had sent orders by courier for all Mexican troops to retreat beyond the Rio Grande. Texas no longer belonged to Mexico; it was a free and sovereign republic, rich in land and hope, but in all other things as poor as Job's turkey.

This was April. Time to go home now and plow the corn.

Muley Dodd pointed westward across the intermittent stretches of water which dotted the greening plain. Heavy rains all month had made eastern Texas a hell for both armies—Mexican and Texan. It would be slow, traveling home. "It's awful far, Josh," Muley worried. "You reckon we can make it there with Antonio?"

Josh shook his head, for he had his doubts. "We'll try."

Except for a bit of sugar, coffee and cornmeal scrounged from among the defeated Mexicans—who were poorly fed themselves—they would have to live off the land. But Texas had deer and wild turkey aplenty, and sometimes bear. Farther west, where the settlements thinned, there would be wild cattle descended from the original mission herds. The diet was monotonous sometimes, but nobody ever starved.

Josh swung carefully up onto his horse, favoring the wounded arm, sucking a sharp breath between his teeth as the pain gripped hard.

Ramón Hernandez' brow creased. "Josh," he said in Spanish, "that arm will give you trouble. Perhaps it is better if you wait a few more days. I can get home alone."

Josh doubted that. A lone Mexican rider caught by a roving Texan patrol would probably be shot before he could bring out his army papers and explain that he had fought in Juan Seguin's Mexican company on the side of Sam Houston. The dark brown man's skin would be taken as evidence enough that he belonged to the enemy.

Josh replied in English. They did that most of the time, the two, each talking in the language that came easiest but understanding the other nevertheless. "I'll heal." He glanced at little Muley Dodd, who was off saying his goodbyes to men he had met in Houston's camp. "Besides, I'll be obliged for your help. Muley's intentions are good, but sometimes his results are poor."

"He fought well," Ramón pointed out.

Josh nodded but held his opinion. Muley had always been what people charitably called "slow." Like some lonesome hound dog, he had attached himself to Josh and Thomas and had trailed along with them all the way down from Tennessee. He had no home, so the Buckalews gave him one. Muley was good help if someone told him what to do; he would break his back without a whimper. But he had to be watched like a child whose curiosity outweighs its judgment.

The matter settled, they rode in silence among the huge old oaks, from which the long beards of Spanish moss hung in cheerless disarray like funeral wreaths. Josh never looked back. Most of the time he gazed through the rain at the trail ahead, though now and again he quietly studied the faces of Muley Dodd and Ramón Hernandez.

Ramón. Pity, what the war had done to Ramón. He had always been the jovial one, quick to smile, quick to sing, the best at roping wild cattle, the quickest to throw a raw-treed Mexican saddle on an unbroken mustang and swing up shouting. His brother Antonio had been the grim one, never smiling, never seeing anything but the flat and the gray and the black. Now Antonio lay wrapped in that blanket, dead, and Ramón had taken on the face of Antonio . . . solemn, unsmiling. It was not a face that fit him. But that was the way of war.

They rode hunched against the slow, chilling rain, minds running over the violence they had put behind them. Ramón's and Josh's, anyway. Muley seldom thought back. His mind was always foraging ahead, flushing out one wild notion after another, the way a pup flushes rabbits but seldom catches one.

Muley's stubbled face twisted as he tried to puzzle through an idea. "Josh, them fellers at camp, they was tellin' me Texas don't belong to Mexico no more. They was tellin' me it's a republic. That's really somethin', ain't it?"

"I reckon so, Muley."

"I thought it must be." He frowned. "Josh, what *is* a republic?"

"Well, Muley, it's . . ." Josh didn't know quite what to tell him. "It means we're free, Muley. We're independent."

"You mean we're like a slave that's had his chains took off?"

"Somethin' like that. We belonged to Mexico and had to do what they told us to. Now we do what we want to."

"Like, we don't have to work no more unless it suits us?"

Josh scratched his head. "Look, Muley, a man is free,

but still he *ain't* free. I mean, nobody can tell him he's got to work, but if he don't, he goes hungry. It's like that with a republic. It's free from other countries, but it ain't ever free from responsibility. It's got to raise food or starve. It's got to make its clothes or go naked. It's got to keep up an army or its enemies will run over it. In other words, it's got to take care of itself. Nobody else is goin' to."

Muley fretted. "Used to, we could just let Mexico worry about all them things. Maybe we was better off when we wasn't free."

Josh shook his head. Trying to explain politics to Muley was like trying to empty a river with a wooden bucket.

Ramón rode along listening, his black-whiskered face furrowed in thought. "His talk is not all foolish, Josh. It is not easy to be free."

"You wishin' we hadn't fought?"

"I wish we had not had to. We fought because of Santa Anna, not because of Mexico herself. It is as if we had to spit in the face of our mother."

"A mother who beat and chastised us?"

Ramón's face was sad. "But still a mother."

Josh knew no way to reply, and he didn't try to. He knew Ramón's tie to Mexico was one of tradition and blood. Josh had felt a strong tie once, too, but mostly one of gratitude for opportunities offered. That tie had not been strong enough to endure, once the trouble began. Josh thought he could understand Ramón's feelings, even though he was unable to share them. And therein lay one of the main factors that had brought difficulty in the first place. The cultural difference between the new

Americano settlers and the native Mexicans had been too great for deep understanding. Even when the hand of friendship was extended, there had been reservations and mistrust. The settlers tried hard, many of them, but even between good friends such as Ramón Hernandez and Joshua Buckalew there remained that last tiny distance they could never quite reach across, that final measure of understanding that never quite came.

It's not our fault, and it's not theirs, Josh thought. *The Bible said all men would be imperfect. Take a horse to a strange country and he'll always try to go back home, to stay with what's familiar to him. Men are no different.*

They made a long ride in the rain and at dusk camped in the ruins of a homestead the Mexicans had put to the torch. Under a caved-in shed they found blackened wood which hadn't been altogether burned away and which was still dry enough to set ablaze. They made coffee and ate cold *tortillas* and huddled around the meager warmth of the little fire, trying to dry out. The damp cold brought a new ache to Josh's arm, and it showed in his face.

"Josh," Muley worried, "you ain't fixin' to get sick on us, are you?"

"Long as we keep travelin' west, I'll make it."

"Don't you worry none, Josh. I'll take care of you."

The thought was pleasant, if not reassuring.

The rain stopped next morning, but they rode across a trackless country, for any sign of recent movement had been washed away. So far as they could tell, they were the first to travel here since the fighting had ended. They came upon mute evidence of the terrible "Runaway Scrape" which had swept across Texas after the fall of the Alamo and the horror of Goliad. They saw burned-out houses. Along the trail they found abandoned sleds and scattered remnants of the loads they had carried. These had been left behind when the livestock broke down and were unable to pull further, or when pressure of the Mexican army forced fleeing settlers to leave their possessions, mount their animals and make a wild run for the Sabine River and the sanctuary which awaited on the other side.

Twice they came across broken-down wagons, only a fractured wheel and the wagon bed itself remaining, the good wheels having been salvaged. Always they searched the relics for food or useful items, but inevitably someone else had done it first. Whatever one man threw away or abandoned, some other man had need of. Texas had nothing to waste, those days. Nothing but land.

Riding, Joshua Buckalew looked back occasionally in cold regret at the burden which trailed behind on the packhorse.

The day was long. His arm throbbed with fever, and each step the horse took came as a jolt of pain. The cold *tortillas* lay like lead in Josh's stomach. Muley frowned. "Josh, you ain't lookin' good."

Ramón reined up and pointed his chin. "*Mira, hombre,* over there. I see a trace leading off into that canebrake. It is so faint I almost missed it. If we follow it, we might find something."

After all the years of exposure, Muley had picked up only a smattering of Spanish. He understood only enough to scare him. "Like what?" he asked, full of doubt.

"Whatever it is, it will be no worse than what we have. Maybe a house the Mexican soldiers missed. Maybe hot food."

"And maybe Mexicans," Muley worried.

Josh had to blink to keep the haze cleared away, for his fever was rising. The trace could have been an old one, not used in a long time. At any rate, it had not been used since the rains. The horses were making tracks six inches deep in the mud. Anyone else's would have done the same. "Let's try it. If we don't find nothin', we can always come back."

The trail meandered through the dense growth. It had been used fairly recently, for cane had been hacked away to clear a path. The horses floundered through the swales, and the packhorse almost fell. Ramón desperately fought to keep it from crushing the body of his brother.

Josh had a futile thought: *It's too far. We'll never get Antonio home.* But he knew that so long as Ramón wanted to, they would keep trying.

They came at length to a sappy-green clearing. A log cabin stood in the center of it. A pair of muddy dogs bounded out to meet them, barking, but they were not hostile. They were tickled to death to see a human being, for they circled around and around the riders and tried to move right under the horses' feet.

"*Hyaww,*" Muley shouted at them, waving his arms. "*Hyaww!*"

The horses snorted and shied. Muley's let fly with a hind foot, narrowly missing the younger and less observant of the dogs. In the yard, hogs grunted and scattered, a pair of them bumping and squealing, teeth flashing. Chickens flapped their wings and fluttered out of the way, clucking and cackling.

Muley grinned, for chickens meant eggs, unless these

two dogs abandoned to hunger had been sucking them all. "I could eat half a dozen of them hens, feathers and all."

Ramón said quietly, "This place belongs to somebody."

Muley replied, "He must've lit out in a right smart of a hurry. Probably figured old Santa Anna was grabbin' at his shirttail, him leavin' all this behind."

"He probably intended to come back to it. If we eat his chickens, he will have no eggs. And if he has no eggs, he will have no more chickens."

Seeing disappointment in Muley's eyes, Josh said, "Don't fret yourself, Muley. If we don't find somethin' else, we can kill one of them fat barrows. Man don't get any pig crop out of a barrow."

Josh eased down from the saddle, cautiously holding the arm tight against his ribs but feeling the pain anyway. Muley took his reins. "Go set, Josh. I'll take care of the horse."

The dogs reared up, licking at Josh's hands. One bumped his arm and caused him to double over from the shock of it. Muley came shouting. "Git, dogs! Git, I say!" The dogs took after Muley then. Seemed natural, somehow. Dogs had always taken a liking to Muley, the way they would to a kid. Perhaps they sensed that in ways he was just a boy.

Rain had caused the rough wooden door to swell tight, but Ramón pushed it open. The cabin smelled musty from the rain, and from the fact that all the shutters had been closed. In those times there probably were not three sheets of glass in a hundred miles. Ramón opened the shutters to let the air circulate and told Josh to sit down.

But Josh had been in the saddle all day. He wanted to move a little. The arm would hurt anyway.

Muley poked around and discovered a cribful of corn, part of which he shelled for the horses. He brought some to the cabin for supper. Josh found the smokehouse, cured hams hanging from the rafters, and abundant supplies of bacon. Muley took dry wood from under a shed and kindled a blaze in the stone fireplace while Ramón whittled the outer edges off of a ham and threw them to the half-starved dogs. Ramón started coffee boiling in a can and from somewhere rustled up a pan. Muley ground the corn for bread, and they all ate as they hadn't eaten in weeks.

Afterwards, a momentary smile crossed Ramón's face as he leaned back, his stomach full. Josh took pleasure in the sight, for he hadn't seen Ramón smile since San Jacinto. For a while then, Ramón had forgotten the blanket-wrapped burden that lay yonder in the shed, out of reach of the hogs.

Josh said, "What are you thinkin' about, Ramón?"

Ramón's voice was quiet. "Of home. Of Miranda, and the baby I have not yet seen. What do you think of, Josh?"

"Of home. And of a girl."

"María? My sister?"

Josh nodded.

Ramón smiled and changed the subject. "It is a good house, this one."

Josh shrugged. Actually, it was a crude cabin built hurriedly of logs and later chinked with liberal slivers of wood and heavy dabs of plaster in an effort to seal out the wind and rain. But they had been so long out of doors, a chicken coop would look good. "By rights," he said, "they ought to've destroyed this so it wouldn't fall into Mexican hands."

Ramón said, "But aren't you glad they didn't?"

Next morning they ate their fill again. Perhaps it was the food; perhaps it was sleeping dry and warm in a house; but at any rate, Josh felt better. The fever had gone down. He stood in the open door and stared across the clearing into the orange sunrise. Not a cloud was in sight.

Muley said, "I wish we could stay here a week."

Ramón looked gravely toward the shed. "We can't."

"Just wishin', is all."

When the three men rode away, they carried one of the hams and some bacon from the smokehouse. The rest they left behind, for it belonged to someone else. Maybe he would return, and maybe he wouldn't. In the Runaway Scrape, many hadn't stopped until they had crossed the Sabine River into United States territory. Once there, some would never return to the uncertainties of a land which lay so near to hostile Mexico, no matter how great Sam Houston's victory. But if this one *did* return, he would not find his property looted. At least, not by Josh and Muley and Ramón. They took only what they needed, and in exchange they left behind a Mexican rifle Muley had picked up on the battlefield. A rifle was something a man could always use.

The dogs followed a long way before they gave up and quit, forlorn as lost children. The three riders did not retrace their steps but instead followed a faint old trace that led southwestward. It hadn't been cleared in a long time and was often slow going. The sun had risen halfway to the meridian before they broke out of the canebrakes and into open prairie.

They hadn't gone two hundred yards when suddenly they wished they had stayed longer at the cabin. Half a dozen horsemen appeared unexpectedly in front of them. Josh had seen enough Mexican cavalry the last few weeks that he recognized these at a glance.

The surprise was as great to the Mexicans. They sat staring, not a hundred yards away. Ramón wheeled his mount and pulled the packhorse after him. "Back to the brakes!"

Whatever worry Josh's arm might have been, he forgot all about it. For a wild instant he could hear the guns of Coleto Creek, and the brutal massacre of Goliad. He spurred like a wild man. The horses tried, but their feet dug deep into the wet ground, and their hoofs left a shower of mud behind them. Shots rattled. Ramón shouted, and his horse went down, sliding on its side. The packhorse jerked free and kept running. Ramón crawled away from his horse as it lay threshing. Josh leaned low to pull Ramón up behind his saddle but to no avail. Ramón tried to get up but went down again. Blood spread across the torn leg of his trousers.

Josh shouted, "Muley, you keep a-ridin'!"

But Muley had stopped. And then there was no use in running, for the Mexican soldiers had closed in around them, and there was nowhere to go. The rifle under Josh's leg might just as well have been in Tennessee for all the good it did. The Mexicans would have put half a dozen holes through him before he could have drawn it. He looked into their rifles and slowly raised his good arm.

Muley drew close, his face paling. "What'll we do now, Josh?"

"Pray some. And do what they tell us to. Climb down

slow, so they won't get nervous and shoot you. We got to see about Ramón."

The Mexicans grabbed the horses as quickly as Josh and Muley touched the ground. Josh knelt by Ramón. "How bad, *compadre*?"

His face pinched in pain, Ramón pointed his chin toward the officer in charge. "Not good. It will be worse, I think. We will all get a bullet in the head."

The officer dismounted with the flair of a man in triumph. Of all the riders in the patrol, only he seemed to carry a pistol. The others carried cumbersome rifles or the clumsy *escopetas* that had enough recoil to knock a man out of his saddle. The officer waved the pistol and announced sharply that all three men were his prisoners.

Josh pointed at Ramón and said in Spanish, "This man is wounded." The officer seemed to ignore Josh. His eyes were hostile as he stared down at the bleeding Ramón. "You are Mexican. Why do you ride with these *Americanos*?" Ramón replied cautiously that they were friends.

"No *Americano* can be friend to Mexicans while there is a war."

"There is no war. Not anymore. Have you not heard?"

The officer showed surprise, but he remained wary. "I have heard nothing."

Ramón gripped his leg, his face twisting as the fire of it began to break through the numbness of the first moments. "The war is over. *El general* Santa Anna has ordered all troops across the Rio Grande."

The officer stared at Josh in puzzlement. "Then we have won. But why are these *Americanos* here?"

Ramón shook his head. "Santa Anna did not win. He lost. There was a big battle at San Jacinto. Houston and the *Tejanos,* they won it."

"You lie!"

"It is the truth, I swear by the Holy Mother."

The officer's hard gaze shifted from one man to another. "Men are sometimes known to lie, even by that which is holy."

Josh said in Spanish, "What he tells you is truth."

The officer's pistol wavered. Josh thought he was likely to fire it at any minute. "No *Americano* is to be believed. And a Mexican who would ride with an *Americano* is even worse. I think I will shoot all of you and end these lies."

One of the Mexicans had ridden out after the packhorse, which had stopped at the edge of the canebrake. Now he came leading the animal. The officer turned to Ramón. "What is tied on the horse?"

"My brother."

The officer's eyes widened. Ramón went on painfully, "My brother died in the battle I told you about. We were trying to get him home to bury him in holy ground with my mother and my father."

The Mexican who had fetched the horse said with face twisting. "He may be telling the truth, *capitán*. Something is dead beneath that blanket."

"Untie it!"

The Mexicans' horses were shying away, their nostrils keenly aware of the smell of death. A couple of the soldiers eased the bundle to the ground. They unwrapped it gingerly, wanting to get the job over with and move away. Josh didn't look as the blanket was pulled back.

He didn't want to see. Ramón turned his head away, too. Muley knew no better than to look, and his face went white.

They would never have gotten home with Antonio.

The officer swore. "That is the uniform of a cavalry-man."

Ramón nodded, his face grave. "My brother was in the army of Santa Anna."

Only then did Joshua Buckalew begin to doubt that they were all about to die.

2

The officer motioned for the two soldiers to spread the blanket back over the body. They did so hurriedly and moved away. The officer studied Ramón, his disbelief fading. "You say we lost. How badly?"

"Very badly. Many hundreds were killed."

"And *el presidente*? Did he fight gallantly?"

"He fled in the uniform of a common soldier. The *Tejanos* found him anyway. Sam Houston has him as a prisoner. *El presidente* sent messages by courier for all Mexican army units to retreat from Texas."

"We have been on a long patrol. We have heard nothing."

The soldiers showed it. They were ragged and dirty, and some of them looked sick and emaciated. Their threadbare uniforms showed evidence of being rain-soaked many times and drying on their chilled bodies. Santa Anna had brought most of his troops up from deep in Mexico, ill-fed, ill-clothed, poorly prepared for a climate far colder than they were accustomed to.

The officer said to Ramón, "Your brother was in uniform. You are not."

Ramón shrugged. "There were not enough uniforms for all who volunteered." It was not in Ramón's nature to tell a deliberate lie, Josh knew. But he *could* tell only that part of the truth which would serve to convey a false idea. Josh held his breath, hoping Ramón could get away with it.

The officer still worried. "You say *el presidente* fled. Did he not first lead the charge against the *Americanos*?"

"He did not charge. He was caught asleep."

The officer nodded bitterly. "That, I believe. He has always been a vain fool, Santa Anna. Mexico will be better off without him."

Listening, Josh was surprised. He had not fully understood that many of the Mexican army officers who gave the tyrant their professed loyalty harbored a carefully hidden contempt. They had little genuine regard for the callous bumbler who fancied himself the new Napoleon but sacrificed his soldiers with no more remorse than if they had been pawns in a chess game.

Ramón said, "He has given Texas away."

The officer swore. "After all the blood that has stained this land?" At length he gave the sad Mexican shrug that signified resignation to fate. "Mexico will be better off without Texas. It is too far from the mother country to be of value. It is a back-breaking land, full of trouble and tears. It is not good enough for Mexicans. Let the accursed *Americanos* have it. It will serve them right."

He ordered his men to bind up Ramón's wound. The

job done, one of the men motioned toward Josh and Muley. "What of these? Are we to leave Texas and not get
to kill even one more *Americano*?"

The officer frowned. "I am tempted, but they are
friends of this man. We shall do them no harm. Let them
stay and struggle in this hell they call Texas. That is a
punishment worse than death." He turned to Ramón and
pointed at the blanket. "You said you were taking him
home. How far is that?"

Ramón told him. The officer shook his head. "You
have carried him too far already. A soldier should be
buried where he falls, with honor. We shall bury him
here."

"It is not holy ground."

"When it receives the body of a Mexican soldier, it
becomes holy."

Ramón made no more protest, for by now he could see
his hope had been in vain. Besides, Ramón would be in
no shape to ride now, not for several days.

The ground was soft from the rains. Muley and the
Mexicans dug with bayonets and their hands and a
bucket that Josh carried for boiling coffee. The hole,
when they finished, was far from six feet deep, but it was
better than the Mexican soldiers were getting at San
Jacinto. It was better than the Texans had gotten at the
Alamo and Goliad.

The Mexicans crossed themselves and the officer said
a short Latin prayer and they covered the hole. They con-
fiscated the ham and bacon, the coffee and corn. They
rode south, leaving the three men at the edge of the canebrake.

Ramón sat on the ground, his bandaged leg stretched

forward, face pale. "It is not what I had hoped for. But it is better than if we had left him on that slaughtering ground."

Josh said, "He saved us, Ramón. If they hadn't seen Antonio's uniform, they'd have killed us by now."

"God's plan, Josh. This war came between Antonio and me. For a while we were brothers no more, until we found him dead among the enemy at San Jacinto." Ramón made the same shrug of resignation as the officer. "God's plan. Man sees only what lies behind him. God sees what lies ahead."

The wounded horse lay still now. One of the cavalrymen had cut its throat as an act of mercy. Josh's mouth was still dry with the realization that he and his friends had almost ended the same way, and not through mercy. He told Muley to maneuver Ramón's saddle off of the dead horse and put it on the pack animal. Then, somehow, he and Muley got Ramón astride. They had no provisions left, and a long ride was out of the question for Ramón.

"We'll go back to the cabin," Josh said.

If they had to be stranded, this was a good place for a couple of cripples and a slow-moving Muley Dodd, he thought. Food was plentiful, and if it rained any-more the roof wouldn't leak. The settler who had built the place had done well for himself, considering the times. Nobody bragged much in Texas those days be-cause nobody had much to brag about, except perhaps endurance. But this man had a decently tight cabin. He had a good field, chickens, hogs, some scattered few cat-tle. And from evidence around the shed Josh was sure there had been a team and a wagon, which the settler no doubt had taken with him on the Scrape. Wagons were exceedingly scarce in pre-revolution Texas. A man who owned a wagon was considered well-to-do. If he owned two wagons, he was rich.

They had had a wagon once, the Buckalews. It had gone up in smoke like almost everything else they owned except the land itself.

Josh's arm healed faster than Ramón's leg, for it had several days' start. Mostly they laid around the cabin sleeping, eating, reading the handful of books they found there. Josh read them, anyway. Ramón could understand spoken English well enough but had to pick his way along slowly with printed words and soon wearied of it. Muley couldn't read at all. Muley spent his time running happily with the dogs, chasing after game but seldom catching any. He hunted bee trees, too, for he always had a knack at that. It didn't worry him that he found none. For Muley the fun was in the chase, not in the catching.

Ramón's leg kept him from pacing the floor, physically. He paced it anyway, in his mind. Josh could read his thoughts almost as well as he could read the books. Up yonder past the Colorado waited Ramón's wife and a new son. Because the time for her delivery was so near, there had been no question of taking her when he went east to join Juan Seguin's Texas-Mexican company. He had counted on the family's Mexican blood to be protection enough from Santa Anna's troops. Though Santa Anna had been ruthless with his own people south of the Rio Grande, up here he considered his war to be with the *Americanos*. His supply lines were stretched a thousand miles or more, so he needed the cooperation of the

Texas Mexican people. In large measure he got it, for he had proclaimed this a racial war, the Mexicans standing shoulder-to-shoulder against the evil blue-eyed *extranjeros* who had come from the other side of the Sabine under a gracious dispensation of the mother country and had then turned against her. But there were those such as the powerful Seguins of Bexar who saw Santa Anna as a blackguard and rallied some of the Mexican people to stand against him. That this made them allies of the *Americanos* could not help but cause them doubt and uneasiness at times. But they rallied just the same.

"We'll get home in due time, Ramón," Josh said.

"There is no due time. I want to be there *now*."

"That baby will wait for you."

"That baby will walk before I ever see him. I want to see them all . . . the baby, Miranda, my sister María . . ."

María . . . Josh went silent then, for he also began thinking of María, a tiny girl with raven hair and dark eyes who laughed and sang. It was a memory to make a man look west, and make him itch to be on the move again.

In a few days Josh's arm was no longer sore. All that remained was a little stiffness. He had read all the books and impatiently watched Ramón cripple around with a crude crutch he had whittled out of a limb, wishing the leg would hurry and heal so they could be on their way. Muley didn't care. He was having a good time with the dogs.

Then one afternoon Muley raced for the cabin, shouting, his face flushed with excitement. One of the dogs ran at his heels. Josh could hear the other one down in the meadow, setting up a racket. Instinctively Josh grabbed up the rifle he had brought from San Jacinto.

"Josh! There's people comin'! I seen them. There's people and horses and mules and some wagons."

"Not soldiers? Not Mexicans?"

Muley vigorously shook his shaggy head. "I seen a couple women."

Ramón pushed up from a chair and reached for the crutch. Josh motioned with his hand. "Stay put. If they're Texans and see you, they're apt to shoot first and ask about you later." He stepped out into the yard with Muley.

Muley eyed Josh's rifle with apprehension. "You reckon they'll come a-fightin', Josh? I already had enough fightin'. I sure don't want no more."

Josh shook his head. "Chances are it's the man who owns this place, come back to claim his own."

"Reckon he'll be mad because we been stayin' here, eatin' his vittles?"

"He'll understand. Anyway, that Mexican rifle we're leavin' will pay for all the vittles we could eat if we stayed a month. We ain't killed none of his layin' hens, or none of his sows. We've left the breedin' stock alone."

Three wagons moved out of a patch of cane and into the open meadow, in good view. Besides the teams, Josh figured there must be a dozen or so extra horses, some running loose, some being ridden by men and boys and one by a little girl. A small boy rode a gray mule.

A man in the lead raised his hand, and the procession stopped. The man touched heels to his horse and rode forward in a slow trot, leaving the others behind him. At the distance, Josh couldn't see their guns, but he had a feeling they bristled on those wagons like cactus. Fifty yards from the cabin the rider slowed to a walk and came in warily.

Muley whispered: "Looky there, Josh. He's got a rifle acrost his lap."

"I see it. Stand easy. Try to grin at him, why don't you?"

He said that to ease Muley's mind, for the violence of the past months had bewildered Muley. He was of a simple nature and had never raised his hand in anger against any man. Muley managed a grin of sorts, but his worried eyes showed it didn't go beyond his teeth.

The rider was tall and gaunt, in ragged homespun. Josh took him to be middle-aged until he came close enough for a look at his face. He was a young man. War and hard times had put years on his shoulders that the calendar didn't account for, Josh reasoned. Well, it had been hell for everybody. Big hands, sun-bleached eyes. Farmer, Josh figured, by the look of him. Most people were, in this country. The call for lawyers and such was none too strong. A man worked with his hands and his back. The rider held his left hand up as a sign his intentions were peaceful, but his right hand still gripped the rifle. Josh got a cold feeling he knew how to use it, and well.

"Howdy," Josh said. "Git down and rest yourself."

The man's eyes touched Muley a moment, then flicked suspiciously back to Josh. "Who be you, mister?"

"My name's Joshua Buckalew. This here is Muley Dodd."

"Names don't mean nothin'. I mean, how come you here? This your place?"

"Nope. Thought maybe it was yours. We was on our way home from San Jacinto."

The eyes narrowed. "How do I know you was at San Jacinto?"

"I just told you."

"If you was there, maybe you can tell me which wing Lamar's cavalry took."

"The right."

"And what horse was General Sam ridin' when the charge started?"

"A big white stallion. I don't know what they called him."

The man relaxed. "They called him Saracen." The hand went easy on the rifle. "I thought we was about the first to come back thisaway. When we seen your tracks dried in the mud, we figured you might be some kind of stragglers or renegades, foragin' around to see what you could steal. You already been here some days, I take it."

"We left pretty soon after the battle. We got this far and ran into a Mexican patrol."

The man's jaw tightened. "A patrol?"

"That was some days ago. I expect it's clear enough now. Of Mexicans, anyway."

"Folks in them wagons, they need a good night's rest. Horses need a feed."

"They can get it here. Mexicans must've missed this place."

"I don't expect they missed many." The rider swung down stiffly, for he had been on horseback a long time.

He held out his hand. "My name's Ocie Quitman." His gaze was steady and not unfriendly, but Josh saw pain deep in the pale eyes. There was no happiness in this man.

When Josh shook hands with him, Quitman noticed the stiff arm. "You get that at San Jacinto?"

"Saber cut. About healed now."

Bitterly Quitman said, "We all lost somethin' to Santa Anna. I wisht they'd of let us hang him. Him and all the rest of them. I wisht there was dead Mexicans strung on every tree limb from here to the Rio Grande!" His eyes hardened, and a cold shudder ran down Josh's back as he sensed the depth of Quitman's hatred.

Man, whatever you lost, it must have been really something.

Quitman waved, and the wagons moved again, the lead wagon's canvas sagging on uneven hoops that seemed to shift with each jolt of the wheels on the rough ground. Towering in the seat, hunched over the leather lines, was a big, square-shouldered, middle-aged farmer. His raw-boned wife sat beside him, her face all but hidden beneath a sagging bonnet. Halting his team, the big farmer handed the reins to the woman and climbed down, walking toward Josh, extending a huge hand that looked as if it could smite a mule to its knees. "Howdy, friend. We're sure glad to see a new face after all these days. My name's Aaron Provost. This here your place?"

Josh told him it wasn't, that they had stopped here to recuperate.

Provost said, "We was a little concerned at first over who you might be, but you got a good face."

Josh felt his bewhiskered cheek and wondered how the

farmer could tell. He couldn't remember when he had shaved. "You got a lot of people here."

"That yonder's my wife Rebecca. Them young'uns you hear whoopin' and hollerin' back there with the stock . . . the missus and I are responsible for all of them but one. The Lord's been more bountiful with children than He has with some of the other blessin's." He didn't say it as if he were complaining, and Josh doubted that Provost regretted sowing the seed. Provost pointed a thick finger. "Fellers on that middle wagon, they're Wiley McAfee and his partner Dent Sessum. That last wagon yonder, it belongs to Ocie Quitman."

Josh saw a woman sitting on the seat, handling the lines. "I suppose that's Mrs. Quitman."

Ocie Quitman turned away. Provost said, "No, it's the Widow Winslow. Heather Winslow. Husband fell to the Mexicans a while back. Ocie let her have the borrow of his wagon. That lad on the gray mule, he belongs to Ocie."

"How far you-all goin'?"

"Long ways yet. Rebecca and me, we had us a place up on the Colorado. The Quitmans, the Winslows, they was all nearby. Sessum and McAfee, they got no land as yet. They're just lookin'."

Josh counted the men who could use guns. "You got four men who can shoot if it comes necessary."

"Five. My eldest, Daniel, ain't but fourteen, but he's a right peart shot when he has to be."

"He might have to be. Last I knew, Comanches was prowlin' the western country, lookin' for easy pickin's. Didn't take them long to find out about the war. Them slow wagons make a good target of you."

Ocie Quitman came back. "Whichaway was *you* headed, Buckalew?"

"West."

"If you was to join up with us, that'd be seven guns."

"Eight. We got one more man in the cabin. Mexican patrol put a bullet in his leg."

Two dusty, lanky men in homespun and buckskins shared a whisky jug, then climbed down from the second wagon and lazily stretched themselves, one of them scratching his ribs. They didn't offer the jug to anyone else. One chunked a rock at the barking dogs. The other hungrily eyed the chickens. Josh featured them as being likely to spend a lot more time in the woods than in the fields.

The woman on the third wagon had her face shaded by a large bonnet similar to Mrs. Provost's, but when she turned toward Josh, he caught a glimpse of her features. He judged she was in her mid-twenties. The little boy reined his gray mule up beside her and stuck close, his large brown eyes abrim with curiosity as he stared at Josh and Muley, and with joy as he looked at the dogs.

Josh said, "She don't look old enough for a widow."

Provost replied, "Wartime, it don't take long."

"She's got no business goin' west again, a woman by herself."

"It's her land, and she's got no place else to go. No people left back in the States."

"She can't work a farm."

"She's stronger than she appears to be. Give her a few years and she'll look like my Rebecca yonder." Josh couldn't see that as a recommendation, but the farmer seemed to think it was. "Anyway, she's got determination. That counts for as much as muscle. And she's a fair handsome woman. I expect there'll be bachelors enough more than willin' to lend a hand." Provost appraised Josh with a wry squint. "You a bachelor, Buckalew?"

The dogs quit barking when the kids started hitting the ground. They made the rounds of first one child, then the next, tails twitching. A smile stretched across Muley's face, for Muley and dogs and kids had always been a happy combination. Before the war, he had gone often to laugh and run with Ramón Hernandez' kid brothers and sisters. Most of them were growing up now, but Muley never would.

Mrs. Provost took charge, shouting orders to the boys and girls from her perch on the wagon seat. The chickens fluttered and cackled in alarm as the youngsters ran around the yard to loosen their tired legs, the dogs yipping merrily after them. The man named Dent Sessum took a few steps in Josh's direction, impatience in his eyes. When Provost strode off to his wagon to speak with his wife, Sessum muttered, "A damned menagerie, that's what it is."

Dryly Ocie Quitman said, "*They* invited *you*."

Provost tramped back in a few minutes, leading his sun-browned wife by one arm. The young widow followed a few paces behind. "Rebecca . . . Heather . . . this here is Joshua Buckalew. I do believe that if we tried right hard we could talk him and his party into throwin' in with us as far as Hopeful Valley. We sure could use their company."

Mrs. Provost smiled pleasantly and proceeded to look Josh up and down as if she were buying a workhorse. She was a weathered but hardy woman who looked as if she could stand up to just about anything chance might decide to throw at her. Most of the early Texas women were that way. Those who weren't either died off or went back to where they had come from. Josh could feature Mrs. Provost skinning game, dressing a baby, quoting Scripture and cussing the weather all at the same time.

Heather Winslow said, "Mister Buckalew may not know me, but I know him."

Surprised, Josh stared. She slipped the bonnet back from her face. "Your farm was west of ours, a good ways. One time you stopped at our cabin on a trip to San Felipe with the old surveyor, Jared Pounce. Whatever became of Mister Pounce?"

"He was in the Alamo."

Her mouth went into a thin, sad line. "He was a good man. They were all good men." She dropped her chin and turned away. Josh figured she was thinking of her husband. He vaguely recalled now, though he wouldn't have if she hadn't spoken up. Jared Pounce, always fond of good vittles, had called her the "corn-dodger woman." She was smallish but strong. She had large blue eyes that would catch a man's gaze so that he didn't pay much attention to whether the rest of her was handsome or not. Josh would have considered her pleasant to look upon, though he would have hesitated to call her pretty. *María Hernandez* was pretty.

He said, "I remember. You-all had you a nice place started."

"It could've been a real good place. Lord knows my Jim tried. Seemed like bad luck always dogged him one way and another. Finally came the Scrape, and the Mexicans caught up to us while we were trying to reach the Sabine." She paused. "Do you remember my Jim?"

He shook his head. "Met him once, is all. I'm afraid I wouldn't know him if he was to come ridin' up here."

Sadness lay like blue ice in her eyes. "I wish he would. But he never will, not ever again."

Dent Sessum shouted to his partner, "Wiley, we're goin' to have fresh meat on the table tonight. See that fat sow yonder? She'd feed all of us for a month." Sessum walked toward her, rifle in hand, moving as if to haze her away from the wagons and shoot her.

Josh called to him, "There's cured meat in the smokehouse. You leave the man's livestock alone."

Sessum turned defiantly. "They ain't yours."

Josh moved closer to him. "They ain't *yours*, either. You'll eat cured pork, and you'll leave the sow to fetch more pigs."

For a moment he figured he was fixing to get an argument from Sessum. And if he did, he'd probably have Wiley McAfee to contend with too. Sessum muttered, "Some people act like they was meant to rule the whole blessed earth." But he turned on his heel and walked away from the sow.

Quitman said, "For what it's worth, Buckalew, they ain't no partners of mine."

Josh glanced at Aaron Provost, who seemed to feel obliged to explain his own position. "They had their own wagon, and they had guns. I figured we needed both."

Josh said, "I been hopin' when the war was over, we'd have a lot of new folks come in . . . folks of the better sort."

Quitman said: "These ain't the ones you been waitin' for, then. They was on the Sabine when the fightin' was goin' on at San Jacinto. But the Lord makes all kinds."

The big farmer remarked, "The buzzard as well as the eagle. The sparrow as well as the hawk."

They turned toward the cabin. Provost said, "We best see if the place can be made comfortable for the women-folk. They'll enjoy sleepin' under a roof. God knows they probably won't find one when they get home."

Ramón Hernandez had pushed to his feet. He hobbled to the door, leaning on the crutch.

Heather Winslow's hands went flat against her cheeks, and she screamed.

A hissing sound broke from Ocie Quitman. His rifle swung up. "A Mexican! A damned dirty Mexican!"

Josh grabbed the gun barrel, thrusting it aside. "Hold on! He's with us!"

He had expected momentary hostility; after the last few months it was only natural. But he was not prepared for the fury in Quitman's tight-drawn face. He wrestled with the man, who tried to wrench the rifle free of Josh's grasp. Instinctively Josh knew Quitman would kill Ramón if given the chance. Sharp pain lancing through his stiff arm, Josh shoved the weapon forward, jamming it into Quitman's belly. He jerked it to one side, wresting it from the big hands as Quitman coughed for breath. Quitman kept grabbing for the rifle as Josh stepped back. Josh blew the powder out of the pan.

"Quitman, I told you he's with us. He fought at San Jacinto too."

Quitman struggled for breath. "The hell! Which side was he on?"

"He was with the Juan Seguin company."

Quitman stopped trying then, his fists still clenched, his face dark. He stared at Ramón with eyes that wanted to kill.

Josh said: "You're not goin' to hurt him. He's my friend."

Quitman stared a moment longer at Ramón, then the sudden rage began to ebb. "To you, maybe, but not to me. No Mexican will ever be a friend of mine again."

He turned and strode toward the wagons, leaving Josh standing there with the rifle in his hand.

3

As Quitman neared Sessum and McAfee, Sessum spoke, "Just say the word, Ocie. We'll kill that Mexican for you."

Quitman made no reply.

Josh dropped Quitman's rifle to the ground and brought up his own, backing toward the cabin door, tensed and ready. The children had stopped running and stood watching open-mouthed. Aaron Provost had turned to watch Quitman, to see what he would do. But Quitman did nothing, except keep walking away. He strode past Sessum and McAfee as if they were not there. He didn't stop until he reached his wagon that the widow had been driving. He leaned against a rear wheel, his back turned, one hand gripping a spoke as he wrestled with whatever private devil was tearing at him.

Mrs. Winslow stood where she had been, except that

she had turned away from Ramón, her face paled, still twisted with the shock.

Josh thought now was the time to make one thing clear to everybody. He brought his rifle up across his chest, not pointing it at anybody but letting it be seen. What he had to say would be blunt, but it would not be misunderstood. "Get this down and be damned sure you swallow it, all of you. We're willin' to join you, but we don't have to. We got by before you came, and we can get by if you leave. If you want us, you got to take all three . . . me and Muley *and* Ramón. Anybody that moves a hand against Ramón has got me to whip."

Sessum muttered, "We fought a war to get rid of them Mexicans."

"Way I hear it," Josh spat, "*you* didn't fight nobody."

"We stood guard at the river. Somebody had to. Ain't our fault we never got to kill no Mexicans."

"You're not killin' this one. You better get that through your head."

Aaron Provost frowned, studying Ramón. "How long you known him, Buckalew?"

"Since we first come down from Tennessee."

"And you're sure of him?"

"As sure as I am of myself."

"Well, you're a man who's pretty sure of himself. Me, I didn't worry over Mexicans one way or the other before the war. They went their way and I went mine. Live and let live, was the way I seen it. If you stand up for him, he's all right as far as I'm concerned." Provost turned to face the other men. "We agreed when we started out that if there come a disagreement, we'd take a vote. So we'll decide whether we want Buckalew and his bunch to go with us. Whichever way it comes out, we don't bother Buckalew's Mexican. How about it, you boys?"

Sessum grumbled, "Damn Mexican is apt to stab a man in the back when he ain't lookin'. We ought to shoot him and be safe."

Provost's voice was as big as the man himself, when he became aroused. "But you ain't goin' to, is that understood?" Sessum reluctantly nodded, and McAfee followed suit. It seemed to Josh that whatever Sessum did, the other one tried to do the same. The farmer turned and called after Quitman. "Ocie, how about you?"

Quitman didn't answer until he was asked the second time. Slowly he turned his head. "Just keep him out of my sight!" He walked off beyond the wagon and stood looking across the meadow.

The farmer turned dourly to Josh. "We'll wait awhile to take that vote. Let Ocie have time to get hold of himself and think things through."

Josh said, "I reckon I already know how he'll vote."

"Don't be too quick to put a judgment on him. That'd be as unfair to him as he was to your Mexican. Ocie's got cause to hate. At least, he thinks so. And he's a good man to have on your side. I don't think I'd want him agin me."

Josh had already decided that. But Ramón had a prior call. Right now it didn't look as if there was a place for both of them.

Provost walked away with his wife. Heather Winslow said, "Buckalew . . ."

"Yes?"

"I didn't mean to set things off. It isn't like me to scream. But I didn't expect to see him. He just bobbed up there all of a sudden. He's the first Mexican I've seen since . . ." She looked at the ground.

Josh said, "Don't blame yourself."

She turned and looked toward Ramón, and Josh could tell it was an effort for her. Ramón stood in the doorway. He hadn't moved an inch.

"I'm sorry," she told him.

Ramón said in forced English, "It is for nothing. I did not mean for to scare you, *señora*."

"And I didn't mean to cause you any trouble."

Josh said, "Looks like trouble would've come whether you'd screamed or not."

Mrs. Winslow said, "I want you to know this, Mister Buckalew, if they let the women vote, I'll vote for all of you to go along."

Josh glanced at the wagon where Quitman had disappeared. "What about him?"

"What *about* him?"

"You ridin' on his wagon and all, I thought . . ."

Her blue eyes hardened a little. "Ocie Quitman is a kind man, inside. He saw I needed help, and he gave it. In return, I've been taking care of his little boy. I still think for myself."

"No offense meant, ma'am. I just didn't want to be the cause of trouble between you and him if there *was* anything . . ."

"There is not. Mister Quitman is a gentleman."

"I never thought no other way."

The new arrivals unloaded what they would need out of the wagons and hobbled the teams out on the meadow. When the men had finished the necessary chores, Aaron Provost summoned them all back beside his wagon. He cast one frowning glance at Josh and Ramón, then turned to the others. "Ain't no need us waitin' no longer to take a vote. We'd just as well get the air cleared so this thing don't lie there and simmer between us all night."

Ocie Quitman jerked his head toward Rebecca Provost and Heather Winslow. "How about the women? They get to vote?"

"You got any objection to it, Ocie?"

"Everything we do affects them the same as us. I say give them a vote."

Aaron nodded. "Suits me. Dent . . . Wiley . . . how do you-all feel about takin' Buckalew and his friends?"

Sessum scowled. "The Mexican too?"

Watching silent anger rise in Ramón, Josh said, "It includes him."

Sessum spat on the ground. "Then I say the hell with it." McAfee agreed. "We got on pretty good so far. We can do without them."

Aaron switched his gaze to Quitman. "Ocie?"

Quitman stared at Ramón. "I say no."

Aaron grimaced. "That's three against. Well, I don't agree. I think we're apt to be glad we took them along, even if one of them *is* a Mexican. I don't reckon the good Lord asked him his preference." He glanced at his wife. "Whatever I say, Rebecca will agree to. So I cast our two votes for takin' them with us. Heather, how do you vote?"

Josh was watching Quitman when Heather Winslow half whispered, "They ought to go with us. I vote yes." Surprise flickered in Quitman's eyes, and disappointment.

Aaron said, "Well, that winds us up in a tie. What do we do now?"

The silence hung so hot Josh thought he could light a fuse with it. Finally Quitman shrugged. "If the women-folk feel better to have them come along, so be it. But keep that Mexican out of my way! I don't even want to look at him!"

Aaron frowned. "Ocie, you have to understand that the war is over. As the Book says, we shall beat our swords into plowshares, and the lion shall lie down with the lamb."

Dryly Quitman replied, "They may lie down together, but the lion will be the only one that gets up."

Ramón moved out of the cabin when the women moved in. Both were silently apologetic. Ramón hobbled out to the shed on his cane while Muley and Josh carried their few belongings. Muley said, "Josh, how come they got it in for old Ramón the way they do?"

"Temper of the times, Muley. Me and you, if we was to go to Mexico we'd get treated the same way."

"It don't hardly seem fair."

"Nothin' is fair in war. Or in what follows after the war, either. Not here, not in Mexico, not noplace."

"Old Provost was right when he said the Lord didn't give Ramón no preference. Reckon if He had, old Ramón would've chosen to be American like us?"

"That's hard to say, Muley."

Muley's face brightened as he examined other angles of the notion. "The Lord didn't give *me* no preference, neither. You know somethin', Josh? If He *had,* I'd of sure been different than I am. I swear, I'd sure ask for a change."

"You would?"

"Yes, sir! I'd have brown eyes instead of blue ones."

They dropped their gear on the packed ground in the rude shed. Ramón carefully lowered himself to a sitting position, stretching his leg out in front of him. His eyes were averted from Josh, but the quiet anger clung to him like heat around a bad stove.

Josh said, "You oughtn't to blame them too much, Ramón."

Ramón gritted in Spanish, "That is what I keep trying to tell myself, but I can't hear it."

"We don't have to go with them. We'd figured all along on goin' by ourselves. We could get up and strike out in the mornin' and on to the Colorado River. We could even leave tonight."

The Provost children and the Quitman boy had followed at a respectful distance. For a few moments they stared from across the open corral that closed off the south side of the shed. Gradually they edged closer, poised to break and run if anybody raised a hand. Their attention was riveted to Ramón, their curiosity gradually overcoming the fear they had for his darker skin. A couple of the children whispered in the little Quitman boy's ear, and he firmly shook his head. They whispered again, nudging him forward. The boy took a few hesitant steps, glancing back over his shoulder to see if his friends were backing him up.

They had been around Mexicans before, Josh reasoned; they *must* have. But Ramón was probably the first they had seen since the Runaway Scrape.

The boy tried to speak but couldn't bring it out. A larger Provost boy stepped up and whispered in his ear again. Finally the little one blurted to Ramón, "Is it true? Are you really Santa Anna?"

Ramón held his silence a moment, his face unreadable. Finally a faint humor gleamed in his black eyes, and for a second Josh thought he was going to smile. "No," Ramón replied in English. "I am not Santa Anna. I am Sam Houston."

The boy's eyes widened in surprise. The other youngsters began to snicker, and the Quitman boy gradually realized he had been taken. "Awwww, you're not."

The other youngsters tittered and ran. The Quitman boy suddenly realized he stood all alone, and he whirled, racing across the corral and scaling the fence.

Ramón watched them go, and the gleam remained. "The wagons are slow. Do you think they will run into trouble?"

Josh said, "You never can tell about Comanches. They could be out west huntin' buffalo, or they could be up thisaway huntin' hair to braid their leggin's with. Not likely there's any Mexican soldiers left, but you couldn't take an ironclad oath on that either."

"And *renegados*?"

"Renegades, you got any time you have a war. Sneakin' around the brush pickin' up the leavin's, stealin' what they can, killin' if it comes handy."

Ramón said, "This war is not the children's doing. I have a son of my own now. If harm came to these little ones, and I had not done what I could, I would not feel entitled to enjoy my own son."

"Folks may treat you dirty, even when you help them."

"I have been treated dirty before. I have not died from it."

Bye and bye Heather Winslow came with a can of steaming coffee and some fried bacon. "Mister Buckalew, Mister Dodd, supper's ready up at the cabin. I brought this out for your friend. With his bad leg and all, I thought he'd rather not have to walk."

She glanced at Josh with apology in her eyes for the weak lie. Ramón accepted the food and coffee with dignity and quiet "*gracias*," but Josh knew he held no illusions.

Heather Winslow paused, looking back at Ramón with regret. "I am sorry, *señor,* for the way things are. Maybe they won't always be."

Ramón thanked her quietly, then stared at the plate. At length he asked, "Do you think it will get better, Josh?" Then he answered his own question. "No, it will get worse. It may get much worse."

They ate breakfast before daylight. Josh and Muley took theirs to the shed, along with Ramón's. They had decided that if Ramón wasn't welcome in the cabin, they wouldn't go either. After breakfast the men and boys hitched teams to the wagons and brought up the loose stock. Muley and Josh saddled their horses.

Ramón said, "Saddle mine too, will you, Josh?"

"With that leg, you'd better ride in a wagon."

"Which wagon?" Ramón grimaced. "The farmer Provost, he might take me, but his wagon is too loaded. McAfee and Sessum, they would not let me ride on their wagon even if I wanted to. And I do not want to."

"There's still the wagon the widow drives . . ."

"She would say yes, but the wagon belongs to Quitman,

no es verdad? I have no wish to cause her trouble from him. She is a widow. She will have need of him, I think."

"I'll talk to Quitman."

Ramón shook his head. "The leg is not so bad that I cannot ride. I will not beg or owe a debt to anyone. No one can later say he did a big good for this Mexican!"

Rebecca Provost took charge of loading her wagon, shouting orders to the children, who seemed endless in number, the way they swarmed over, around and through the wagon, getting the load settled and tied. Before long the Provost and Winslow wagons were ready to go.

"You-all roll out," Sessum told Provost. "Me and Wiley, we got somethin' to fix. We'll catch up to you directly."

Josh rode by their wagon and failed to see anything that appeared to be broken down. It would have suited him just as well if the two didn't catch up at all. Aaron Provost flipped his lines, shouting roughly, and his team strained against the traces. Heather Winslow followed, shouting in a voice that lacked the coarseness of Rebecca Provost's but which carried authority, nevertheless. Quitman's small son rode the gray mule again, dropping back to join the Provost youngsters in herding the loose stock a short way behind the wagons. The children whooped and frisked along. Whatever terror they had been through, they had shrugged it off. Or at least it appeared they had. Josh wondered, though, if sometimes it would not come back to them in the night, in the screaming horror of a nightmare that the mind is helpless to shut out. War had a way of leaving scars that didn't show.

The dogs followed the youngsters. Aaron yelled back for the kids to chase the dogs home, but nothing worked, not even chunking rocks at them. The dogs would tuck their tails between their legs, drop back a little but continue to follow.

Josh rode up beside the Provost wagon. "Looks like they're bound and determined to go. They been left here too long to want to stay."

Provost frowned. "I hate to git away with a man's dogs."

"He may not come back. You don't mind your kids havin' the dogs, do you?"

Aaron shook his head. "They ain't likely to have much else when we get home." Rebecca Provost nodded in solemn agreement. "War and hard times has robbed these young'uns. A dog or two would be good for them."

"Then," Josh said, "let's don't worry about it. A hog or a cow is property, but a dog is a free agent. He goes where he wants to and does as he pleases. If it pleases him to tag along with your young'uns, who's to blame?"

Presently, looking back, Josh could see the third wagon moving along, making some progress but showing no hurry about catching up. Every little while he would look back and gauge how much distance it had closed. The rate Sessum and McAfee were traveling, they wouldn't be up to the other two wagons till the noonday stop.

Suspicious, Josh turned his horse and started back toward the trailing wagons. Muley shouted, "Josh, where you goin'?"

"You stay here, Muley. I'll be back directly."

He heard a horse loping up behind him and turned to

speak sharply to Muley. He saw Ramón instead, the wounded leg thrust out. "Ramón, you just as well stay with the wagons."

"I am curious too."

"It'd tickle them to find an excuse to shoot you."

"I have been shot at by better men."

"You bein' there might cause trouble that I wouldn't otherwise have. I'd rather you stayed here, Ramón."

Reluctantly Ramón reined up. "I will watch from here. If it looks like a fight, I will come."

Josh rode in a slow trot. Approaching the wagon, he could see hostility. Sessum said, "You needn't have fretted none about us, Buckalew. We're gettin' along just fine."

Josh didn't say so, but that was the thought which made him fret. Tied to the rear of their wagon he saw chicken coops, quickly and crudely put together. He said brittlely, "Looks to me like you're doin' a mite *too* well. I told you yesterday, the breedin' stock belongs to somebody. You got no business takin' it."

"He may never come back."

"On the other hand, he might come back today. Ain't no use you robbin' him."

Sessum argued, "Think how good it'll be, havin' fresh eggs every day we're on the trail."

Josh was sure that even if they *did* have eggs, they wouldn't give him any. He judged the distance back to the cabin and decided the chickens would work their way home if he released them here. "You'll open them coops and dump them chickens out."

Sessum said stiffly, "We hadn't figured on it."

"Then figure on it now. Either you dump them out or *I* will."

Sessum's eyes narrowed. "Just because you done a little soldierin', you don't need to think you can run over the rest of us."

McAfee put in with a sneer, "Anybody who runs around with a stinkin' Mexican has got no call to think he's so much."

Josh rode toward the coops. The two men had packed so many chickens that half the birds would smother before the day was out.

Josh heard a metallic click that brought up the hair on his neck. Sessum gritted, "You touch that coop, Buckalew, and that Mexican is goin' to be awful lonesome, just him and that halfwit."

That was what did it, his calling Muley a halfwit. Josh reined around, turning his back on the coop. He took a hard look into Sessum's eyes and decided the man didn't have the guts to pull that trigger. Josh moved straight at the rifle. He grabbed the barrel of it with both hands and thrust the stock back as hard as he could. Caught by surprise, Sessum took the blow in the belly. He doubled over, coughing for breath as Josh jerked the rifle out of his slackened hands. Josh eased the hammer down and pitched the weapon out into the grass. Turning, he slipped a knife out of its sheath at his belt and slashed at the nearest coop. It was almost open when he heard the scuffling of heavy boots. He looked back to see Sessum climbing across the loaded wagon.

Sessum leaped at him. The impact and Sessum's weight dragged Josh out of the saddle and jarred him against the ground. The horse jerked loose and trotted away. Sessum pounded Josh with his fists. Josh tried to fend him off with his stiff arm while he struggled to free the other arm, pinned beneath him. He gripped Sessum's collar and yanked, then shifted his own weight and pulled the good arm out. Wrestling in the grass, the two men rolled into a narrow ditch that runoff waters had cut across the sloping hillside. Somehow Josh landed on top of him. He shoved his knee into Sessum's belly and took most of Sessum's breath. That put both of them on a fairly even basis, for the fall from the horse had taken most of Josh's.

Sessum wheezed, "Wiley, come help me."

But the struggle had excited the team, and McAfee's hands were full with the reins, fighting to keep the horses from running away. Josh picked up the knife from where it had fallen and finished slashing the coop open. The chickens rushed out with a flapping of wings and a sudden burst of squawking. Some landed on Sessum in their first attempt at flight. He threw his arms over his face, cursing. The horses kept dancing, wanting to run.

Josh started on the second coop as Sessum brushed the chickens away and pushed to his feet, feathers clinging to his dusty clothes. He rushed, cursing. Josh dropped the knife and met him halfway. He gave him a couple of underhanded licks he had learned back in Tennessee. They weren't fair, but no fight is fair unless you win it. Josh had no intention of losing this one.

Sessum doubled over. The horses had quit straining, and McAfee jumped down, ready to join the fight. But he stopped as a dark shadow fell across him. Ocie Quitman sat there on his horse. Behind Quitman, Ramón loped up, his leg outthrust.

Quitman said, "You better hold on, McAfee."

McAfee protested, "He don't look like God to me. He's got no call to be a-tellin' us what to do."

Quitman said calmly, "Then forget what he told you, and listen to what *I* tell you. Turn the rest of them chickens out."

McAfee pointed toward the other two wagons, which had halted. "They're takin' the dogs with them. I don't see where there's no difference in takin' the chickens and takin' the dogs."

"Only way them dogs would stay here would be if you tied them, and then they'd starve to death. But the chickens will stay if you don't tote them off. And you're not goin' to." His eyes were sharp as fine-honed steel. "Now do what I said and open them other coops."

Sessum was on his feet now, glaring at Josh but not putting up any resistance to Quitman. There was a look about Quitman which reminded a man of a loaded rifle, pointed straight at him. Sessum picked up Josh's knife from the ground and cut the coops open, releasing the rest of the chickens. Feathers floated in the morning breeze. Done, Sessum hefted the knife, then hurled it sideways at Josh. Josh's instinct was to duck away from it, and he had to go and fetch it after it fell.

By now Ramón had arrived, but there was nothing for him to do except watch. He did that in silence.

Sessum jerked his chin at Josh and said to Quitman, "I don't know what you have to go and take up his fight for. None of us ever even seen him till yesterday."

"It ain't for him. I just believe in doin' what's right, and carryin' off a man's chickens ain't right. You ought to see that for yourselves."

"All I can see is this Buckalew, makin' out like he was the Lord of all Creation."

"Forget about Buckalew, then. You just worry about *me*."

Quitman turned his horse and started back toward the other wagons. As if he considered the incident over and done with, he never looked behind him.

"That man," Ramón murmured, "is like ice in the river."

Josh said: "I'd sure rather have him for me than against me. Right now I don't think he's either."

Ramón observed, "He is against *me*."

4

Heather Winslow let the leather lines sag in her hands as the wagon creaked slowly through the greening grass. Now and again her eyes followed the hopping frogs, brought out by the recent long spell of rains. She flinched each time a wagon wheel crushed one, its body making a distinct "pop" as it exploded under the weight of the iron rim. She was glad Quitman's boy Patrick was back yonder on that gray mule, riding with the Provost youngsters, for it upset him to see the frogs die. He had seen too much of death already for a boy of five.

She glanced back over her shoulder when she sensed that the children had grown quiet for the first time all day. They rode sleepily in the pleasant warmth of the mid-afternoon sun, loose-herding the extra stock, keeping it drifting along after the wagons. She sought out Patrick and beckoned until he saw her. He rode up, trying to push the lazy mule into a fast trot but unable to get him out of a walk.

"Sleepy, Patrick? Why don't you crawl up here with me and take a nap?"

He nodded. "All right, Mrs. Winslow." She had tried to get him to call her Heather, but the training was too strong in him. A boy called a grown woman Miss or Mrs. That was Ocie Quitman's teaching. She stopped the wagon to let him tie the mule at the tailgate. Climbing up, he stretched his short frame in the wagonseat, legs hanging over the edge, his head in the woman's lap. She flipped the reins and set the team to moving again.

She stared down at Patrick as he drifted into slumber, trying to find in his features those points that resembled his father.

It had always been a disappointment to her that she had never been able to give Jim a son. She didn't know whether the trouble had been with him or with her, and it didn't matter now. At least Quitman had the boy as a tangible reminder of his wife. Heather Winslow had only a memory of Jim, and a piece of land that might have nothing left on it but ashes.

Ahead yonder, a few days up the trail, waited the farm. She had tried to make plans, tried to decide how she could operate it by herself. There would be the fields to work, the garden to tend, the stock to take care of . . . if she had any left. In all probability there would even be a cabin to build. In all the long miles west from the Sabine she had seen only one left intact.

The farm had been hard enough even when Jim was alive. Lord knew he had tried. He'd always had good intentions, Jim had. He had been given to melancholy periods when things didn't go right, but he never complained aloud or blamed anybody. He always tried again. And often as not, he fell short again. Seemed things had a knack of going only halfway for Jim. Never total failure, but never actual success. Heather had tried to rationalize that they expected too much from this raw land, that they should be content with less. But other men did better. Other men worked no harder but came up with better crops. Other men seemed to go farther on good luck than Jim did by breaking his back.

Heather hadn't realized this when she married him. Orphaned young back in Missouri, she had been brought up by her grandmother and grandfather, who were kindly and well-meaning but hard-pressed to raise her after having finished with their own brood and being well along in years. Jim Winslow had come along, a handsome young man full of promise if short of the world's goods. He talked of going to the new land of Texas to seek his fortune and of wanting a nice girl to share it with him. The old folks pushed her to take advantage of the opportunity before some wiser girl beat her to it. She accepted their judgment and his proposal and headed west with him in a wagon. They were forced to trade the wagon for supplies before they ever got past Louisiana, and they made it into Austin's colony riding two horses and leading a packmule. Their luck had run to the same pattern ever since.

Though their marriage had been arranged more by mutual agreement than by any actual romance, she gradually developed a genuine affection for him, and he for her. If sometimes she looked at other young married couples and sensed a fire which her own marriage lacked, she tried not to let herself dwell upon the thought. Sure, life was hard. The country itself was hard. But surely there would be better times ahead. Surely luck would change. Anyway, she had observed that the fire of young love inevitably died down, and in doing so it often left the couple with a sense of loss and frustration. Better to have an affection that was genuine even if it never blazed. At least, Jim would always be there.

But Jim was not here, and he never would be again. As always, luck had run against him. Heather Winslow looked down upon the peaceful face of the sleeping boy and wished for that kind of peace. The terror still came to her, sometimes, in a nightmare. She could only hope it would fade . . . that she could forget the awful morning Jim Winslow had made his final sacrifice to let Heather go on to safety. Seeing the Mexican patrol catching up, knowing the two of them could never make the timber, he had given his protesting wife the fastest horse, kissed her goodbye and had ridden back with a rifle to hold up the patrol.

The firing had stopped about the time she reached the timber. Under cover of the trees, Heather had waited, praying desperately. When she saw the patrol come over the hill, she knew the outcome of the fight. She rode on alone, pushing all night, leaving the patrol far behind.

That one time, at least, Jim Winslow accomplished what he set out to do.

Heather Winslow could see Ocie Quitman now, riding the point position far out ahead of the wagons. He rode now as he always rode . . . alone. She remembered the way she had seen him the morning after Jim had died. Near exhaustion, the horse so tired he was barely walking, she had come out of the timber and into a clearing. A bewildered little boy had stood there by a wagon, and a man sat with his head in his hands beside a newly filled grave. Easing down from the saddle, she had reached Ocie Quitman before he even sensed that anyone was near. Looking up and seeing she was a woman, he had cried out, "Oh God, why couldn't you have come sooner?"

She had remembered him as being from the same general part of the colony, out on the Colorado. Brokenly he told her he had just buried his wife and a newborn son. The Runaway Scrape had killed her. It had been too much—the hard trip, the rough flight barely ahead of the Mexican army at the time for her delivery.

"There was no one to help her," Quitman had cried. "No one but me."

After a while, when he had time to think, he decided what to do. "My boy needs a woman's care. I need your horse, and you need my wagon. So you take the wagon, ma'am, and get my boy to the Sabine. I'll take the horse and catch up to Houston's army."

"How'll I get the boy back to you, and the wagon?"

"I'll find you. You stay put, the other side of the river. When the fightin' is over, I'll come and find you."

She had already seen what could happen to a man. "And if you *don't* come?"

"I got folks in the States. You can send the boy to them. And the wagon is yours." He gave her what little money he had and rode off across the valley and out of sight.

She never got across the Sabine. With hundreds of

other refugees, she had been stranded on the Texas side by high water, within sound of the cannon at San Jacinto. The day after the cannons stopped, Ocie Quitman came.

All that was behind her now. She could not afford to dwell upon it too much. What mattered was the times that lay ahead. She hated to think of them, but she knew she must. The thought of operating the farm alone was staggering. She didn't know how she could do it all by herself. But what else could she do? Hire a man? With what? How could she pay him? All the cash money she owned in this world probably wouldn't add up to three dollars.

There was one possibility, of course, though even to think about it so early was brazen, and her conscience plagued her. She knew it must be considered shameful, her husband just a few weeks dead.

She could marry again.

Surely she would, in time. She was still a young woman, not yet even twenty-five. And though the years of hard work and frustration had left their mark on her face and on her hands, she knew she was still considered a comely woman. Not as pretty as some who hadn't been through so much toil and care, but still not bad to look upon. She was credited with being a right smart of a cook. And in this land where unattached women were far fewer than the men, she should not have to worry that she would be passed over unnoticed. She would have to wait a while, of course, for it would not be seemly to show interest in men so soon. And in the meantime there was the farm, and the problem of operating it. There was the problem of how she would live and how she would eat, how she would protect herself in this big, lonely, savage land where tranquillity and happiness stood always in jeopardy of being shattered in a few short moments of violence and terror.

If there had been anywhere else to go after the Scrape, she would never have started west again. But the grandparents were dead now. There had been nowhere else, unless she decided to cross over the Sabine and throw herself upon the pity of some unknown community that already had problems enough of its own, some community that did not know her and owed her nothing more than the impersonal charity which all mankind owes to the unfortunate. In the west, at least, she had the farm.

That was it, then. She would follow along and trust the Lord to mark the way. But she would keep her own eyes open, too. She always had.

Joshua Buckalew rode close to the wagons. Heather Winslow found herself looking at him often, wondering. He had told little, and all she could remember of him was once when he and the happy little man, Muley Dodd, had come by her cabin with the surveyor Jared Pounce. She smiled, remembering how Pounce had bragged about her corn dodgers. He'd been a great one for eating, old Pounce. And he had been fond of Buckalew, she remembered. That spoke well of him, for Pounce had been a shrewd judge of character.

Now Muley Dodd spent most of his time back with the youngsters and the stock. He came up once and took a long look at little Patrick, still asleep with his head on

Heather's lap. Muley tipped his hat and smiled. "Sure do look peaceful, don't he, ma'am?"

She nodded and gave him back his smile. "He'll be with you again directly, when he gets his nap."

"Just wanted to be sure he was all right, ma'am. Didn't ever want to see him sick or nothin'."

Muley turned to ride back to the other youngsters. Heather Winslow's gaze followed him. Joshua Buckalew dropped back beside her wagon. "Muley's a good hand with kids, Mrs. Winslow. He'll take care of the boy."

"I'm glad you two came along. Little Patrick thinks the sun rises and sets with Muley."

The breeze carried the sound of Muley's tuneless whistling, as if there had never been any trouble in the world. Josh said, "Sometimes I think maybe it does. Times, I'd swap places with him and never look back."

"You've known him a long time?"

"Since back home in Tennessee. He needed a friend. So did I."

Her gaze found Ramón Hernandez, riding alone on one flank of the wagons. "And *him*?"

"We were neighbors. And we were friends, long before the war was ever thought of. We decided to stay friends, no matter what."

"Hasn't been easy, has it?"

"Been a strain. I lost my brother Thomas at Goliad. For a while it was hard for me to look at Ramón and see anything but his brown skin. But I had to get it through my head that he wasn't noway to blame for whatever Santa Anna did. I had to get it straight that I wasn't just lookin' at a Mexican . . . I was lookin' at an old friend.

It wasn't him that had changed . . . it was the times." Josh frowned. "Ramón worries you, don't he?"

Heather nodded, her lips drawn tight as she glanced down at the sleeping boy. "I know better, but I can't help it. The feeling crawls over my skin every time I look at him. I know it wasn't his fault about my Jim, but the feeling is there, just the same."

"You tried to be kind, takin' him his supper, tryin' to save him from the treatment some of them would've given him in the cabin."

"Guilty conscience, I suppose. I knew I was doing him a wrong, and something inside of me was trying to make up for it. I hope he understands. I can't help the way I feel."

"He understands, ma'am."

Joshua Buckalew pulled away and drifted out toward Ramón Hernandez. Heather Winslow watched him from under the shadow of her bonnet, wondering what kind of farmer *he* was.

5

Ocie Quitman was riding point, up ahead of the wagons. In late afternoon he turned back, looking over his shoulder, his worried manner indicating something was wrong. Josh rode forward and met him abreast of the Provost wagon. Quitman spoke to Josh and Aaron Provost together. "Men up yonder a-horseback. Five or six, at least. Maybe more."

"Indians?" Josh asked.

"Not Indian, and from the looks of them I'd say probably not Mexican either. They're movin' in our direction."

Aaron squinted. "Could be settlers like us, on their way home."

"Possible. But if they was, they'd be movin' in a different direction. Unless, of course, they seen us and decided to come down and get acquainted." Quitman's hands moved restlessly on the rifle held across his lap.

Tensing, Josh reached down and brought up his own rifle. In the backwash of every war roam the scavengers feeding on other people's misery. In this one, that breed rode along behind the fleeing settlers during the Runaway Scrape, falsely telling them the Mexicans were about to catch up, then plundering the goods the frightened people dumped in their haste.

Rebecca Provost groaned. "Aaron, look how far the young'uns have dropped back." The children had allowed the loose stock to graze, and now they were at least a quarter mile behind. But Muley had come forward hungry, wanting to know how long it would be before they stopped to camp. He was still with the wagons.

Josh said urgently, "Muley, you go fetch them kids up here and do it in a hurry. Leave the stock. We can pick them up later. Get them kids to the wagons before those riders reach here."

Alarmed, Muley held back to ask questions. Impatiently Josh shouted, "Muley, I said move!" Muley spurred away, but he kept looking back.

Sessum and McAfee had lagged with their wagon, sulking all day since they had lost the chickens. Now they caught the excitement and saw the riders. They brought their team up in a hurry. Sessum's eyes were big with alarm. "What's happenin'?"

Provost said tightly, "We got company comin'."

Rebecca had stood up in the wagonbed, looking back worriedly toward the children. Heather Winslow had stopped her wagon, and Mrs. Provost was telling her about the horsemen. Aaron Provost threw out a question which didn't seem to be pointed at anybody in particular. "What do we do?"

Josh waited to see if anybody else said anything. "First thing is to see that every gun we got is loaded and in hand. Rifles, shotguns, whatever we have."

Wiley McAfee hadn't grasped the situation. "If they ain't Mexicans, and they ain't Indians, what we need to worry about? The war's over."

Quitman clipped, "Not everywhere, it ain't. See after your guns."

Josh quickly took inventory. He and Quitman each had a rifle. Provost had a shotgun, which probably was best because Josh suspected the farmer might have a bad case of buck fever if it came to a shooting. A shotgun was good insurance against bad marksmanship. McAfee and Sessum each had rifles. An extra rifle lay in the Provost wagon. It belonged to the oldest Provost boy, Daniel, but he was back yonder with the youngsters. Josh glanced in that direction, then once more at the approaching horsemen. It was too late. The kids weren't going to reach the wagons before the visitors did.

"Mrs. Provost," Josh said, "you better take charge of your son's rifle. You may have to use it."

"Lord, not me," she protested, fright beginning to show. "I can do lots of things, but I can't shoot a man."

"Have it ready, anyway," Quitman said.

Josh glanced back at Heather Winslow, who was watching the children, her fist balled against her mouth. Josh dug a Mexican pistol out of his blanket roll and loaded it. It was his first intention to hand it to Mrs. Winslow, but on second thought he doubted she would use it. Better he keep it, for he *would* use it.

The riders were close now, and he could tell that Quitman hadn't seen them all. There were nine. Josh totted up the odds and didn't like them. One of the riders peeled away from the rest and spurred out to intercept Muley and the youngsters. Josh felt his heart go down. Muley had a rifle with him, but he wouldn't use it.

Josh found Ramón watching the youngsters. He could read the thought in the Mexican's mind: ride to them.

"Forget it, Ramón. If they got mischief on their minds—and they act like it—they'd never let you live long enough to reach them kids. Sit tight. We'll need all our guns right here in a bunch."

The riders slowed to a trot, then to a walk. They approached in a ragged line, some carrying pistols, some carrying rifles, one toting a Mexican *escopeta*. The man who appeared to be the leader pulled a length ahead and raised his hand to signal a halt. He moved a little closer, but not close enough to reach.

"Howdy." A thin smile flitted briefly across his bearded face. His eyes hungrily surveyed the wagons. "Nice outfit you folks got here. Headin' west, I take it?"

Aaron Provost waited until he saw that neither Josh nor Quitman seemed inclined to answer. "We're goin' back to our homes. We understand the Mexican soldiers have all gone. It's safe now."

The bearded man slouched lazily in his saddle. "Not altogether, it ain't. There's still a chance some stragglin' Mexicans are left. And then there's always the Indians. You-all think about the Indians? Man thinks he's got everything goin' on a nice downhill grade and then some sneakin' Comanche goes and takes his hair. It ain't right, good folks havin' to fret over things like that. So us boys here, we have done gone and formed us a kind of a frontier rifle company. We're here to kill any stray Mexicans and Indians we come across and make this country safe for the good folks." His gaze fell on Ramón. "This one here a prisoner of yours? We'd be right tickled to take care of him."

They were a dirty, unkempt, hungry-looking bunch, all of them. Josh had seen their kind, and he thought he had them pegged already: renegades operating out of the noman's territory known as the Redlands, that wild and lawless region that lay between the Texas colonies and the settled regions of Louisiana. These people turned their hands to all sorts of mischief: smuggling, counterfeiting, making bad whisky, stealing horses and waging a bloody brand of banditry, preying on travelers who tried to use the dim traces across western Louisiana and eastern Texas. Stephen F. Austin had organized militia bands against them and had driven them out of the colonies. But now, in the turmoil of Santa Anna's invasion and defeat, they were back again, straggling across Texas like roving, hungry wolves dogging the buffalo herds to pick up the weak and the unwary. They were as bad as the Comanches. Worse even than the Mexicans, for at least the Mexicans had considered that they had a cause.

Provost looked over his shoulder. "One of your men has stopped our children. I'd like to know what he done that for."

"That's Beau," came the smiling reply. "He's partial to young'uns." The smile faded. "Them is good-lookin' wagons. They're loaded too. Looks like you-all have come out of the war pretty good."

"Everything that's in these wagons is rightfully ours."

"I didn't go to make it look like we doubt you none. Anybody can tell, you're quality folks. What I'm gettin' to is, we're poor men, all of us. You can see that for yourselves. They ain't nobody payin' us nothin' or feedin' us nothin' for the protection we're givin' folks and their property. We got to live off of the land or starve. And starvin' ain't much to our likin', I'll guarantee."

Quitman asked, "Anybody authorize you to give all this . . . protection?"

"We're doin' it on our own. Not everybody can fight with old General Sam and git the glory of it. Some has got to do the dirty little jobs that don't rate even a thank-you or a howdy-do. We ain't complainin' none, but we figure you owe us, friends."

"Owe you what?" demanded Aaron Provost.

"Depends. Depends on what-all you got in them wagons."

He made a move toward the wagon which carried the widow Winslow. Ocie Quitman blocked him. "That's as far as you go, *friend*."

The black-bearded one darkened. "I don't believe you-all have quite understood the situation yet."

Josh said, "We understand it. You come to rob us."

"Not rob. *Rob* ain't a good word. *Commandeer* is better. Got a military ring to it, *commandeer* has. Sounds nice and legal too."

"There ain't nothin' legal about you," Josh declared. "You ain't militia. You probably never fired a shot at a Mexican, unless he was some helpless settler or stragglin' soldier you caught out by himself. You got nothin' comin' to you from us. If you're hungry, there's game enough around here. You got no call to starve."

The leader shrugged broad shoulders that stretched a ragged old black coat almost to the ripping point. Evidently the coat hadn't been made for him. Josh guessed he stole it from somebody. Somebody dead, more than likely. The man said, "We'd intended to handle this nice, but looks like you-all are bound and determined not to have it that way. So, we'll have it your way instead. You'll notice there's more of *us* than there is of you. And you'll remember we got one man down yonder close-herdin' that bunch of young'uns. Now, I sent old Beau on purpose, because he don't shrink from nothin', Beau don't. If I was to tell him to put his pistol up to some young'un's head and blow his brains out, he'd do it and not wink an eye. He's mean, Beau is."

Rebecca Provost cried out, and Heather Winslow's face went white.

The man nodded with satisfaction. "I do believe you-all are gettin' to see things the way I do. Women always seem to understand quicker'n men."

Shaken, Aaron Provost rubbed his whiskered chin. "What do you want from us?"

The dark-clad man slouched a little more, exuding an air of victory. "Well now, we ain't sure till we see what you got. We find we're needin' a little bit of everything."

Josh knew that was what they would take. *Everything.*

Provost looked at Josh and Quitman, his eyes begging for help. He said to the renegade, "You let our young'uns come on up and join us. Then we'll talk to you."

"You'll talk a right smart better the way things is. Beau'll take good care of them."

Provost said, "We got to have a few minutes to talk this over."

"We'll give you a few minutes, then. Here's our proposition: you turn them wagons over to us and walk away from here. You get yourselves good and clear of the wagons and we'll let the kids come on up. Afoot, of course. We find we sure do need us some horses."

"You'll want our guns too," Josh said dryly.

"Naturally. We need more guns. How else we goin' to fight Mexicans and Comanches?" He started to rein the horse around. "We'll give you three minutes to talk it over. If you ain't made up your mind by then, I'll have to send a little message down to Beau. I'd sure hate to do that. Like I told you, Beau is mean."

He rode off a short distance, he and his men. Then they turned to watch. But at least it was too far for them to hear.

Quitman's face had darkened. "You thinkin' the same as me, Buckalew?"

Aaron Provost broke in gravely, "There ain't no

thinkin' to be done. They outnumber us, and they got the kids. We can't take no risks with them young'uns."

Quitman's gaze went back to Josh. Josh said, "Years ago, when me and Muley and my brother Thomas were comin' to Texas from Tennessee, we ran into this kind of trouble over in the Redlands."

"What did you do?"

"We killed them before they could kill us. They was sure goin' to. And if we walk away from these wagons, we're all dead. Us *and* the kids. Don't you see, Aaron, they can't steal a bunch of slow wagons and leave us to tell about it. Too much risk of people findin' us before they've had time to get in the clear. Soon's they get us afoot and helpless, they'll kill us all and make out like it was Indians or Mexicans. It's the only thing they *could* do."

Provost repeated, "They got us outnumbered."

"Only by three, and they've sent one man down to the kids. That leaves two more men here than we got. Bad luck that your oldest boy and Muley both got cut off, but we got to make do without them."

Quitman glanced doubtfully at Ramón. "What about him? Can he shoot?"

"He can pick your teeth at fifty yards."

Quitman counted on his fingers. "If every one of us hits a man, that leaves two of them alive here and us with empty rifles. Chances are one or maybe both of them will turn tail and run."

Incredulous, Aaron demanded, "You mean we're just goin' to shoot them down? That don't hardly seem Christian."

"What they're figurin' on doin' to us ain't Christian, either," Josh pointed out. "And remember, they'll do it to the women and the children same as us. Your damned right we'll shoot them down." He remembered that other time, in the Redlands. He'd had the same feeling as Provost then, but Thomas had been older and tougher. Thomas had made him see it through. Looking back afterwards Josh had realized it was the only way. Hard, even brutal. But you don't make deals with a hungry wolf. You may bribe him off so long as you keep feeding him, but when you've nothing else to give him, he'll take you.

Dent Sessum and Wiley McAfee had pulled their wagon in close so they could listen. Cold sweat broke out on their faces. Any enmity between them and Josh was momentarily shoved away in the face of this outside threat. Sessum asked, "What if two or three of us shoot at the same man?"

Quitman replied, "We got to parcel them out. McAfee, you get the one with that Mexican-lookin' sombrero. Aaron can shoot the one with the beaver hat. Hernandez'll take the one sittin' next to him, the one with the crooked neck that looks like he'd been hung and cut down early. Buckalew can take the one on the end, and I'll get the man that done all the talkin'."

Ramón had kept quiet. Now he motioned back down the trail toward the youngsters. Normally he spoke in Spanish, but now he had to force himself into broken English that came hard for him. "The children. That *hombre* Beau. Somebody got to shoot Beau."

Quitman frowned. "I was figurin' him for Sessum. From where you're at, Sessum, you got the best chance to shoot Beau. You can rest your rifle barrel across that stack of goods and draw a fine bead."

That would leave three men here alive, even if everybody hit his target.

Provost was murmuring, "I sure as sin don't like it."

Josh said, "What they got in mind, you'd like a lot less. Everybody better shoot straight. Kill them the first shot and you won't have anything to do over."

The three minutes passed, and the scavengers closed in, fanning out to form a semi-circle. Every one of them carried a gun of some kind, and every gun was ready. The only thing Josh figured his group could count on was the renegades' conviction that this was to be easy pickings, that the settlers would give up.

That, he thought, *gives us a couple seconds jump on them, because at least we know what we're going to do.*

The leader was coming close to the wagons, so sure was he of surrender. That would make an easy shot for Quitman, anyway. Josh let his attention settle then on the man at the end who was to be his target. He hoped the man wouldn't see it in his eyes.

Josh had shot a few men in the war, and he'd always wondered about it afterwards . . . who they were, where they had come from, how it came that they were destined to be at that particular place at that particular moment and to die by his hand rather than someone else's. It wasn't a pleasant thing to dwell on, after the bloody task was done. It was even less pleasant to dwell on *before* the deed. All he could see in the flesh was a wind-reddened face, a heavy cover of dirty whiskers streaked by tobacco, a set of pale eyes that found Josh's and stayed there. That and a pair of rough hands gripping a rifle that he intended to use for killing. Josh wondered if he had a family back home . . . a wife, maybe, and even some kids who would always wonder what had become of him, kids who would grow up wild and unrestrained and perhaps turn out in his own cruel image, not wholly at fault because they had known no other way. And was it really even *this* man's fault that he was here now, about to die but not knowing it? Had a careless fate pointed him in this direction when he was too young to understand? Josh would always wonder, but there would never be any way for him to know.

The men were so close now that he knew he could not miss. Cold sweat made the rifle slick in his hands. He felt the man must see the tension drawing his face tight, and he hoped it would be taken for fear.

"You made up your minds yet?" the leader asked casually.

"We have," Quitman replied. He waited a moment, then shouted, "NOW!"

Six weapons roared. Horses plunged and squealed. Men shrieked and cursed and fell. Through a cloud of black powdersmoke drifting out from the wagons, Josh watched his man jerk backward, clutching his stomach, then slide off and crumple in an awkward heap. Another man crawled on the ground, screeching, going limp as a terrified horse trampled him. The smoke was heavy, but Josh could see that at least four men had been left untouched. Someone had completely missed his target.

The fusillade had caught the renegades by surprise. Two of the ones not hit wheeled their horses and ran, coattails flapping as they spurred in panic. Josh saw a rifle flash from one of the two men who were left, but he didn't turn to see if one of his party was hit. He kicked his horse and moved quickly through the smoke, drawing the pistol out of his waistband. Ocie Quitman swung his riflebarrel, clubbing one rider out of the saddle. Josh saw the other one holding the *escopeta,* trying to find a target in the gray smoke. Josh brought up the pistol and squeezed the trigger. The man went down.

He heard Wiley McAfee scream, "Help me, somebody. He's got me!"

Josh wheeled. On the wagonseat, Aaron Provost sat frozen, the smoking shotgun in his hands, as he stared in hypnotic dismay at the renegade in the beaver hat, writhing on the ground. This was probably the first man Provost had ever shot.

On the far side of the wagon, Wiley McAfee and one of the Redlanders rolled in the grass. A knifeblade caught the sunshine for an instant. McAfee had failed to kill his man, and now he was fighting for his life.

Josh remembered the extra rifle in the Provost wagon, the one that belonged to the oldest boy. He made a move, but Ramón had thought of it before him. Ramón was closer, and he got to it first.

McAfee saw him, for he was shrieking, "Help me, Mexican! Help before he kills me!" He had never even bothered to learn Ramón's name.

Ramón climbed out of his saddle and onto the Provost wagon, moving awkwardly because of his bad leg. He grabbed the rifle, and for a moment Josh thought he was going to shoot the renegade who had McAfee down. But Ramón brought the rifle to a level and propped it across a box to fire it. Josh saw then what he was aiming at.

Sessum had missed his shot at the man called Beau.

Now Beau pursued the little Provost girl, evidently trying to gain a hostage.

McAfee screamed again, "For God's sake, help before he kills me!"

But Ramón ignored him. Beads of sweat broke on the dark forehead as the barrel followed the moving Beau. The rifle roared. Beau slumped, grabbing at his horse's mane. In an instant Provost's oldest boy and Muley together had pounced on him and dragged him to the ground.

Josh ran to help McAfee. He was too late. The renegade plunged the knife into McAfee's throat. Quitman got there first. He leaned down from his saddle and jabbed the butt of his empty rifle savagely against the renegade's head. The man went slack, and Quitman clubbed him again. The skull broke like a melon.

Josh hadn't seen Sessum all this time, but now the man came running, eyes big as a washtub. "Wiley! What's happened, Wiley? Wiley!"

Wiley McAfee lay gasping, struggling as his lifeblood spread a stain in the grass. His hands reached up in fearful supplication, but no one could help him.

Sessum crouched over him a moment in shock, then grabbed up McAfee's fallen rifle and frenziedly began to club the fallen renegade.

Quitman said, "Sessum, that won't help none. He's already dead."

Sessum shouted, "I heard Wiley holler to the Mexican for help. Why didn't he help him?" His gaze fastened on Ramón, and he gripped the rifle barrel as if to use the weapon for a club. "Answer me, Mexican! How come you didn't help him? You wanted him dead!"

"The children," Ramón gritted. "McAfee was a man. First came the children."

Sessum seemed not to hear him. "You had a rifle in your hands, and you stood there and let him die."

Ramón shrugged. He'd made his explanation. Sessum could accept it, or he could go to hell.

Josh put in, "Sessum, it was your job to shoot Beau. You missed him and left them young'uns in his hands. Ramón had to finish your job." Pausing, he saw no sign that his words were taking any effect. "If you'd done what you was supposed to, McAfee would not have had to die."

Sessum gave no indication he had even heard. "That Mexican could've saved him. He let him be killed." Sessum made a move forward with the rifle barrel gripped in his hands. Josh caught him by the shoulder, spun him around and struck him on the chin. Sessum sprawled. Josh picked up the fallen rifle to keep it out of Sessum's hands.

Over the hill he could see two men riding away, still spurring. The wise thing would be to go after them, to make sure the whole den was killed out. But here with the smoke still thick enough to choke a man, and with the dying men groaning on the ground and women sobbing softly in the wagons, he was glad to let them go.

Muley and the oldest Provost boy rode up with the children, and with the wounded Beau staggering at the end of a rope.

Muley said quickly in self-defense, "There wasn't nothin' I could do, Josh. He taken my rifle before I even knowed what was goin' on."

Josh looked at the captured man. "You did fine, Muley. So did you, Daniel."

The Provost boy sat straight and proud, though he trembled from the excitement. "We wasn't afraid of him, Mister Buckalew. Quick as we got the chance, we grabbed onto him."

Muley shouted, "He was fixin' to kill the children. That's what he told us. Said if anything went wrong he was goin' to kill them off one by one, like he'd wring chicken necks. He was tryin' to catch the girl when somebody shot him."

Quitman's eyes were sharp. He told Beau: "Your friends are dead, most of them. You know any reason we ought to have mercy on you?"

"I'm bleedin' to death," Beau whined. "You can't let a man stand here and bleed to death."

"No," said Quitman, "we can't." He squeezed the trigger. Beau jerked, stared in horror till his eyes went blank, then he pitched forward in a heap.

Quitman said to no one in particular, "That's what he was fixin' to do to the young'uns." He switched his gaze to Josh. "What you waitin' for? Any others still alive, we better do the same to them. No use them healin' up and pullin' this on somebody else."

Josh said, "We're not the law."

"Aren't we? There ain't no law right now except the law we make. Mexican government is gone. We got no Texas government except on paper."

"There's still God's law."

"God ain't come west of the Sabine River."

"You're not goin' to kill anybody else, Quitman."

"You figure on stoppin' me?"

"If I have to."

Quitman's gaze could cut steel. All Josh knew was to

stare back. They watched each other like buck deer trying to decide whether to lower their horns and fight. Finally Quitman shrugged. "You could take lessons from that Mexican of yours. He knows when to let his blood run cold."

Provost came out of his daze and climbed shakily down from his wagon. They all scouted around, picking up the guns and looking over the blood-soaked renegades, scattered in a grisly semi-circle where they had fallen. It would have been a sickening sight, had Josh not already seen so many others, most of them worse. The man Josh had shot with the pistol lay breathing raggedly, already unconscious. He would never open his eyes. The rest appeared dead except the one who had worn the beaver hat. The hat lay crushed beneath him. Provost had shot him, but nervousness had spoiled his aim. The blue whistlers had shattered the leg.

Quitman said, "Leave him be and he'll bleed to death."

This one, of all the renegades, showed no whiskers. Bending over for a close look, Josh exclaimed: "He's a young'un, is all. Not much older than Daniel Provost. Seventeen . . . maybe eighteen."

Quitman frowned. "A young'un can kill you as dead as an old one. He's part of that trash."

"He's not old enough to know what he's doin'."

"The hell he ain't. He's old enough to kill a man. That means he's old enough for somebody to kill *him* and not worry over it none."

Searching the lad, Josh found a knife but no other weapon. He slit the shot-torn trouser leg. The youngster choked off a cry. Josh grimaced. "Busted into little bitty pieces. We got to do somethin'."

Quitman growled, "Leave him."

"He's just a kid."

"We was all kids, one time or another. I knew right from wrong by the time I was six. He's growed up with a wolfpack, Buckalew. You can't change a wolf's habits. Save him now and he'll kill again. Leave him die. It's best for everybody."

"We can't."

"While ago you helped me plan how we'd kill them all. It didn't bother you then."

"He had a gun in his hands. Now it's different. He's helpless."

"You think he'd of fixed *you* up? He'd of cut your throat."

Aaron Provost said, "Ocie, it was me that shot him. We got to give him a chance."

Quitman shrugged. "Do it then. But remember, if you save him he'll like as not be at your throat first chance he gets."

Josh looked to Muley for help, but Muley's face was clabber-white at the sight of so much blood. "Muley, you gather the young'uns and take them to the shade of that tree yonder to wait and rest. No use them bein' here at this slaughterhouse."

Still shaken, Aaron Provost said, "I'll help you with the boy, Josh. I feel like it's my responsibility. What you want me to do?"

"Let's take a better look at this wound." Josh ripped away the trouser leg, his brow furrowing. It was even worse than he thought. A chill crawled up his back. Looking away, he saw that Aaron's boy Daniel had taken it upon himself to round up the renegades' horses.

Nobody had had to tell him. And Josh remembered how Daniel had pounced on Beau the moment Ramón's rifleball struck. Good boy, that Daniel. Aaron and Rebecca had pointed him right. Pity there hadn't been somebody to point *this* boy right. "Aaron, why don't you look through them saddlebags and find out if any of them had a bottle of whisky or somethin'? This boy is goin' to need it. He's goin' to need a-plenty of it."

Josh made a tourniquet of the trouserleg, then walked to the widow Winslow's wagon where Ocie Quitman had his arms around his little son Patrick. "Mrs. Winslow, could you get a fire goin' and heat some water, please? We're goin' to need it directly."

Aaron found a couple of bottles. Josh removed the stopper from one and tilted it up to drink. He gasped and wiped his sleeve across his mouth. "Man who'd sell that stuff would club his grandmother. But it'll do the job. Here, boy, drink. Drink it all."

By the time the water was boiling, the boy was floating away in a drunken stupor. Josh had whetted his knife until the blade was keen. He held it in the boiling water, glanced at Aaron and said, "You hold him."

The boy surged against Aaron, screaming, then fell back in a faint. Cold sweat broke out on Josh's forehead. Once he turned away to be sick. But he came back, and presently the job was done. Heather Winslow fled while Josh and Aaron cauterized the stump. Then she forced herself forward with some homespun cotton cloth. "You'll need bandages."

Quitman and Dent Sessum had placed Wiley McAfee's body in the Sessum wagon. Josh walked up to Quitman.

"We got to put that boy in a wagon too. We want to use yours."

Quitman frowned. "What if I said no?"

"You and me would have to fight. And when it was over, we'd put the boy in your wagon anyhow."

Quitman shook his head in resignation. "You got a soft heart, Buckalew, and a soft head to match. Like as not, it'll get you killed someday. But go ahead. If it's all right with Mrs. Winslow, you can use the wagon."

They put a couple of miles behind them, leaving the battlefield with the bodies lying where they had fallen. They camped on a little creek beneath a canopy of freshly-leafed pecan trees. Josh and Muley and Aaron gathered old leaves into a soft mat, spread blankets and placed the wounded boy on them. The lad was groaning.

Dent Sessum and Ocie Quitman carried shovels up to a high point and dug a grave for Wiley McAfee. After supper, Aaron read from the Bible, they all bowed their heads, and each man took a turn with the shovel.

Josh watched Sessum carve McAfee's name onto a cross Muley had fashioned. He suspected Sessum had misspelled the name, but he saw no need in making an issue of it. He asked, "Did McAfee have any relatives you know of? Is there somebody we ought to send a letter to?"

Sessum shook his head. "We was partners, him and me. There wasn't nobody else."

"Bound to be somebody . . . a mother, maybe, or a sister or brother . . . somebody who ought to get the stuff that belonged to him."

Sessum put aside the cross and clenched his fists, his face darkening. "We was partners. Whatever belonged to him belongs to me now. Everything in that wagon, it belongs to me. Just me! You ain't goin' to take away or give away what's mine!"

"I had no intention . . ."

"I'm warnin' you, Buckalew. Touch one thing on that wagon and there'll be big trouble. It's all mine now, do you hear?"

Josh turned away, disgust welling in him. He picked up a shovel and started toward the wagon. Aaron Provost trudged out to meet him, his shoulders slumped, his face grim. "Don't put the shovel away, Josh."

"The boy?"

The farmer's voice broke. "He died fightin'."

Somberly Josh pondered the waste and the futility of it all. At length he made a Mexican shrug of resignation. "At least we tried."

Anguished, Aaron cried, "It was me that shot him, Josh. How am I goin' to carry that burden? He was a boy like my Daniel."

"No, Aaron, not like your boy. This one was suckled on wolf's milk, taught to kill like an animal. It wasn't your fault. The blame goes on the people who raised him that way."

6

The days were long and the miles passed slowly under the wheels, but gradually the Spanish moss country of the coastal lands fell behind them and the gently rising prairies marked the way into the higher, dryer inland regions of Texas . . . across the Brazos, past the charred ruins of Stephen F. Austin's San Felipe, across the San Bernard and finally west to the Colorado.

Ocie Quitman had never talked much, and as the wagons rolled farther west he said even less than before. He rode ahead, alone, a morose silence gathered about him like some dark cloud. Now and again Josh spoke to him and received no answer, for Quitman's mind was somewhere far away.

Aaron Provost said, "We're gettin' close to home country now, to the place we all called Hopeful Valley. I'm right uneasy, Josh, how he's goin' to take it when he first sets eyes on his farm. You can tell, lately he's done a lot of thinkin' about *her*."

The farther they moved across the prairies, the more uneasy Josh became about Comanches. The only horse tracks they had encountered crossing their trail had proved to be bands of wild mustangs, grazing free. While Quitman rode his solitary point, Josh and Ramón would each move far out on the flank, watching. They stirred up deer, which would bound away in long, fleet leaps. Sometimes antelope raced across the prairie ahead of them, their white-puff tails bobbing. The riders found wild cattle, a few of which they promptly brought in for beef. But they saw no Indians, and no sign of any.

A day came when Quitman rode forward to the top of a hill and sat his horse there unmoving. After a long time Josh became uneasy and loped up from his flank position. From on the other side, he could see Ramón follow his lead. At the hilltop, Josh stopped and looked down upon a small field, evidently plowed last winter but now growing up in weeds. His searching gaze picked up a small, crooked stream, its green banks lined with massive pecan trees. Finally, just above the stream, he saw the black skeleton of a cabin, the charred logs of its tumbled walls spread out like burned ribs.

He knew with a cold certainty. "Your place?"

Quitman made no answer. Josh thought he had never seen a face so sad. He held his silence, studying the place. He could tell it had been a good farm. It would be again, with some work. "Cabin's easy to build," he offered finally. "Soon's we all get our field work caught up with, we'll help you put it back up."

Quitman shook his head. "Cabin don't mean nothin' to me. Mary is what mattered, and there ain't no way to bring her back."

Josh thought, *A man has to put his dead behind him and go on living.* But he figured it would sound cruel, no matter how he said it.

Quitman pointed at the remains of the cabin. "It wasn't much, but she loved it there. Had her some flowers in front of it, and her garden out back, where you see that square plot with the log fence. I remember how aggravated she'd get when the coons would come slippin' in at night and tear the garden up. She'd take a broom and chase them out—she wouldn't hurt one for the world. Then she'd go out next mornin' and try to fix the damage. She could make anything grow, Mary could. She had the touch of life about her. She could take a sick plant or a sick animal or a sick bird—didn't matter which— and she could make it live." His eyes pinched. "But when her own time come, she couldn't help herself. Whatever touch she had, it wouldn't work for *her*."

"It was a hard go of luck, but I reckon there wasn't anything anybody could do."

Quitman gave a quick, hard glance at Ramón. "There *was* somebody could've done somethin', but they wouldn't." His head turned slowly, and Josh followed his gaze southward. He thought he saw a wisp of light-colored smoke beyond the trees. He glanced at Quitman, but he didn't ask the question.

Quitman's voice was barbed. "Faustino Marquez." His hands balled into fists. He stared toward the thin column of smoke, his face darkening. Finally he said, "Buck-alew, you want to do me a favor?"

Josh frowned, dubious. "If I can."

"Come along with me, then. I want you to stand back and keep quiet. I don't want you to interfere or get in the way of whatever I do except for one thing. The last second before I kill him, I want you to stop me. Let me burn him out. Let me beat him to within an inch of his life. But don't let me kill him."

"I don't know . . ." Josh rubbed his jaw. "Before I'm a party to this, I better know how come you hate him so bad."

Quitman turned to Ramón. "I'd rather *you* didn't go with us."

Ramón glanced at Josh, his eyes asking. Josh said, "It's all right, Ramón. I'll go with him. Maybe you better go help watch out for the wagons anyway."

Quitman touched heels to his horse's ribs and started down the hill toward the smoke. Josh hurried to follow.

"Quitman, you didn't answer me."

Without slowing his horse, Quitman painfully spilled out his story. "Time I'm finished, you'll know why I can't stand the sight of a Mexican. Not even that pet of yours. Faustino Marquez as good as killed my wife. He could've saved her, but he wouldn't lift a hand." Quitman spat. "Two years, we was neighbors. Faustino was the hungry kind, never satisfied with what he had, takin' everything else he could get. A grasper. Whatever he needed, he come borrowin' from us, and I'd have hell gettin' it back. But the times him or his wife got sick, Mary would go over and take care of them. The big fever come last year. Mary stayed there most of a week, nursin' Alicia Marquez, pullin' her back after the fever all but took her away. Faustino swore if there was ever anything Mary needed, he'd give up his life to help her.

"Well, the time come. We had another baby on the way when the war commenced. I went off to help fight. After the Alamo and Goliad, when the Scrape started, I got leave to go home and see after Mary. All our *Americano* friends had packed up and left. They'd tried to get Mary to go with them, but she'd waited for me. I got home and found her so close to her time that it was dangerous for her to travel. Santa Anna's Mexicans was almost on top of us by then. I was afraid ridin' in a wagon would kill her.

"Bein' Mexicans themselves, Faustino and his wife didn't see no need in them runnin' from Santa Anna. I decided that if Mary stayed with the Marquez family, the soldiers wouldn't bother her none, so I put her and Patrick in the wagon and took them over there. Faustino met me at the door with a gun in his hand. Said for us damned *Americanos* to get off of his land. I told him he owed Mary protection, but he said if we didn't get away, he'd shoot us all and maybe Santa Anna would give him a medal. Said this land was for the Mexicans anyway, and the only reason they'd ever let any *Ameri-*

canos in here in the first place was to help them fight off the Comanches. Said our place was *his* place from now on.

"We rode all that day and through the night and hid in a thicket at daylight. It kept rainin' and washin' our tracks out behind us. While we was in the thicket, a bunch of Mexican soldiers come ridin' by, tryin' to find us. And up front, helpin' them, was Faustino Marquez." Ocie Quitman's eyes closed. "We traveled by night and hid by day. But it turned out like I was afraid it would. Mary's time came, and the trip had been too much for her. She died hard. The baby never drew a breath. I reckon you know the rest of it."

Josh said, "Heather Winslow told me."

"Mrs. Winslow was in a lot the same shape as I was. She'd lost her husband, and I'd lost my wife. I gave her Patrick and the wagon and went on to find Sam Houston. I'd made up my mind to kill as many Mexicans as I could. And I did, Buckalew. I made them pay."

"But it wasn't enough, was it?"

Quitman shook his head. "No, it wasn't enough. All the time I knew Faustino was still here. I laid awake nights, thinkin' about all the slow, hard ways I could use to kill him. None of them was good enough. Once he was dead, he wouldn't feel anything, and I wanted him to feel. Then I got to thinkin' about how greedy he was. I decided the way to punish him most was to run him off of his place with nothin' but the shirt on his back and let him spend the rest of his miserable life rememberin' what he had thrown away. That's a way you can kill a man and still leave him alive."

"That's what you want me to help you do?"

"Not help me. I'll do it all myself. You just be there to make sure I don't forget myself and kill him. Agreed?"

Josh hesitated. "I reckon you got cause enough to hate him. But I'll stop you whenever I think it's time."

The Marquez house lay beyond a recently-tilled field. It was of stone, Mexican style, rather than the log type the *Americano* settlers favored. Smoke curled from the chimney, and Josh thought he saw movement inside. No one came out. Quitman's eyes narrowed.

"Faustino!"

No answer.

"Faustino! You drag yourself out here, and be damned quick!"

A broad-hipped Mexican man showed himself uncertainly in the open doorway. He stared at Quitman with the horrified eyes of a man who has seen the dead spring to life. "Quitman!"

Ocie Quitman carried his rifle across the pommel of his saddle. His voice was quieter now but keen-edged. "Thought they'd got me, didn't you? Thought I'd never come back." Quitman's gaze swept over the yard. It fastened on a plow, and his eyes crackled. "That's *my* plow you got. And that chair under the arbor . . . it's one I made for Mary."

Marquez stammered. "All this I save for you, Quitman. I say to myself, that Santa Anna, he burn everything. I bring it over here, and I save it for my good friend Quitman and his wife." He trembled. "I save it for you, Quitman."

"You stole it. You didn't think I'd be back."

"No, Quitman, I no steal from you. You and me, we friends."

"So friendly you led the Mexican troops to try and find us? You wanted us dead, Faustino. You wanted to steal everything for yourself."

"Long time we are friends," Marquez quailed. "You and me, your wife, my Alicia. Do you forget that?"

"*You're* the one that forgot it." Quitman swung down slowly, the rifle's muzzle pointing in Marquez's general direction. Marquez began shrinking back inside the door.

"Faustino! You stay out here or I'll put a bullet in you!"

The Mexican slumped, stricken with fear. "Please, you don't kill me, Quitman. Please."

"You killed my Mary. Why shouldn't I kill you?"

"I did nothing."

"You did nothin', and that is why she's dead. You owed her a debt, but you let her die. Now I owe *you,* Faustino, and I'm goin' to pay."

The butt of his rifle caught Marquez in the stomach. The man bent forward, arms coming around instinctively for protection. Quitman jabbed the butt straight forward, hitting him again. Marquez stumbled backward into the house. A woman screamed. Josh dismounted, looped the reins through the brush fence and moved quickly through the open door. He saw a plump Mexican woman cowering in a corner, face covered with her hands, but her fingers spread enough that she could see. Each time Quitman hit her husband, she screamed. An old rifle stood in another corner, but neither she nor Marquez made any move toward it. Josh picked it up and took it out of contention.

What Quitman did to Marquez was slow, methodical and brutal. He drove him back against a stone wall and there proceeded to beat him with his fists. Each time Marquez slipped to the packed-earth floor, Quitman hauled him up again. Marquez made only a small attempt to defend himself. He whimpered and pleaded that he did not want to die.

About the time Josh was preparing to step in and stop it, Quitman flung Marquez halfway across the room. "Get up, Faustino. Get up and get out!"

Marquez pushed himself up onto hands and knees, staring without comprehension. *"No entiendo." I do not understand.*

"I said get out. You and your wife, get your oxen and hook up your *carreta* and go. Don't you ever come back."

The woman spoke for the first time. Up to now, all she had done was scream. "This is our home."

"It *was* your home. You're leavin'."

"Where?" she pleaded in Spanish. "We have nowhere to go."

Quitman strode across the room and hauled Marquez to his feet. "You hear me, Faustino?" The man nodded in terror. Quitman said, "If I was you I wouldn't stop till I got plumb the other side of the Rio Grande. Don't stop in Bexar, because I might go there sometime. Don't stop at the Neuces, because I might be *there* sometime too. I promise you this, Faustino: if I ever see you again . . . any time, any place . . . I'll kill you on sight!" He turned loose. The Mexican fell to his hands and knees, scrambling for the door, not pushing to his feet until he was outside. The woman began gathering up clothes and cooking utensils. Quitman raised his hand. "Leave them."

She stared in disbelief.

He repeated, "Leave them. I'm givin' you Faustino. That's all you're leavin' here with."

Josh said: "You're makin' it awful tough. How're they goin' to live?"

"That's their problem. They didn't give a damn what happened to Mary."

Josh watched somberly as the Mexican yoked his oxen to a high-wheeled wooden cart. The couple left without so much as the old rifle.

Josh said, "They might run into Comanches."

"They might."

"They'd have no chance at all."

"They'd have all the chance they gave Mary." Quitman turned back inside the little rock house. The anger still rode high in his face. "Damn near everything in here—the chairs, the table, all of it—came from our house. Faustino cleaned it out. Then he burned it."

"So now you've cleaned him out."

"Clean as a hound's tooth."

Quitman walked toward the homemade wooden bed. Josh guessed by the way he looked at it that it had been his—his and Mary's. Quitman picked up a pillow and let his fingers run over the fine embroidery work, and he turned away, his head down. Josh decided to leave the cabin and give the man his moments of peace . . . if ever he had any.

They rode in silence across the field and over the hill to Quitman's own place. Quitman moved his horse in a slow walk around the rock pens, the burned cabin, the weed-grown garden. He kept his eyes away from Josh's, and Josh tried not to intrude. He held back, willing to listen if it would help but not wanting to put himself in where he wasn't needed.

At length Quitman reined up, shoulders slumped. "I don't think I can do it, Buckalew."

"Do what?"

"Live here again. I could come here and work the land, maybe, but I couldn't live here anymore. There's too much that'd try to take me back, and there's no goin' back. Like as not, I'd go out of my mind."

"What do you think you'll do?"

"Texas owes me free land for my soldierin'. Didn't you say there's good land up your way?"

Josh nodded. "There's a lot that ain't been claimed."

"Then I'll pick me a piece of it bye and bye and put in my claim. This place I'll keep for my boy Patrick."

"You'll be welcome." Josh frowned. "There's just one thing . . ."

"What's that?"

"You'll have Mexican neighbors again. You'll have Ramón Hernandez. It won't be like it was with Faustino. Push Ramón and he'll fight. What's more, I'll help him."

Quitman stared at him unflinchingly. "I got a notion I'll have to fight you sooner or later anyhow."

7

Heather Winslow had thought she would be prepared to face the sight of her burned-out home, for she had seen enough others along the way to know she could expect nothing else. But the tears came anyway as she stared at the cold, blackened chimney which towered as a silent sentinel over a pile of charred logs.

Gaunt Rebecca Provost stood behind her, strong hands gripping Heather's shoulders. "Go ahead, child, cry if it'll help you any. But there's plenty more logs where them come from. The men'll put you up another one. All it takes is time and labor and some good timber. You'll have you a home again."

It will take more to make this a home, Heather thought. *Without Jim, there will be no man in the house. And without a man in the house, it won't be a home.*

She heard a quiet voice which she knew belonged to Joshua Buckalew. "Mrs. Provost is right. First thing we got to do is see after the crops, includin' yours. Then we'll get to work buildin' the cabins back the way they was, or better, even. We'll put a good roof over your head, you don't need to be worryin' about that."

Aaron Provost declared confidently, "Bound to be one of us has a cabin that didn't get burned. We'll all stay together till we know it's safe for us to break off on our own. If Rebecca and me has been lucky, you'll share our house, Heather. You'll share it as long as you need it."

But the Provosts hadn't been lucky either. Their big double cabin lay in black ruins, even one of its two tall chimneys broken off and lying in a heap of rubble.

Heather was not much surprised to see a lone tear roll down Rebecca Provost's tight-stretched cheek, nor was she surprised to see the tall woman square her shoulders and jut her chin forward, shutting off the tears like she would shutter and bar a window.

Aaron Provost's eyes were grim. "Where to from here? Think your cabin might still be standin', Josh?"

Josh shook his head. "It was already burned the last time I came this way. Indians, I figured. No use us goin' by there."

Sitting on his horse, Ocie Quitman shook his head in resignation. "Then there's noplace else. We'd just as well set up camp here."

Josh said, "Wrong. There's still Ramón's. It's a good ways from Hopeful Valley, but I know the place will still be there. His family stayed. Be all right with you, Ramón, if we set up camp there till we get everybody's fields plowed out and the cabins rebuilt?"

Ramón nodded. "We would be happy."

Ocie Quitman's gaze fixed itself on the Mexican. "You don't need to be doin' us no favors."

Ramón shrugged. "Would you not do the same for me?"

Quitman looked away, not answering. Heather thought she knew the answer, and she suspected Ramón knew it too. She wondered if Hernandez might purposely be twisting the knife a little.

Josh said, "They got a good rock house that the Indians have never tried to hit. It'd be a safe place for the women and children till we find out about the Comanches. We can't afford to go scatterin' right now anyway before we know how much of a hazard the Indians will be."

Quitman glared at Ramón. "I've always been careful who I let myself owe favors to."

Heather looked for resentment in Ramón's eyes, but if it was there he kept it well concealed. He said, "You owe me nothing. It is protection for my family if all of you go there. Everything is even."

Ocie did not yield. "I won't be beholden. I'll pay you out of my crops this fall. There ain't goin' to be no debt."

Ramón shrugged. *"No le hace."*

Josh looked at Dent Sessum. "How do you feel about it?"

Sessum glowered, not liking the situation but accepting it sourly. "I'll go along with whatever the majority wants. But I'll tell you this: I think if I help provide protection, that's pay enough. I ain't payin' that Mexican no extry."

Ramón repeated, "Nobody owes me."

Muley Dodd grinned happily. "Does that mean we're goin' to Ramón's now, Josh? Does that mean we're goin' to see all them Hernandez kids?"

Josh smiled. "And your old dog Hickory, too."

Muley rubbed his hands together, laughing. "Lordy, Josh, I'd almost forgot old Hickory. Bet he'll be right tickled to see us come. I can't hardly wait to go huntin' with him again."

Josh placed his hand on Muley's shoulder. Heather watched, admiring Buckalew for the friendship and the sense of duty which held him to the smaller man. Muley Dodd was like a child, she had realized from the first time she saw him. His heart was good and his intentions were honest, but an adolescent helplessness held him dependent upon Joshua Buckalew. She suspected that at times Muley must be burden enough to make a man weep.

If he's gentle like that with Muley, he'd be even gentler with a woman, she thought.

Jim had been gentle. In that respect he had been like Buckalew. Yet in other ways he'd been a bit like Muley Dodd, too. Not slow-thinking, the way Muley was, but somehow dependent, unsure. He had leaned on Heather for strength and she had tried to give it, even when she was stricken with anxiety herself.

Heather stared at Buckalew, then at Ocie Quitman. She doubted that either man ever leaned on anybody. They were strong men, self-confident, able to stand on their own feet and well aware of it. Either one of them would make a woman a good home. *Either one would make me a good home,* she told herself. Again she felt a touch of shame for this errant direction her thoughts were taking. It didn't seem there had been proper time yet for her to begin measuring other men as candidates to take Jim's place. But, then, these were not normal times, and this was not the settled homeland of her girlhood where the old rules could be applied without question. Out here a woman alone was a woman in jeopardy.

Well, she wouldn't be brazen about it. She would observe the amenities of widowhood and show all the proper respect. But she had to be realistic about the facts of the situation. The facts were that she was alone and couldn't afford to remain that way indefinitely. So she would watch and weigh and compare. When time had erased the obligations of propriety, and when Jim's face quit coming back unbidden in her dreams, she would know which man—if either—she wanted. And she would get him.

The most direct way to the Hernandez place did not include Joshua Buckalew's land, but it passed within a few miles of there. Heather could see nervousness building in Buckalew until he could stand it no longer.

"Aaron," he told the big farmer, "I just got to ride over and take a look. I'll catch up to you later."

He rode off over the hill, Muley Dodd spurring desperately to catch up. For hours Heather found herself watching, hoping to see them. At last they came, and she smiled a little, relieved. But she stopped smiling when she saw the sober expression in Buckalew's face. She asked no questions. She sat impatiently on the wagon-seat and listened for Aaron Provost to do the asking.

"Burned out, was you, Josh?"

He nodded. "I knew that, of course. I'd seen it before."

"How do your fields look?"

"Muley got the corn planted before he and Ramón took and went to join Houston. Rain's got the field growed up in weeds pretty bad. It sure needs plowin'. And then, there's the garden to plant and all."

"That don't sound so bad, then. By your face, I thought it was goin' to be worse."

Buckalew glanced at Rebecca Provost and then back to Heather Winslow. "Ladies, I don't want to get you-all upset or nothin', but me and Muley, we found horsetracks. They was made in the mud, maybe a week or more ago, but tracks just the same. And they wasn't just wild mustangs wanderin' over the country. They had riders on them."

Provost's mouth curved downward. "Indians?"

"I expect."

"Could've been just a huntin' party, already long gone back west where they come from."

"Could've been."

"Might not see any more Indians around here for months . . . maybe not for a year."

"Might not. But if they *are* here, I damn sure want to see *them* before they see *me*."

Without being told, Heather sensed that they were nearing the Hernandez place. Ramón Hernandez kept drifting farther and farther forward, till he was up even with Ocie Quitman on the point. Rather than ride with him, Quitman stopped his horse and waited for the wagons to catch up, then he drifted out to Ramón's customary place on the flank. Often Heather could see Ramón turn to look back over his shoulder as if to ask why the wagons were moving so slowly.

And finally she saw him take off his hat and wave it in a wide circle over his head. The warm south breeze brought the sound of lusty shouting. Beyond him she saw two horses and made out the figures sitting on them. The riders moved into a lope toward Ramón, and Ramón spurred into a run. When they all reined up together, she could see Ramón throw his arms around first one of the riders, then the other.

She heard Dent Sessum grumble, "Hell of a lot of guardin' he's doin' for us right now. A whole herd of Indians could ride in on us and he'd never even see them."

Heather felt compelled to speak. "He's found some of his family. You can't blame him for that."

"I didn't know Mexicans had families. I figured they just had litters, like dogs."

Heather wished she could have seen Joshua Buckalew beat Dent Sessum instead of simply having to hear about it.

She could see that the two riders with Ramón were boys, wearing plain homemade cotton shirts and trousers, with floppy straw hats perched on their heads. Their feet were bare except for simple leather *huaraches* which covered little but the soles. Joshua Buckalew rode forward and embraced them. Muley Dodd jumped off of his horse, pulled the boys down and whirled around and around with first one of them, then the other. From fifty yards away, Heather could hear his happy laugh.

As the wagons pulled up, Ramón put his hands on the two boys' shoulders and led them to the Provost wagon. "Mrs. Provost, Mr. Provost . . ." He glanced toward Heather. ". . . Mrs. Winslow, I want you all to meet my brothers. Demons, these two. But good demons."

The boys stared at the wagons and the people on them and made their *mucho gustos* with cautious grace and bubbling curiosity. Aaron climbed down and shook hands with them as if they were adults, and Heather could tell that the gesture had made him their friend for life. Aaron asked, "Ramón, did they give you a good report on the rest of your family?"

Ramón grinned. English failed him, and he replied in Spanish, which Heather understood imperfectly. "Everyone is well. My baby son is almost big enough to smoke tobacco, and I have not even seen him yet. Josh, I think I will ride on ahead."

"Go on, Ramón. We wouldn't have it no other way."

"Perhaps you would like to go in with me?"

Muley nodded his enthusiasm, but Josh waved him back. "No, Ramón, you have your reunion first. We'll be in with the wagons directly."

Muley was still eager. "Josh, I'd like to go with him."

"We'll need you here, Muley. With Ramón goin' on ahead, and all, we're a man short."

One of the boys spoke, "We'll tell María you are coming, Josh."

"You do that, Gregorio."

Heather frowned, for she had understood enough Spanish to catch that. She wondered who María was. It suddenly occurred to her that Josh had taken time this morning to shave his face clean. She hadn't given it much thought at the time except to note that he looked strongly handsome with the whiskers off.

Heather, she told herself, *it's none of your business. You've got no claim on the man. Maybe someone else has.*

But she wondered, nevertheless.

It was an hour before the wagons climbed the last hill and Heather looked down on the Hernandez *rancho*. At first glance she almost missed seeing the buildings. They were made of rock that blended with the color of the land around them. Their roofs were almost flat, so that the main house and the little buildings clustered close around it seemed to huddle just barely above the ground, and seemed to be almost a part of it. A scattering of gardens and green little fields lay on the slope and down in the shallow valley below the house. The fields had been freshly worked. They weren't weed-grown like those of the *Americano* settlers who had been forced to flee ahead of Santa Anna's army.

She heard Sessum grumble loudly to Ocie Quitman, "Looky yonder, will you? Everything neat as ever was. House standin', kids playin' in the yard. Couldn't even tell there was a war. A lot different than for all the white folks. All he's got to do is pick up things right where he left off. And him just a black-eyed Mexican. Kind of gorges you a little, don't it?"

Heather could not hear Quitman's reply, if he gave one. For a moment she found herself sharing a little of Sessum's resentment, until she realized that Ramón had fought for Texas, and Sessum hadn't fought for anything. He had been sitting on the Sabine, he and his partner McAfee, waiting for others to shed their blood and make the ground safe for him.

Aaron Provost spoke reprovingly, "Don't be envious, Sessum. Rejoice in another man's good fortune. Next time it may be yours."

"Damn it, Provost, there's that Mexican down yonder got him a good house and a bunch of fresh-plowed fields and it don't even make you a little bit mad. Don't *nothin'* ever provoke you?"

Aaron's eyes narrowed, and his voice went deliberately flat. "*You* provoke me sometimes, Sessum. It'd please me a right smart if you'd just tend your wagon and hold your silence."

Resentment flared in Sessum's face, but he said nothing more. Heather had an idea that one hard blow from the farmer's big fist could knock him off his wagon, and Sessum probably knew it. She had a devilish wish to see it happen but knew it was unlikely she ever would. Aaron Provost used his great strength for labor, not for strife. She had seen him grieve over that renegade boy he had shot. Provost would fight if he had to, but it would be with reluctance.

Josh and Muley rode down the hill a little ahead of the wagons. Muley broke loose and raced on, sliding his horse to a stop, jumping down and scooping up the smaller members of the Hernandez family one at a time, swinging them round and round. The youngsters then would run to Josh and throw their arms around him.

Heather could see Ramón and a tiny woman standing proudly by the door of the stone house, Ramón holding a red-blanketed bundle in his arms. Then she saw another woman who had moved out into the yard, behind the children but well in front of Ramón and his wife. This, Heather knew, would be the María whose name she had heard. María was watching Josh intently, her hands clasped in nervousness as she obviously fought a strong wish to run out and meet him halfway. Josh broke free of the youngsters finally, and he turned toward María. He stood there a moment, looking at her, then moved. She broke into a run and threw her arms around him.

The proper thing, Heather knew, would have been to look the other way and give them their moment of privacy. But she watched. She glanced at Ocie Quitman, finally, and she found he was watching, too. His eyes disapproved.

"You look troubled, Mister Quitman."

"Never did set good with me, seein' American men dally with these Mexican women. Always thought they ought to have more pride."

"Every man needs a woman sometime. There aren't enough American women to go around."

"Then a man ought to do without." Quitman looked at the ground. Face twisting, he swung down and dropped to one knee to examine a wide mark. "*Carreta* track. Been one of them big Mexican carts along here."

"I expect these people have one."

"This one passed not very long ago." Anger welled in his face, anger Heather could not understand. "Faustino!" he said bitterly.

"What is Faustino?"

"Never mind."

Ramón had all of his family line up. He introduced Aaron and Rebecca and Heather. He made no effort to introduce all the Provost children because he simply hadn't had a chance to get them all separated in his own mind. Last of all he named Ocie Quitman and Dent Sessum. Neither man did more than nod.

Heather said quietly to Quitman, "I know I have no right to criticize you . . ."

"No, you don't."

Muley's old hound Hickory made a fuss over him, then he and the Provosts' dogs warily circled, sizing each other up, testing one end and then the other.

Heather somehow thought at first that the Mexican children were sons and daughters of Ramón, but it was made clear to her they were his brothers and sisters. His father and mother had been taken by the fever before the war began. The only child he had of his own was the baby he proudly held in his arms, opening the blanket so everyone could see the tiny brown face, the dark eyes blinking defensively against the brightness of the sun. Ramón's wife Miranda stood beside him, smiling happily, her small hands tightly holding onto his arm as if she never intended ever again to let Ramón out of her grasp.

Heather had seen Mexicans before, but she had never been around them much. The few she saw were transient horse traders and the like, and the handful of resident Mexicans who lived in Austin's capital town of San Felipe. She could not remember that she had ever seen a family group like this one, at their own home and wholly at ease.

"They don't seem so different, do they, Mister Quitman? I mean, they remind me of when I was a girl, back home."

"They're different, Mrs. Winslow."

Ocie Quitman tied his horse to the wagon wheel and walked up to Ramón. Ramón opened the blanket a little to show his child, but Quitman didn't look down. He stared at Ramón. "How long since Faustino left here?"

Ramón's smile faded. "Forget Faustino. He is gone."

"I asked you, how long?"

"When I came. I saw him here, I told him go."

"You gave him stuff?"

"Food, blankets."

"I didn't want nobody helpin' them."

Ramón reverted to Spanish. "This is *my* place, Mister Quitman. *I* say who is helped here, and who is not. You are my guest, and *only* my guest."

Quitman turned toward his horse. "I can fix that. I don't have to stay here."

"Wait." Ramón pointed at the boy Patrick. "Your son has need of this place. Where would you take him?"

Quitman fought for control of his temper. He glanced toward Heather Winslow as if to ask her for help. She had none to give him. She said, "He's right, Mister Quitman."

Quitman stood with his back to Ramón. His fists clenched a moment, but slowly he gave in and turned.

"All right, Hernandez. Long as Faustino has left for Mexico—long as he don't ever come back—I reckon that's the last I'll say of it. But I want you to understand one thing: you're not givin' me nothin'. Whatever you do for me or my boy, I'll pay for it. I'll pay you in work or in goods or in money, but I'll pay you. I'll not stand beholden."

Ramón nodded. "Then, I see no argument. We are agreed."

The first thing they had to do was to place the wagons, for they would have to continue to live out of them until the crops were planted and the cabins rebuilt. The teams were maneuvered so that the Provost wagon and Quitman's sat a few steps apart, not far from the stone house. Aaron Provost motioned for Dent Sessum to pull his into the same line, but Sessum hauled his team around and moved off down toward one of the sheds.

"No use us gettin' our stuff mixed up with each other," Sessum grunted. "Keep 'em apart, I say. Then there ain't no chance of one of us gettin' off with things that belong to somebody else and causin' hard feelin's." He spat, his gaze touching the house, then falling on some of the Hernandez youngsters. "Besides, the further I stay away from *them* people, the better I'll sleep of a night."

Provost made no argument. When Sessum was out of earshot, the big farmer sighed in relief, "I'll sleep a lot better knowin' he's that far away from *me*. He'd bust a gut if he thought somebody would get off with a tin cup or a piece of rope that belonged to him. I believe he's the greediest livin' thing I ever seen, outside of a hog pen."

Quitman turned toward Josh. "Where do you intend to camp?"

Josh grimaced. "I *had* figured on the shed. But with Sessum down there, Muley and me will have to find us some other place. That arbor, I expect."

Quitman frowned toward the door of the rock house, where María Hernandez had gone. "Kind of thought you might choose to camp with her."

Josh's voice sharpened. "You better get one thing straight, Quitman, and get it now. She's as honest as the best you ever met."

"If you say so." Quitman paused. "Mind if I camp with you?"

"Suit yourself. I'm surprised you'd want to."

"It's either you or Sessum. There's some things you do that I don't care for, but at least you're open about them."

Josh stared at him, still surprised. "I'd have to say the same for you, Quitman. Times, I'd like to take a club to you. But I always know where you stand."

As she had been doing on the trail each night, Heather Winslow shared camping chores with Rebecca Provost. Cooking together, washing the utensils together, they managed to make the load easier than if each tried to maintain a separate camp. The children helped unload what they would need out of the wagons. Aaron Provost dug a pit for the fire.

Heather noticed that the Hernandez youngsters gathered around, well out of the way, watching the Provost boys and girls and Ocie Quitman's son. The Provost children gawked back.

"Come on, young'uns," Mrs. Provost scolded, "we got work to be done." But it wasn't being done very efficiently. The oldest Provost boy had his eye on the oldest of the Hernandez girls. Suddenly he leaped toward her and shouted, "Boo!" She jumped. The others giggled and laughed. Mrs. Provost shooed them all away. "Go on, all of you. You're no help here anyway. Go on out yonder and get yourselves acquainted."

Heather smiled. "You're not afraid they'll be contaminated?"

"You been listenin' to Ocie Quitman. A lot he knows . . ."

María Hernandez came out again and approached the two women hesitantly. "Pardon. Is there anything I can do to help?"

Mrs. Provost stretched, her hands pressing against her back. "I reckon we got it in order . . . as much order as we're goin' to have."

The Mexican girl said apologetically, "If the house was larger . . ."

Mrs. Provost shrugged, smiling. "Well, it ain't, and there's nothin' you can do about that, child. We'll have our own cabins in due time."

Heather Winslow studied María. She found her slight in build, not weighing much over a hundred pounds. Long black hair, carefully brushed and ribbon-tied at the back of her neck, framed a pretty oval face. It was the skin Heather noticed most—olive skin, clear and smooth, as if it had never known the harshness of the sun and the wind. Heather felt of her own face and knew it must be chapped and rough, for this had been a hard trip, and exposure had been extreme.

The girl's gaze moved to Heather, and Heather looked down, embarrassed to be caught staring. "I like your place here."

María Hernandez smiled. "It is home. Not pretty, like some places in Bexar. Have you ever been to Bexar?"

Heather shook her head. María went on, "It is very pretty in Bexar, or was before the trouble. Big stone houses by the river, tall churches, pretty gardens . . . You would like it."

"I like it here."

"I would be pleased to show you all of it."

"I'd like that. How about you, Rebecca?"

Mrs. Provost shook her head. "I'm a little tired, and anyway I got a meal to start. You young folks go ahead. I'll see it in due time, I expect."

María led Heather first to the house. Heather paused at the arbor in front of the door and looked at a couple of crude willow crates, which stood open and empty.

"For the roosters," María said. "The fighting roosters. My father, my older brothers, they all liked the fighting roosters. But the war came, and there was no more time."

"You mean people raise roosters just to fight?"

"They fight to the death, if you let them."

"How do they provoke them into it?"

"They do not have to. It is bred into the birds to hate and to fight. There does not have to be a reason. You put them together and they fight, that is all." Sadness touched her. "With people, it is the same. They do not need a reason. They just fight. They fight and they die, and they know not why they do it."

The house was as plain inside as outside, Heather found. The furniture was handmade from materials found close to home. The walls were mostly bare, coats hanging from pegs secured by the mortar between the stones. Heather's eye was caught by a huge hand-carved crucifix hanging in a corner, the figure of Christ meticulously done.

María said, "My father made that. He had the priest to bless it because we are so far from the church. We look at it, and we do not forget what is holy."

María started to lead her into another room but stopped. Heather caught a glimpse of Ramón and Miranda sitting on a bed, their hands clasped as they looked down on their sleeping baby. María smiled and whispered, "They have no need of us."

She led Heather outside and up the slope. Occasionally María would stop to point out one thing or another, and tell of some incident that had happened there.

Heather noticed a tall rock corral, quite close to the house. "A lot of work went into that. Why did it have to be built so strong? No animal is going to break out of it anyway."

"The Comanche might try to break in. When we know the Indians are close, we put the horses and mules in the rock corral. The gate is on the side by the house. When the Indians try to take the bars away and open it, we can stop them. Never have we lost an animal out of that corral."

"Do the Indians come often?"

"Not often. But when they come, they want horses."

The two women walked on up the slope and stopped finally at a small family cemetery where tall wooden markers stood stark against the blue sky. María crossed herself and pointed to the two tallest. "My mother and father. Next to them, a little brother who died of the fever at the same time."

On another cross Heather read the word. "Teresa."

"My sister," said María. "It was many years ago she died."

"The fever?"

"No, the Comanches. They found her on the road." She looked at the ground. "Do you know Joshua very well?"

"Not really. We came across him and your brother and Muley west of San Jacinto."

"Joshua was in love with Teresa. He wanted to marry her. That was a very long time ago."

Heather waited a little before she asked, "And now you want to marry *him?*" When María stared in surprise, Heather continued, "I saw the way you greeted him. It was plain to anyone with eyes that you were in love with him. Is he in love with you?"

María shook her head soberly. "I don't know. I don't think *he* knows. People all say I look like my sister. I know how he felt about *her.*"

"How long have you been in love with him?"

"Since I was a little girl. He came here, he taught us English while we taught him Spanish."

"You speak it very well."

"Even as a girl, I wanted to please him. I studied hard. I learned English better than anyone here, even Ramón, and he knew it before, from Bexar. But I was foolish. I was only a little girl. Teresa was a woman."

"You're a woman now."

"Perhaps it is still not enough. Perhaps another woman will come along and he will love her instead of me."

Heather got an uneasy feeling María meant her. "I am not your rival, María."

María managed a thin smile. "I meant nothing. But I could not blame you if you wanted Josh. He has been wanted before."

"But no one ever got him."

"One day someone will. I hope it is me."

Down on the flat, Ocie Quitman rode alone, walking his horse, studying the fields, looking over the scattering of Hernandez cattle. María's eyes hardened with dislike as she watched him. "He is a strange one, your Mister Quitman."

"*My* Mister Quitman?"

"Well, Mister Quitman, anyway. Ramón told us he would be so. Before you came, a Mexican man and woman stopped here in an oxcart." They were in such a hurry they would not even let us cook for them. They were afraid Mister Quitman would come."

Heather's eyes widened, for now she started putting odd bits of fact together, and she thought she could figure the rest of the story. She told María about Faustino and about Quitman's wife.

María's voice softened a little. "That, then, is why he dislikes us all."

"It's more than just dislike. He's a good man in many ways, but he's like one of your fighting roosters. He fights because it is in him to do it. Give him room, María. He's been hurt, badly. He may hurt a lot of others before he gets it burned out of his system."

8

It took only a couple of days to catch up with what work the men needed to do around the Hernandez place, for the women and the youngsters had stayed busy while Ramón was off to the war.

Dent Sessum bent his back but little. Most of the time he walked around admiring the fields or riding one of his horses bareback over the grassland. The longer he looked at it, the better he liked it. While Ramón squatted with Joshua Buckalew beside Josh's coffee bucket one evening, Sessum strode up and made a blunt offer. "I'll buy this place from you, Hernandez. I'll pay you in American cash money."

Surprised, Ramón shook his head. "It is not to be sold."

"Better take my offer, *hombre*. Next time I won't likely bid as much."

"Next time I don't sell, either. This is my home."

"Home is where a man lays his head down to sleep. You can sleep comfortable someplace else, with American money in your pockets."

"I will sleep here."

"You can take and buy you some more land."

"Why? I do not want other land. Why would I sell?"

Sessum squinted one eye. "Because you're a foreigner livin' in a white man's country, that's why. The war's over. Goin' to be a lot of new people move in here now, people from the States. They ain't goin' to take well to havin' Mexicans livin' in their midst. Like as not they'd up and run you off and you wouldn't get paid a thing.

Better you take my offer and go hunt you a place where you're welcome."

Ramón pointed up the slope. "See that cemetery? My father is there, and my mother. Some others too. This is Hernandez land, for always. I have fought for it against Santa Anna."

"Them new people movin' in, they ain't goin' to know that, or care. All they'll see is that you're a Mexican. Believe me, Hernandez, they'll move you. Or they'll bury you up in that cemetery with the rest of your folks."

Ramón set his cup aside and stood up straight. His leg had healed enough that he no longer walked with a stick. "Do you make a threat?"

"A prediction. And you can mark it down as the gospel."

Joshua Buckalew pushed to his feet and stepped in front of Sessum. "You heard him tell you he don't want to sell. Now you leave him alone."

"Let him fight his own battles."

"He did, at San Jacinto. If you'd seen him there, you wouldn't be so damned anxious to stir up a fight with him now."

Glaring, Sessum turned and walked away resentfully.

Ramón went back to Spanish. "Josh, do you really believe he has the money he talks about?"

Josh nodded. "I expect. I've had a feelin' for a long time that he and McAfee had somethin' hidden in that wagon."

"Where do you think they got it?"

"Not much tellin'. They didn't earn it. And wherever it was, you can bet they left there in the middle of the night."

* * *

It was time for the men to go back and work their own
farms in Hopeful Valley, to break their weed-grown
fields and plant spring crops. They agreed to stay together for mutual protection as well as for the speed
and efficiency they would gain by working as a team.
They wanted to take Sessum's wagon, for it would be
sitting idle and unneeded here.

Josh was sure that by now Sessum had gone off somewhere in the dark and had buried his money, so the wagon
wasn't needed to store it. But Sessum argued that a wagon
was a tremendously valuable piece of equipment these
days, well-nigh impossible to replace. The trip would be a
hazard to it that he felt no obligation to suffer, especially
because he had no land yet and was, in his view, already
contributing more than his share by the labor he was
performing. That he worked at all was simply a demon-
stration of the goodness of his heart, Sessum declared.

The upshot was that they took Ocie Quitman's wagon.
Heather Winslow said she could do without it. The men
loaded Ramón's wooden plows and tied his work oxen
behind the wagon. They loaded axes and shovels, seed
corn and coffee. In the way of food, there was not much
more they could take. For the most part they would live
off of the land.

Muley watched the children at play, his eyes aglow.
"Josh, how about me stayin' here and kind of helpin' tend
to things? I could be a right smart of protection for the
womenfolk."

Josh smiled. He knew Muley wouldn't be very watch-
ful protection, for he would be playing games with the

kids every minute the women didn't have him busy on some job or other. "Muley, we need you too bad ourselves. We've decided to leave Aaron's boy Daniel. He's not far from bein' a man, and he can shoot as good as any of us, just about. María can handle a rifle, and I expect Heather Winslow and Rebecca Provost could too, if the need come. They'll be all right, long as nobody strays far from the house."

Muley looked crestfallen. "Josh, I was helpin' them Provost boys learn to talk Mexican. They're startin' to do pretty good."

Josh's observation was that the boys had learned a lot more from the Hernandez brood than from Muley. Muley's Spanish was rudimentary and mostly wrong. "They won't forget what you've taught them. When we get back, you can take up where you left off."

Miranda Hernandez stood leaning against Ramón, and it was hard to tell which one was holding the baby, for each had an arm beneath it. Miranda wept silently, and Ramón tenderly assured her it wouldn't be long before they would be back.

Josh took María's hand. "If there's any sign of Indians, we'll come back in a hurry. Meantime, you-all stick close by. Don't let anybody get so far from the house that they could be cut off."

"You are the ones to be careful, Josh." Pain was in her eyes. "You will be a long way from help."

"We're takin' along our own. There's six of us."

Patrick Quitman was in his father's arms. "Now, son," Quitman was telling him, "you mind whatever Mrs. Winslow tells you, and don't you be causin' her no grief. I'll be back soon's I can."

"You goin' to take us home before long, Daddy?"

Quitman winced. "I don't know, son. We'll just have to see."

"I sure do wish we could go home."

Quitman looked away, and Josh could read the thought betrayed by the heavy furrows in the man's face. How could they go to a home that no longer existed, that could never exist again the way it had been?

Quitman warned, "You stay close to Mrs. Winslow. Don't you be runnin' off out of sight."

The boy hugged his father's neck. "All right, Daddy. *Vaya con Dios.*"

Quitman stiffened. "Where'd you learn that?"

"From Gregorio." Patrick pointed to the largest of the Hernandez boys. "Gregorio knows everything."

The brown-skinned lad shrank back in consternation from the hostility in Quitman's eyes. Quitman said, "Mrs. Winslow!"

Heather Winslow stepped forward. Quitman handed Patrick to her and said sternly, "Whatever teachin' is to be done for my boy, I want you to do it, or me. There's too many things he needs to learn a lot more than talkin' Mexican."

María Hernandez spoke, her voice edged with quick anger. "Gregorio has meant no harm, Mister Quitman."

Quitman stared at her a long moment. "And let's see that no harm is done, Miss Hernandez. If I decide I want him to learn Mexican, or to learn anything else you people can teach him, I'll let you know."

He climbed up onto the wagon seat and flipped the reins, the team quickly settling into the traces.

María watched him with eyes as hard as black shale. "Josh, will you do something for me?"

"Whatever you want."

"Run over him with his wagon, first time you have the chance. Don't kill him dead. Just kill him a little bit."

Hopeful Valley had no town, no store, no central settlement. It was simply a name some optimistic settler had hung on the whole general area which included the Provost place and Winslow's and Quitman's and a dozen others. Someday perhaps there would be a town, or at least a tiny crossroads settlement, when enough people came. It was a long way short of that yet.

The men halted first at the Provost place, hobbling the horses, staking the oxen, unloading the plows in Aaron's weedy field. The farmer took off his floppy hat and ran his huge hands through his graying hair, shaking his head as he gazed across the ragged, overgrown rows. "There's a heap of back strain ahead of us if we're to get any corn and cotton out of that mess this year."

Dent Sessum grunted. "Well, I'll stand guard and keep the Indians off of the rest of you, but I'll be damned if I see why I ought to break my back tryin' to make the other man a crop."

Josh flung a hard glance at him. At times, he wished it had been Sessum instead of his unlucky partner McAfee who had died under that Redlander's knife. "Don't you fret, Aaron. With all those kids you got, we have to see that you make a crop. Else it'll be up to the rest of us to feed you."

Aaron grinned. He called, "Hey, Muley, want to help me dig up a couple of graves?"

Muley looked stunned. "Well, Aaron, I was fixin' to help Ramón skin out this here deer we shot. We'll be needin' some supper."

"The deer can wait. Grab you a shovel, Muley."

Muley looked anxiously to Josh, but Josh jerked his thumb after Aaron in silent command. Muley put away his skinning knife, picked up a shovel and went trailing with no enthusiasm. Josh winked at Ramón and followed the farmer.

Provost stopped where three crosses stood over a set of mounds beneath a huge old live oak tree. He wrapped his muscular arms around one of the crosses and pulled it up, dropping it to one side. Muley's gaze followed the cross, then cut back to Aaron, scandalized as the farmer said, "All right now, let's get to diggin'."

"Aaron!"

Grinning, the farmer rammed his shovel into the mud. "Go ahead, Muley. Anything that's down there ain't alive."

"No, sir, I wouldn't hardly think so."

Muley made a few perfunctory jabs with the shovel, his spirit not in it. Aaron had to do most of the digging. Presently his blade struck something. The sharp sound brought Muley's eyes wide open. Aaron knelt and cleared the wet earth from around a plowhandle. "Help me pull it up, Muley." Muley didn't move. Aaron finally had to tell him, "It's not nothin' like you think it is. Help me, Muley."

"It ain't nothin' dead?"

"No, Muley. I was funnin' you."

Muley stepped into the hole and helped tug. Josh

reached down and took hold. They brought up a muddy plow.

Aaron said, "We buried everything we couldn't haul with us on the Scrape. We put the crosses up to fool the Mexicans."

Muley wiped his face. "Mexicans wasn't all you fooled, Aaron. That was a real funny joke." But he wasn't laughing.

In a little while they had dug up a considerable variety of tools from the first two "graves." Aaron said, "We'd best smooth these holes over and leave the third one like it is. Mostly it's got Rebecca's kitchen things in it. They'll be safer right where they're at."

The labor was hard and steady, for the weeds were rank and clung stubbornly to life. But the soil had dried enough on top that it worked without balling on the plows. The men used all the equipment they had, and all the animals, methodically turning up the fresh brown earth in rows straight as an arrow. They finished Aaron's fields, planting the corn and putting in the garden. Next they moved to the widow Winslow's place and did the same. That done, they went on to Ocie Quitman's.

Muley Dodd had a strong back, and work held no terror for him. But his was not a nature that could go indefinitely on hard labor without some relief. The third day at Quitman's, Josh noticed Muley's plow leaned idle in the row, the horse standing switching flies. Josh could see the rust color of Muley's holey shirt moving through the timber. Presently Muley came to the field in a trot, his face aglow with excitement.

"I seen some wild bees, Josh. I could find us some honey if you'd give me leave."

Josh looked across the field, surveying the large amount of work still to be done. But he knew Muley wouldn't be much help when his thoughts turned to bee-hunting. Muley's mind had a hard time keeping track of more than one thing at a time.

"I reckon it'd be all right if you had somebody to go with you for protection. Try Dent Sessum. He ain't been much help to us anyway." It would be a relief to get Sessum out of sight anyway. An idle man is always an irritant to the one who has to work. Besides, Josh knew the others were getting as tired of their straight venison diet as he was. They were low on coffee and cornmeal and hadn't had any sugar at all.

For days now, Muley had been watching for bees. He had already made his preparations, stripping a deerhide off without slitting it down the belly. He had turned it wrongside out, sewed up the bullethole and tied off the legs with buckskin strings. Then he had blown it up tight and let it dry in the sun. Now it was a tight case, big enough to hold all the honey a strong man could carry.

Muley slung the empty skin case over his shoulder. He carried an ax in one hand and a rifle in the other. Dent Sessum frowned, dubious about the whole adventure. He eased up to Josh and asked suspiciously, "You sure you ain't just sendin' me off on a fool's errand? Muley ain't smart enough to know a bee from a hummin' bird."

"Everybody's got his own talent. Bee-huntin' is Muley's."

Sessum snorted. "I'll wager he can't even find a wasp's nest. Tell you what, Buckalew: ever bit of honey he gits, I'll tote in on my own back."

Josh said to Muley, "You remember that now. He made

you a promise." Muley grinned in excitement. Josh pointed a finger at him. "Don't you get so wrought up over your bees that you forget to watch out for Indian sign. You keep a sharp eye open, Muley."

"I will, Josh. You comin', Mister Sessum?"

When they were gone out of sight, Josh went back to his plow. They put in a long day of it and had the biggest part of the field turned by sundown. Josh stood stretching, both hands on his hips, and searched the landscape futilely for a sign of Muley and Sessum.

Aaron Provost climbed up from the creek where he had been washing the dirt and sweat from his face and hands. "You don't reckon somethin' went with them?"

Josh shook his head. "We'd of heard shootin'. Once Muley gets on a bee trail, he just don't know when to quit." He turned and watched Ramón Hernandez limp in from the field, walking his oxen.

Aaron followed Josh's gaze. "That leg's still gimpy."

"Mornin's, it looks like Ramón has healed up. You don't see much of a limp. Evenin's, time he's put in a hard day, it comes back."

"He's workin' too hard. You better talk to him, Josh."

"That's always been Ramón's nature. When he works, he works hard. When he plays, he plays like it's for the last time."

"You better talk to him anyway." Aaron turned his attention to Josh. "By the bye, how's your arm?"

Josh blinked, and he rubbed the place where the saber had cut. He couldn't feel anything. In fact, he hadn't even thought about it. "I'd forgotten anything happened."

Ocie Quitman brought in the team he had been working to a heavy plow. He walked them over the steep creek bank, a way downstream from where Ramón was watering the oxen.

Aaron frowned. "Bank's almost flat where Ramón is. Plenty of room for all of them. Ocie don't have to go down the steep place."

"Just can't bring himself to get that close to Ramón."

"Think he'll ever come around?"

"He's been burned awful deep."

"You notice the way he's acted since we been here on his farm? Hasn't said three words in three days."

Josh nodded. "He told me he didn't think he could ever live here again. Too many ghosts. It'll be a good thing for him when we finish up and get off of this place."

Aaron kindled a campfire out of the banked coals. "It'll be better when he gets married again and has a soft, warm woman to smooth the rough edges off of him. I got an idea a woman like Heather Winslow could help make a man forget that one that died."

"He ain't said he figures to marry her. And I don't re-call she's said anything about it, either."

"It'll happen. They need each other too bad." Aaron smiled tolerantly. "Besides, Rebecca has made up her mind to it. When that wife of mine decides a thing is goin' to be, you better take it for gospel."

Ramón turned the oxen loose to graze on the lush green grass along the creek. At dark the men would have to gather all the stock and pen them in a brush corral thrown together for protection against befeathered horse thieves. Finishing, Ramón picked up the empty water bucket. Aaron took it from him. "You set your-self down and rest. That leg must be givin' you fits. I'll tote the water."

"Leg's all right," Ramón protested. But he didn't argue much, so Josh took it that the leg was aching.

Slicing venison from a deer leg hanging suspended below a live oak branch, Josh said, "You got to go a little easier, Ramón. That leg is liable to cripple on you, permanent."

"The sooner we get all the fields plowed out and planted, the sooner I get home to Miranda and the baby."

"You don't want to go home on a bad leg. Tomorrow we'll find you somethin' easier to do. You won't be lookin' them oxen in the rear."

"I am not Dent Sessum."

"You're lame. He's just lazy. It's a religion with him."

Ramón sat up straight and pointed. "Then he is losing his religion."

Turning, Josh began to laugh. Muley Dodd came striding out of the timber, rifle in one hand, ax in the other. Behind him—way behind—Sessum struggled along, his back bent under the heavy load of the bulging deerskin.

Muley shouted long before he reached the camp. "Told you, Josh. Told you I could course me some bees. You ought to see what I found."

Josh waited until Muley came up to him. "I *do* see. If you'd of found any more, you'd of broken Sessum's back."

"That'd be a good idea," Aaron grumbled.

Muley glanced over his shoulder, then back to Josh. His voice dropped almost to a whisper. "Josh, I think I ought to tell you somethin'. That Mister Sessum, he ain't a nice feller."

Josh tried to act surprised. "What did he do?"

"He wanted to go back on his promise. He kept settin' the honey down and swearin' he wouldn't carry it another step. But a promise is a promise, ain't it, Josh? You always told me if I promised to do somethin' I got to do it. I told him that, and he wouldn't listen." Muley's voice reflected his disapproval. "But I foxed him, Josh. I told him I was fixin' to run off and leave him out in them woods all by hisself. He'd holler a little bit and then pick up the honey again. He'd carry it a ways, and then it was all to do over. He ain't very nice."

Dent Sessum struggled into camp and let the honey skin down. His face and hands were swollen, for the bees hadn't taken the robbery without a fight. Muley showed not a wound. This one thing, at least, he knew how to do.

Aaron Provost ran his finger through some honey that had seeped out around the bullethole. "First honey I've tasted since I don't remember when. You fellers'll have to do this some more."

Sessum groaned. "Like hell. I'd rather follow a mule backwards and forwards over that field than follow this halfwit across all creation."

Angering, Josh said, "Tomorrow you remember you said that, because that's just what you're goin' to do."

Sessum flared. "I still ain't got no land of my own. I don't see as I need to do anything I don't want to."

Ocie Quitman had walked up, shoulders slumped in weariness, eyes bleak from the strain of being on this place that held so many memories. Somehow Sessum's complaint sparked a sudden blaze of anger. Quitman grabbed Sessum's collar and jerked. "You'd sure as hell better want to, or you'll sack your plunder and move out of here. Tomorrow you're goin' to sweat, Sessum, or I'm goin' to see you leave."

Sessum swallowed. He trembled a little after Quitman

turned loose of his collar. He finally collected enough strength to declare, "All right, I been abused enough. First thing in the mornin' I'll head up to the Mexican's place and get my wagon and clear out. I got nothin' at stake with you people. You can just get along without me."

Quitman strode angrily away, past the other men. He grabbed the ax and began chopping firewood with a fury that couldn't have been caused by Sessum alone. Sessum had merely set off the fuse. Aaron rubbed his whiskery chin and stared through narrowed eyes. "He's got a terrible anger buildin' in him, Josh. He's takin' out a little of it on that ax. But it's goin' to be dangerous for the man that ever causes him to let all that steam out at once. You better keep Ramón clear of him."

Next morning, true to his word, Sessum saddled after a hasty breakfast and took off, riding north. In a way Josh hated to see him go. Little as Sessum had done, at least he had been an extra gun in case trouble came.

Before noon Sessum came riding back. Quietly he unsaddled and hobbled his horse. He carried his saddle and blanket and bridle up close to the camp fire and dropped them. He stared into the blaze a few moments before he could bring himself to look anybody in the eye. Finally he said in a subdued voice, "A man'd be a fool to ride across that country by hisself. It ain't nothin' you can see, but I swear you can almost smell the paint and feathers in every thicket. Bad as I hate it, I reckon we need each other."

Josh and Muley's corn crop was already well underway because Muley had planted it before he left with Ramón to join Sam Houston. It was overgrown now in weeds, so the main task was to hoe it without uprooting the corn. They turned in on the job with hands and hoes.

A day's work done, they huddled around the campfire, frying venison. Aaron pointed his square chin at Josh's field. "Josh, you're goin' to have you a corn crop laid by while the rest of us is still just thinkin' about it."

"There'll be enough here to feed everybody till the harvest comes in for the rest of you."

"Thanks, Josh. We knowed you'd feel that way. We'll pay you back when the time comes." His gaze drifted northward. "Sure am missin' Rebecca and the young'uns. Wisht we had our cabin up so we could all be closer home."

Josh said, "I been studyin' how'd be the best way to handle it, and whose cabin we ought to put up first. Way I see it, we ought to go ahead and build yours, Aaron, soon's we get my fields weeded."

Sessum spoke up, though it wasn't any of his business whose house was built first. "Why his? Why not somebody else's?"

"First place, Aaron's about as well located as anybody . . . in the center of things, I mean. Second place, he's got far and away the biggest family. Way I see it, we build Aaron's first. We build it big enough to take care of the extra folks awhile. By extra folks I mean Mrs. Winslow, and Quitman and his boy. And you too, Sessum, till you find a place for yourself. Muley and me, our place is closer to Ramón's than it is to Hopeful Valley. Anyway, we can camp on the creek bank all summer if we have to. We don't have to have a roof before winter." He glanced at Quitman. "How does that sound to you?"

Quitman nodded. "Makes sense."

"Way I see it," Aaron put in, "Mrs. Winslow is a special kind of case. Even if we was to go and build her a cabin, she couldn't hardly live there by herself. And she sure couldn't live with you, Ocie, 'less the minister come around first. It wouldn't look right. So what I'd figured was that Rebecca and me would make a place for her at our house. She can read and write good, so I figured she could teach all them young'uns of ours. Your boy too, Ocie. In return for her teachin', we'd give her a roof and take care of her till you two figure a proper time has passed and you marry each other."

Quitman poked a fresh chunk of wood into the fire. "You're takin' a right smart for granted, Aaron. Mrs. Winslow and me, we haven't talked about the idea of marriage."

"You will," Aaron said confidently. "Nature will get to you bye and bye. A man needs a woman, even if he *ain't* got a boy that's without a mother. And a woman needs a man, especially if she's ever had one and got used to it. You'll both get to thinkin' about it as cold weather comes on. Them two farms would make one nice big place, once you join them together."

Quitman's eyes narrowed. "I'm not ready to think about things like that."

Aaron nodded. "I know, so your friends have got to do that thinkin' for you, and have things prepared when you do get ready."

"Aaron, you meddle like an old woman."

"One of life's little pleasures. Costs nothin' and does a heap of good in the world."

After supper they lay on their blankets in the grass

beside the log corral Josh and Muley and Thomas Buckalew had built years ago. Josh stared into the darkening
sky, wishing the work were done, wishing he could get
back and see María again. He thought of her much these
long days, and these nights. He thought of the shining
laughter in her dark eyes, like the laughter he remembered in the eyes of Teresa so awfully long ago. Sometimes, it was hard to be sure which sister he thought
of, for they had looked alike, these two.

Time had slowly healed the pain of Teresa's death. He
had almost forgotten what she looked like, though
the emptiness remained. Then one day he had gazed
into the eyes of María and had seen Teresa there. The
love he had once felt for Teresa had been born again,
this time for María. The loneliness of the years between
had left him in the light of María's smile.

Muley's voice came in a shout. "Josh! There's somebody out yonder horseback. Josh!"

Josh was on his feet instantly, grabbing for his rifle.
The men around him scrambled for their guns. The fire
had burned down to coals, but everyone hurried to get
away from it. If these were Indians, they would be looking for targets by the red glow.

A long call came from the edge of the timber. "Hello-
o-o! Hello the house!"

Josh relaxed a little. It wasn't Indians. It occurred
to him that was a hell of a poor choice for a call,
because there was no house unless you counted the
charred heap of rubble. He thought he detected something familiar about the voice. He shouted. "Who's
out there?"

"Josh! Is that you, Joshua Buckalew?"

Josh gritted, "Damn!," for he knew the voice now. He shouted back, "Come on in. It's all right."

Ocie Quitman lowered his rifle. "I take it this is some friend of yours?"

"Don't know as I'd want to call him a friend. Acquaintance is more like it. He neighbors me to the north. Name is Alfred Noonan. He's a lazy old hound dog of a man who'd talk the bark off of a tree. Quarrelsome, got a tendency to be a little mean. Don't never lend him nothin'."

Alfred Noonan rode in the lead, his gray beard streaming a little in the breeze. A second man rode half a length behind him, and Josh couldn't see him well in the poor light.

"Josh, boy!" Old Noonan's gravelly voice rubbed like splintery wood. "I'd of swore you was killed in the big war. Didn't have no idea you'd come back till we seen your smoke awhile ago."

"Who's with you, Noonan?"

"See for yourself, Josh. It's Jacob Phipps, come back from the dead. Him that the Mexicans thought they'd killed way down below the Nueces. He come back, Josh, same as you did." Noonan quickly glanced over the faces. "I don't see Thomas. Was he . . ."

"He was killed."

Noonan nodded. "I'd of swore he was. Thought you was too. Thought everybody was but me. Then I come up on Jacob Phipps, and now you. The Lord's been bountiful in His mercy."

Jacob Phipps rode forward. He was thinner than Josh remembered him, and gray before his time, for Phipps was a young man yet, not even thirty. What Josh noticed most was the stiff left arm, hanging useless at Phipps' side. "Get down, Jacob. You had any supper?"

Phipps swung down and stretched out his right hand uncertainly. Josh gripped it. Phipps said, "I wasn't sure how you'd take it, me comin' here. We didn't always get along, me and you."

That was true, for Jacob Phipps and his brother Ezekiel, together with Noonan, had often been a thorn in Josh's side. From what Josh had heard, Ezekiel lay somewhere down near the Rio Grande, his head blown off by Mexican cavalry who had ambushed a foolhardy Texan patrol as Santa Anna's column started its march toward the Alamo.

Josh said, "Good to see you alive, Jacob. As for the rest, forget it. The past is gone." He pointed to the ruins of his cabin. "The future is all we got."

Phipps nodded sadly. "That's the truth if ever was. They didn't leave us nothin' but prospects. You say you got somethin' to eat?"

Josh introduced them around, though he found they'd met Aaron before, and there seemed a slight recognition of Ocie Quitman. They came finally to Ramón. Phipps shook hands with him, but Noonan stepped back, disapproving. "You mean, Josh, after all that's happened, you're still runnin' with *that* tribe?"

Regretfully Josh said, "I hoped the war would've changed you, Noonan."

"I hoped it'd change *you*. Your brother dead, and still you make friends with the likes of this?"

"Ramón fought on *our* side."

Noonan shrugged. "Knowed us Texans was bound to win, that's why. They're a shifty lot, them people. Always watch whichaway the wind blows, and they go with it. He knowed we'd come out on top of old Santy Anna."

Josh's voice took on a barb. "Last time I seen you, Noonan, *you* didn't think so. You had your tail between your legs, runnin' for the Sabine River just as hard as you could go."

Noonan's reddish face got even redder, but he made no direct reply. "You watch. Hernandez and his kind will turn against us first time they see a chance. You can't trust them a minute."

Ramón limped away, angry but carrying it with him rather than be the cause of trouble. Dent Sessum took old Noonan by the arm. "You look hungry, friend. Come on and we'll see what we can stir up for you. You sound like a man after my own heart."

Josh glanced at Jacob Phipps. "How about you, Jacob? Noonan speakin' for you, too?"

Phipps shook his head. "Me, I had all the fightin' I ever want. I'm ready to be friends with everybody, white, brown, black or green. I stick with Noonan because I need him." He touched his dead arm. "But he don't do my talkin' for me, not anymore."

9

María Hernandez stopped in the edge of the garden and leaned on her hoe, gazing across the fields at the children, scattered up and down the long rows with hoes or bare hands, cutting or pulling the upstart young weeds that still tried to take hold among the cornstalks and the cotton. They had gone farther from the house than María had told them to. Squinting, she could see the oldest Provost boy Daniel, way down at the far end of the field, near his tied horse. Daniel held a rifle and was supposed to be keeping watch. But María noted that he was bending a lot, evidently pulling weeds with the rest of them.

"They have gone too far, Heather," María said. "We must speak to them about that."

Heather Winslow was on her knees, digging up onions. She pushed her bonnet back away from her eyes. "Children don't always listen. Do you see Patrick?"

"Way out yonder by Daniel."

"He's always tagging after one of the older boys, either Daniel or Gregorio. He's gotten awfully attached to that young brother of yours."

"I know. And your Mister Quitman will not like it."

Mrs. Winslow reddened. "I wish you wouldn't call him *my* Mister Quitman."

"Mrs. Provost talks as if it is all settled."

"It isn't. I wish people would stop trying to push us into something I'm not sure either one of us wants."

"He is not a bad man to look upon. I cannot say I like his temper."

"He is bitter. He suffered a terrible loss."

"So did you. You do not seem bitter."

"Some people accept things, and others don't. I've accepted what happened to Jim. It was part of the war. In a way I guess it was to be expected. But what happened to Mister Quitman's wife was not to be expected. It was too cruel even for war."

"He seems a hard man, but he is gentle with you, Mrs. Winslow. That means something, yes?"

"I think he must always have been gentle with *her*."

María frowned. "And so maybe you only remind him of her."

"Maybe."

María's eyes pinched. "I hope it is not so. One should be loved for oneself, not because one reminds a man of someone else. That would be a long and empty road, I think."

The corner of her eye caught a sudden flurry of movement, and she turned half around, staring out across the field. She saw the Provost boy running, leading the horse. The boy Patrick was racing alongside him. Near them, some of the girls had dropped their sticks and hoes and were running toward young Provost. Daniel lifted them up and put them on the horse one at a time until four girls were astride. María saw him wave his hat and start the horse running toward the house. Then Daniel was running again, keeping his pace slow enough that Patrick could stay up.

Daniel shouted, though María could make out nothing he said. Nearer the house, the other children had caught the importance of the sudden movement and seemed to be hearing what Daniel was shouting at them. They dropped everything and started to run.

Heather Winslow's face went pale. "María, what is it?" But she must already have known.

María was already running. "There is a rifle in the house. Come on!" She grabbed the rifle, a powderhorn and a pouch of shot. She was out of the house again in seconds. She paused only long enough to prime the weapon. Then she was running for the field, racing toward the children. Heather hurried just behind her.

The four girls on the horse came galloping past the other running children. María threw her hands in the air as the horse approached her. The biggest girl reined to a stop, and María started helping the girls to the ground. "Run!" she shouted. "Run for the house!" Then she motioned for Heather. "Up! I'll give you a foot-lift."

Heather's long skirts got in her way, but she swung up, sliding the skirts far up her legs. She reached down and caught María's hand, helping María swing up too. María's bare heels thumped against the horse's ribs as she reined it around. The horse reluctantly went into a lope again. It had caught the excitement and wanted only to go to the house. María kept her heels drumming till she came up even with the second group of running children. She shouted, "Down, Heather. Take the rifle and get these children to the house. I'll go for the boys."

Heather pointed to a line of horsemen on the hill, riding down toward the field. "No, María, you can't. Look yonder."

"I think I can beat them to the boys."

Heather slid to the ground, falling to hands and knees and pushing herself up immediately. She reached for the rifle and horn and pouch. María said breathlessly, "You can reach the house before them, but keep the children moving fast. Use the gun if you have to."

María moved away from Heather in a lope, her heels drumming again. Heather began pushing the children. "Hurry. Run, girls. Boys, rush it up. You've got to run." For herself, she was running backward much of the time, watching María.

The horse galloped through the fresh green corn, trampling the stalks, almost losing his footing in the soft plowed ground. María was shouting first at the horse, then at the boys. "Run, run!"

The riders were coming down off of the hill, yipping and shouting. María's blood ran like ice, and her scalp prickled. Comanches, smelling blood. It mattered not to them whether they killed men or women or children, or whether they were American or Mexican.

I'm not going to get there in time. The terrible thought ran through her mind, and scalding tears burned her eyes. Neither boy was hers, or even of her blood, but the thought of seeing them slain like helpless deer brought an anguished "No!" from her tight throat. She drummed her heels harder. Another thought came. What if they did not kill the boys? What if they took them? The Comanches did that sometimes with children. She had known of many cases. The boys, if they survived the first hard days and weeks, might be treated first as slaves and later taken into the tribe. The girls might also be enslaved, and when they were old enough, taken for wife.

Better they die, she thought. *But better still if I reach them first. Then at least they'll have a chance.*

María held no illusions about what the Indians would do if they caught *her.* Years ago, they had caught her sister Teresa.

The boys were only fifty yards from her now . . . forty . . . thirty. She dared not look for the Indians, but some terrible curiosity forced her to do it anyway. She saw that they were not coming straight at her now. They were angling off.

The ravine. She remembered the ravine which cut across above the field. It was too deep, too steep. They were having to go around it. She remembered the many times Ramón had cursed that ravine for stealing runoff water the field needed, and now she thanked God for it.

She stopped the horse and reached down for Patrick's arm. The Provost boy gave the lad a boost. Then, almost in the same motion, Daniel swung up too, the rifle still unfired but ready.

Three on one horse, and the Indians all riding single. That made for a desperate risk, but there was no way to ease it, for which boy would she leave? She shouted, "Hold me, Patrick," and put her heels to work again. They quartered across the field, trying to get out of the plowed soil and onto the solid ground. She glanced back once, just long enough to see the Indians coming around the head of the ravine. They were close enough that she could hear their shouts, even over the hoofs and the little boy's sobs.

Ahead, Heather Winslow was almost out of the field with the other children. There remained a run of fifty yards to the house. They could make it. Heather turned and faced back across the field, the rifle coming up to her shoulder. María saw the fire and the smoke and saw Heather drop the rifle butt to the ground, preparing to ram down another load.

"She's trying to help us," María told the boys.

Daniel Provost's voice was frightened. "She can't hit them at that distance."

"She will worry them," María said.

Daniel looked back and gasped. "There's one of them way out in the lead. He's goin' to catch us, María."

She saw an arrow go by like the flash of a light, suddenly gone. "Can you shoot him?"

He tried to aim the rifle. "Not with us goin' thisaway."

"Then be ready. I'll stop. Shoot him."

She reined to a quick halt. The rifle boomed. Daniel shouted, "He's down. I got the horse."

María put the plowhorse back into a run. Ahead of her, Heather Winslow fired again and began to retreat, moving backward, watching, reloading as she moved. María shouted, "To the house, Heather. Run!"

Heather fired once more, then turned and ran. María allowed herself another glance over her shoulder. The Indians were coming, but now María was certain she would beat them to the house. She slid to a stop as Heather reached the arbor. Rebecca Provost held the door open. "You-all come a-runnin'! Come a-runnin', I say!"

María shoved both boys off of the horse. Patrick sprawled, sobbing. Heather grabbed him into her arms. María turned the horse into the stone corral and took time to shut the gate. Rebecca Provost shouted desperately at her, and at her oldest son. But Daniel stood his ground at the arbor, rifle to his shoulder, protecting María. She sprinted for the house. The Provost boy walked backward, keeping the rifle ready. The dogs scurried through the door ahead of María. The boy turned and ran. Rebecca Provost slammed the door shut behind them and dropped the heavy bar.

María's lungs ached. She had held her breath much of the time, taking it in gasps. She found herself trembling now, tears starting to flow. She looked fearfully around the room, counting. "The children . . ."

Rebecca Provost hugged Heather, then María. "They're all here, praise God. Hadn't been for you two girls, we'd of lost them all." The older woman let her tears stream without any effort to blink them away. María broke free, still struggling for breath. "Heather . . . you have the rifle . . . Will you use it . . . or you want me to?"

Hands shaking, Heather extended the rifle to arm's length. "If you can shoot straight, you'd better do it."

Miranda Hernandez sat on the floor, cradling her baby to her bosom and praying softly to her saint. Rebecca and Heather got all the whimpering children to lie flat around Miranda. María went to a shuttered window. Daniel Provost was at another, peering intently through the port.

Rebecca said, "Heather, you got more learnin' than me. Miranda's prayin' in her language. You pray in English. The good Lord ought to understand *one* of you."

Heather asked, "What're *you* going to do?"

Rebecca had brought the chopping ax in from the woodpile during the excitement. Now she picked it up. "I'm goin' to be holdin' this, just in case."

Hoofs pounded in the yard outside. An Indian made for the corral where María had penned the horse. Daniel's rifle roared. The bullet whined angrily off of the rock fence. "Didn't hit him," the boy shouted, "but he sure turned back." He began reloading.

An Indian galloped straight toward the house, lance poised. He hurled it, and the heavy wooden door trembled. María fired. The rider shrieked and flopped back, almost losing his leg-hold on the gotch-eared pony. As he whirled away, María glimpsed a blood-splotch on his side. She had creased his ribs, if she hadn't shattered them.

She took count of the Indians now. Six. Horse-stealing

party, likely, but a party out for horses would not pass up any easy opportunity to bleed their enemies.

She saw two Indians riding one horse. One of them must have been the warrior Daniel had set afoot. For all practical purposes, then, they had put two Indians out of any real chance at action.

"Watch the corral!" she said to Daniel. "They'll try again for the horse. They have a man afoot."

One Indian got as far as the gate. His pony went down threshing, a slug in its belly. The Indian scuttled away.

The Comanches pulled back, shouting in anger. María knew none of the words, but the message was clear. Six men had only four horses between them now, and all the enemy were forted up in a strong rock house. Under normal circumstances the Indians would have left, for the Comanche was not one to throw his life away in a mad gamble. He killed when the odds were in his favor, and he melted with the whistling wind when the risk became too great. He was never ashamed to retreat, for retreat to him was not surrender. It was merely a realistic acceptance of a bad situation. He always intended to come back another time, when perhaps the spirits were smiling upon him.

For these men, retreat must be coming a little harder. They had seen nothing here but women and children. They probably were figuring accurately that if there had been any men here they would have come out to protect their families. It would be a galling thing for a Comanche warrior to go into camp and admit he had been set afoot and chased away by a few women and children.

"Be ready," said María. "I think they will try again."

She wished for more rifles. The Indians seemed to

have none at all. They had used nothing but arrows and the lance, which she felt sure must still be stuck in the heavy door. "Can you see them, Daniel?"

"No. They're off to one side someplace. I can't see them through the porthole."

María moved across the room to watch the back of the house. She could see them out there milling around, uncertain, four men on horses, one standing, one sitting hunched on the ground, holding his side.

In the tightly closed room the dogs were barking and some of the children were whimpering. Their ears all rang from the roar of the rifles. Smoke hung thick and acrid. The children who weren't crying were coughing, choking on the smoke.

María saw one Indian come running, afoot. The horsemen gave him a few seconds, then came in a gallop, yipping and shouting.

"Two are coming your way, Daniel."

Two riders rushed toward the back of the house, but at such an oblique angle María could not take aim through the port. She held her fire and waited. An arrow thumped into the wooden shutters. Another struck the wood at the edge of the port and came flying in, its force blunted. It hit the rifle, glancing off. María's heart leaped with fright, but she forced herself to glance through the port. She saw the Indian afoot hurl his body against the shutters. The bar bulged and cracked. Almost in panic, María shoved the muzzle through the port and fired.

She realized instantly that had been a mistake, for now she had to take time to reload. The Indian threw his shoulder against the shutters again. The bar splintered, and the shutters swung open. For a second the Comanche paused there, blinking against the darkness of the interior while María fought to reload.

Mrs. Provost shouted, "You bloody heathen!" She ran at the Indian, the ax poised over her shoulder. The Indian tried to swing his bow into position to loose an arrow at her, but he was off balance. Just as the ax swung, he threw himself backward, out of the window. The blade split the bow and sank deep into the wooden sash. Mrs. Provost yanked it free, shouting in fury: "Hyahh-h-h, you red heathen! Git! Git, I say!"

Weaponless now, he got. One of the dogs jumped through the window and raced after him, teeth bared.

María had her rifle reloaded. She stood back away from the window a little, trying not to make a target but ready to shoot when she had to.

Across the room, Daniel's rifle roared. "I got another horse!"

The Indians didn't try again. There were still six of them, and only three horses now. Even as it was, they would all have to ride double. They couldn't afford to lose another horse.

From her vantage point behind the broken shutters, María watched the Indians gather out of range. For a long time they milled, hands gesturing in argument. But cool heads prevailed, and presently the six Comanches melted away.

It was a long time before anyone ventured to open the door. When at last they worked up the nerve, Rebecca Provost slid the bar away, and Daniel pushed the door open. The lance bumped against a post supporting the arbor, and it clattered to the ground. Daniel moved out first, rifle poised. María and Heather went next, and finally Rebecca and Miranda.

Daniel picked up the lance, touching his thumb experimentally to the sharp metal point. "Filed out of a barrel hoop." He stepped into the yard. There two Indian horses lay, one dead, one slowly dying. Out at the field's edge lay another. There was no powder or lead to be wasted. He moved to the dying horse, slipped his Bowie knife from its sheath and cut the animal's throat. Walking back to the arbor, he said, "We didn't kill any Indians, looks like, but we sure played hell with their horses." He glanced at his mother, and his face reddened. "Mama, I hadn't ought to've said that."

Rebecca Provost threw her arms around him. "A boy ain't supposed to, but today you're a man. And a man can say anything he damn pleases."

10

Aaron Provost backed off and took a long look at the big new double cabin with its opening through the center, a loft over the dog-run for the boys to sleep in. "I swun, it's better even than what we had before. Rebecca'll be right proud."

The builders were gathering their tools and putting them in the dog-run to keep them dry. Josh leaned on his ax and admired the new structure with Aaron. "Still a right smart of finishin'-up work to be done, but I expect you and your boys can be doin' that along as you get to it."

Aaron grinned. "You fellers will all be my guests tonight. You can roll your blankets on the floor and sleep under my new roof. Once we bring the womenfolk, you ain't likely to have another chance." The grin slowly left him. "Been right concerned about the women, Josh."

"Aaron, we been back and forth over all these farms the last three-four weeks, and we ain't seen a sign."

"Sometimes the first sign you see of the Comanch is when he sends a dogwood arrow singin' at you."

"They're all right. María and the Hernandez family stayed there all by themselves while Ramón was gone to the war."

"Just the same, I'll be tickled to see Rebecca and them young'uns."

They left Quitman's wagon, for it would slow them down, and what few belongings Mrs. Winslow had could easily be carried in the Provost wagon anyway. They struck off southwestward, horseback. Homesick, Ramón held the lead. Once Josh felt compelled to catch up to him and slow him down.

"It could be dangerous, you gettin' so far out front by yourself."

Ramón said sheepishly, "I didn't notice. My mind was with Miranda and the baby. I hate to think of Miranda sleeping alone in that big, cold bed."

"You stay a little closer to the rest of us or she might sleep by herself for a long, long time."

They rode steadily through the morning, stopping at a creek to water the horses and to eat some jerked venison. Ramón was out front again as they topped the last hill and looked down on the Hernandez house. He waved his hat frantically. Josh and the others moved up in a hurry.

Ramón pointed to a blackened pile of charred timber and bones. "Josh, something has happened here."

Josh swung down and kicked at the remnants. A chill ran up his back as he counted three skulls. "Horses. Somebody's drug three dead horses up here and burned them."

Fright came into Ramón's voice. "We didn't have three horses here." Suddenly desperate, he set his mount into a hard lope.

Ramón was too far in the lead for anyone to catch him. Riding hard, Josh looked across the fields toward the house, hoping to see some sign of life. He saw none. He knew with a terrible certainty that something had gone wrong here. Then the door opened and the women hurried out under the brush arbor. The children spilled around them. Josh could see rifles in María's and Daniel's hands. *They thought we was Indians.*

Tiny Miranda ran forward to meet Ramón. Ramón slid to a stop and jumped down, grabbing her fiercely. Josh noted that Ramón's bad leg didn't seem to be bothering him much.

The dogs came running, barking. Patrick hurried out toward his father. "Daddy, Daddy, the Indians came!"

Ocie Quitman reached down and scooped the boy up into the saddle, crushing him in his arms. Quitman's voice quavered. "Son, what's that about Indians?"

"They came, Daddy, and they tried to get us."

Josh broke in, "Anybody hurt, Patrick?"

"Just Indians. María saved us, Daddy. Them old Indians was a-fixin' to get me and Daniel, but María came a-runnin'."

Quitman seemed to freeze. He stared into his son's

face, dazed by the realization that he had come close to losing the boy.

Aaron Provost hugged first one of his children, then another. Rebecca waited patiently, and he squeezed her hardest of all. "Aaron, we been needin' you."

Josh dismounted slowly, his eyes on María. He reached for her hands. "María, I heard what Patrick said. Are you all right?"

She nodded, smiling. He opened his arms, drawing her to him violently. He whispered, "Thank God. If something had happened again . . ." He held her so tightly that she gasped for breath. "Sorry, María, I didn't go to hurt you. But all of a sudden I was rememberin' what happened to Teresa, a long time ago . . ."

She stiffened a little. "Nothing happened to me. Everything is fine." She dropped her head forward, against his chest. In a moment she said, "Teresa is still much on your mind, isn't she, Josh?"

He fumbled for an answer. "No, María, no. What happened here just brought it back, that's all."

The men gathered around and demanded a full account. Rebecca said, "You're the one to tell them, María." When María shook her head, Rebecca went on, "Then I'll tell it." She gave the whole story in rousing detail.

Ocie Quitman held his son tightly. Now and again, listening, he would glance covertly at María. Patrick would break in occasionally to say, "What you scared for, Daddy? It's over with."

When Rebecca had told it all, Aaron Provost took a long, thankful look at all his children. He reached out and clasped María's fingers in one of his big hands,

Heather Winslow's in the other. "You little ladies, there ain't nothin' I can say that would be half enough."

Heather put in quietly, "María did most of it."

Aaron blinked. "It beats all nature, the way a woman can come through when she has to. Girls, I know you got no daddy—either one of you—but from now on you got the next thing to a real one. If ever there comes a time you need help—no matter what or how much of it—you don't have to go no farther than the Provost house." He glanced at Josh. "Boy, you hug that girl María and do it proper. If you don't, I swear *I* will."

Ramón and Miranda heard the baby crying—or said they did—and walked into the house, arms around each other. Muley led off his and Ramón's horses, the children following after him. Aaron moved toward his wagon, one hand on Rebecca's shoulder, the other on Daniel's. Dent Sessum tramped away to examine his own wagon, fearful the Indians might have done him some damage. Josh figured he would be looking after his money, too, wherever he had hidden it. Josh said to María, "I best see after the horses. But later I'll do what Aaron said, and I'll do it right."

Ocie Quitman stared at María, even as he clung to his son. She stared after Josh, but it was evident she knew Quitman was watching her. At length she turned toward the house. Quitman said, "Miss Hernandez . . ."

She stopped. He picked around for the words, and they came with difficulty. "I need to tell you . . ."

"It's not necessary."

"This boy's the only thing I got left in the world that means anything to me. They say you saved him."

María's voice was cool. She spoke in Spanish, throwing it in his face. "If I did, it was not because he was your son. It was in spite of that. Don't hurt yourself trying to say thank you."

Stung, Quitman watched her enter the house. Patrick stuck to him like a burr as he led his horse out and turned him loose. That done, he returned to the arbor and sat on a log bench, face furrowed, his hands absently running through his son's hair. He nodded while Patrick told him again about all that had happened, coloring it with a child's fears and fantasies. The Indians had all been nine feet tall, painted and feathered and riding horses big as a house. But María had come out for him and Daniel and hadn't been scared at all. Her pony had run like the wind. At length Quitman tried to switch the subject. "What else has happened, son? What all did you do before the Indians came?"

"We hoed the fields, and we played a lot. Gregorio's my favorite, Daddy. You know Gregorio?" Quitman only nodded. The boy said eagerly, "Gregorio's goin' to teach me how to twist a rabbit out of a hole. Did you ever twist a rabbit, Daddy?" When Quitman shook his head, the boy said, "He twisted one the other day. Got it up out of its hole and caught it."

Quitman frowned. "I hope you didn't eat it? That'd be like a bunch of Mexicans."

"No, sir, Gregorio turned it loose. Said no use killin' somethin' unless it's hurtin' you or you aim to eat it. I've learned lots of things from Gregorio. He's goin' to teach me a lot more."

Quitman's gaze ranged down around the sheds, where

Muley and the Provost youngsters and the Hernandez children milled. "I don't reckon he'll have the chance, son. We're fixin' to leave here."

The boy's face fell. "Leave María, and Gregorio?"

Quitman nodded. "We've built a house on the Provost place. You'll live there awhile, Patrick. Mrs. Winslow will be there too. She'll look out for you when I can't be around. She's goin' to teach all you young'uns. You'll enjoy that."

"I'd rather we was stayin' here."

"We can't. This is too far from the valley. Anyway, you like Mrs. Winslow, don't you?"

"Sure, Daddy, but I wish María and Gregorio was goin' with us too. Couldn't we take them?"

"Their home is here, son. Everybody has to live where his land is."

"I wish our land was here."

Presently Patrick ran off to join the other children. Heather Winslow came out and took another bench, near Quitman. He was frowning in disapproval as he saw his son pair up with the dark-skinned Gregorio.

Heather Winslow said, "Don't worry about it, Mister Quitman. Gregorio is all right."

"I'd just rather see Patrick take up with the Provost boys more. Better he stays with his own kind."

"It won't matter long. Aaron says we're leaving here."

"Tomorrow. We've made a place for you to live at the Provosts'. Have they talked to you about givin' the young'uns some learnin'?"

"Yes. I said I'd be glad to, as much as I can do. It's a way to help earn my keep. Anyway, there doesn't seem to be anywhere else I can go. I can't live on my place alone."

Hesitantly Quitman said, "Teachin' ain't all they got in mind. They got other plans worked out for you. And for me."

Heather blushed. "I know."

"I hope you don't let it embarrass you. Far as I'm concerned, you needn't even think about it."

She looked away. "I'll confess, Mister Quitman, I have done some thinking about it."

He stared blankly. "Come to any conclusions?"

She shook her head. "No conclusions. It's still too soon after . . . I need more time."

Quitman looked relieved. "The same with me. I'm in no mood to be pushed into somethin' by other people, no matter how good their intentions are. Whatever I decide to do—and if I do *anything*—it'll be because I made up my own mind."

"They'll keep pushing us. Rebecca keeps saying your son needs a woman's care. She keeps saying *you* need a woman, and I owe you what a woman can give."

He looked at her in surprise. "It's hard on a man, once he's been married. But don't ever feel for a minute that you owe me anything like that. You don't. I wouldn't ask you to."

Her eyes were grateful. "I know you wouldn't, Mister Quitman. But let me tell you this: if I ever decided I wanted to, you wouldn't have to ask me."

María Hernandez walked outside. She glanced a moment at Heather and Quitman, then moved out to the garden. Heather's gaze followed her. "Mister Quitman, I don't mean to tell you what you ought to do, but it would be a bad thing if you left here without telling that girl you're sorry."

"Sorry about what?"

"I shouldn't have to tell you. In spite of everything, she went out there and brought Patrick back with those devils yapping at her heels. They would've killed her if they had caught her, or they would've carried her away. If it hadn't been for her, you wouldn't have a boy."

"What can I say to her?"

Heather smiled. "You're a straightforward man, Mister Quitman. The words will come to you." Heather arose from the bench and walked down toward the Provost wagon.

Reluctantly, feeling somehow trapped, Quitman stood up. He stared at the dark-haired girl, who was pulling beans and dropping them into a tightly woven willow basket. He took a few steps toward her, stopped, clenched his fists and took a few steps more. He stood behind her, trying for words that didn't want to come. "Miss Hernandez . . ."

She turned to look at him over her shoulder. "Yes?" He stood in awkward silence. She said, "You were about to say something?"

He frowned, his fist balling up. "Yes, and I expect you know what."

"I think so. I can see the pain in your face. It hurts."

"Like pullin' out my own teeth."

"Then forget about it, Mister Quitman."

"No. I always been one to pay my debts."

"I am just a Mexican. You have said so. You owe me nothing."

A touch of anger came, and he wasn't sure whether it was at her or at himself. "Yes, you're a Mexican. I won't lie about it: that's what makes it so hard for me to say.

But I *will* say it if it kills me. I oughtn't to've treated you the way I done. I reckon it ain't your fault bein' born what you was. And what you done for my boy leaves me a debt I can never pay you for."

Her eyes were hard. "I think you resent that it was me. You wish it had been anybody else—Heather Winslow, or Rebecca—anybody but this Mexican girl."

His face pinched. "You see right through a man, don't you?" He shrugged. "I reckon you got cause to hate me, but that's the way it is. I can't help the way I feel. I can't cover it up and act like it ain't there."

Some of the harsh dislike faded from her eyes. She looked at him strangely. "That is true, Mister Quitman. You can't, and you don't try. There are some who smile and talk nice but hate inside. You are not one of those." She looked down at the willow basket. "She must have been a good woman, your wife."

His voice tightened. "Yes, she was."

"I am sorry you lost her."

"It had nothin' to do with you. I got no reason to make you share the blame for it. It's just somethin' inside me I can't control. I can apologize for it, but I can't stop it."

"Then the best thing is for you to stay away . . . from all my people."

"That's what I been tryin' to do. Luck just keeps throwin' us together. And now I'm owin' you . . ."

"I do not accept the debt. Some of my people did you a bad wrong. Whatever I did, take it as a payment on what my people owe to *you*."

She carried the basket back to the house. He watched till she passed through the door and out of view. He stopped to pick up a long string bean she had dropped,

and he shifted his gaze down to the shed where Buckalew was.

He remembered then the talk of Buckalew marrying
this girl. He thought, *Maybe Buckalew isn't as far wrong
as I figured him.*

11

It was a busy summer, for there were not only the crops
to be weeded and garden plots to be tended and stock to
be worked, but there was also all the rebuilding to be
done, the war scars to be rubbed away with muscle strain
and sweat and determination. Josh's cattle had scattered.
Many were completely gone, taken perhaps by beef-
hungry Mexican troops. In the unsettled country to the
west roamed wild cattle, descended in freedom from
those which had strayed long ago out of the Spanish mission herds. These cattle were spotted and striped and
every color a man had ever seen, their horns long and
their legs longer. They fleshened well on grass and were
far less gamey than the wild deer and turkey and bear
which kept so many settlers' ribs from showing through
the skin. Brought home, gentled enough to stay, they
would be good for trading in the settlements. When they
had time, Josh and Muley and Ramón and Gregorio rode
west, picking up wild cattle where they could find them.
Often they had to rope them with rawhide *reatas* and
throw them down and tie up a leg to slow them and make
them workable. Sometimes they necked them to gentler
cattle brought along from home. Slowly through the

summer they built their herds by going out and bringing in what Nature had provided. Some cattle they kept;
some strayed right back where they had come from.

There was this about early Texas: if it *was* a big and
untamed land, and if its people *were* poor and ragged
and ever standing in the presence of danger, at least Nature herself was bountiful. No man went hungry if he
had a horse and a rope, or if he had a rifle and powder
and ball, or if he had the knowledge and material to build
even a snare.

When they weren't after cattle, Josh and Muley and
Ramón were sometimes out searching for the mustangs
which roamed these hills and valleys in numbers beyond
counting. They built wings and traps and hazed the
horses into them, then caught them Mexican style with
their heavy rawhide *reatas* and brought them to hand.
These were grand days, these fleeting days of summer,
and it pleased Josh that Ramón was once more learn-
ing to laugh. It was not the high, easy laughter of the
old days, but that would never come back. That was
killed forever. Even the little chuckle that followed a
good ride on a mustang bronc was an improvement,
though, and Josh was gratified.

They spent so much time gentling these captured
horses that summer was far gone before Josh realized
they had not made any preparations for building a cabin.
They'd slept in the open through the warm weather, but
he and Muley would need tight walls and a roof before
the fall northers began moving in with the chilling bite
of raw prairie wind.

After the corn crop was harvested, Josh and Muley
started looking for cabin timber. They chopped down

trees, stripped off the branches and dragged in logs at the end of a *reata*. As he could, Josh measured off the size the structure was to be and started cutting and shaping the logs, notching the ends to fit together. He fashioned this cabin bigger than his old one had been, for in the back of his mind was the notion that one day he would bring María here to live. He would ask her someday, when he had the place fixed up the way he wanted it, the way it ought to be for a woman. A man could live in any kind of a house, so long as it kept the rain off of his head. But he couldn't expect a woman to live that way, not if he had any real feeling for her.

Because his crop was the earliest in, Josh had shared his corn. He hauled roasting ears to the neighbors. Later, as the ears hardened, he had carried grinding corn to the Provosts and Mrs. Winslow and Quitman, and Jacob Phipps. He had even given some to Dent Sessum and Alfred Noonan, living like a pair of boar hogs in the squalor of old Noonan's place. This, with the game they killed, saw the settlers through until their own crops could ripen.

In return, they owed Josh and Muley a cabin-raising. They would have done it debt or not—all, perhaps, but Sessum and Noonan. Those damned reprobates didn't seem to feel they owed anybody anything. Josh was surprised to see Sessum and Noonan ride in the morning everybody was to gather and start raising the cabin. He was not made joyful by their coming. Nevertheless, he tried to be civil.

"Didn't figure I'd see you-all." He might have added that the only time he *ever* saw them was when he took them something, like the roasting ears.

"Never miss a cabin-raisin'," Noonan enthused. "Been to many a one in my day. I do hope you got some drinkin'-whisky. Me and Sessum, we been whettin' our bills."

Josh hesitated to admit it. He and Muley had taken some cattle down into the settlements for trade and had come back with several jugs of whisky, among other things. It would be neighborly to furnish an occasional snort to friends helping bring up a cabin. He told the old man, "I expect we can dig up a swig or two when the time comes."

"It's always time," Noonan said. But Josh didn't offer.

Sessum said, "Buckalew, you got somethin' me and Noonan could be doin' to help you?" He didn't sound particularly eager, but maybe he thought it would help hurry the whisky. Josh decided to see how much work he might get out of them. He knew they would get plenty of his whisky.

"We'll need more clapboards for the roof. I got logs sawed for the job if you-all would like to rive them for me."

Normally one man could rive logs, but Sessum and Noonan made a two-man job of it. They would place the sharp edge of the froe on the upended short log and drive it down by pounding on its blunt upper edge with a wooden hammer, splitting off a board about an inch thick. The rate they started, Josh calculated they could spend a week. But it would keep them out from under foot.

"Where's Jacob Phipps?" he asked. "Surprised you didn't bring him."

Old Noonan grunted. "Tell you the truth, Josh, I been

a mite disappointed in him. He ain't been none too friendly of late. You know one day he even had the gall to tell me and Sessum to git ourselves off of his place? And us old friends, the way we was. I swear, you can't put your faith in nobody anymore."

The war had cost Phipps an arm, Josh thought, but it seemed to have sharpened his judgment. He asked Sessum, "How about you? Still huntin' you a place to buy?"

Sessum shook his head. "I still got my eye on the place your Mexican friend has got, if he'd just talk business."

In Josh's view, the thing that had drawn Sessum's interest at Ramón's was the neatness of it, the way the fields were clean-worked and the crops coming along well. Sessum didn't recognize the work that had gone into it to get it that way, and the work it would take to maintain it in that condition. If a man like Sessum got hold of it, the place would look like a disaster had struck inside of six months. "Ramón won't sell. You'd just as well forget it."

Sessum shrugged. "Man never can tell what may happen. The Mexicans are liable to decide they want to leave, and I'll be in a position to buy."

"They been here longer than any of us. Nothin' is apt to change their minds. You leave them alone, Sessum. You'll likely find somebody else willin' to sell, if you'll look around."

"I been watchin' Jacob Phipps. He's havin' hell tryin' to work that place of his with just one good arm. I figure one of these days he'll give up and take an offer. Who knows? I might be able to buy his land and the Hernandez place both if they go cheap enough. You'd have me for a neighbor on both sides of you, Buckalew."

Josh turned away, scowling. He'd as soon have a Comanche village on one flank and the cannibalistic Karankawans on the other.

A couple of horses showed up to the west, and a high-wheeled Mexican cart drawn by mules. Ramón Hernandez led the way on a big, brown horse. He was bringing the whole family—Miranda, the baby, María, and all the brothers and sisters. Hickory loped out to greet them, barking all the way. From east came Aaron and Rebecca Provost in their wagon, bringing with them Mrs. Winslow and Patrick and all the young Provosts. Ocie Quitman rode alongside with lanky Daniel Provost. Their dogs bounced in front of them, setting up a barking contest with Hickory. The Provost children jumped out of their wagon and raced toward the Hernandez family. Patrick climbed down shouting, "Gregorio! Hey, Gregorio!" Quitman tried to stop him, but the boy was away like a deer.

It took a while for everybody to get through with the hugging and the howdying. Presently the women hauled out their cooking utensils and took a critical look at a side of beef which had been placed over the coals early in the morning. Josh and Muley squatted on their heels with Aaron and Ramón to swap talk. Pretty soon Muley became bored with it all and trailed off after the youngsters. Ocie Quitman listened, but his gaze absently followed the women.

Been a long time now since he lost his wife, Josh thought. *Nature's starting to work on him. He's probably gone to thinking more and more about Heather Winslow. And he ought to. She's a right handsome woman.*

Old Noonan came around and began wedging into the

conversation. And once he started, he had a way of taking it over, asking the questions and giving the answers. One by one the men commenced getting up and looking for work to do. The foundation logs went down first. Then the builders started "rolling up" the side walls. By dusk, when Josh called a halt, they had the project well started. They were a long way from reaching the roofline, but the women would have a place to sleep tonight, "indoors."

Off and on during the day, as appetite hit them, the men had gone to the beef, slicing hot strips of barbecue from the carcass which had slow-cooked over the gentle heat of the coals. Now the women were preparing a regular supper. The smoke from their fire smelled good to Josh, for his stomach growled in complaint, and his muscles ached from straining with the heavy logs. He took a cup and walked to the fire, where Heather Winslow was stirring beans in a pot. He filled the cup with coffee and paused to visit a little.

"How's the school comin', Mrs. Winslow?"

"Not good, not bad. We just have to make do with what little we've got. Do you know we have only two books for the children to learn from? The Bible and *Pilgrim's Progress*. We have a copy of the United States Constitution, too, but we never got past the part about the pursuit of happiness. Daniel Provost said he's pursued deer, but he didn't know you had to pursue happiness. He'd never seen it run."

She smiled, but Josh didn't. It didn't strike him that way. He said, "Happiness is a hard thing to catch hold of, sometimes. Maybe it don't run, exactly, but it's got a habit of slippin' away from you."

"This ought to be a happy place you have here, Mister Buckalew. I like the way the creek lies, and all those trees. I like the view as you stand here and look off to the south and east. It will be a good place to bring a woman." She nodded toward the cabin. "It's going to be a big one. Of course you'll have to find a place to put Muley, once María comes here to live."

"I'll build him another cabin."

"You sound as if you already have your plans made."

"I done a lot of studyin'."

"Then maybe you ought to talk with María. I gather that she's not sure what your intentions are."

"I figured they've always been understood without me sayin'."

"By you, maybe, but not by her, Mister Buckalew. A woman doesn't like things taken for granted. She wants to hear them said out loud."

He grimaced. "Truth is, Mrs. Winslow, I never have been around women much. I had some sisters, but they was older, and I never did understand them anyway. They all cussed about men, then up and married the first ones that come along and asked them. María . . . she was not much more than a little girl first time I ever saw her. I reckon that's the way I've thought of her, till just lately."

"Till you realized all of a sudden that she was a grown woman, like her sister had been?"

He stared into the coffee. "I rode up to their house one day, and for a minute I would've sworn she was Teresa. It was like all the years had rolled away and Teresa had come back from the long ago. You've got no idea the way I felt."

Heather Winslow mused, "I can imagine. It would be

as if Jim were to ride in here right now, come back to life." She frowned, "It could happen, you know . . . I mean, somebody could come along who looked like Jim, who talked like him. But it wouldn't *be* Jim. Nobody else could ever be him, no matter how much he looked like him, or how much I wanted him to be. Jim's dead. There's no use me looking for him."

Josh studied her over the cup. "Is the teacher tryin' to teach *me* somethin'?"

"Just this, Mister Buckalew: María is a woman with a love in her, and she'd be good for a man who really loved her. But a person who has room for so much love also has room for a lot of hurt. Don't you hurt her."

"I wouldn't for the world."

"You might, and not mean to. Be careful with her, Mister Buckalew."

After supper, María took a bucket and walked down toward the creek in the near darkness. Ocie Quitman sat on his heels by a small campfire, old Noonan's incessant rattling falling upon his ears but not penetrating the mental shield Quitman had raised. He watched the girl go out of sight over the creekbank. Quitman pushed to his feet, stretched, then began moving toward the line of trees, taking his time as if he had no place to go, nothing to do but exercise his legs. He walked down the creek bank and met María starting up, straining. "That looks heavy," he said. "I'll carry it for you."

She stood frozen in surprise, the bucket at arm's length.

He said again, "I'll take it."

"Why?"

"I told you. It's too heavy."

"I've been carrying buckets like this for years. I'll carry them the rest of my life."

"Well, I'll carry this one." He reached for it, and she gave it to him. He made no move to start up the bank, however. She stared, her eyes still showing surprise.

Finally she said experimentally, "How have you been, Mister Quitman?"

"All right. Been workin' awful hard."

"It seems to do you good. You look well."

"I look like a tired man older than I really am. But work's good for a man, especially if he's got heavy things on his mind. Keeps him too busy to worry much, or grieve. Work's a good healer."

"I suppose."

Frowning, he looked away from her. "Miss Hernandez, I followed you down here on purpose."

"For what reason?"

"To talk to you, to unload a little bit of guilt, maybe. I've said things I'm not proud of. I been wantin' you to know. I carried an awful anger, before. I've worked a lot of it off, I think."

"Have you changed your thinking, about . . . *things?*"

He shook his head. "I wouldn't lie to you. Some things burn so deep in a man that he can't root them out, no matter how much he'd like to. But I want you to know I'm sorry for the pain I've caused you. I had no right."

"I have no grudge against you, Mister Quitman."

"I didn't have the right. It was just in me to hurt you . . . to hurt *all* of you."

She shrugged. "That's all behind us. Anyway, you apologized before."

"The way I apologized was an insult in itself. I didn't mean it, and you could tell I didn't. Now I *do* mean it."

Her narrowed eyes held to his for a long time before a faint smile tugged at her mouth. He was hunched over, leaning strongly to the side where he held the bucket of water.

"That looks heavy, Mister Quitman. Maybe you should let me carry it."

He eased at the sight of her smile. A tiny hint of one crossed his face and disappeared, for smiling did not come easily to Ocie Quitman. "You've just taken a heavy load off of my shoulders, Miss Hernandez. I reckon I can carry the bucket."

Josh kept the jugs hidden out and fetched them one at a time at a deliberate rate calculated to keep anyone from getting drunk. There was no stopping old man Noonan, though. For every swallow anyone else took, he took three. His Adam's apple bobbed up and down several times with each lifting of the jug. The more he drank, the wilder, louder and more continuously he talked. It occurred to Josh finally that the old scoundrel probably had found his jug cache, so he had Muley slip out and move it. Surely enough, they were one jug shy. Old Noonan was hiding it out.

Against his protests Josh found the cabin getting completely out of hand. Aaron Provost virtually took over the project. What Josh had seen as a two-day job turned into quite a bit more, and his envisioned one-room cabin became a big double cabin with a liberal dog-run separating the two halves, one common roof over the whole structure. When the roof finally went up, it didn't lack much being as big as the one they had built for the Provosts.

To all of Josh's protests, Aaron waved his hand in dismissal. "One fine day you'll be bringin' María home to this place, and first thing you know there'll be some black-headed young'uns runnin' around and we'd all have to come back over and build it bigger anyway. Just as well do it now when we won't be in the way of nothin'."

So, up it went. The one-armed Jacob Phipps mixed mortar and fitted stone and put up a fireplace in each section of the cabin, smiling in pride as he backed away to admire his handiwork. This was something he could do and do well despite the handicap war had thrust upon him.

Noonan and Sessum were out of sight half the time, sleeping on the creek bank. Noonan, in particular, had a lot to sleep off.

When the cabin was finished, Aaron Provost gathered the others around him and walked out a hundred feet, turning to look back in the dusk. He made a sweeping gesture with his hand. "What it lacks for purty, it sure makes up for stout. You can live to be a hundred and six, Josh, but you'll never have a better house."

Josh nodded his appreciation. "I don't know why I'd ever *want* a better one. All I can say is thank you."

"You're welcome. We owed it to you, and by johnny there can't nobody say a Texan don't pay his debts. It's all complete, Josh, floor to the roof. Got fireplaces, got tables and benches and a bed. All you lack now is a woman to put in it. That's somethin' you'll just have to take care of for yourself." Aaron squeezed María's shoulder. She looked down, her face reddening.

"There'll be time enough," Josh said.

"Not as much as you think, maybe," Aaron responded. "Winter's comin'. Fireplace ain't goin' to be enough to keep you warm."

Ocie Quitman watched María's face, and his eyebrows furrowed as he listened to Aaron's good-natured joking.

Aaron said, "Josh, you still got another jug hid out?"

"Just one more. That's all that's left."

"Let's get it, then. No house is finished proper till the builders have had them a chance to take a drink under its roof." Aaron put his arm around Josh's shoulder and pulled him toward the cabin. The others followed. Only María waited there, and Quitman. She stared at the new cabin, her dark eyes beginning to glisten.

Quitman's voice was quiet. "You oughtn't to be sheddin' tears, Miss Hernandez. It's a good house. From what I hear, it's goin' to be yours."

She shook her head. "That's what everybody says. Everybody but Josh."

"He hasn't asked you?"

"No."

"You want him to?"

She cut her gaze to him a moment. "For a long time I've wanted him to. Now I'm not sure anymore."

"I thought you were in love with him."

"I thought so too. I've thought so ever since I was a girl. But love has to come from two people . . . it can't be all with one."

"You don't think he loves you?"

"I think he thinks he does. But it isn't really me. It never was."

Quitman found himself walking slowly toward the cabin, beside her. Worriedly he asked, "So, what're you goin' to do about it?"

"What *can* I do? Wait till he asks me, then tell him we've both been wrong."

"It'll be a disappointment to him."

"At first, till he realizes I'm right."

"And this cabin, that's been built for you?"

"There will be another woman sometime, one who doesn't look like my sister Teresa . . . one he can love for herself and not for somebody else."

They were at the side of the cabin now. Quitman halted, hands flexing nervously. "María . . ." He broke off. Always before he had called her Miss Hernandez, if he had given her a name at all.

She turned. "Yes?"

"María, I lost somebody once. She didn't look anything like you." His chin dropped, and he groped for the right words. "I don't hardly know how to say it . . ."

Her face pinched. "I think I know what you're trying to say. Be careful . . ."

"María, I wronged you, and I worried over it. I couldn't figure out why it ought to bother me so much. The last few days here, seein' you all the time, I knew why."

"Mister Quitman, don't . . ."

"You got every cause to hate me; I got no right to expect anything else. And if I told you I'd lost all the feelin' I've had against your people, I'd be lyin' to you. But damn it, María, in spite of all that . . ."

She stared at him in painful silence.

He said, "The last few days I've fought it. My eyes have followed you everywhere you moved, and I've fought it. I didn't noway want it to happen, but it's happened anyhow. So, help me, María. Curse me . . . hit me. Do somethin' to make me stop bein' in love with you."

She said quietly, "I'm not sure I want to."

"It isn't any good. I oughtn't to've told you."

"You didn't have to. I've sensed it as long as you have."

"You must've been laughin' at me."

"No, it wasn't funny."

"Then you must've hated me."

Her fingers reached out and gently closed over his hand. "I don't hate you. I never did."

He took a step forward, close to her. He reached a hand behind her neck and pulled her toward him, bending. Her face turned upward, and her eyes closed as he found her lips. He kissed her with a cautious gentleness. Her arms went around him, and her mouth pressed tighter, and he cast away the caution, the gentleness. He let loose the pent-up anger and the hunger and the aching loneliness that had built so long. She gasped for breath.

A sharp voice jerked him back and brought him halfway around.

"María!"

Joshua Buckalew stood at the corner, face creased in surprise. "Quitman, what in the . . ."

Ocie Quitman turned loose of the girl and faced Josh. Josh seemed frozen in his tracks. Then he moved, fists clenched.

Quitman said, "Buckalew, it ain't like it looks . . ."

"Ain't it? María, you go in the cabin. He ain't goin' to bother you no more."

María didn't move. Her eyes were big and dark and frightened.

Josh swung his fist. It struck Quitman solidly on the chin and he staggered back into María. She tried to grab him, but he fell, almost tripping her when he went down. She cried out as Josh reached down to grab Quitman's shirt and haul him back to his feet. She grasped at Josh's hands. "Josh, don't do it . . . Don't . . ."

Josh wasn't listening to her. "Damn your soul, Quitman! After all the things you've said . . . and then you try to take her like this. I'll beat you to death."

María had hold of Josh's arm. "Josh, listen to me . . ."

Josh pulled away from her and struck Quitman again, sending him stumbling backward into the log wall. Quitman hunched there, shaking his head, clearing his eyes. Then the anger rushed into his face and he surged out swinging. The two men rammed into each other like a pair of bulls fighting. Arms muscled by hard work, hands toughened by rain and wind and sun, they swung and pounded and slashed and jabbed, one pushing awhile, the other giving ground, then reversing. They circled and fell and rolled and pushed to their feet and pounded again until their shirts hung in ribbons and blood streaked their faces like Indian war paint. They grunted and cursed and shouted in their anger. One went to his knees, and then the other. They fought until they were far out from the cabin, almost to the bank of the creek. At the end they were staggering, and each man almost fell every time he swung. Ocie Quitman finally stumbled and went to his knees and couldn't come up anymore. Josh teetered on the edge of the bank, trying to keep his footing, trying to focus his eyes, trying to find Quitman one more time.

Aaron Provost's strong voice broke through to him. "Josh, for God's sake, don't you think there's been enough?"

María Hernandez cried, "Josh, it's over."

Josh gritted stubbornly, "Where's he at?"

In fury María gave Josh a push that sent him stumbling backward over the bank and into the cold water of the creek. He splashed and floundered, sputtering. "There!" she cried. "Cool off a little!"

Weeping, she knelt to try to help Ocie Quitman to his feet. Bewildered, Ramón came to her aid. He got Quitman up, staggering. Aaron Provost strode over the bank and climbed down to extend a huge hand to Josh. "Boy, I got no idea what's happened between you two, but you sure have tore each other up. This is a hell of a way to celebrate a new cabin."

Jug in his hand, old Noonan was snickering to Dent Sessum. "It's that gal, Dent. They'll do it every time. I been knowin' Mexican gals for years and years, and that's the way they'll do you. Hug and kiss and sweet-do you while you're there, and the minute you're out of sight they're flashin' their eyes at somebody else."

Ramón Hernandez reached down for a handful of mud from the edge of an old rain puddle. Noonan's mouth was wide open when Ramón came up with his hand and plopped the mud in. The old man coughed and spluttered and cursed.

Aaron brought Josh up out of the creek. Ocie Quitman waited there, leaning on María's thin shoulder for strength. Their eyes met, anger still crackling in Josh's. But the anger had burned out of Quitman. The ashes held only a cold regret.

"I didn't mean it to happen, Buckalew. But God help me, I'm in love with your Mexican girl."

12

The festive mood which had lasted through the building of the cabin was gone like summer smoke. Even the children sensed the change and bedded down quietly, the play gone out of them. Ocie Quitman moved his bedroll out beyond anyone else's, and though he awakened with morning's first light and rolled up his blankets, he made no move toward the house. He sat out there alone, brooding, his gaze lost in the light fog which masked off the sunrise.

Old Alfred Noonan held his head in his hands as he raised up in his blankets beside the corral and watched Quitman, half hoping there might be another fight but knowing there wouldn't be. That was why Quitman was staying out there by himself.

"Damn," Noonan complained hoarsely, "looks like Buckalew could've got a better grade of drinkin'-whisky, us buildin' him a cabin and all."

Dent Sessum only groaned and turned over. Noonan pushed him with his foot. "Dent, stir yourself."

Sessum raised up irritably, blinking in a sleepy confusion. "What the hell's the matter?"

Noonan shook his head. "Ain't nothin' the matter. All

of a sudden I got me a notion things is fixin' to get better." He could see Ramón Hernandez up and moving around, loading his high-wheeled cart.

Sessum rubbed his forehead and whispered some choice words about how it felt like somebody was splitting his head with a chopping ax.

Noonan growled. "You ain't no worse off than me. I got an awful taste in my mouth this mornin'. Can't figure out whether it's like bad whisky or black mud."

"Mud, likely. You got the Mexican to thank for that."

Noonan scowled and cut a hard glance toward the distant Ramón. "And I do intend to thank him good and proper. Man can't go around lettin' them chili-eaters get away with insults, or first thing you know they'll think they own this country again."

Sessum's eyes were rimmed with red. "What you intend to do about it?"

Noonan looked around him furtively. "Dent, I think I've figured out somethin' that'll be good for both of us. Me, I got a grudge to settle with Ramón, and anyway, I just don't like Mexicans. You, you been wantin' to buy that piece of land from him but he won't listen. I bet his *widow* would listen."

"He ain't got no widow."

"He's fixin' to have. It could happen today . . . this very mornin'."

Sessum blinked, trying to absorb the meaning of it all, but it was too big for him.

Noonan said, "Everybody's had Indians on the brain since that raid over at the Hernandez place. Now, if somebody was to shoot Ramón, who do you reckon would catch the blame for it?"

"The Comanch."

"You're soberin' up, Dent. Now, the way I see it, them Mexicans'll eat breakfast pretty soon and start home. Way things went to hell here last night, they'll be wantin' to leave. We could do the same, only we could double back, ride in the creek aways to lose our tracks, then lay in wait where the brush comes up close to the trail. After it's done, we just follow the creek till we lose our tracks again, then we go on home with nobody the wiser, and Ramón Hernandez a hell of a lot deader."

"What'll Jacob Phipps think?"

"He don't need to know. We come here without him; we can leave without him."

Sessum rubbed his chin, his eyes gradually coming alive. "It's a pleasure to know you, Noonan. I'm proud to ride with a man who uses his head for somethin' besides a place to put his hat. You goin' to give me first shot?"

"Think you're sober enough to hit him?"

"I'll *be* sober enough, if there's one more drink left in that jug." Sessum pawed around beneath the blankets. Finding the jug, he tipped it up and shook it. But they'd been too diligent the night before. It was empty.

Sourly Noonan said, "Looks like a host would see to it he had enough whisky so a man didn't run out."

As a smuggler and a filibusterer in Texas even before the days of Stephen F. Austin, old Noonan had done his share of fighting against Mexican soldiers and customs officers as well as against Indians. When Dent Sessum started to tie his horse in the brush, the old man impatiently grabbed the reins. "Damn it, Dent, you're as green as a gourd vine. Your horse is liable to jerk loose when the shootin' starts and leave you afoot. Tie a rope to your reins and hang onto it. That way you always got hold of him."

Noonan showed Sessum how to tie a length of rawhide *reata* to his reins, then loop the end over his arm. "A horse is lots of things, but smart ain't one of them. He don't like a rifle goin' off in his face. This way you get far enough from him that he don't spook so bad. You got both arms free, and still you don't let him run loose."

A thin fog still clung to the ground and obscured the view of anything more than fifty yards away. They crouched a long time in the brush, till Dent Sessum's legs went stiff. His fingers played nervously up and down the stock of his long rifle. "Sure do wish I had me another jug."

"You'd be drinkin' out of it, and you couldn't shoot straight."

"Why don't they hurry up and come on? You sure we got out ahead of them, Noonan? They could've already passed this way."

Noonan gritted, "Calm down, Dent. You're gettin' the shakes, and that ain't goin' to help none. They'll be along directly."

Sessum hunched his shoulders. "I swear it's gettin' cold. Fall ain't far enough along for it to be this cold."

"It's just you. You got the trembles from that whisky wearin' off. Scared, Dent?"

"What I got to be scared of?"

"Nothin'. That's what I'm tryin' to tell you. A Mexican's easy to kill. Just send a bullet whistlin' by his ear and he'll die of fright."

"That ain't the way I heard tell about the war."

"Folks lie. There ain't nothin' to killin' a Mexican. You'll see. Square yourself up."

From east it came, out of the fog, the wailing of wooden wheels rubbing against a wooden axle. Noonan turned in triumph. "See what I told you, Dent? You can hear one of them Mexican carts a mile away. Now, you get ahold of yourself."

They crouched lower and waited. Sessum's hands still played nervously up and down the rifle stock and on the barrel. Cold sweat popped out on his forehead, and he rubbed his sleeved arm across his face.

Noonan turned and frowned at him. "Dent, you sure you still want the first shot? Maybe I better take it."

Sessum shook his head. "I've took a right smart off of him too. I've took it off *all* of them. I want my bullet in him first."

Noonan shrugged. "All right, but don't you miss."

The groaning of the wheels came louder. Both men squinted and tried to see into the fog. Sessum's tongue darted back and forth across dry lips, and again he rubbed his sleeve over his face.

Noonan pointed. "There they come. You can see them now."

Ramón Hernandez rode his brown horse a little in front of the cart. He held a rifle balanced across his lap. His head moved slowly from left to right as his gaze swept the patches of brush that lay on either side of the trail. It touched the thick oak where Noonan and Sessum crouched, but they were hidden by the heavy green foliage.

The two Mexican women and the children rode in the cart, all but the boy Gregorio. He trailed behind, a-horse-back. In his hands was an old blunderbuss.

Noonan whispered, "Now, Dent, you just move slow, and don't be in no hurry. He'll be in your sights plenty long enough."

Sessum licked his lips nervously and leveled the rifle, resting its long barrel across a limb. He blinked hard, turned his cheek to wipe the sweat onto his shoulder, then returned to the sights. His hands trembled.

"Wait, Dent . . ." Noonan warned. "You're goin' to miss."

But Sessum jerked the trigger. The rifle belched.

Noonan spat in disgust. "See there, Dent, I told you; you missed him." Noonan brought his own rifle into line. The children were screaming, and Ramón reined around to lope back to the cart. In the swirling confusion Noonan took aim at what he thought was Ramón. After the roar of the rifle, he heard a high-pitched scream. Through the black smoke he saw a small figure lurch forward in the cart. "Hit one of the women," Noonan hissed. The horses danced in fright, jerking against the reins looped over Noonan's and Sessum's arms.

A ball tore through the leaves over their heads. Noonan gritted, "He'll be comin' in a minute, that Mexican. If he sees us, we'll have to kill them all."

"What'll we do?"

"We've spilt our chance. We better be gettin' the hell up and gone."

Rifles still empty, they swung onto the horses and

moved out in a lope. Noonan looked back over his shoulder, thankful for the fog. "One good thing," he muttered, "he'll move cautious, thinkin' we was a passel of Indians. It'll give us time to clear out."

They rode in a hard run for a few hundred yards, then slowed to an easier lope to spare the horses. After a couple of miles they gradually came to a stop. Noonan turned his head so that his right ear was toward the direction from which they had come.

Sessum asked anxiously, "Hear anything?"

"Only you. My old ears ain't the best anyhow. Maybe you better listen for both of us."

Sessum stood in the stirrups, turning his head slowly. "Quiet as a grave."

Noonan nodded in satisfaction. "Didn't figure he'd come chasin' us and leave the women and kids. Especially, him not knowin' but what we was Indians."

Sessum frowned. "I seen that woman fall. You shot her instead of Ramón, didn't you?"

Noonan shrugged. "Ain't no way to tell. Never pleasured me none to kill a woman, but them Mexican women breed more little ones anyway, and little ones grow into big ones, and we'd just have to kill them someday."

They rode west until they struck a creek, then rode down the bank into the water. They rode in the water's edge for a couple of miles, glancing back occasionally for sign of pursuit. Noonan saw no reason there ought to be, and he found no evidence of any.

Finally he said "I reckon we been far enough. Let's get up out of this creek and head for home."

"Suits me," Sessum replied, and reined his horse

around. He touched spurs to him and climbed up the steep bank, Noonan trailing. As he reached the top, Sessum suddenly jerked on the reins.

"Noonan!" he shouted in terror.

An arrow thumped into his chest and drove halfway through. Before he had time to fall, another arrow thudded between his ribs. His eyes rolled back and he slipped out of the saddle, tumbling, skidding, sliding down the muddy bank.

Sessum's horse lost its footing and slid back into Noonan's with an impact that jarred the old man loose from the saddle. Still gripping his rifle, he slammed against the muddy ground and pushed himself to his feet. He grabbed at the reins, but the horse broke away from him and ran. He shouted at Sessum's horse, which almost ran him down in its mad break to escape.

Mouth open, Noonan stood on wobbly legs and stared in helpless fear at the half dozen riders who suddenly towered above him on the creekbank. He got a glimpse of feathers and bare chests and bows, of gotch-eared ponies and bull-hide shields. He raised the rifle and remembered he never had taken time to reload it. Dropping it, he turned to run in the soft mud. A sharp pain stopped him in midstride. He grabbed at his side and felt his fingers clasp the shaft of an arrow, imbedded between his ribs. The numbness passed and the pain rushed on with the sudden intensity of hellfire. He tried again to run but found his legs would not bend, his feet would not move. He heard the thump of another arrow and felt it like the blow of a huge hammer against his back.

Twisting half around, Noonan stared in wordless horror at the warrior heeling his pony down the bank and coming at him in a run. He stared in deadly fascination at the heavy stone ax in the Indian's hand. He saw the strong brown arm come up. His eyes followed the downward arc of the stone as it swung savagely toward his head. The last sound he heard was his own terrified scream.

13

Heather Winslow came back into the cabin with a plate and an empty coffee cup. She was shaking her head. "Mister Quitman didn't eat much. Said he wasn't hungry. Drank the coffee, was about all."

Joshua Buckalew sat frowning down at his heavy cowhide boots. He said nothing.

Heather added, "He wants to know how long before we're ready to leave. He's impatient."

Aaron Provost grunted and turned to look sharply at Josh. "Ain't no use you two partin' with this thing hangin' over you. Sooner or later you both got to come to some understandin'. Why not start now and get done with it?"

Irritably Josh said, "What's there to talk about? We try to talk, like as not we'll end up fightin' again. He done what he done, and that's all there is to it."

Aaron argued, "He didn't go to. You ought to know him well enough to realize that of all the women on earth, María would be one of the last he'd want to fall in love with. Man just can't always help himself."

Josh arose and impatiently slapped a hand against his hip. "The whole subject pains me. I'd as soon not talk no more."

Aaron shrugged. He glanced around for his wife. "Rebecca, you got them kids about all ready to go? No use us wastin' any more time around here. It's a long ways."

"You and the boys can load the wagon," she said, her level gaze on Josh rather than on her husband. Josh couldn't tell whether she sympathized with him or blamed him. In the lingering of hurt and anger, he couldn't bring himself to care much.

He said, "I appreciate all you done, buildin' me this cabin. I'm sorry things went to hell at the last."

Aaron grimaced. "Life's thataway. 'Bout the time you figure you finally got everything on a downhill pull, somethin' comes along and stands you on your head." He walked out of the cabin, paused in the dog-run to frown at the lingering fog, then strode on out into the yard, hollering orders at the young ones. Most times Josh would have helped them tote their goods to the wagon, but this morning it wasn't in him. He leaned against the log wall and watched disconsolately. He hated to see them all leave; yet, he wanted to be alone awhile, to think things clear. A man couldn't study a problem out with people waiting around to hear what his decision was.

Josh cast a glance toward Ocie Quitman, who sat on his rolled blankets way out yonder. His fists knotted, and he found them painfully sore. *Dammit,* he thought with a surge of self-anger, *keep control of yourself. The world hasn't come to an end yet.*

It came to him that Aaron had been right about one thing. Feeling the way he did about Mexican people,

Ocie Quitman wouldn't have wanted to let himself de-
velop any feeling for María Hernandez . . . not even a
passing physical desire, much less anything stronger or
more lasting. Josh let his gaze follow Quitman as the
man pushed to his feet and began to pace restlessly.
Bet he feels guilty about the whole thing. The kind of
pride he's got, it probably torments his soul to find out
just how human he really is.

Under other circumstances, Josh might have found it
in himself to pity Quitman, even. If it had been some
other Mexican girl . . . But not María. *He's not good*
enough for her. After all the things he's said, he's not fit
to walk the same ground where she's been.

Daniel Provost brought up the horses and began to
help Aaron harness the team. Ocie Quitman came near
the cabin for the first time and saddled his own horse.
He carefully avoided looking at Josh.

Heather Winslow stopped beside Joshua Buckalew
and fidgeted, plainly wanting to say something but finding nothing that didn't sound hollow to her. "It's a good
house, Mister Buckalew. And this thing with María . . .
you'll get it straightened out. I never met a better girl."

"Thank you." He was surprised at the hoarseness of
his voice. "I'm sorry you had to be around and see it. I
expect you were disappointed with Ocie Quitman . . .
and with me."

"I'll live over it, Mister Buckalew. And so will you."

She walked out to the wagon and helped Patrick Quitman up into the bed of it, with the Provost youngsters.
Muley stood there, sadly telling them all goodbye. Aaron
Provost gave each of the two women a lift up, then placed
his foot on the right front wheel and swung his big frame

onto the seat. "Come over when you can, Josh. We'll shoot a fat doe." He hollered at the team, and the wagon began to roll.

Ocie Quitman sat on his horse, waiting for the wagon to come even with him. When it did, he pulled in beside it, Daniel Provost a-horseback on the other side. Quitman looked back over his shoulder at Josh. He rode a few yards, pulled around and came to the cabin.

"Buckalew . . ."

Josh watched him distrustfully. "Yes?"

"Buckalew, I . . ." Quitman broke off, his face twisting. He held silent a moment, then said bitterly, "Aw, hell, what can a man say?" He turned and started after the wagon.

The first shot came from somewhere out in the fog, a long way off. Josh stiffened. He heard another shot, and a third, in quick succession.

Three guns. Even counting the old blunderbuss, Ramón had left here with only two. The fog seemed to close in on Josh. A hard chill paralyzed him. "Quitman, they're in trouble."

Quitman's face was grave. "Get your horse."

Aaron Provost wheeled the wagon around and brought his team back in a long trot. He shouted, "Daniel, give me your horse. You women and kids . . . back into the cabin!"

Josh told Muley to help Daniel guard the cabin. Quitman was out forty yards in the lead when Josh and Aaron and Jacob Phipps swung into their saddles. Josh spurred hard to catch up. Aaron and Phipps never did catch up, quite.

The cart's tracks were easy to follow, the wheels having pressed the curing grass deep into the soft, wet ground. Riding in a run, Josh listened for other shots. He heard none. Why hadn't there been more? The question ran again and again through his brain. Maybe they'd been overrun. He could think of several reasons, and he didn't like any of them.

Once he glimpsed Quitman's face and found it as fearful as his own.

Through the fog he saw the dark shape that must be the cart. "Yonder, Quitman, ahead of us."

They slowed their horses to a trot, wary, and only then did Aaron and Phipps catch up. Rifle cradled high, ready for trouble, Josh squinted, trying to see. The fog drifted a little, and he could make out the huddle of figures around the cart.

"There! They look like they're all right."

Ramón whirled, the rifle in his hands. He lowered it as recognition came. "Careful," he called. "They may still be around here."

Josh heard some of the children sobbing. He tried to see through the tight group of frightened figures. "Ramón, is everybody all right?"

The Mexican's face answered him before his voice did. "Josh, María is shot."

Josh hit the ground and dropped the reins. The children pulled aside to make room for him, but they stayed close to the cart, crouched in fear. María lay still.

"María!" Josh dropped to one knee. Miranda Hernandez gave him a quick glance, and he could see dread in her eyes. She had torn open the neck of María's dress and was pressing a crimson-soaked handkerchief to a wound above María's breast. Tears streaked Miranda's face. "It is bad, Josh."

Josh lifted the handkerchief. He gasped as he saw the ragged hole which a rifleball had torn. He put the handkerchief back in place. "Did it go all the way through?"

Miranda shook her head. "The ball is still in there."

"Then we got to get her to the cabin, and quick."

He looked up, and his gaze stopped at Ocie Quitman. The man's face was drained of color.

Aaron Provost was asking, "Ramón, where was they shootin' from?"

Ramón pointed toward the brush. In his nervousness he made no effort at English. "There. Two shots. I fired back one time. I heard two horses run away."

"Reckon they're all gone?"

"I have not tried to go and see."

Quitman's voice was cold. "*I'll* go see." He started walking.

Aaron shouted, "Quitman, if they're there, they'll kill you!"

Quitman did not slow down or look back. He kept walking, the rifle up and ready. He moved stiffly, as if whittled from wood.

María groaned. Voice breaking, Josh could only whisper. "You'll be all right, María, I promise. You'll be all right." He bent down and placed his cheek against her forehead, his eyes afire.

From out in the brush, Quitman called, "They're gone."

Cautiously Aaron and Jacob Phipps followed him. Josh looked up and saw Ramón through a blur. "Ramón, let's put her into the cart." They rolled out blankets to make as soft a bed as possible. It would be a rough ride back to the cabin, for there was no kind of spring or leather sling on these Mexican carts to take up any of the shock. By the time they had placed María on the blankets, the other three men were back.

Ocie Quitman looked gravely at the girl. "How is she?"

Josh shook his head. "Bad."

Quitman's chin dropped. His eyes were hidden by the brim of his hat. When he looked up again, his face was dark with a fury Josh had never seen. His voice was quiet and deadly. "It wasn't Indians. We found boot-heel marks out there, and tobacco juice."

Jacob Phipps said regretfully, "It was Dent Sessum and old Noonan."

Aaron said, "They must've thought we'd never look at their tracks. They been drinkin'; maybe they didn't think at all."

Ramón's eyes filled with tears. "They must have been after me. They hit María instead."

Josh held the girl's shock-cold hand. "We'll settle with them later. Let's get María back where we can take care of her."

Quitman reached out. "You got a pistol in your belt, Buckalew. I want it."

"What for?"

"I'm not waitin'. I'm goin' after them now. I can't go up against two men with just a rifle. Whichever one I shot, the other would get me while I reloaded."

"We'll all go, Quitman, together. But first we got to think of María."

"I *am* thinkin' of her, and I'm thinkin' of them that shot her. You stay with her, Buckalew. It's your place;

she's your girl. She always was." Quitman reached and took the pistol out of Josh's belt.

Josh could see murder in his eyes. "We could be wrong. It could've been somebody else. It's the government's place to pass judgment."

"We're not wrong. And we got no government, not out here. I'll see you when I get back. You take good care of that girl, Buckalew."

Jacob Phipps blocked Quitman's path. "You figurin' on shootin' them wherever you find them?"

"Like a pair of killer wolves."

"I'll go with you, Quitman."

"Old Noonan's a friend of yours, ain't he, Phipps?"

"He used to be."

"Then you stay here. I don't want to fight *three* men." He shoved Phipps aside. Phipps called, "Wait, Quitman."

Quitman turned, eyes narrowed. "Don't you give me no trouble, Phipps." He stood a moment, his terrible eyes boring into Phipps until Phipps' chin dropped. Quitman swung onto his horse, rode out to the brush, paused a moment, then moved into the fog, following the tracks.

Phipps looked after him, frowning. "Old Noonan's a big talker and all, but he *has* been a fighter in his time. He'd fight again if Quitman was to corner him."

Josh said, "If we get the bullet out, and if we can tell María is goin' to do all right, we'll go help Quitman."

"That may not be soon enough. I think I'd best trail after him."

"You worried about him, or about Noonan?"

Phipps shrugged. "Both, I reckon. There was a time I thought a right smart of that old man, even with all his faults. I'd rather see him take his chances with a court than have Quitman shoot him down like a mad dog."

"There's no stoppin' Quitman right now. He's after blood."

"Maybe he'll cool off before he catches them. Anyway, I'll trail along."

Phipps rode off into the fog.

Josh rode in the cart, holding María's cold hand, feeling tears burn his eyes each time she moaned. Every little bit he would take up the handkerchief to let the blood wash the wound clean, then put it back again. Without help, she would have bled to death before now. Times, when he felt he was going to break down, Miranda would reach across and grip his arm. For a little woman, Ramón's wife had a lot of strength. "Faith, Josh. Faith."

They carried María into the cabin, the white-faced Rebecca Provost and Heather Winslow rushing ahead to clear a place for her. "The table," Josh said breathlessly. "We got to put her on the table and get the bullet out. You-all get some hot water started."

Aaron had planed down some boards riven from logs and had built Josh a heavy table, held together with stout pegs. Josh and Ramón placed María there on blankets Heather had spread. Josh stood back, looking down on the still girl.

"We got to dig that bullet out. Who's goin' to do it?"

Everybody looked at somebody else. All eyes came back to Josh. He shook his head. "You women—you got skilled fingers."

Rebecca demurred. "It'll take a man to have the stomach for it."

Josh looked in vain to Ramón, for he could see Ramón beginning to weep. Aaron raised his own trembling hands. "A thing like this, Josh, I got ten thumbs. It's up to you."

María's eyes came partially open. She tried to speak, but the words were unclear. Josh leaned over anxiously. "Don't talk now, *querida*."

"Ocie . . ." she murmured. "Where is Ocie?"

Josh swallowed and looked away. Quietly he said, "He's around."

"I want him. I want him here."

A taste came to Josh's mouth, a taste like gall. But he whispered: "He'll be here, María. Don't you fret; he'll be here."

She lapsed back into unconsciousness. Cold sweat broke on Josh's face. "I don't know if I can do it."

"You operated on that bushwacker boy," Aaron said.

"And he died."

When the water was hot, he picked up a knife with a stiletto blade. He had to go by feel rather than sight because the blood kept welling up. Each time his hands started to tremble, he paused, taking a deep breath or two. And while he worked, he prayed. María stirred, the pain reaching her through her unconsciousness. Once Josh thought he would have to give up, for sickness rolled in his stomach. But from somewhere he took strength to keep on. And finally the ball came out. He dropped it, and it rolled against his boot on the dirt floor. He realized he'd held his breath a long, long time. He let out what had been compressed in his lungs and took a deep breath of fresh air. He let the wound bleed a moment to wash it clean, then called for a hot iron to sear it over. María lunged against him and cried out, then went limp.

Josh's tears flowed unchecked. "Jesus, don't let her die again!"

14

Sitting in a rough chair beside the bed, he heard a horse running. He raised his head to listen. He blinked the haze from his burning eyes and saw that Aaron and Ramón were listening too. Aaron went to the door.

"Can't see him for the fog. Way he's ridin', there's somethin' wrong."

There's a lot wrong, Josh thought numbly. *There's an awful lot wrong.* He pushed stiffly to his feet and dragged himself across the dirt floor to stand beside Aaron. Ramón had stepped into the yard. Jacob Phipps broke out of the fog, splashing across the creek and up the steep bank.

"Quitman's in trouble!" he shouted. "Indians!"

Josh heard, but he was too numb to move. It took a moment for the message to soak in on him.

Phipps shouted, "They got him cornered up in the limestone bluffs. I don't know how long he can hold out."

Aaron grabbed his rifle and went out the door. "How many?"

"Couldn't tell for the fog, not for sure. Seven or eight, maybe ten. Too many, that's for certain."

Ramón came for his rifle. He paused. "Josh, you coming?"

Josh looked at the girl. She hadn't moved or moaned or anything since he had seared the wound. Her face was almost gray. "María . . ." He clenched his fist. "We can't leave her now." Resentment came in an angry rush. "Dammit, he got himself into this. We tried to tell him."

"Maybe you should stay, then. We'll go to Quitman."

Josh touched the girl's hand and found it cold as ever. But there was still a pulse. "I don't want to leave her, Ramón. But she'd want me to go. Wait, and I'll get my rifle."

He rode hunched, his mind and soul still in that cabin and only the shell of him out here on horseback, riding in the fall chill. He only half heard Jacob Phipps telling what had happened.

"I trailed along behind him aways, and he must've caught on. All of a sudden he rode out from behind a live oak tree with his rifle on me and told me to get away and stay away, or he was liable to put a rifle ball through my other arm. I tell you, I was sore tempted to come on back. But I decided maybe I still ought to be around, so I let him have a long start, and I trailed him again. He come to the creek. The tracks led off down into the water. I reckon he figured the same as I did, that they was tryin' to throw off anybody that might come after them. But bein' who they was, they'd head in the general direction of Noonan's cabin. Quitman's tracks led thataway, so I followed.

"It was the fog that saved me when the Indians jumped him. They was so interested in him that they didn't see me. He must've had a little warnin', because I heard his horse runnin' before they ever started to whoopin'. He took out across the creek and headed west toward the

bluffs, them Indians after him like hounds after a rabbit. There was too many of them for me to help him. I
trailed along till I knowed he made the bluffs. I heard
him fire a shot or two. After that, I turned and came back
here." Phipps was apologetic. "I'd of stayed if there'd of
been anything I could do. But they had him hemmed,
and I couldn't have got through to him."

Aaron said, "You done the right thing."

Phipps turned to Josh. "How's the girl?"

Josh shook his head. "I don't know. I just don't know."

They came to the creek, and Josh could see the tracks
where the Indians had gone up the opposite bank. Ramón
pointed. "They were coming down the creek. Quitman
was going up the creek, following Sessum and Noonan."

That brought Josh up with a shudder. "Then the Indians must've run into Sessum and Noonan before they
found Quitman."

Phipps shivered. "I thought of that awhile ago. I figure
Quitman wasted his trip. Them Indians likely already
done to Sessum and Noonan what *he* was intendin' to do.
More, even."

Josh managed to collect his wits. Perhaps what brought
him to reality was the brutal certainty of what must have
happened to that hapless pair of scoundrels. He wondered if it had been quick, or if the Indians had taken
their time. When they weren't in any hurry, the Comanches had their ways. It wasn't a thing Josh would wish
on anybody. But thinking of María, the cold clay color
of her face when he had left her, he didn't care whether
death had come quickly or not for Sessum and Noonan.
He found no sympathy.

A vagrant thought ran through his mind: that hidden

money wouldn't do Sessum any good now. Or anybody else, either. Chances were it would never be found.

Josh knew the bluffs Phipps had spoken of. He had sought wild cattle here many times, and mustangs. This ground was almost as familiar to him as his own yard and fields that he had plowed and harvested and built his cabin upon. "It's not far anymore," he said cautiously. "We better spread out a little and keep a careful watch. We don't want them jumpin' us by surprise. We'd rather have it the other way."

It worried him, the fact that by Phipps' account the Indians had them somewhat outnumbered. Josh had long heard people brag that a white man was the equal of several Indians in a fight, but he had taken that as idle boasting. The few hostile Indians he'd met hadn't been anything to mess around with. If Quitman was still alive, the best chance they had to rescue him was by using their one bit of leverage—surprise.

Somewhere ahead of them, he heard a shot. He saw some of the anxiety lift from Aaron's face. The farmer edged over to Josh. "Quitman's rifle. I know the sound of it. They ain't got him yet."

Josh eased a little. "He's likely found him a good place with the bluff to his back. They can't get to him except straight on."

Aaron nodded. "The Comanch, he loves a good fight, long as he knows he's goin' to win it. But he don't fancy suicide. They're probably just laid up there, figurin' on wearin' him down."

"Quitman's got his rifle and my pistol," Josh reasoned. "Long's he don't let both of them get empty at the same time, they'll show him a lot of respect. They know that sooner or later he's either got to come out or starve. Time don't mean much to an Indian."

Phipps said nervously, "Right now we need old Sam Houston to general for us. I don't like suicide any more than the Comanches do."

Josh found all the men looking to him for leadership. He didn't want it. He wasn't sure he knew enough to give it to them. He had no plan. All he'd thought of was that Quitman was trapped, and it was up to them to get him out of trouble. How, he didn't know.

Finally he said, "Since we know he's still there, let's go easy; take our time and figure how we can do this right. Fog ought to let us get in pretty close."

They rode in silence, Josh watching for the outline of the bluffs to begin showing. Presently he heard another shot. Quitman's rifle. It occurred to him that the Indians probably had no guns, for he hadn't heard any. Only a scattered few rifles had fallen into Indian hands by trade, plus an occasional one stolen in a raid or taken from a murdered white man. Most Indians still didn't know how to load and fire a rifle even if they came into possession. But the bow could be as deadly as a rifle, within its range. Even more so, in one way, for a Comanche could unleash several arrows while a white man was reloading a rifle for just one more shot.

They were near the bluffs now. Josh knew, though he could not yet see them. He raised his hand for a halt. He leaned forward in the saddle, listening. He couldn't hear anything. He pushed on, slower now, watching where his horse stepped, keeping him away from rocks that he might kick and cause a noise. Josh's hand tightened on the stock of his rifle. He found himself breathing faster.

Then, from out in the fog, he heard the restless stamping of horses' hoofs. He held up his hand again and halted to listen. Somewhere up there, he reasoned, the Indians' horses were being held in a safe place away from fire. Josh swung down from the saddle and looked back. "Ramón," he whispered, "you want to go with me? Aaron, you and Jacob watch after our horses."

Ramón beside him, Josh walked carefully, watching his footing, peering cautiously through the fog. At length he saw something move, and he dropped to one knee, pointing. Ramón nodded.

There were the Indian horses. As the fog drifted, Josh glimpsed an Indian a-horseback, tending them. The brave's attention was not on the horses, however; he was looking westward, where the bluffs lay. After a few moments another rifle shot echoed against the unseen limestone walls, and the horses stirred restlessly.

Josh whispered, "He's not lookin' for any trouble from thisaway."

Ramón said, "You want to try to get him? I could use my knife."

Josh shook his head. "Not yet. If somethin' went wrong, he might raise an alarm before we're ready. Let's ease around him and see how the rest of them are spread out."

Crouching, they moved at a tangent from the Indian horses, carefully keeping to the live oak brush for cover, because now and again the fog drifted enough to leave them exposed for anyone who happened to be looking in their direction. In a little while the picture was clear to Josh. As he had expected, the warriors had spread themselves in a ragged line just back from Quitman's position at the base of the bluff. He was bottled up in there like whisky stoppered in a jug. Josh couldn't see him, though once he caught the flash of the rifle. He pointed, and Ramón nodded. He had seen too. Josh made a sign for retreat.

When they were back with Aaron and Phipps, Josh knelt and brushed away the mat of old live oak leaves and acorns so he could draw a rough map on the ground. "This here is the bluff. Right here is Quitman. The Comanches are scattered along like this . . . here, and here, and here. We couldn't see them all, but we took a count on their horses. There was ten, plus Quitman's." He glanced at Phipps. "Two of them horses belonged to Sessum and Noonan."

Phipps grimaced. "I figured that."

"If all the Indians was mounted to start with, and they picked up Sessum's and Noonan's horses extra, that comes out to eight men."

Aaron counted on his fingers. "Four of us. That's two to one."

"Quitman makes five. From where he's at, he can help."

Aaron frowned. "Never did go much for Indian-fightin', not even when the odds was in our favor."

"We got no choice, except to leave Quitman there. Likely these are braves out on a horse raid. If we don't stop them here they'll come on and hit one of us any-way . . . maybe all of us. We'll still have to fight."

Phipps asked, "You got a plan, Josh?"

Josh shrugged. "Not much. We just hit them and hope the surprise makes up for the difference in numbers."

Ramón said regretfully in Spanish, "Lately it seems

all we've done is fight. The war, first. Then Mexican army stragglers, then that group of Redland renegades. Now the Indians."

Josh said, "It's a raw country. If we stay here there'll be more fightin' yet before we've won this land free and clear. And I intend to stay!"

Ramón replied, "If I fight now, perhaps my sons will never have to."

"Everybody has to fight, in his own way and in his own time. You're all ready to go, I hope."

They made a long arc to the left, walking their mounts slowly and watchfully. At length Josh put up his hand. "We've got them outflanked now. From here we can ride in on them and take them one at a time. The horses will be yonder." He pointed. "We'll rush the horses first and drive them right in on top of the Indians. If that don't confuse them, nothin' will."

He started to go on, but he hesitated. There was one more thing which needed to be said. His gaze moved from one man to another, and he spoke gravely. "Quitman's just one man. If he lives but one of us dies, we haven't gained anything. We've just swapped lives. I'm no hero and got no wish to ever be one. Let's just hit them hard and fast and make as little target as we can get by with."

They moved into a trot toward the horses. From up against the bluff, the rifle fired again. *Good,* thought Josh, *that'll hold their attention for a minute.* He leaned forward, straining to see the horses. When suddenly they showed through the fog, he saw that the Indian guarding them was still mounted, looking toward the cliff. Josh touched spurs to his horse and moved into a run.

Hearing him, the Indian turned, surprised. For a second or two he stared in disbelief. Then he brought up his bow with his left hand as his right hand reached back for an arrow from his quiver. Before the arrow touched the bowstring, Josh plowed into him. He drove the rifle butt into the warrior's ribs, then swung it up and jammed it against the chin. Grunting, the Indian slid over his horse's side, still clutching the bow, trying to bring the arrow to the string. Then Ramón was there, knife blade flashing. He leaned out of the saddle, the knife streaking down and coming up red.

The horses shied away, moving toward the Indians, Josh waved his hat and shouted. The other men started shouting, too. The horses broke into a run.

The first Indian jumped up from behind a scrub oak, consternation in his eyes. Not quite comprehending, he waved his arms and shouted, trying to turn the horses. They split around him. Josh's rifle butt slashed, and the Indian fell.

The racket stirred the others, who could not see clearly through the fog but knew instinctively that something had gone wrong. One by one the running horses sped past them or split around them. An arrow sang past Josh, and he saw an Indian whipping another arrow into place. Josh fired, knowing as he did so that for the rest of this run he was carrying an empty rifle. Well, by George, at least it would make a damn good club. He spurred and shouted and fell right in behind the running horses.

Another Indian arose, arrow fitted. Josh dropped down over his horse's off-shoulder. He felt the impact as it struck his saddle, and a sudden burn told him it had at

least creased his thigh. Another shot sounded behind
him. The Indian fell.

Two shots gone. Only two shots left among us.

His horse stumbled, almost fell, caught its footing and
ran again. But its movement was labored, and Josh saw
the arrow driven into its shoulder.

I'll be lucky to finish this run before he falls.

In front of him, behind him, he could see the bewildered Indians, loosing arrows. The horse stumbled. Josh
kicked free of the stirrups and hit the ground rolling,
holding onto his rifle. He heard the rip of cloth and realized the arrow which grazed his thigh had pinned him
to the saddle. He jumped to his feet, hopping, looking
around desperately. He held the rifle in both hands, like
a club.

Through the fog he had a clear view of the bluff now.
He saw an Indian rise up and take aim at him, too far
away for the clubbed rifle to help him. Partway up the
bluff, fire flashed, and the Indian fell.

Then Phipps reined up beside him. "Up, Josh. Hurry!"

He offered Josh an empty stirrup, and Josh swung up
behind him.

Ramón Hernandez spurred to the base of the cliff.
Ocie Quitman clambored down to meet him. Ramón
leaned over, extending his arm. Quitman caught it and
swung up, landing on the horse's hips. An Indian came
running to stop them. Ramón fired. The Indian dropped
his bow and sank to his knees.

One shot left, Josh thought. *Wonder who has it?*

Aaron Provost slowed to wait for Ramón and Quitman. As a Comanche stepped from behind a live oak,
Aaron squeezed off a shot. It missed, but it clipped leaves

above the Comanche's head and showered them on him. His arrow went astray.

"Let's get out of here!" Josh shouted. Aaron came in a lope, waving his hat at the loose horses. Ramón and Quitman were just behind him. Looking back over his shoulder, Josh saw a couple of arrows in flight, but they would fall short.

We're out of their range.

They circled around the horses and brought them finally to a nervous, milling stop. Josh slid off, going to one knee and pushing back to his feet. He felt the thigh, and his hand came away with a small streak of blood. The arrow had not cut deep. "Anybody hit?" he asked anxiously.

No one else was except Ocie Quitman. Quitman's arm was bleeding. Stepping to the ground, Quitman slid up his sleeve and examined the wound. "Just enough to teach me humility," he said, "I'll live." His gaze lifted to Ramón, then went to Phipps and Aaron and Josh. "Men, I don't know what to say. I hope *thanks* will do."

Josh waited for someone to reply, but no one did. He said, "That's good enough. I expect you'd of done the same for any of us."

"They as good as had me. I was almost out of powder." He looked at Jacob Phipps. "You went and trailed me, even after I told you not to."

Phipps nodded. "Seemed like the thing to do."

Quitman turned to Ramón. "And you . . . you're the one who went in there and picked me up. You're the last one who had any reason to do it."

Ramón shrugged. "I had a reason. María."

A frown came over Ocie Quitman. He turned his face

to Josh. "She's all right, isn't she? You wouldn't have left her if she wasn't all right, would you?"

Josh said tightly, "She looked bad when we left her."

"Then, you ought to've stayed."

"The women were there. They could do as much as I could."

Quitman stared at the ground. "Josh, I wonder why you came after me atall. I've caused you a right smart of trouble." He gripped his arm, where the stain was still spreading. "I think the best thing for me to do is take my son and go somewhere . . . to get away from here."

Josh said, "Let's talk about it later." He pointed to Quitman's horse, which stamped nervously among the Indian ponies, the saddle still on its back. "Right now you better catch that bay. I'll take Sessum's. I don't have the nerve to try to get my saddle . . . not right now."

Aaron gave him a boost up. Josh motioned. "Let's go see about María."

Rebecca Provost and Heather Winslow waited anxiously in the doorway as the men rode into view. Josh could see them counting fearfully, making sure no one was missing. Rebecca hurried out and threw her arms around Aaron as he stepped out of the saddle. Muley and the children came running, and Josh dropped his reins into the first pair of eager hands. Ocie Quitman grabbed up his son and gave him a fierce hug, then set him down. Together he and Josh walked to the door. Heather Winslow met them there. Tears stained her cheeks.

Josh asked with anxiety, "What about María?"

"She's conscious now. We tried to lie to her about where you'd all gone, but I think she knew."

Josh and Quitman stepped into the room and haltingly moved toward the bed where María lay. Her eyes opened, and she blinked, trying to recognize the men against the light of the open door. Her hand came up weakly, and she gave a sharp little cry. "Josh!"

"I'm right here, María."

"Did you find Ocie? Did you bring him?"

Josh halted. "We found him, María. He's here."

Quitman glanced at him in surprise. Josh gave him a nudge forward. "Go on. It's you she was callin' for when we took the bullet out. It's you she really wants, not me."

Quitman dropped his hat to the earthen floor and moved forward with slow, uncertain steps. He knelt beside the girl and said hoarsely, "I'm here. I'm here if you want me."

Her hand reached out, and he took it. "Yes, Ocie," she whispered. "I want you." He dropped himself down beside her, his cheek to her own. Josh could hear her sobbing quietly and thanking the saints.

Quitman was telling her, "I'm not a good man for you. You know me. I'm hard and I'm mean, and when I get an idea in my stubborn head, nobody can tell me I'm wrong."

"I am stubborn too."

"It won't be easy. You know how I've been. I'll be hard to change."

"But I want you, Ocie."

Throat tight, Josh turned and walked toward the door, where Heather waited. He tried to smile, but it was a poor attempt, and he gave it up. It hurt too much. "She'll live, Heather. She wants to, and she's a strong little woman, that María. Anything she wants bad enough, she'll get."

"And she wants Ocie Quitman."

Josh nodded.

Heather stared at him in wonder. "You'd give her up, just like that?"

Josh flinched. "What I'm givin' up is a dream, Heather, a mirage. María never was mine to give up, really. There was a time she thought she loved me, I guess, but she was just a girl. She hadn't met anybody else. I thought I loved her too, and in a way I did. I still do. But it was never right, not from the start."

He stepped outside and leaned against the wall, his gaze drifting aimlessly over the field, over the rolling prairie and the sun-cured grass. "She took me back, Heather; that's all it ever really was. When I was with María it was like she had come to me from somewhere out of the past, out of a time that was gone but that I never could quite turn loose of. She wasn't really María, not to me. She was always somebody else, somebody I had to say goodbye to years ago but never quite let go of. Deep inside me, I guess I've sensed it awhile now. That's why I never could bring myself to talk to her about marryin' me. While ago, when I took the bullet out, I found myself prayin' she wouldn't die again." His fist clenched. "Die *again*. It wasn't María I prayed for; it was her sister Teresa. It was *always* Teresa."

Heather waited a long time before she asked, "Do you think you can turn loose now?"

He nodded slowly. "It won't be easy, but I'll have to."

Heather took his hand. "Josh, I had to, once. Maybe, if you wanted me to, I could teach you how."

He turned and looked at her as if he had never seen her before. It occurred to him that he never really had. "Maybe you can, Heather. Maybe you can."

LLANO
RIVER

1

Some men seem blessed with a Jovial nature, an even humor that lets them take reversal and insult in stride without losing their smile or clenching a fist.

Dundee was not one of these. His temper was like a hammer cocked back over forty grains of black powder. The echo racketed for miles when Old Man Farraday brought a new son-in-law out to the ranch and handed him Dundee's job as foreman. A man with any self-respect couldn't just stand there like a sheep and abjectly accept demotion to cowhand thataway. So after the discussion was over, Dundee painfully rubbed his bruised knuckles and asked for his time.

He had stopped in a ragtag shipping-pen settlement later to wash away the indignities and suffered one more: he lost most of his payoff money over a whiskey-splashed card table.

He had no clear idea where he was riding to. In the Texas free-range days of the '80s, a man seeking fresh grass usually drifted in a westerly direction. He might veer a little northward, or southward, but the main direction was always west, for that was where the "new" was, where a man could cut a fresh deck and hope for a new deal all around. Dundee had ridden several days. Now darkness was about to catch him as his half-Thoroughbred bay splashed across a narrow creek toward a dusty little cowtown which the sign said was Titusville. His outlook hadn't improved much as the bay had slowly put the long miles behind him. Dundee was tired, hungry, near broke, and ringy enough to do bare-handed battle with a bobcat.

The two-rut wagon road widened into a many-rutted street. At the head of it Dundee passed a set of horse corrals and a big barn that said "Titus Livery." He thought how much the bay would like a clean stall and a good bait of oats. A little way down the hoof-softened street he saw a thin little man lighting a lantern on the front gallery of a long frame building. The sign by the front door said "Titus Hotel." Dundee looked with appreciation at the deep, narrow windows and imagined how soft the mattresses were, how pleasant must be the bright colors of the wallpaper. But he jingled the few coins left in his pockets and knew that after a drink and a meal, he'd retrace his steps down to the creekbank, stake the bay on grass and stretch his own frame on a blanket, looking up at stars instead of wallpaper.

Slim pickings, sure enough, but there wasn't any use a man biting himself like a stirred-up rattler. If he was strong he took the hand which was dealt him and played it through, even when it was all jokers. Tomorrow he'd scout around and try to find him a ranch job. Tonight, the hell with it.

He saw the words "Titus Mercantile" on a big, false-fronted building, and "Titus Saloon" on still another. *Ain't there nobody here but Titus?* he asked himself irritably.

Across the street lay a narrow, deep building which

he took to be a second saloon, and he angled the bay toward it. On the porch, a lanky man sat rocked back in a rawhide chair, balanced against the clapboard wall. The sign over his head read: "Texas Bar." Since it didn't say anything about Titus, Dundee decided to give the place a try. *That Titus is already rich enough*, he thought. *No use giving him my business*. He stepped off of the horse and dropped the reins through a ring in a cedar post, taking a hitch to be sure the bay didn't get a fool notion to wander off in search of Titus, whoever the Samhill that was.

Dundee stretched himself. He dusted his felt hat across his leg, raising a small cloud. He glanced at the stubbled oldtimer in the chair and found the man sitting motionless, watching him. The man finally spoke: "Evenin'." Saloon bum, Dundee judged him by his look, by the dusty, threadbare clothes he wore, the runover old boots. If he was figuring on Dundee buying him a drink, he was out of luck. But it didn't cost anything to be civil. "Evenin'."

The tail of his eye caught a movement, and he turned. From around the side of the building three young men came ambling along as if they had all night to do whatever it might be that they had in mind. Cowboys, Dundee figured. Boil them all down and you wouldn't have fifty cents worth of tallow, or anything else. They paused at the edge of the low porch and eyed Dundee like they were appraising a bronc at a first-Monday horse sale. One of them looked at the bay, finally, and foolishly asked, "That your horse, friend?"

Dundee's voice was sharply impatient. "I ain't had a friend since a year ago last March. And you just try riding him off. You'll find out right quick whose horse he is."

His voice was rougher than he meant it to be. Damn Old Man Farraday and his flat-chested daughter and his ignorant new son-in-law, anyway! He saw a flash of anger in the young man's eyes. *I'm too touchy,* he thought. *I cut him off a little quick. But when a man asks a foolish question, he ought to expect an answer in kind.*

He went into the saloon and leaned his elbows heavily on the dark-stained bar. "A drink," he said. He glanced at his own scowling face in the cracked mirror behind the bar and quickly looked away, for he didn't like what he saw. Even as a baby, he hadn't been called pretty by anybody but his mother, and thirty years hadn't improved the situation. Right now he looked forty, face dusty and bewhiskered, brown eyes hostile, when deep down he knew he didn't have anybody to be mad at, really, except Old Man Farraday, who was a long way behind him.

The heavy-jowled bartender studied him as if trying to decide whether Dundee could pay. "Good whiskey or cheap whisky?"

"It better not cost much. I'm almost as broke as I look."

The bartender's heavy moustache tugged with the beginnings of a grin. "That don't leave a man but little choice." He brought up a plain bottle from beneath the bar. "The quality ain't much, but it sure does carry authority."

Dundee choked on the first swallow and cut a hard glance at the bartender. But he couldn't say he'd been lied to. He poured himself a second glass and lifted it. "Here's to truth."

"I *told* you the truth."

"That is purely a fact."

He heard a commotion outside, and a stirring of hoofs. It struck him that that crazy cowboy just might be taking him up on his dare. In three long strides he reached the door and stopped. One cowboy was holding the bay's reins up close to the bit, trying to make the horse stand still. Behind, a second cowboy had hold of the bay's tail, stretching it taut. The third—the one who had asked the question—was using a pocket-knife in an attempt to bob the tail off short.

Roaring, Dundee left the porch like a firebrand flung in fury. He barreled into the man who was holding the horse's tail and sent him staggering. The cowboy with the knife stared in disbelief at the speed of Dundee's fist streaking toward his eyes. The cowboy reeled backward and fell in the dust, a believer.

The third man turned loose of the reins and trudged forward, his fists up in a bare-knuckle boxer stance. Dundee didn't know the rules. He just went under and caught him in the belly. The cowboy buckled, gasping for breath. He went to his knees, out of the fight.

The first cowboy charged back into the fray. Dundee turned to meet him, his fists doubled hard as a sledge. Of a sudden this wasn't just any cowboy; he was Old Man Farraday, young enough to hit. Dundee thought the man got in a lick or two, but he didn't feel them. In a moment the cowboy was on the ground, out of it.

Only the pocketknife man was left. His nose was bleeding, his eyes wild, and somehow he looked a little like Old Man Farraday's son-in-law. Dundee gathered the pent-up anger of many days and delivered it into the cowboy's ribs. It was a considerable load. The cowboy cried out in pain, but he didn't stop coming. He swung fists awkwardly, trying for any kind of contact he could make. Dundee fetched him a hard lick on the chin, and another in the belly. They hurt; he could tell. But the cowboy stayed. He got his arms around Dundee and wrestled until Dundee lost his footing. Falling, he managed to twist so that the cowboy didn't land on top of him. The instant he hit the dirt he was pushing himself up again. He dropped the cowboy onto his back and straddled him, grabbing at the swinging fists.

"Boy," he gritted, "you better give up. I got you by the short hair."

Raging, the cowboy continued his struggle. Somehow now he didn't look quite so much like Farraday's son-in-law, who hadn't fought this hard. But Dundee thought of the pocketknife and the bay horse's tail, and his conscience didn't twinge as he swung at the jutting jaw. The cowboy stiffened, then went to struggling again. He was game, anyway.

"Boy," Dundee warned, "I tell you, I'm fixing to get out of sorts with you."

The struggling went on, so Dundee fetched him another lick.

The nondescript old man on the porch slowly let his chair away from the wall and pushed himself to his feet. He looked down calmly at the cowboy pinned to the ground. "Son Titus, I believe you've caused this stranger trouble enough. You better let him go."

The cowboy twisted and fought beneath Dundee's weight.

The man on the porch said a little firmer, "Son Titus, you get up and leave that stranger alone."

The cowboy relaxed. "All right, Pa. But I could've whipped him."

The older man snorted. "The day we have six inches of snow here in July, maybe you can whip him. Git up from there and dust yourself off."

Dundee pushed away from the cowboy but kept his fists clenched. That crazy button might decide to try just one more spin of the wheel. Dundee's knuckles were bruised, his breath short. He couldn't rightly remember when he'd had so satisfying a little fight.

The young cowboy's face was red-smeared. From his eyes, Dundee judged he hadn't had quite enough yet. But the older man's voice was strong with authority. "Son Titus, go wash yourself."

Son Titus turned away, looking back over his shoulder at Dundee. The look spoke of things unfinished, and things to come.

The other two cowboys got shakily to their feet, but they didn't seem much inclined to continue what they had started. *Some people*, Dundee thought, *just can't stay interested in one thing very long at a time.*

He turned back to check his horse. Wonder the bay hadn't jerked loose and run off, all that scuffling going on around him. Dundee patted the horse reassuringly. He took hold of the tail, stretching it out to see how much damage the cowboy had done, while at the same time he warily watched the bay's hind feet. It would be just like a horse to kick now that the trouble was over.

He couldn't see they had cut much hair. Dull boy, dull knife.

The man on the porch said, "Stranger, I apologize for my boy. He was just by way of having a little fun."

"It wasn't very funny to my horse."

"Little town like this, there ain't much for a young man to do to entertain himself. So it's natural they turn their hand to mischief when they see a stranger. Hope they didn't spoil the looks of your horse."

"They didn't, but it's no thanks to you. You sat right there and let them do it."

"I was curious to see if I'd judged you right."

"Well, did you?"

"Sized you up when you first come. You did just about what I expected you would. A little quicker, even. Nice job you done on them three buttons."

"If one of them was your son, you take it awful calm."

The man shrugged. "Does a boy good to get himself whipped once in a while. Teaches him humility. Come on back in. I'll stand you to a drink."

The heavy-jawed barkeep with the smiling moustache reached beneath the bar and came up with a bottle that even *looked* better than the one Dundee had tried. He poured two glasses.

The man from the porch said, "I didn't hear your name."

"No, I don't reckon you did."

"It's none of my business, but I got to call you something."

"Dundee will do. I answer to that."

"I doubt that you answer to anybody. I'm John Titus."

Dundee nodded. "I gathered that when the boy called you Pa. You the Titus that owns everything in town?"

"Most of it. Whichaway did you ride in from?"

"Northeast."

"You been on my ranch the last twenty . . . twenty-five miles."

"You don't look like a big rancher."

"Meaning my clothes?" Titus shook his head. "Hell, everybody here knows me. I don't have to impress anybody."

"You dress up different when you go away from home?"

Titus shook his head again. "Why should I? Nobody would know me anyhow."

Dundee mulled that a while and finished his drink. He glanced at the big barkeep and back at Titus. "This saloon ain't got your name on it. How come you're in here buying whisky from the competition?"

"It's better than the kind *I* sell. Anyhow, the people who work in *my* saloon wear the knees out of their britches trying to please me. I get tired of being 'Mistered' all over the place. Badger here, he's so independent that even his mother hates him. I like a man who's a little contrary. Shows he's got character." His eyes narrowed. "*You're* a contrary man, Dundee."

Dundee didn't reply, for this was no news to him. He'd been only about fourteen when his brothers had decided they couldn't stand him any more. They had ganged up and run him off from home.

Titus picked up the bottle and his glass and carried it to a small round table. Dundee followed suit. Titus said, "You look tired. I hope you're figuring on spending the night in my *ho*tel."

"I expect I'll sleep out on the creekbank."

Titus gazed at him intently. "That's what I thought. Broke, ain't you?"

"What gives you that kind of a notion?"

"The look of you. It's all over you, like dark skin on a Comanche. Anyway, you're a cowboy. Cowboys are stone broke nine-tenths of the time."

"I won't go hungry."

"You don't have to. You need a job, I need a man. I bet we could work up a deal." Titus passed. "I seen a carbine on your saddle. You know how to use it, I expect."

"I generally hit what I aim at."

"How about a pistol?"

"Got one in my saddlebag. Always liked a carbine better."

"Ever hire your guns out?"

Dundee scowled. "You got somebody you want killed, you just go and shoot him yourself. I do honest work."

He thought he saw a flicker of a smile across Titus' face, and a look of satisfaction. "I'm sure you do, Dundee. What I had in mind would be honest. I wouldn't lie to you, though. It's so damned honest it just *could* get you killed."

"How's that?"

"Where I want you to go, honest men are as rare as fresh peaches in January. They're in open season the year around."

"If somebody was to shoot me, I don't see where that money of yours would do me any good."

"I got a notion you can take care of yourself. Anyway, man, think of the challenge."

"I'm not a schoolboy. A challenge don't stir me anymore."

"But I'll bet money does."

Dundee took the bottle and poured himself a fresh drink. "You got the money; I got the time. Long as your whiskey holds out, I'll at least listen. What's your problem?"

"Cowthieves. Hideburners. They're after me like heelflies after an old bull. I need them stopped."

"Why don't you just call in the Texas Rangers? That's their line of work."

"It's *my* cattle; I'll pay for my own remedies. Man runs to the government with all his trouble, it's a sign of weakness. When I itch, I scratch for myself."

Or hire somebody to do the scratching for you, Dundee thought. "How come you think I'm the man to do it for you? You don't know me. For all you know, *I* could be a cowthief." He grunted. "For all *I* know, I *could* be one, if the profit looked big enough."

Titus shook his head. "You're not one of that kind. Some people are easy to read, minute you set eyes on them. I got a strong notion you could go down into that den of snakes and bite as hard as *they* do."

"Where is this snake den?"

"You ever been down in the Llano River country, south of here?"

Dundee said he hadn't. Titus said, "It's rough country, lots of brush and timber. A regular outlaw paradise. They even got a town of their own, if you'd *call* it a town . . . a place by the name of 'Runaway.' Ever hear of it?"

Dundee shook his head. "Never even heard of Titusville till I rode in here."

"Runaway's not on any map. It's just down there, like a boil on a man's backside. It's outside of this county.

Local sheriff's got no jurisdiction down there, and what's more, he don't want any. Runaway's a far piece from its own county seat, and they don't even keep a deputy there. Bad climate, hard on your health."

"Looks like the thing to do is just to hire you a couple or three dozen gunslingers, go down there and clean house. Be done with it once and for all."

"I will. But I got to go about it right. Old days, a man could just go down and throw a nice, big hanging party and burn the damned place and be shed of it, and no questions asked. But now people have got awful righteous about things like that. They get upset and call for investigations and such . . . cause a heap of bother. Anyway, I'm not a hard man, Dundee. There's some good people down there—a few, at least—and I don't want to have to hurt them all just to get at the heelflies. Trouble is, I don't know just who-all's doing the stealing. That'd be one of the things I'd want you to find out. Once I know the guilty ones, I'll get me some men and go down there and throw one hell of a good party."

Dundee's opinion of Titus was slowly on the rise. Some cowmen he knew would simply ride down on such a town like a cyclone, sweep it clean and tell God they'd all just died.

"Titus, you're a wealthy man. A few cowthieves won't break you."

"No?" Titus clenched a big fist on the table. Dundee could tell by the rough look of it that it had known a long lifetime of hard work. "You've heard the old saying: the bigger a man is, the harder he goes down. I got debts, Dundee, debts that would scare old Jim Fisk himself. The cattle I'm losing can be the difference between me hanging on and going under. I got to stop the leaks, and I will. I want to do it the right way: get the people who are hurting me and leave the innocent folks alone. But if I wind up with my back to the wall, I'll take desperate measures. I *will* go down there and wipe the whole slate clean. When a man comes up to the snubbing post, he's got to save himself."

"And what about the innocent ones?"

"I expect there was a few good people in Jericho, Dundee. But when Joshua blew that trumpet, they all went down."

Dundee shrugged. It wasn't any skin off of his nose, one way or the other. But he had a feeling he could get to like this Titus, if he stayed around. Dundee liked contrary men, too. "You asked me if I'd ever hired out my guns. I have, but only when I liked the deal."

"I'm not asking you to go down there and kill out all them varmints. I'm not asking you to kill *anybody*, unless there comes a need for it. I just want you to go find out who's running off my stock. I'll handle it from there. I'll pay you more than you could make in two years if you was to try to earn it cowboying."

Dundee thought about Titus' hotel, and the beds in it, and the colored wallpaper. "How much in advance?"

"Say, two hundred dollars. The balance when you get back."

"What if I don't *get* back?"

"Then I save the rest of the money." Titus let a tiny smile flicker, then go out. "I'll be square with you, Dundee. I've sent two men down there already. One of them acted like a broke cowpuncher riding the chuckline. Figured that would give him a chance to see a lot.

They dumped his body in the street here one night, right in front of my *hotel*. The other one went down there acting like a cattle buyer. I never *did* see him again."

Dundee reached for the bottle, then changed his mind. He could already feel a glow starting. If he was going to dicker on a deal, he didn't want any cobwebs on his brain. "Saying I was to decide to go down there, I don't intend to do it acting like somebody I ain't. Been times in my life I ain't told all there was to the story, but there's never been a time I ever out-and-out lied about anything. I won't make any big point of it, but if anybody asks me, my name is Dundee and I'm working for you. No lies, no play-acting."

Titus shrugged. "How you do it is up to you. I just want to be damn sure it gets done."

Son Titus stepped through the door. He had washed the blood from his face and dusted his clothes a little. But around one eye a blue spot the size of a half dollar was beginning to show up. And one cheek was skinned down to the color of calf meat. Dundee nodded in satisfaction. It had always pleasured him to see a job well done.

Son Titus said suspiciously, "Pa, what you talking to this drifter about?"

Titus stirred in annoyance. "Nothing that's any concern of yours. Go find yourself something to do, and this time leave that knife in your pocket."

"There ain't nothing to do, Pa, and you know it. You don't allow no high-stepping women in Titusville, or no high-limit poker games. Anyhow, I wouldn't ask you if I didn't want to know. What you getting mixed up with this stranger for?"

"Hiring him for a little job of work, is all. Go play marbles, or something."

Dundee judged Son Titus to be about twenty-one or two, somewhat beyond the age for marbles.

Son said, "I heard a little of it from the porch. You're sending him to Runaway, ain't you? You think maybe he's going to catch them cowthieves." The young man answered his own question with a show of contempt. "He won't. He'll take whatever you give him, then go down there and join up with them. That is, if that's not where he come from in the first place. I can tell by the look of him. I bet you a million dollars he's a cowthief himself."

Dundee slowly got to his feet. He clenched a first, wincing as pain lanced through a battered knuckle. "Boy, if you keep working at it, you're finally going to make me take a disliking to you."

John Titus said, "Son Titus, you get along out of here. You haven't *got* a million dollars, and you never will. You haven't got much sense sometimes, either."

"I got sense enough to take care of that Runaway job for you, if you'd let me. You don't have to go hiring some drifter."

The father's voice was sharp. "Son Titus, if you don't want to spend all this summer roundup jingling horses and holding the cut, you better do what I tell you."

Son Titus turned and walked out talking to himself. He paused on the porch, looking back, his eyes hot with resentment.

John Titus said, and not without pride, "He's contrary. I reckon that's why I like him."

Only a father could, Dundee thought. *And maybe a*

mother. He settled back into his chair. "If I was to take this job, you got any ideas where I ought to start at?"

"I'll give you the names of some people I think are honest. And I'll tell you about a few of the other kind. Main name to begin with, I think, is old Blue Roan."

"What kind of a name is *that*?"

"It's the name of a cowthief, the daddy of them all. Smart as a mustang, mean as a one-eyed polecat. Whatever you find down there, I expect old Roan Hardesty is at the center of it.

"Sounds like you know him."

"I do. Long time ago, down in deep South Texas, him and me used to steal cattle together." Titus paused, seeing surprise in Dundee's eyes. "Hell yes, I used to steal cattle. How else do you think I got my start? We all did, them days. But I reformed. Blue Roan never did."

Titus sat in silence, waiting. "Well, how about it, Dundee? You want to take the job?"

Dundee bit off the end of a cigar and then lighted a match. He drew, getting the tobacco worked up to a glow.

"The beds in that *hotel* of yours . . . they good and soft?"

2

In the 1880s, much of the Texas hill country which shed its waters into the Llano River, and down into the Frio and the Nueces, was known far and wide as thieves' territory, for it was a big land of high, rough hills, of rocky ranges, of deep valleys and heavy, protective timber—liveoak, Spanish oak, cedar and mesquite—of hundreds of clear-water springs and dozens of creeks and streams—of the Llanos themselves, the North, the South and the main Llano. Here great herds of cattle could be swallowed up and lost. Bold men could make fortunes in the light of the moon by the ambitious use of long ropes and fast horses, fanning out in all directions to take other men's cattle, other men's horses, bringing them here to this favored land of strong grass and abundant water, far from law, far from the harsh hand of retribution.

Riding the bay, leading a packhorse lent him by John Titus, Dundee took his time heading south and west into the Llano River country. Carrying a generous amount of Titus grub in his pack, and *most* of two hundred dollars in his pocket—that hotel had overcharged him—he saw no reason to be in a hurry. He doubted the cowthieves would leave before he got there.

He took a long, leisurely look at the Titus cattle he came across. He decided they weren't different from most other people's. Some places, cowmen had brought in improved bulls such as the imported Shorthorn to start a gradual upgrading. Titus still held onto the pure Longhorn, the native Texas "mustang" breed. The only visible step toward improvement was that he had steered all the male produce except the ones he had selected as best—and the ones he couldn't catch. The latter bequeathed a certain hardihood to their progeny, whatever shortcomings they might have had as beef. Some of the Titus bulls showed strong Mexican blood, and even beyond that, the fighting strains that went back to ancient Spain. Most range cattle fought horsemen only when provoked. Twice Dundee found bulls coming to meet him halfway, pawing their challenge.

He guessed Titus liked his cattle contrary too.

One thing he noted was the form of the Titus T Bar brand, made with three stamps of a straight bar iron, the bar under the T. Every time Dundee sat awhile on the ground, whether to eat, rest the horses or just ease his tired rump, he would take a stick and draw the T Bar in the dirt. Then he would start improvising various ways it could be burned over with a running iron and converted into something else. He was amazed at the many variations. He could join the T to the bar and then cross a line through it and make a Double E. He could run the upright through the top of the T and make a Cross Bar. He could make a Double Cross, a TE, a TF Bar, a Big I, a Rocking R, a JE. There was little limit other than a man's ingenuity, and Dundee had observed that when it came to thievery, many a dull man was transported into genius.

John Titus must surely know his brand was easy to alter. Its lines were too simple. If he would use something complicated, after the Mexican style, he would present the hideburners a challenge. But this was probably a measure of the man's stubbornness. The brand was *his*. He would hang onto it come hell or high losses.

As he drew the various brands that he could conceive from the T Bar, Dundee catalogued them in his mind. As far as he was concerned, any cattle he came across with such a brand belonged to Titus.

The country became rougher and brushier, the farther he went south. He never was sure when he passed beyond the boundaries of the Titus ranch. Actually, he knew Titus didn't own more than a fraction of the land he used. What he had done—what a great many early Texas cowmen had done when the land showed signs of settling up—was to buy or lease all the land he could get that had natural water on it. The man who controlled the water thus controlled all the land within a cow's practical walking distance of it, for the land was valueless without water. A dry ranch up in the hills wasn't worth the shirt on a man's back. Dundee figured that a map of Titus' deeded land would be little more than a map of springs, creeks and streams. It was legal enough, and ingeniously simple. Dundee didn't begrudge him his holdings. He only regretted that he hadn't gotten here early enough to do the same thing himself.

The breaks of the game, he reasoned. *Them as has, gits.*

He found awesomely-twisted gray-green liveoaks edging the shell-studded limestone hills, and Mexican cedars growing in dense brakes, single cedars dotting the hills all the way to the rimrocks. There was often a tangly type of underbrush in the valleys, rustling with the wind and with the unseen movement of animals and rodents and Lord knew what. Now and again he would catch a glimpse of a big rack of horns an instant before a whitetail buck deer darted off into the protection of the heavy sumac and Spanish oak. Once in a while he stirred up a few wild turkeys, which sprinted away like racehorses, or flew up explosively like the bob-white quail. Once the bay snorted and jumped and almost lost him as a long-nosed, thick-plated armadillo scurried out from underfoot.

Good country for wild animals, Dundee thought. *No wonder it appeals to wild men.*

The first scattered bunch of cattle he found in the roughs were standing around a half-dried waterhole in a rocky draw. He rode up on them quietly and with care. He managed to see the brands before the first old cow jerked her head up high, took one good look at him and went clattering off for the thickets. The rest followed close behind her, their tails up, their dignity injured.

Most of them carried what he took to be a Rocker M, or maybe it was meant for a Hat. Either way, it wasn't a conversion from the T Bar. However, Dundee saw one which looked suspicious. Best he could tell in the second or two he'd had a view, it was a box with a straight line down through it. That one could very easily have been made over from the Titus brand. He took a small tally book from his pocket and sketched the brand as he had seen it. He recorded the Rocker M, too, just for reference. As he went along, tallying every brand, he would begin to find out who claimed each one. There would come a time, someday, for a reckoning.

He spent long days quietly riding out the creeks and streams as he came across them, noting brands, jotting each new one in the book, sketching a rough map. During that time he found at least half a dozen brands which could have been—and most probably were—the illegitimate offspring of the T Bar.

Somewhere he had read about the big fish living off of the little ones. Here it looked more like the little ones living off of the big.

Dundee studiously avoided people. Now and again

he would see a picket cabin or a small rock house·or even a tent pitched somewhere close to water, with perhaps a few brush corrals and a rude barn or two. These he observed at length and committed to map and memory, but he didn't go down for a talk.

He found few cattle carrying the Titus brand. That, he thought, was a little odd. Even with Titus riders patrolling the outer edges of what Titus considered to be his rightful range, it seemed probable that on an outfit so large, some cattle would naturally stray out of bounds. It was to be expected. Seemed like the bigger the ranch, the farther the cattle wandered.

Dundee figured they wandered, all right, and probably a good many were encouraged more than somewhat. Any strays which showed up this far from home likely didn't carry the T Bar very long. It would be converted into something else in no more time than it took somebody to get a fire going and an iron hot.

One morning, moving the bay and the packhorse down a ridge, he heard cattle bawling. He paused to listen. From the sound of it he knew they were being driven. A cow bawling for a strayed calf sounds one way. Bawling of a cow forcibly separated from a calf under stress sounds another. And the bawling of many cows at one time means a herd being moved. Dundee eased into the protection of a cedar motte and waited patiently, smoking himself a leisurely cigarette.

In due time the cattle came into sight. At a distance he estimated seventy or eighty head. As they gradually came nearer, he counted about fifty cows and twenty-five or thirty calves. Dundee reached into his saddlebag and brought out a small spyglass Titus had lent him. It was too far yet to read the brands and earmarks, so he studied the four riders. Best he could tell, the one in charge was a tall, heavy man in a Mexican sombrero. At least he seemed to be giving orders, what few were being given. These men knew their business without needing much instruction. It occurred to Dundee they were moving the cattle too fast, though. No bigger than this bunch was, if they would let the cows set their own pace, the calves would keep up with their mammies and there wouldn't be all this bawling. A real cowman wouldn't push his own cattle this way except for a short distance. These had been walking a long time. They had a trail-drawn look about them.

The riders were putting the cattle across a nice grassy flat, one of the best Dundee had seen this side of the T Bar. Most of the cattle he had found in this region carried the Rocker M, or the Hat, or whatever it was. A little before sundown yesterday Dundee had scouted what appeared to be the headquarters, on up about three or four miles beside a nice spring. He had sat on the brow of a hill and looked down with the spyglass for an hour or more, studying the layout. A double cabin there, built of logs, was better constructed than most he had seen. Whoever these people were, they had built with every intention of staying. He had seen a picket saddleshed and a set of corrals, part of them built of brush and some of stone, laboriously stacked.

A couple of times he had seen a woman. At the distance he couldn't tell much about her. She was small, and by the ease of her movements he guessed she was young. He hadn't seen any children. About sundown two horsemen had come in from somewhere above, had unsaddled their horses and put the saddles in the shed. One man was a bit heavy and moved with the stiffness of age. The other had the movements of a young man, and the energy. While the older of the two limped slowly to the cabin and flopped beneath a brush arbor to rest, the younger strode to a pile of rocks beside the corral and carried several to the fence he was building, setting them in place. He didn't stop until the woman came out and waved him to supper. About that time Dundee had decided he was hungry too, so he had pulled back a safe distance and made camp.

He had thought about that stone fence some as he sat around his own campfire, chewing venison and sipping boiled coffee. Stone fences and laziness didn't go together.

He noted that none of the riders pushing these cattle sat their horses like the two he had observed yesterday. Eventually the small herd came close enough that with the spyglass he could read the brands. Most of the calves were still slick-eared, but the cows weren't. They belonged to Titus.

Sitting there, Dundee tried again to study out a way the T Bar could be altered into the Rocker M. It couldn't be done.

This don't add up, he thought. *I reckon I'll just follow along.*

As he was fixing to ride out from the motte, he hauled up short. Three riders were coming from the south. Another minute and he would have been in their view. They came upon the trail of the cattle, paused a moment and followed the tracks. Dundee scratched his head, wondering. He decided to stay on the higher ground and see without being seen. Some games, it was better to watch than to play in.

Presently the three riders overtook the cattle. They howdied and shook with the drovers and sat their horses in a circle, taking time to smoke and parley. One man rode off. Before long he came back, pointing.

Across the big flat, from the southwest, a rider pushed along in an easy trot. Dundee dismounted with the spyglass. He could recognize people sometimes by the way they sat their horses. He knew this was the man he had observed yesterday working on the corral.

Three men peeled away from the herd and rode to intercept the rider. Dundee could see angry gestures. At length the heavy man in the Mexican sombrero turned back and spoke to the two who sat a little behind him. The heavy man held a pistol. The two men dismounted slowly, deliberately, and walked to the fence-builder's horse. One reached up and grabbed. The horseman slid out of the saddle, and they sprawled together in the dust. The two set in to beat him with their fists.

The other man abandoned the cattle and spurred up to watch the fight. They formed a semi-circle around the sombreroed horseman who had done their initial arguing and had given the orders. The breeze brought Dundee their shouts of encouragement.

Though it was two against one, the lone man put up a good fight of it, for a while. Toting those rocks had put a good set of muscles on him, Dundee reasoned. One of the two who was beating him finally stretched out on the ground and didn't get up. The heavy man ordered fresh blood into the fray.

The unequal contest raised a resentful anger in

Dundee, and he considered going down there. But the odds were too long. There were too many guns. He reasoned that if they had intended to kill the man, they would have done it at the start.

Anyway, it wasn't any of his put-in.

The fencebuilder didn't have the chance of a one-legged pullet in a coyote den, but he resisted with all he had. Wearying, he swayed, staggered, swung without strength. Someone's fist hit him every time he opened up. He went down, pushed to his feet, went down again, came up as far as his knees, got struck in the jaw and went down to stay. The man in the sombrero dismounted and delivered him a couple of hard kicks in the ribs. Gritting his teeth, Dundee held the spyglass on that man long enough to decide he wasn't a Mexican, despite the hat.

You got something coming to you, hoss, Dundee thought. *I hope I'm there when it's delivered.*

The leader pointed back to the slowly-scattering herd. The horsemen grudgingly turned away from the downed fighter and trailed in a ragged line to the cattle. After a bit they drove the cows and calves by the beaten man, and on beyond him.

Even in the shade, the close heat was oppressive here in the cedars, where the thin breeze could not move through the dense foliage. Dundee wondered about that man down yonder, sprawled on the ground in the open sun. *Least they could do was drag him to the shade.* His impulse was to go on down and help, but he made himself wait until the cattle passed over a rise and out of view.

The lone man heard him coming. He raised up onto

hands and knees, defiance in his eyes. He reached back to his hip, but they had thrown his pistol away into the grass.

Dundee raised his hand in the peace sign. "I don't mean you no harm." The young man tried to push to his feet. Dundee said: "Wait and I'll help you. Go slow. If they've busted anything, you don't want to lose the pieces."

The man swayed. His face was bloody and torn, his beribboned shirt crusted with dust and sweat. His hands were laced and bleeding.

Dundee said, "They done a right smart of a job on you."

The man licked his bleeding lip. "Where'd my horse go?"

"He run off. That's the way with horses." Dundee hunted around till he found the pistol and returned it. "You gave them a good fight."

A suspicious gaze bore into Dundee. "Who are you?"

"You wouldn't know me. Name's Dundee."

"You saw the fight?"

"Had me a spyglass."

"And you didn't do a thing to help me?"

Dundee shrugged. "I spent a lot of money across a poker table before I learned there's no use going against a stacked deck. Figured your health was lost anyway and I'd keep mine so I could come down here and put the pieces back together." He jerked his thumb toward the bay. "Think you can get on my horse? I'll take you to the creek. You'll feel better once you wash the dirt and blood off."

Dundee had to help him into the saddle, then swung

up behind the cantle and sat on the bay's hips. "I'd as soon not have to keep calling you *'You.'* You got a name?"

"McCown. Warren McCown."

McCown. That would fit with the Rocker M brand.

Dundee squatted patiently on his heels and flipped rocks into the creek while McCown stripped off his clothes and waded into the water. He noted that McCown's face, neck, and hands were brown, but the rest of his body was white. Most early cowboys buttoned their collars and their sleeves. They believed it was cooler if you kept the sun out, the skin covered.

McCown soaked till the dirt and blood were washed away.

Lord help the fish, Dundee thought.

Now that he could see the cowboy's face plainer, he judged him to be in his late twenties. Presently McCown came out and sat on the gravelly bank to let the wind dry him. "Feel better?" Dundee asked.

McCown only nodded.

"Some of them marks didn't wash off. You'll carry them a spell." McCown still only nodded. Dundee said, "You sore about me not coming down and throwing in with you?"

McCown shrugged. "You didn't know me."

"I still don't."

McCown glanced at him sharply. "And *I* don't know *you.* I do know that packhorse is carrying a T Bar brand on him. You steal him?"

Dundee's eyes narrowed. "Make any difference to you if I did?"

"I got worries enough of my own. Old Titus can watch out for himself."

Dundee reflected a moment. "Who *were* them jolly lads you was entertaining back there?"

McCown stared him straight in the eye. "While ago you didn't want to get involved. You'd better just stay clear of it all around. What you don't know won't cause you no trouble."

McCown put on his hat first, then his long underwear, then his boots, his remnant of a shirt, and his trousers. "Mind letting me ride double with you to my cabin? Ain't far."

"I know where it is."

When McCown showed surprise, Dundee said: "I know more than you think I do. I know you got a log cabin and brush pens and you're building yourself a set of rock corrals. I know you got an old man living with you, and a wife."

McCown's eyes narrowed, but he held his tongue.

Dundee said: "What's more, I know you brand a Rocker M, and that there ain't no way to make a Rocker M out of a T Bar. I already tried."

"Who the hell *are* you?"

"Told you, my name's Dundee."

"A man can change names like he changes shirts. A name don't mean nothing."

"I'm working for John Titus. I come to see what's been doing with his cattle."

"And you been watching me, figuring me for a thief."

"Not necessarily. I thought you *might* be."

"Now you figure I'm not?"

"Not necessarily. Mount up. I'll ride behind again."

"I think I'd as soon walk as ride with a man who thinks I'm a thief."

"I ain't said you are, and I ain't said you're not. I got a wide open mind. Now, if you want to ride home, you better get up on that horse."

They moved up the creek in an easy trot, McCown silently nursing his resentment, Dundee making no apology and, indeed, not even considering the possibility that he should. To him, apology was a sign either of weakness or of being wrong, and he seldom conceded either.

A mile or so from headquarters, he saw a rider approaching, leading a horse. "Hope this is a friend of yours, McCown."

McCown squinted. "It's Uncle Ollie. He's bringing my horse."

An elderly man slouched gracelessly in the saddle, taking his time. His face furrowed in concern, though worry didn't seem to enhance his speed. "Horse come in without you, Warren. Millie like to've had a fit." He cocked his head over. "Look at you! I been telling you this horse'd throw you off."

"It wasn't the horse, Uncle Ollie. It was. . . ." He turned half around to look at Dundee. "I run into some boys back yonder."

"Was old Blue Roan with them?"

Dundee listened intently, remembering what Titus had said about Roan. McCown frowned. "I didn't say it was Roan's bunch."

"They marked you, boy, they surely did. They'll kill you, you don't watch out." The old man turned his squinting attention to Dundee, his eyes light gray, set against a sun-darkened skin wrinkled and dried like neglected leather. "And who might you be?"

McCown answered for Dundee. "You can call him the silent observer."

Dundee said, "The name's Dundee."

The old man reached out, his grip casual. "Mine's Ollie McCown."

To dismount without Dundee's having to get down first, McCown threw his right leg over the bay's neck and jumped to the ground. Weaker than he thought, he went to his hands and knees. He straightened. "I do thank you, Dundee, for what help you *have* been. Maybe I'll get to do the same for you sometime . . . if I'm real lucky." There was a touch of malice in it. McCown took the reins from his uncle's hands and swung up onto his own horse. Then a thought struck him. "How come you home when my horse came in, Uncle Ollie? You were supposed to be out rocking up that spring on the south branch."

The old man shrugged like a kid caught at mischief. "I got tired. Anyway, I thought it'd be nice to go down to the creek and catch a nice mess of fish for Millie to fix for supper."

McCown grumbled: "You and that fishing pole! I'd burn it, but you'd just fix another."

Glad I don't work for him, Dundee thought. *All he lacks is a whip.*

Dundee noticed Uncle Ollie looking with concern at the brand on the packhorse. Warren McCown saw, too. "Dundee works for John Titus. He's down here to find out where the Titus cattle are going."

The old man said, "Reckon people might think we're taking sides with him, Warren?"

"Let them."

"They done beat you up. Next time they might kill you!"

"This is my place, and I'll do as I please on it." Mc-Cown turned to Dundee. "Since you're this close, you might as well come and have supper. I owe you that much for the ride."

"Much obliged." Dundee decided if he kept his mouth shut and his ears open, he might learn something. And even if he didn't learn anything, he'd get something in his belly besides old bacon and gamy venison and poor coffee and promises. If a man couldn't get rich—and Dundee doubted he ever would—the next best thing was to get fat.

There was nothing elaborate about the McCown place, for this was not a country given to fancy things. Poor for pretty but hell for stout. They passed the incomplete stone corrals, and the piles of wagon-hauled rocks which one day would find their place in the fences. The stones had been selected for size and shape up in the hills, more than likely, through long, hot days of back-breaking toil.

McCown pointed to a finished rock corral in which stood the saddleshed. "You can put your horses in there and feed them. You'll likely want to be a-riding again come morning."

Dundee carried his saddle into the shed and set it across a rack that was simply a smoothed-off log placed atop a pair of posts. He noted that the shed's walls were upright cedar pickets, axe-hewn for a close fit and set well into the ground to hold them solid. The roof was tightly built of liveoak timbers, cedar and sod.

Another contrary man, Dundee thought. He'd have to be to drive himself to this kind of work.

Somehow Dundee thought McCown might have oats
for his horses, but instead the rancher dug into a barrel
and came up with dried mesquite beans. Well, what they
lacked in feed value, they made up in convenience. And
they didn't cost anything.

McCown paused at the gate and looked toward the unfinished rock fence. "I reckon I'll come back out here
after supper and work till dark. Don't lack too much finishing me another pen."

Uncle Ollie said: "After that beating you got? You better go to bed, Warren McCown."

A woman stood in the open dog-run that separated the
two sections of the cabin. Moving in that direction, walking to the right of the hobbling Uncle Ollie, Dundee
found himself studying her. She was slender; he could
tell that at a distance. Nearer, he could see she was
younger than he had thought, watching at a distance
through the spyglass. Now he could see her long brown
hair, strands of it lifting in the wind, strands that when
down to full length must reach nearly to her waist. She
had a thinnish oval face, not yet sun-hardened but still
clean and soft. It was a natural face, one that probably
had never known powder or rouge or any form of lip-
reddening like the town women sometimes used.

The young woman—she might have been twenty or
so—gasped at sight of McCown's face. "Warren . . ."

McCown gestured that it didn't amount to anything.
"You about got supper ready? I want to do a little more
work before it gets too late."

Uncle Ollie shrugged in futility.

The woman turned to stare at Dundee in curiosity
and, perhaps, a touch of fear. Dundee ran his hand over

his face and realized his whiskers hadn't felt a razor since he had left Titusville. Moreover, he was dusty and streaked with grime and woodsmoke. To her, he must look like some robber chieftain, some brigand out of employ.

Dundee ventured, "I know I appear fearsome, ma'am, but I got a good heart."

Warren McCown added drily: "And a good appetite too, I expect. We just as well feed him some of Uncle Ollie's fish."

The woman glanced at Uncle Ollie and began to smile. The old man said to Dundee, "We had it made up that if Warren raised cain about me fishing instead of working on that spring, we'd say it was Millie caught them."

Looked like nobody was going to introduce him, so he would have to do it for himself. "Mrs. McCown, my name is Dundee."

She smiled shyly. Dundee suspected the beard still worried her. "I'm Millie McCown. And it's not Mrs.; it's *Miss*."

Warren McCown said in a small triumph: "You see, you didn't know everything after all, Dundee. She's my sister, not my wife."

Dundee let it pass. A man was entitled to a small mistake now and again. For no reason he would have admitted to himself, he was somehow pleased to find she was unmarried.

The kitchen was the biggest room in the double cabin. On one wall stood a black Charter Oak stove. At a time when most people in Western Texas still cooked in an open fireplace, this was an uncommon luxury worth a dozen head of cattle or several fair-to-middling horses.

A woodbox beside it was heaped full with mesquite and oak wood, chopped to length. The fish was sizzling in a deep iron skillet. Millie McCown had set three chipped plates on a plain wooden table. Now, allowing for Dundee, she set a fourth. Waiting, Dundee looked around at the plain lumber shelves, the homemade rawhide-and-cedar chairs, the two cots that would be Warren's and Uncle Ollie's. The place was built for utility. The stove was the only thing in it that would sell for three pieces of Mexican silver.

On a shelf Dundee saw an old tintype propped against a big family Bible. It pictured two soldiers in what appeared to be Confederate uniforms. One, he realized, was Uncle Ollie. This had been a good many years ago.

Ollie McCown said: "That's me on the left. I was still full of vinegar, them days. I ain't changed much in looks, just the vinegar has about run out." Dundee glanced at the old man. If Ollie didn't think he'd changed, he hadn't stood close to a mirror lately. The old man said: "That other feller, that's my brother George, the daddy of Millie and Warren. He's gone now. We buried him a long ways back."

"I'm sorry," Dundee said, and he meant it.

Dundee approached the fish with some uncertainty. He'd been seeing them in the clear-water streams and wished he could catch some, but he'd never lived in a part of the country where there were creeks to fish in. He didn't know how to start. Even if he had caught any, he wouldn't have known whether to skin them like a beef or eat them with the hide on.

Dundee found himself looking at the girl through supper, cutting his eyes away when she glanced in his di-

rection. He knew she was aware of his staring, for once
her face reddened a little. She'd been sheltered, this girl.

After supper, Warren McCown did just what he said
he would do; he went out and stacked rock for the fence,
despite the soreness, despite his bruises. Dundee thought
he owed it to him to help, but McCown shook his head
when Dundee picked up the first stone. "Wrong shape,
wrong size for the tie I'm making here. I can do it better
by myself."

Dundee dropped the rock and left McCown to handle the job all by his lonesome. He walked down to the
saddle-shed, rubbing his beard and looking back at
the cabin. He fished around in the pack for his razor and
soap. He shaved in the cold water of the creek, wincing
as the razor scraped. Done with it, he asked himself why
he had gone to the trouble. He had no intentions to jus-
tify it. When a man courted a country girl like this Millie McCown, he had to have one thing in mind: marriage.
Anything less would draw immediate rebuff from the
girl and very possibly a bellyful of buckshot from an
outraged father or brother.

Dundee knew marriage was not for him. His itchy feet
hadn't been to the far side of all the hills yet. Tempo-
rary female companionship could be had in most any
town, if the urge got so strong a man had to give in to it.
It could be bought and paid for, then he could turn his
back and ride away from her with no regrets, no sense
of shirked responsibilities.

He had no thought of despoiling this country girl, even
if there were no penalty for it. This was a man's country, good women as scarce as gold and as highly valued,
to be treasured and protected from all that was thought

dirty and raw and unpleasant. He subscribed to an old cowboy code that put a woman on a pedestal. She didn't leave it unless she deliberately stepped down. Unless a man had marriage in mind, he tipped his hat, as the knights of old tipped their visors, and held himself afar.

Uncle Ollie had stayed long at the table. Now he was stretched on the ground beneath the arbor, belching. The sun had gone down, and there was no longer any need for shade, but habit is a slavemaster. Dundee joined him, sitting on the ground, crossing his legs. Ollie's eyes narrowed as he studied Dundee's shaven face. "Don't expect you'd win no prize, but you look a *little* better. You still got a dab of soap under your left ear."

Dundee wiped it off onto his sleeve. He pointed his chin toward the distant figure of Warren McCown, working in the dusk. "Is he thataway all the time?"

Ollie nodded. "He expects a lot out of a man, but he drives hisself the most of all."

"What's his hurry? Nobody gets out of this world alive."

"Maybe it was seeing his old daddy die without a dollar in his pocket, hardly. This here place is Warren's . . . his and Millie's, anyway. He's worked for it and fought for it. It's like a fever in him. I ain't sure sometimes whether Warren owns the land or the land owns him."

Millie McCown walked out into the dog-run, drying her hands on a cloth. Dundee pushed to his feet and took off his hat, bowing slightly, awkwardly. She smiled, and he sensed she was pleased he had taken time to shave. He noticed she had brushed her long hair. He wanted to pay her a compliment, but he didn't know what to say.

She said: "You don't have to get up for me. Please, be comfortable."

Dundee fetched her a rawhide chair from against the house. Then he stepped back beside Uncle Ollie and once more seated himself upon the ground. Dundee watched the girl until he knew she was nervously aware of his eyes. He looked away.

She said, "It's a nice, cool evening after such a warm day."

Dundee thought a man could hardly argue with a statement like that. "Yes, ma'am."

"Maybe it'll be the same again tomorrow."

"I expect."

"It was like this yesterday."

"Yes, ma'am."

A long silence followed. But Dundee could see Millie McCown's lips working a little. She was biting them, working up nerve to ask him: "Mister Dundee, I couldn't get Warren to tell me what happened to him, how he got so skinned up and bruised. Will *you* tell me?"

Dundee hesitated. If McCown wanted her to know, he would have told her.

"Please, Mister Dundee?"

The pleading tone of her voice melted him like butter. McCown *ought* to have told her. "I don't know who the men was, ma'am. They was driving a herd of cattle that sure as he . . . heck didn't belong to them. Your brother rode up, and a fight started."

"Maybe they were our cattle."

"No, ma'am, they was carrying the T Bar, old John Titus' brand." Maybe no one had told her. "I work for John Titus."

She nodded. "Oh. And you were trailing the cattle to see where they were being taken."

"That's about it, ma'am."

"And you helped my brother."

He squirmed. "I ain't fixing to lie to you; I didn't get in the fight. But later I went down and done what I could."

"If I know Warren, he didn't even think to thank you. So *I* thank you, Mister Dundee."

"No trouble, ma'am. I'd of done as much for a broken-legged dog." He rubbed his neck. *That* hadn't come out the way he meant it.

She seemed not to notice. "It was old Blue Roan, or some of his men; I'd bet on that. Warren's had trouble with them. They keep bringing cattle across our land, cattle that don't belong to them."

Uncle Ollie stirred nervously. "Millie . . ."

She went on: "We're minding our own business, or trying to. If Roan Hardesty steals cattle, that's between him and the law, or between him and the people he takes the cattle away from. But he's got no right to drive them across our land and draw us into it. One of these days there'll come a reckoning. We don't want to be caught up in it."

Uncle Ollie's eyes were narrowed. "Millie, you better hush up and not be making loose talk. That'll get us in trouble too."

"I'm just saying what's true."

"You're saying it to a man who represents John Titus.

Ain't no use having Roan and his crowd come over here some fine day and shut all of us up for good. They could do it, you know."

She said with confidence, "Warren can take care of us."

The old man grunted. "He ain't but one man. I'm only half a man, and you're no man atall. If it comes a show-down, we won't last long."

Guardedly Dundee suggested: "You wouldn't have to be alone. I think John Titus would help anybody who helps *him*."

She asked, "What kind of help could we give him?"

Dundee brought out his tallybook. "I been jotting down brands. I'd be much obliged if you'd tell me who claims them."

Uncle Ollie said tightly: "Dundee, I was in the big war. I didn't own no slaves; it wasn't none of my business. But I got in it anyway. All I got for it was a hole in my leg and some sense in my head. I learned one thing; take care of your own self and stay out of a fight any way you can. Us McCowns, we're not messing into John Titus' trouble. We don't owe John Titus nothing."

"If I tell him you helped me, he might figure he owes *you* something."

"So might Blue Roan." The old man gritted, "Dundee, you go riding down into old Roan's backyard and you may not ever *see* John Titus again."

Dundee had seen ranches where it didn't take long to spend the night, but this place was extreme. McCown was up and stirring two hours before good daylight. Dundee had spread his blankets outdoors, beneath the arbor. Through the open window he could hear McCown poking a fire into life in the big cookstove and fussing at Uncle Ollie to rouse his lazy bones and get his clothes on so Millie could come in from her side of the cabin and start breakfast. Dundee dressed in the dark, hiding himself beneath the blanket until he had his pants on.

McCown put in an hour of work on the fence before breakfast. Dundee felt he ought to do something to pay for the hospitality, so he jerked an axe loose from the chopping block and cut stovewood until Millie McCown called the men in.

They ate hurriedly, McCown impatient to get on with work. Nobody talked much. Dundee stole glances at the girl by lamplight.

The sun came up. McCown blew out the lamp to save coal oil. "Well, Dundee, Uncle Ollie and I have got work to do, and I expect you're anxious to be on your way."

As a matter of fact, Dundee wasn't, for he kind of liked sitting here looking at the girl. But he knew an invitation to leave when he heard one. "I reckon. I got a right smart of ground to cover."

He was behind the saddleshed, lashing down the pack when he heard horses. He glanced cautiously around the cedar-stake wall. Five riders were nearing the cabin. A heavy-set old man with a hunch to his shoulders raised a big hand, and the riders stopped. The old man rode on a couple more yards. His voice was deep and loud and carried well in the cool morning air.

"McCown, I came to parley with you."

Warren McCown stepped out onto the small porch, followed by a cringing Uncle Ollie. Both had six-shooters strapped around their waists. Millie McCown's frightened face appeared in the doorway. Seeing her, the old man took off his floppy old hat. His gray hair sparkled like frost in the early sun. His voice seemed almost pleasant for a moment. "Morning, Miss McCown. I swear, you do get prettier every time I see you."

If she made any reply, Dundee couldn't hear it. As yet unseen, he decided to stay put awhile.

The big old man said: "Little lady, what I got to say to your brother ain't of no concern to you, and if they was any cusswords to be accidentally dropped, I wouldn't want them falling on your ears. Ain't you got some chickens to feed or a cow to milk or something?"

Millie didn't move. The old man said: "I promise you, ma'am, there's not a man here would harm a hair on your head. I'd shoot ary one that tried. Now, why don't you go on off and take care of the chores or something, so me and your brother can have us a talk?"

Warren McCown said, "Go on, Millie."

Millie McCown glanced fearfully at the men, then walked briskly toward the saddleshed. Dundee stepped out of sight, knowing the men's gaze would follow her.

When she came around the shed, Dundee put his finger to his lips. He said quietly, "I reckon that's be Blue Roan?"

She grabbed Dundee's arm. "If there's trouble, will you help my brother?" Her fingers were tight. "I'll take another look at that tallybook. I'll give you the names of all the people I know."

Right then he'd have charged hell with a bucket of water if she'd asked him to. And not for any tallybook.

He stepped to his bay and gingerly slipped the carbine up out of the scabbard. He peered around the wall. The riders had their backs turned partially to him and all their attention riveted on the McCowns. He could hear Roan Hardesty's bull voice.

"McCown, I understand you and some of my boys butted heads yesterday."

McCown only stared in defiance. Hardesty said: "Now boy, I thought you and me had come to an understanding. I told you how things was going to be. Now, they're going to *be* thataway, whether it suits your pleasure or not."

McCown gritted, "This is my land."

"You got some papers that was signed in Austin, but you're a long ways from Austin now. I was here before you ever come. I expect to stay here a long time yet. Whether you stay or not depends on you." He paused. "McCown, you got guts; I'll give you credit for that. Now, I'm not a mean sort of a man. I don't like to have to go and get hard with anybody. And killing just ain't my idea of the right way atall. But, boy, there's an end to my patience."

"You got no right to dictate what goes on in this whole section of the country. You're just one man," McCown said.

"But I got a lot of men with me. *You're* just one man, McCown. Your uncle here makes two. You don't have to have no schooling to figure out that two is an awful little number."

Dundee thought, *And two and one makes three.* He stepped out from behind the shed, the saddlegun cradled across his left arm, one finger in the trigger guard. He walked slowly toward the horsemen, until one of them heard the jingle of his spurs and turned, stiffening. The others saw him. Big old Roan Hardesty twisted slowly in the saddle, surprised, squinting for recognition that wouldn't come.

Dundee stopped, the rifle not pointed at anybody in particular but in a position that it could, quickly.

Hardesty stared. "Boy, I reckon you know how to shoot that thing?"

Dundee nodded.

Hardesty sighed in resignation. "I got a feeling you do. You some kin of McCown's?"

"Never seen him till yesterday."

"Then how come you're siding him?"

"I owe him for breakfast."

The old man's round face softened a little, for he seemed to find some odd kind of humor here. "It must've been a better breakfast than the one *I* got. Don't it occur to you that you may be paying too high a price? You could be making an awful big mistake."

"I've made a few in my time. One more won't hurt me."

"Don't bet on it." The old man pointed his heavy jaw toward the men who flanked him. "You can count, can't you? And there's plenty more where these come from. There ain't but three of you."

Dundee said evenly: "If trouble starts, I shoot you first. It wouldn't help you none if you had a *hundred* men."

The old man shrugged. "Logic like that, there ain't no use arguing with. I never did think I'd want to die in the cool of the morning; it's too pleasant a time to leave. Boys, let's be moving on. I think McCown has got a pretty good notion what I was meaning to tell him."

The men reined about, but they did it so as to keep Dundee in view. It seemed they knew Dundee was the man to contend with, rather than McCown. Roan Hardesty edged his dappled gray horse up closer to Dundee and halted. Only then did Dundee get a good look at the aging but strong face, the full power of stern gray eyes that fastened on a man like a pair of spikes. And he saw—without being told—why they called him Blue Roan. Across the side of his face, as if flung there by an angry hand, was a scattering of large blotches, like freckles almost, except that they were blue.

"Young fellow," Roan said, "nerve is a nice thing to have, long as you don't abuse it."

"I never was noted for good sense."

"You'd best cultivate it, then, or you may not be noted for long life, either." The old man turned and rode out of the McCown yard.

Warren and Ollie McCown didn't move a toe until Hardesty's men were a good two hundred yards away. Then McCown stepped down from the little porch and slowly walked to Dundee. "You didn't have to come out."

"I owed you."

"They wasn't fixing to do any shooting."

"How do you know?"

"I just know. You could've stayed put, like yesterday. Then *I* wouldn't be left owing *you*."

Dundee frowned, his patience thinning. "Does it bother you, owing somebody?"

"It chews on me like a dog worrying a bone."

"Then forget it. Like I told Hardesty, I just paid for my breakfast."

Dundee turned away sharply and left him standing there. At the saddleshed, Millie McCown waited, her face a shade whiter. She watched as he slipped the saddlegun back into the scabbard.

"Thank you, Mister Dundee."

He turned slowly, facing her. "Thank *you*, ma'am, for saying 'thanks.' You must've learned it from your old daddy. It didn't come from your brother."

"You're a good man, Mister Dundee."

"Some people would argue with that," Dundee said.

"Not with *me* they wouldn't. Now where's that tally-book?"

It turned out she didn't know but a couple of the brands. She didn't get away from this house much. But anything was good for a start. Dundee swung into the saddle, then took off his hat. "Thanks for the good meals, ma'am. They'll be long remembered."

"So will you. Come back again, when you get hungry. I'd be glad to cook some more."

"You can expect me, ma'am." He gave the lead rope a tug to bring along the packhorse. He didn't put his hat back on until he was out of the gate.

He cut across country and found the trail of the T Bar cattle still almost as plain as yesterday. Wind had begun to smooth the tracks, but he figured a blind man could still follow them, riding backwards. He moved along at a steady trot, his gaze sweeping the cedars and the live-oaks, up the valley ahead of him and back down the valley behind him. It wasn't hard to figure why the rustlers chose this route to move cattle. The grass was good and water was plentiful. They didn't have to climb up and down a lot of rocky hills. That would appeal to a lazy man. In Dundee's reckoning, the average rustler was inclined to be basically a lazy man, shunning honest work. He had little sympathy for the breed.

Hard work, he had always figured, was not something to be feared. *Avoided*, if possible, but not feared. And not avoided at the cost of making oneself an outlaw. He had seen some of the running kind through the years, always looking back over their shoulders, always wearing guns loose in their holsters, checking the back door before they trusted the front. That, he had decided long ago, was too high a price to avoid honest work. Most of the long-riders he had ever known had lived in fear, then died broke and hungry and in mortal pain. It was a coyote life . . . and death. Badly as he disliked sweat, sometimes, it was better than blood.

He came to a grassy pecan bottom where the herd evidently had been held a while to settle down and allow the cows and calves to pair. Then the cattle had been split into two bunches. One set had been pushed westward, the other south. Dundee arbitrarily chose the south.

He had to devote closer attention to the trail now, for the ground was rockier. The cattle had been moved into rougher country where limestone hills were more rugged, the postoak and cedar thicker, the grass thinner. Times he could not be sure where the driven cattle's prints stopped and loose range cattle began. He would circle and hunt till he found a horsetrack, and then he knew he was still right.

He was about to concede defeat when he heard the bawling of a calf in pain and fear. He knew the sound. He would bet the calf had been roped, or perhaps it was being branded. Drawing the saddlegun, he walked the horse slowly, watching the ground to avoid loose rocks or fallen timber. He paused every so often to listen. Now and again he heard the bawling of another calf. Each time he could tell he was closer. Afraid to crowd his luck, he finally tied the two horses and moved on afoot, cradling the carbine. He crouched to see under the low timber, and to be able to drop instantly into cover. He picked his footing carefully amid treacherous loose stones and rotted scrub brush. He climbed a hill and tried vainly to see a way down the other side that would keep him under cover. He had to backtrack partway and circle the long way around, staying well below the hill's crest to remain in the brush.

Lying on his belly, he looked down the small valley below him to cattle bunched in one end of a crude brush corral, two men and a horse with them. Every so often one of the men would climb onto the horse, swing a loop and drag a big calf by its heels. The other man would grab the calf's tail and jerk the bawling critter down on its side, then kneel on the neck and hold a foreleg. The horse would hold the rope taut and keep the animal helpless. The rider would step down, walk to a small fire and pick out a long iron. Dundee couldn't tell at the distance, but he would bet a keg of snakehead whisky that this was a running iron, designed to change brands.

He wished for the spyglass he had left in the saddlebag. He wanted to be sure about those brands. Now the only way was to move in closer. Keeping to the brush, he crept downhill toward the corral.

He stopped again, for now he saw a rude log cabin he had overlooked from up on the hill. He studied it a long time, wondering if somebody was in it. He saw no smoke curling out of the chimney. He waited, warily watching for movement. None came.

The man throwing the calves was the big rider who had been in charge of the stolen herd, the one who had seen to it that Warren McCown was beaten to the ground. He still wore that Mexican sombrero.

Dundee didn't intend to show himself. All he wanted was to get close enough to see the brands, and to get a good look at these men's faces. Intent on watching the men, he missed seeing a downed cedar. He went down sliding, sending rocks clattering, the dead cedar limb cracking like the angry strike of buckhorns.

Damn a country where a man busts his ribs on a rock!

The men ran for cover of the heavy brush fence. Almost before Dundee quit sliding, flame lanced from between logs. A bullet ricocheted off of rocks near his face.

Dundee, you've went and spilled the buttermilk again!

He was exposed, and he knew it. What he didn't know was how good a pistol shot old Mexican Hat might be. Dundee swung the saddlegun up, took reckless aim and dropped a bullet at the place he had seen the flash. The moment the woodchips flew, he sprinted for a rock the size of a washtub. A bullet whined by him, striking sparks and scattering small rocks like buckshot. Dundee fired again, taking more time to aim. He heard a howl of pain. From behind the fence he caught a frenzy of movement. At first he thought it was the cattle, stirred into panic by the firing. Then he saw the smaller of the men jump upon the horse and spur hard, shouting. The horse went up over the low brush fence in a long leap, caught his hind feet and almost fell, straightened and went on, the rider spurring him all the way.

Dundee aimed, reconsidered and lowered the muzzle. He had never shot a man in the back, and he didn't want to cultivate any bad habits at this late date. He turned his attention back to the fence.

Well, Mexican Hat, it's your move now. Do something.

He waited, but nothing happened. Impatient, Dundee aimed at the same spot where he had fired before. Once more the chips flew.

He heard a man cry weakly: "Quit your shooting. I already been hit."

"Raise up and drop your arms over this side of the fence where I can see them."

"I'm hit in the leg. I can't get up."

"You can if you want to bad enough. I want to see you before I move."

A hand showed at the top of the fence, then another, then the mashed-in, greasy sombrero, and finally a grimy, stubbled face. The big man painfully dragged himself up onto his legs—or leg, Dundee judged—and hung his arms over the fence where Dundee could see them.

Dundee pushed to his feet, the saddlegun pointed at the man. "Now, you just stand there thataway. Make one move and I'll put a bullet through the third button on that dirty shirt."

"I'm bleeding, I tell you."

"You *could* bleed a lot worse."

Dundee had forgotten the cabin in the excitement. He glanced that way again but saw no one. He cautiously approached the wounded cowthief. The man's face was rapidly draining of color. Just as Dundee reached him, the rustler's good leg gave way, and he slid slowly down on the inside of the fence.

Fearing a trick, Dundee sprinted the last three strides to the fence and shoved the carbine across. The rustler's six-shooter lay on the ground. The man wasn't going to reach for it anyway; he was all but unconscious. Dundee climbed over the fence and set the carbine against a post, where he could reach it in a hurry. He dropped to one knee. He saw a small pool of blood beneath the leg, and a spreading stain on the trousers.

"Looks like I can still shoot a little."

"Damn you," the man muttered, eyes glazing.

"You shot at me first," Dundee pointed out. "Or else your partner did. Great partner he was. Took to the tulies like a boogered rabbit."

"Damn him, too."

Dundee slit the pants leg open. The bottom of it had sealed and was holding blood like a sagging canvas holds rain. Best he could tell, the bullet had gone clean through.

"First thing we got to do is stop this bleeding, or you'll just lie here and drain your life away." He wrapped his neckerchief around the leg, above the wound. He stuck the closed pocketknife inside and used it to twist with. The flow of blood eased to a tiny trickle. "I expect you need a good shot of whisky. You got any in the cabin?" The rustler shook his head. Dundee said: "I got some on my packhorse. I'll go fetch it. Don't you run off noplace."

He saw no guns, other than the rustler's six-shooter. Examining it, he was tempted to keep it. But on reflection he decided some town-raised judge might find him guilty of theft, even though he had taken it off of a cowthief. Courts had a way of doing off-center things like that. He hurled the pistol as far as he could throw it out into the tall grass.

The cattle moved out of a corner as he crowded them a little. He saw one cow lying dead. She had caught a bullet.

It'd be like old John Titus to dock my pay by the price of that cow. What he don't know won't never hurt him.

A horse tied to a tree back of the corral had broken one leather rein in the excitement, but the other rein had held him. Dundee opened the corral gate so the cattle could wander out, then strode to the horse. It rolled its eyes at him, hinting trouble. Warily Dundee swung up and took a tight grip with his knees, expecting the horse to pitch. It humped a little, but that was all. Dundee rode him over the rocky hill, got his own two horses and came back. The rustler still lay in the same spot.

"Nice of you to stay around," Dundee said. He tilted a bottle of Titusville whisky to take a drink himself first, then handed it to the outlaw. "Here, you better have yourself a strong snort. It won't cure anything, but it'll fuzz the edges a little." He loosened the neckerchief and found the blood had almost stopped. "We better clean this wound out or you'll get an infection in it, and somebody'll have a job of digging to do, in these rocks."

He poured whisky into the bullethole.

Dundee had thought the rustler was only half conscious, but the searing of the raw whisky brought him up cursing and fighting. Dundee poured until the bottle was almost empty. Then he held it up and stared ruefully. "See there what you went and made me do? I brought this whisky along to drink, not to pour it down some cowthief. Here, you'd just as well finish what little is left."

Done with the bandage, he leaned on the fence and studied the wounded outlaw. "Your partner may not come back. He left here in an awful hurry."

"Damn him."

"If you just lay here and nobody comes, you'll likely fade away to the Unhappy Hunting Grounds. That leg'll go to gangrene."

"Damn the leg."

"I ought to just leave you, you having a penful of burnt cattle that rightfully belong to another man." Dundee frowned thoughtfully. He had never left a man alone in this kind of shape, not even a cowthief. He knew what he had to do and he regretted it, for he hadn't intended to show himself until he had finished scouting this whole Llano River country. "Seeing as I'm the one that shot you, looks like I'm duty-bound to haul you in to Runaway."

"Damn Runaway!"

In the cabin, Dundee found a lantern and a can of coal oil. He poured the oil on the floor and walls, stepped to the door and flipped a match inside.

The whole shack wasn't worth three dollars Confederate. Burning it was a gesture rather than any real damage to the cowthieves. But a man had to start someplace.

That done, he managed to get the wounded man onto his horse and head in the direction where town ought to be.

4

The pleasant smell of woodsmoke reached him before he came over the hill, and he knew he was nearing Runaway. Dundee stopped the bay horse at the crest and looked down on the rock and log and picket houses clustered west from the sun-bright limestone face of a bluff, just back from the riverbank. He recalled John Titus' words about Runaway being not so much a town as simply a boil on a man's backside. The description was apt.

Down the valley perhaps three quarters of a mile he saw men lined up a-horseback, waving their hats and cheering. In front of them, two riders spurred and whipped their horses in a tight race, coming to the turn-around point, sliding and then spurring back to the finish line. Dundee had lost track of days, but he figured this was Sunday. Horseracing wasn't decent, except on a Sunday. Other days, a man was supposed to work.

The wounded rustler was slumped in the saddle, tied

on so he couldn't slide off if he lapsed into unconsciousness. Dundee considered turning the man's horse loose
here and letting it carry him on down into town where
somebody would find him. But that was chancy. It would
be like a fool horse to stop and graze, or even head home
again, so long as the man in the saddle was unable to
rein him or spur him any.

If I got it to do, I'd just as well get on with it. He led
the horses down off of the hill.

Dundee had seen a few army-camp "Chihuahuas" and
"scabtowns" in his time, the sort of makeshift cutthroat
communities that followed in the wake of the military
like scavenging dogs. This looked like one of those, except there weren't any soldiers. Studying an aimless scatter of ugly buildings—most of them saloons plain and
simple—he remembered what Titus had said about there
possibly being a few good people here.

Damn few, if any, Dundee judged.

The first place he came to was a wagonyard, its fence
built of cedar pickets sunk into the ground and tied
together at the top by strips of green rawhide. Most
wagonyards had a good-sized livery barn, but not this
one. Where men slept beneath the stars much of the
time themselves, nobody thought of putting *horses* under a roof. The barn was nothing more than a big shed.
A be-whiskered man slouched out front on an upended
barrel. A considerable pile of wood shavings lay in front
of him, and he was adding to it right along. He squinted
at the horses and said: "It'll be two bits a head. They'll
run loose in the corral. You can sleep under the shed
for nothing, provided you don't get careless and set fire
to the hay. That comes extra."

"I ain't trying to put the horses up. I got a man here with a bad wound in his leg. Is there a doctor in this town?"

The man got up and lazily walked around to Mexican Hat's horse. "Who is he?"

"Can't rightly say. Maybe his name is Damn. That's about the only word I been able to get out of him."

"Who shot him?"

"I did."

The stableman frowned. "Your aim ain't much good, is it?"

"I asked you if there's a doctor here."

"No doctor. Far as I know, there never was. I reckon most people here are straight-enough shots that when a man gets hit he don't need no doctor; he needs a preacher. But there ain't no preacher, neither."

"There ought to be somebody to look after a wounded man."

"You might carry him down to the Llano River Saloon. There's a woman down there pretty good at patching up after other people's sloppy shooting. Ask for Katy Long." The stableman's eyes narrowed. "Stranger here, ain't you?"

Dundee nodded.

"Well, that feller you got there, I recognize him now. He belongs to old Blue Roan. You won't be a stranger here very long." His gaze drifted to the T Bar brand on the packhorse. "I expect you got that one awful cheap."

Dundee shrugged. They'd know soon enough. "I came by him legal. I work for John Titus."

The stableman said quietly, "May you rest in peace."

Dundee took his time, studying the town as he moved

along. Most of the buildings, he noted, were devoted to the sale of strong spirits and sundry types of entertainment. They ranged from little picket shacks that reminded him of a chicken crate up to one big, long structure built of stone. That one bore a small painted sign saying "Llano River Salon." They'd left an O out of the last word, but he doubted that many people noticed.

He tied the horses and said to Mexican Hat, "Don't you run off."

"Go to hell," the man mumbled.

Gratitude, Dundee reflected, had gone the way of the buffalo.

A skinny little bartender scowled. From his looks, Dundee judged that he drank vinegar instead of whisky. "What's your pleasure, friend?"

"I don't know as it *is* a pleasure. I'm looking for a woman by the name of Katy Long."

The frown didn't change. "I expect Katy is taking her siesta."

"Wake her up. I can't wait."

The frown deepened. "You been steered wrong about Katy, friend. Anyhow, there's a couple of places down the street where the girls don't ever sleep. Go try one of them."

"I got a man outside bleeding to death. I'm told she's pretty good at patching up things like that."

The bartender sighed. "She won't like it, but she'll come." He walked through a double door and down a hall. Dundee could hear him knock and call for Katy. In a moment he was back. "She'll be here directly. Let's me and you see if we can get your friend in."

A rider came jogging down the street, half asleep from

some long celebration, almost bumping into the tied horses. He came awake at sight of the slumped-over man in the sombrero. "Jayce! Jason Karnes! What in hell happened to you?"

Karnes just mumbled. The rider glanced at Dundee and the bartender. "I better go tell Bunch. And Roan." He jerked the horse around and spurred into a lope toward the races.

Dundee said to the bartender: "Well, I've found out who this is. Now, who is Bunch?"

"Bunch Karnes. He's a brother to Jayce."

"Tough?"

"Mixes rattlesnake juice with his whisky."

Physically, there wasn't much strength in the little bartender. He lent moral support but not much else. Dundee supported most of the weight as they carried Karnes, dropping his sombrero in the dust. A young woman came through the double doors at the back of the room, still buttoning a high-necked dress. "Bring him on back. We'll put him on a cot and see what we can do."

She was a good-looking woman, and Dundee figured she ought to be successful in her trade. She held a door open. He brushed against her, not altogether by accident.

The woman said to the bartender: "Cricket, we'll need hot water. You better go start a fire in my cookstove."

Dundee pulled the wounded man's boots off and pitched them under the cot. "I reckon he's yours now, Katy."

She showed resentment at the familiar use of her name. "You can call me Miss Long. You don't know me, and I don't know you."

He started to say, *I know you, even if I never saw you*

before. She must have seen it in his eyes. Her dislike of him was instantaneous. "You've got the wrong idea, cowboy. I make enough money selling whisky. I don't have to sell anything else." Curtly she said, "Let's see what we can do for your friend Jayce."

"He's not my friend."

"You brought him in."

"Figured I ought to. I shot him."

"Accident?"

"Not especially."

She carefully unwrapped the cloth Dundee had bound around the leg. Karnes moaned and cursed. The woman said contemptuously: "Why didn't you just go ahead and kill him? Don't you know a dirty bandage can kill a man just as dead as a bullet can?"

"I had to make do with what was there."

"Lucky thing the wound bled some and washed itself clean."

The bartender brought hot water in a pan. Katy Long cleansed the area around the wound with the skill of a trained nurse. Karnes sucked air between his teeth, but she was careful not to hurt him more than she had to.

Dundee decided to give credit where it was due. "You know your business."

"My business is whisky, and nothing else. There's no profit in this." To Karnes she said, "Grit your teeth and hang on." Karnes gripped the cotframe, his knuckles going white. He cursed and raved.

The woman glanced accusingly at Dundee. "I'm glad you had to watch."

Dundee wanted to defend himself, but pride stopped

him. He didn't owe any explanation to a saloon woman. Let her think what she damn pleased.

He heard the strike of heavy boots in the hall. A gruff voice shouted: "Jayce! Where you at, Jayce?"

The woman called impatiently: "You don't have to holler. He's here."

A tall figure filled the narrow doorway. Dundee's gaze lifted to a dirty, tobacco-stained beard, to a pair of angry, blood-tinged eyes. The tall man demanded, "Who was it done this to you, Jayce?"

Katy Long tried to head him off. "He'll be all right."

Dundee tensed. He knew this would be Bunch Karnes, the brother.

Karnes seemed not to hear the woman. "Jayce!" His voice was more demanding. "I said, who done this to you? I want to know."

Dundee was glad he had strapped on his pistol. He let his hands rest at his hips, handy. He suggested: "Maybe you ought to leave him be."

Hard eyes cut to Dundee's face. "What business is it of yours?"

The wounded man rasped: "He's the one done it, Bunch. He's the one shot me."

Karnes' hand dropped. Dundee brought his pistol up so fast that Karnes froze, blinking. At this range Dundee couldn't miss. Karnes swallowed.

Katy Long watched open-mouthed. For long seconds she held her breath until Karnes slowly raised his hand. Then, the moment of crisis past, she pointed to the door. "Bunch Karnes, this is *my* place, and I'm telling you to clear out. If you two have got to kill each other, do it someplace else. I don't want to clean up the mess."

The gunman's fingers flexed, his flashing eyes watching Dundee's pistol. Dundee didn't let the pistol waver from Karnes' belly. He didn't speak, for at times like this he'd never seen much gain in conversation.

Anger high in her face, the woman said sternly: "Karnes, I told you to *git!* You-all do any shooting in here, one of you is liable to hit your brother. Damn if I want to see all my work wasted."

Karnes sullenly backed toward the door. "When you come out, cowboy, I'll be waiting in the saloon."

His eyes didn't leave Dundee until he was in the hall and out of the line of vision. Dundee listened to the heavy footsteps tromping across the floor. His lungs cried out for air, and only then did he realize he had held his breath the whole time.

Katy stood in silence, her face paled.

Dundee told her, "It's all right now."

Her voice was sharp. "I don't know how you figure that, with him waiting out yonder in the saloon. You don't know this town. You don't know people like Bunch and Jason Karnes."

"I've run into a few."

"Bunch Karnes isn't the smartest man on earth, but he's hard. Minute you step out into that hall, he'll put a bullet in you."

"What difference would that make to you?"

"Blood leaves a dark stain on the floor. It's hard to get out."

"I'll try not to cause you no extra work." Dundee moved to the deep, narrow window. Its frame was set so that the window moved sluggishly to one side. He didn't know that he trusted the woman to keep quiet, but circumstances didn't permit him much choice. He slipped out the window and eased to the ground.

Pistol in hand, Dundee edged up to the one side window of the saloon and peered cautiously with one eye. The bartender saw him but gave no sign. Bunch Karnes sat facing the double doors, pistol lying in front of him on a small square table.

Dundee moved hurriedly past the window and on to the front of the building. He still held the pistol, but in a fight, the carbine would suit him better. He walked up to the bay at the hitching rail, drew the carbine and dropped his pistol back into its holster. He moved quietly up to the door. Inside, he could see Karnes seated, back turned, his attention still fixed on the double doors. The bartender saw Dundee and dropped out of sight behind the bar.

Dundee leveled the carbine. "Karnes, back away from that table. And leave your six-shooter right where it's at."

Karnes went stiff. Dundee said: "I got a gun pointed at you. Give me a reason and I'll blow a hole in you they could run a wagon through."

Karnes slowly stood up. Dundee held his breath, watching the pistol. Karnes' hand was only inches from it. He drew clear of the table and turned, hands empty, face raging.

Dundee said: "Why don't you just quit? I got no wish to kill you."

"But I'm going to kill *you*, cowboy."

"Your brother's alive. Why don't you just let it go at that?"

He wasn't reaching Bunch Karnes and knew it. *I ought to shoot him where he stands,* Dundee thought. *That would be the end of it. There won't be an end to it till I do.*

The man was a thief, and in all likelihood a killer. The world would shed few tears if Dundee cut him down. In fact, it would be a better place. But Dundee knew he couldn't pull the trigger, not this way.

"Step away from that table, and leave the pistol."

"I can get another pistol."

A voice in Dundee kept telling him, *Go on and kill him.*

Boots clomped on the front steps. Dundee stepped backward toward the corner, not letting the carbine waver from Karnes.

A big man blocked off most of the light from the doorway, the same heavy-built old man who had been at McCown's.

This was Blue Roan.

Roan Hardesty paused in the door, as if undecided whether to come in or to step back out into the street. He saw then that Karnes was out of reach of his pistol. He cast a long look at Dundee. "You again. They told me some stranger had brung Jayce Karnes to town with a bullethole in him. I ought to've knowed it'd turn out to be you."

Dundee said, "If you got any influence over this man, you better use it."

Hardesty turned to Karnes. "Well?"

"It was him that shot Jayce. I'm fixing to kill him."

"With your six-shooter lying over there on the table? You're just fixing to get your light blowed out, is all. This cowboy looks like he means business, Bunch."

"So do I."

"I need you alive, Bunch. Anyway, the weather's too hot for a funeral. You git yourself along."

"But I . . ."

"I said git on along. I'll talk to you later."

Karnes stared resentfully at Roan Hardesty, his eyes then drifting to Dundee and spilling their hatred. "I'm going because Roan says to. But don't think it's over, cowboy. I ain't even started yet."

He stomped to the door, down the steps and out into the street, leaving the pistol on the table. Dundee held the carbine, not pointing it directly at Hardesty but not letting the muzzle drop far, either.

Hardesty's voice was deep and gravelly. "You can put away the hardware. I ain't going to do you no harm."

"You can bet your life you're not."

"I promise you. I don't ever break a promise." He turned. "Who the hell is tending bar around here? Where's Cricket?"

The little bartender's head tentatively rose from behind the pine bar, eyes cautiously appraising the situation before he stood up to full height.

Hardesty said, "Whisky, Cricket." He started toward the few small tables. Dundee picked up Karnes' pistol and shoved it into his waistband. Hardesty pulled out a chair. "Set yourself down."

Dundee sat in a corner, where nobody could come up behind him. He watched Hardesty with distrust. The bartender set down a bottle and two glasses. Hardesty pulled the cork and poured the glasses full. "Here's to all the bold and foolish men. And there's a hell of a lot of them." He downed his drink in one swallow. Dundee didn't touch his own. Hardesty noticed. "You don't trust me?"

"I make it a practice not to trust nobody."

"A safe policy. But I gave a promise. Old Blue Roan has broke most of the laws that was ever passed, but he don't break a promise."

Dundee looked at the blue spots on the old man's broad face. "I didn't figure they called you that where you could hear it."

"I'm not ashamed of my face, boy. I bear it like a medal, a thing to be proud of. I got it in the line of duty. I was in the late war, boy, the war between the states. We charged into an artillery emplacement, and the whole thing went up . . . right in my face. I was lucky I kept my eyes. When it was over, I had these marks for life. Sure, I fretted over them awhile, but bye and bye it come to me that they was honest marks. They was like a medal that a man wears all the time and don't even take off with his clothes. They tell the world that Roan Hardesty done his job." He paused to take another drink. "People has said some hard things about me, but there's one thing they can't take away. I done my duty, and I got the marks to prove it." He refilled his glass. "Anyway, I didn't come here to talk about me. I want to find out about *you*. How come you to shoot Jason Karnes?"

"I come up on him and his partner venting the brands on some cattle. He shot at me first."

"Where was this?"

"Back up in the hills, close to a cabin." Dundee pointed his chin.

"How come you fooling around up there, anyway?"

Dundee figured he'd just as well tell it all. "To see what I could find out."

"What *did* you find out?"

"Where some of John Titus' cattle been going."

Roan Hardesty got up from the table. Dundee took a firm grip on the saddlegun. Hardesty walked to the door and looked out at Dundee's horses. "I'm getting old, I guess. Never even noticed the brand on that packhorse when I come in. You working for John Titus?"

Dundee nodded.

Hardesty spat on the floor. "What's old John figure on doing?"

"If I told you that, you'd know as much as *I* do."

Hardesty sat down again, taking another sip out of the glass. "Old Honest John. Bet he never told you he was a pretty good hand with a long rope once. As good a thief as *I* was, pretty near. But he got to letting his conscience talk to him. And then he went and married. Churchgoing kind, she was. She ruint him; he went honest. Got rich and turned his back on all his old friends."

"Maybe you ought to've done the same."

"No need to. I always had women. Never had to marry one."

"I mean, you should've turned honest."

"The meanest, dullest, most miserable people I know are honest. I like it better where I'm at."

"Somebody may kill you one of these days."

"You, maybe?"

"I hope not." Dundee wouldn't have admitted it, but he found himself drawn to this old reprobate. The old man had the same disarming frankness as John Titus.

"I'd as soon not have to shoot you neither, Dundee. I always had a soft spot for an honest man with guts. Wisht I'd had you with me in the war. A few more like me and you, we'd of whipped them Yankees."

"We might have."

Blue Roan stared at him through narrowed eyes, appraising him like he would judge a horse. "Dundee, I know John Titus. Whatever he's paying you, it ain't enough for the risk. Join up with me and I'll show you where the money's at."

"Venting other people's brands? I reckon not."

"Look at it this way: it's free range, most of it. Biggest part of the land John Titus uses still belongs to the state of Texas. He's taking the use of it free, not paying a dime. And who is the state of Texas? Why, it's me and you and everybody else. John Titus is robbing all us taxpayers. If we run off a few piddling head now and then, it's just our way of making sure he pays something for the grass. We're doing the state of Texas a service, you might say."

The reasoning brought Dundee a smile. He wondered if Roan Hardesty had ever actually paid a dollar of tax to the state of Texas. "I made John Titus a promise. I'll keep it."

The outlaw regretfully accepted Dundee's judgment. "I like a man who keeps a promise. But I can't guarantee you your safety. I can't be responsible for people like Bunch Karnes who think slow but shoot fast."

"I've always took care of myself."

"Keep on doing it. I'd sooner not have you on my conscience." Hardesty stood up to leave, then turned again. "What connection you got with the McCowns?"

"Like I told you, I stopped there and they fed me."

"That's all?"

Worry started building in Dundee. He hadn't intended to get the McCowns any deeper in trouble than they already were. "That's all, and I'll swear to it. I never saw them before."

Hardesty paused in the doorway. "You're worried because you think this is going to cause me to bear down on them. Don't fret yourself. Them and me, we had our trouble before you ever come here." A faint smile tugged at his big mouth. "That girl is the one you're really thinking about, ain't she? You know, she reminds me of the one old John Titus married. Pass her by, Dundee. She's not for you, all that honeysuckle and home cooking. She'd hogtie you like a slick-eared yearling."

When the old man was gone, Katy Long came back. "I heard most of that. You really come from John Titus?"

"Yep."

"And you tell anybody who asks you?"

"I never been one to lie."

"There's a time and a place for everything. In your place, I'd lie."

"Way I heard it, a couple of other fellers come into this country and lied. They got killed. Me, I just come to find out who's been taking John Titus' cattle, and where they're going with them, that's all. Maybe you'd like to tell me, and save me some trouble."

"You're *already* in trouble. I'm keeping clear of it."

Through the front door Dundee could see the corner of a small mercantile building across the rutted road that passed for a street. He saw a shadow move. He stood up, the carbine in his hands.

Katy Long caught the tension. "What is it?"

"You said you didn't want no trouble. Just stay put." Keeping within the darkness of the room, he moved to a point where he had a better view of the mercantile. He watched a few minutes, waiting for more movement. He saw a hatbrim edge out, and then part of Bunch Karnes' face as the tall man peeked around the corner. He saw a little of a gunbarrel.

Well, Dundee thought regretfully, *I tried. I could as well have shot him a while ago.*

He maneuvered toward the door, staying close to the wall. He paused a moment, his shoulder to the wall, gauging where the horses were tied. He didn't want a stray shot to kill his bay or the pack animal. He glanced at the wide-eyed bartender, at the silent woman. He took a deep breath, leaped out the door and lit running.

He took Karnes by surprise. Dundee made three long strides before Karnes stepped out into the open, the pistol extended almost to arm's length in front of him, swinging to try to bring it in line with the running target. Dundee threw himself to the ground. He saw the flash as he brought the carbine up. He aimed at Karnes' chest and squeezed the trigger.

Karnes was flung back grabbing at his shirt in open-mouthed bewilderment, the pistol falling from his hand. He crumpled in a heap.

Cautiously Dundee moved forward, trying to watch Karnes and at the same time looking up and down the street for trouble. He kicked the pistol away, then knelt. He touched Karnes and drew his hand back. Karnes shuddered once, then lay still.

Dundee arose, turned and walked back to the saloon, the carbine smoking in his hands. In the front door stood Katy Long and the little bartender.

A bitter taste in his mouth, Dundee said, "Well, at least we didn't leak blood on your floor."

She didn't back away from him. "Don't take it out on me. When you came here for John Titus, you knew you might kill somebody, or maybe get killed yourself."

He nodded darkly, watching a small crowd begin to gather around the body.

"Then don't blame me. All I do is operate a saloon."

"In an outlaw town."

"Look, cowboy, nobody's taken care of me since I was fourteen. I've minded my own business and left everybody else's alone. I just sell whisky. And you're shooting my customers."

From down the hall Jason Karnes' voice called weakly: "What's happened out there? Somebody tell me what's happened!" In a moment, when no one went to him, he shouted again, anxiety rising: "Bunch! Bunch! Where you at, Bunch? What's happened out there? Bunch!"

Katy Long's handsome face twisted with regret. "I suppose now it's up to me to tell him. Cowboy, I wish to hell you'd ride out of here."

"I was just fixing to leave."

5

Dundee had had a bellyful of Runaway. The hour or so he had whiled away in its contentious clime would do him till hell froze over. As far as he was concerned, they could burn the place to the ground. He even studied a bit about dropping a match in the dry grass, but the wind was blowing in the wrong direction.

Bunch Karnes' blood drying in the sand was not the first Dundee had ever seen, or even the first he'd ever spilled. But this was one experience not improved by repetition. It was a thing that curdled a man's stomach, made him want to get off someplace and face up to his own private demons alone, with no eyes watching. Dundee couldn't see that it would benefit his mission any to hang around Runaway. Chances were somebody would just crowd him into smoking up the carbine again. Let John Titus do the shooting, he thought. They were *his* cattle.

So, looking over his shoulder to be sure the only thing behind him was his shadow, he left Runaway. He rode west awhile, then south. Long days stretched into weeks while he prowled the endless hills, leading the pack-horse, looking, mapping, noting brands. Sometimes when he found a cabin or a camp, he would sit among the cedars on some high vantage point and watch for hours with that spyglass, until he was sure he knew what brand went with what people, and whether it was a bonafide brand or some optimistic conversion.

Times, he knew he was not only watching but being watched. Times he would look back and see a horseman or two patiently trailing after him, keeping their distance. When he stopped, they stopped. When he rode, they rode.

Nobody made a threatening move, but no longer did he enjoy that feeling of obscurity he had had before the trip to Runaway. He was sure the word about him had spread through all these hills. Maybe they didn't know exactly what he was up to, but they knew he was here. He had to watch for more than cattle now. He took to eating his supper before dark, then riding into the darkness before making cold camp in a thicket somewhere. If they caught him in his blankets, they had to be doing a good job of hunting.

The list of blotted brands kept growing in his tallybook. It had worried him at first because he had so few names to go with the brands. He had no one to go to, no one to ask. But in time he quit stewing about it. He knew the greasy-sack spreads where these brands were claimed. He knew many of the men by appearance, even if he didn't know their names. Besides, most of them probably weren't using the names their mothers had given them anyway. A cowthief by any name was still a cowthief.

There came a point, south, where Dundee found no more T Bar cattle. He came across other fresh brands on grown cattle, and he didn't doubt they'd originally been something else, but not the T Bar. These likely had been rustled in the south and brought north, just as Titus cattle had been stolen in the north and brought south. The way Dundee pictured it, these Llano hills were kind of a crossroads for livestock that had made a nocturnal change in ownership. Some of the cattle he saw here bore all the trademarks of Mexico. They had, no doubt, crossed the Rio Grande in a right smart of a rush.

Well, they were a problem for *somebody*, but not for Dundee. His wages were being paid by John Titus. He began bearing east again, and some to the north. Slowly he was completing a wide circle, and with it, his map. The circle would be closed when he returned to the part of the country where he had started, the Rocker M.

That ranch had been stirring in his mind like a restless squirrel worrying a pile of leaves. Every time he came across a valley which in any way resembled the McCown country, he remembered the young woman standing in the dog-run between the two sections of the sturdy log cabin, her long brown hair floating gently in the wind. He remembered the slenderness of her, the voice, the eyes, the soft woman smell.

She came to him in the golden sunlight of morning, and in the dark of night. She came like a song that has been once heard, and not clearly, but which echoes on and on in memory.

Sometimes, staring at the darkness in a liveoak motte or cedar thicket, he would rub his scratchy beard, smell the dry dust and the smoke that had sifted into the fiber of all his clothes and clung there. He was glad she could not see him this way. He would try to be sure that she never saw him like that again.

He was carrying close to two hundred dollars now, about as much money as he had ever owned at one time in his life. That wasn't much prospect to offer a woman. Times, when he thought of her, he also thought of the free-wheeling, easy-drifting life he'd led, and wondered if he was really ready to change. Damn, but it had been fun. Hard, hungry, stifling hot or freezing cold . . . but fun, just the same. A restlessness still stirred in him, a prickly feeling that came over him every so often and set him to moving without direction, without any purpose except simply to *go*. It wasn't much recommendation to present to a woman. Not *that* kind of woman.

Times, too, he got to wondering if word had drifted back to her about the shooting in Runaway. It probably had. When she next looked at him, would she see Dundee, or would she just see the blood on his hands?

This was mostly a cattle country, but now and again he would run across a band of sheep, usually but not always herded by a Mexican. One sheep outfit he watched was made up of three bands, each band totaling twelve or fifteen hundred sheep.

These, Dundee figured, he didn't have to worry about. A man with a flock of sheep on his hands was too busy to be stealing cows. Maybe more sheep was what it would take to civilize this country.

He was nearing the close-up point on his circle when the heavy rain came. It poured bountifully from a leaden sky, the thunder rolling, the water singing as it filtered down through the hillside grass in a growing flood. Dundee had no idea where to find a ranchhouse. He searched for an overhang he could squeeze under, but he couldn't find one. He huddled beneath the liveoaks until the rain trickled down through the leaves and reached him. The horses hung their heads and took it, for they had never known a roof. But Dundee was soaked to the skin and shivering, his shoulders hunched and his teeth clicking. He decided he had as well be miserable on the move as miserable hunkered on the ground beneath these leaky trees.

At length he came down off of a hill and saw a picket shack. It was a miserable hovel, and any other time he wouldn't have given it a second glance. But now with the rain and the wind chilling him to the bone, it looked as pretty as a marble church. In a set of brush pens he saw goats hunched against the cold. They weren't leggy and spotted and made up of all colors like the Mexican goats he had often seen. These were Angoras, carrying fine, long white mohair which tended to curl into ringlets, even wet. But he was too cold to wonder much or pause to admire a penful of drenched goats. He shouted, "Hello the house!"

A slump-shouldered old man stood in the open door, the wind whipping his snowy beard as he squinted through the rain. He pointed a long, bony finger. "Shed's yonderway. Put your horses up and git yourself back here to the dry."

The shed was mostly just an arbor closed on three sides and given a liberal cover of sod and brush on top to turn the water. He took off saddle and pack and turned the horses loose. He stood a moment under the shed, the first time in hours the rain hadn't been beating down on his back. It felt good here. But the shack would feel even better, for he could see smoke curling up from a stone chimney.

He stopped abruptly as he saw a cowhide stretched across the top of a fence. It was fresh, maybe two or three days old. He started to pass it by, but curiosity was stronger than the cold. The flesh side was turned up, the brand easily visible through it.

The T Bar.

Hell of a country, he thought, where even a goatherder steals cattle.

He dug the pistol out of his saddlebag and strapped it around his waist, beneath his yellow slicker. He stalked across the yard and into the cabin. The old man stared at him with pale gray eyes that were almost lost beneath bushy gray brows. A Mexican boy of eighteen or so sat on a wooden-framed goathide cot in a corner, rolling a brown-paper cigarette.

Dundee was too cold to play games. He flung the challenge. "You got a cowhide out yonder with a T Bar on it!"

The old man nodded as if it wasn't any news to him. "I bet you're that feller I been hearing about. Ain't your name *Dandy?*"

"It's *Dun*dee. And I asked you about that hide."

The old man looked sympathetic. "You're cold. And I bet you ain't yet et."

"I'm asking you for an answer."

"I bet you're hungry. Well, you peel some of them wet clothes off and we'll have dinner here directly. You'll feel like a new man when you've surrounded some of this fresh beef."

"About that hide . . ."

"Let's don't talk business right now. You're cold and hungry, and I never did like to argue with a hungry man. A man just ain't reasonable. You git your belly filled, then we'll talk."

A Dutch oven sat astraddle some blazing oakwood in the open fireplace, steak sizzling. Dundee pointed his chin. "That steak yonder, I reckon it came out from under that hide?"

The old fellow nodded.

Dundee exclaimed: "That's T Bar beef. You expect me to eat it?"

"Why not? You work for old Titus, don't you? And if you was on the home ranch you'd be eating Titus beef, wouldn't you? So what's the difference if you eat it *here?* Who's better entitled to it?"

The off-center logic went by Dundee so fast he couldn't argue with it. The steak smelled good. And the old man had called the tune: Dundee was hungry as a she-wolf with six pups.

The Mexican wasn't saying anything. Dundee didn't know if he understood English, even. But the herder sat like a suspicious watchdog, glancing protectively at the old man, most of the time keeping his narrowed eyes fastened on Dundee. Dundee had a cold feeling that if he made any manacing move toward the old goat man, he'd have to beat that young Mexican to the floor or be crushed himself. In addition, there was a black and white dog of a breed or mixture that Dundee didn't know. It sat under the Mexican's feet, gaze never wavering from the stranger. Dundee might have to fight *him,* too.

Coffee boiled in a pot in the corner of the fireplace. The old man poured a cup of cold water in to settle the grounds and brought the pot up to set it on the rough table. It left black ash marks, but they were hardly noticeable; the table was already as discolored as it could get. "Steak's done. Got a pot of beans, too. Hope you don't mind cold bread."

The tinware was battered and tarnished, but that was of no matter. The food was good. Dundee's eyebrows went up when the old man lifted one piece of steak out of the popping grease and dropped it into an old tin plate on the dirt floor, for the dog. The dog sniffed it eagerly but knew enough to wait for it to cool. The old man dropped him a couple of cold biscuits to keep him busy. "Man's got a good working dog, he's got to take care of him," he said.

Dundee wondered how John Titus would appreciate it, seeing his beef fed to a goatherder's dog.

The meal over, Dundee leaned back and rubbed his stomach. "That was sure fine."

The old man took the compliment with grace. "No trick to it if you got good beef."

"Such as Titus beef?"

"I tried not to notice the brand." The old man smiled gently. "While ago I said you'd be eating T Bar beef if you was on the home ranch. Fact is, I bet you'd be eating some neighbor's. John Titus kills strays, just like everybody else. A man's own beef don't ever taste as good."

"Titus might not see it your way."

"The fact is, Dandy, I kept that steer from being stole."

"What do you mean?"

"Some fellers brought a herd of cattle through here three . . . four days ago, heading south. They scattered my goats by accident, so to make it right they offered me this steer. He was lame and couldn't keep up anyway."

"The rest of the cattle . . . they carry a T Bar brand?"

"Like I said, in this country I don't ever see no brands."

"The men driving those cattle . . . who were they?"

The oldtimer smiled thinly. "Now, Dandy, the way I lived to get so old was by not seeing anything that wasn't my business, and not saying nothing about what I didn't see."

"I could tell John Titus you been eating his beef."

"If you think it'll make things right, I'll swap you for that steer. He was lame and not worth much. I'll pick out two of my top goats, and you can take them along."

"What would I do with two goats?"

"That'd be up to you. All I want is to pay a debt if I got one. And I ain't sure as I do. After all, I *did* save that steer from being stole."

Dundee shrugged. He didn't figure John Titus would be very hard on a man who just butchered a steer once in a while to eat. Especially if Dundee never told him. Dundee changed the subject. "Them are unusual-looking goats you got. They work good in this country?"

"Them is Angorys . . . *hair*-goats. You shear mohair off of them, like you shear wool off of a sheep. They're the coming thing for this part of the country, once the cowthieves leave. They eat brush and stuff like that. If he has to, a goat can live on next to nothing. And a man can live on goat. Hard to starve a goat man to death."

The old man stared through the door at the rain still pelting down. "Looks like it's liable to hang on awhile. You're welcome to stay here, Dandy."

"Much obliged."

"Where you headed when it's over with? You figuring on trying to trail them cattle?"

Dundee shook his head. "Won't be no tracks left after this rain. No, I reckon I'll go see some folks. Then I'll head back to the T Bar."

"This is a good country down here. You could do worse than stay."

"What for? I got no cattle, and I don't aim to steal any."

"You could start small and build as the country builds."

"This is nothing but an outlaw country."

"The outlaws won't last. They're just part of a country's growing up, like a kid has to put up with measles and chickenpox. One day they'll all be gone, but the country'll be here. All we need in these hills is some good people . . . and a little more rain."

"That," said Dundee, "is all *hell* needs."

6

Dundee had jogged along in a deliberate trot all day, keeping a checkrein on his patience. Now the double log cabin lay ahead of him, and patience evaporated like a summer mist He touched spurs to the bay picking up into an easy lope.

All morning he had watched for signs of Warren Mc-Cown or Uncle Ollie. He thought they might be riding these hills and the long valleys to check their cattle after the rains. Now, approaching the homeplace spring and the corrals, he looked for the men again. He still didn't see them. A single horse stood in the pen, near the saddleshed. Unsaddling his bay and dropping the pack, Dundee noticed that Uncle Ollie's saddle hung on its rack, but Warren's was gone.

The lazy old whelp probably waited till Warren was out of sight, then snuck back to loaf, Dundee thought. He spread dry mesquite beans for the horses, then set out afoot toward the cabin.

Millie stood in the dog-run, smiling, her long hair adrift in the south wind which had come up strong now that the rains were over and the clouds broken away. He walked briskly toward her. She didn't wait; she hurried to meet him halfway. She stopped when they were three paces apart, her eyes ashine. She made an instinctive gesture of opening her arms to receive him, realized what she had done and brought her hands together.

Dundee stopped. He fought a compelling urge to scoop her into his arms. A man didn't do that . . . not to a woman like this. He swallowed and remembered his place. He had no right.

He crushed his hat in his hands the way he wanted to crush *her*.

"Dundee! I don't know when I've ever been so glad to see somebody."

"Been a while, ain't it?" He rubbed his face and managed a nervous smile. "This time I shaved *before* I got here." He had washed out his clothes, too, though they had dried with the wrinkles of wadded-up paper.

"You didn't have to," she said.

"Yes, I had to."

She smiled, and watching her warmed him like a long drink of whisky. He'd never seen a woman before that a man could get drunk just looking at.

She said, "Dundee, I hope you can stay."

"Well. . . ."

"Warren's not here, and Uncle Ollie's had a fall."

"Bad hurt?"

"Doesn't seem like he's got any bones broken. But he's sore and stiff, and it pains him to move. I need help with him till Warren gets back."

He wondered suspiciously whether the old man was really lame or just lazy. "Where did Warren go?"

"Went south to buy cattle."

Dundee stopped walking. "South, you say? Why south?"

She saw the look on his face and stared in puzzlement. "North of us there's nothing much but T Bar. There are already too many T Bar cattle running around here with somebody else's brand on them. Warren didn't want any, not even *with* a bill of sale."

Remembering what the old goat man had told him, Dundee counted back. "How many days since Warren left?"

"Six. Six days and seven hours." There was sadness in the way she said it.

Six. He frowned, counting on his fingers, finally shaking his head. *Not Warren. Surely not Warren.*

"Come on," Millie said, "let me take you to Uncle Ollie. He'll be real tickled to see a friendly face."

If I find the old codger faking, it ain't going to be none too friendly.

Uncle Ollie lay on his cot, atop the old woolen blankets. He had his britches on for propriety, a concession to Millie, Dundee guessed. But his faded red underwear was his cover from the waist up. It bore patches that must have been stitched there by Millie McCown's patient fingers. Ollie raised himself up on his left elbow and stuck out his right hand, wincing as if it caused him great pain. "Howdy, Dundee. Millie said she seen you ride in, but I didn't hear you. Used to could hear a grasshopper spit from a hundred yards. Used to do a heap of things I can't do no more."

Dundee asked with suspicion, "Horse throw you off?"

Sheepishly the old man said: "Wisht one had. There's

a little bit of glory in that. Truth is, I was fishing and fell off of the bank."

Dundee nodded. It was in character, all right. The old man was probably spreading it on thicker than it really was, but he was likely telling the truth in the main.

Millie said: "Just the same, we'll tell Warren it was a horse."

Dundee shrugged. "I reckon a little lie once in a while don't hurt nothing, long's it's for a good cause."

Ollie smiled thinly. "Glad you see it my way, Dundee. Wisht Warren did."

I expect he sees more than you think he does, Dundee said to himself.

Ollie complained: "Way he goes all the time, he'll be old before long hisself. Then maybe he'll know. Only it'll be too late then for me. I'll be dead and in the grave." He sat up and dropped his legs off the cot, wincing and groaning. Millie had moved across the room to the cabinet, where she had some biscuit dough working. Ollie whispered, "Help me outside, will you?"

Dundee took a thin arm around his shoulder and assisted the old man to his feet. Ollie moved slowly, sucking breath between his teeth. Outside, he waved for a pause to rest. "Much obliged. Some things a man can't have a woman help him do. Been having to make this trip all by myself, an it's been pure hell."

"Ollie, when did you take this fall?"

"Why, it was the day Warren left. The very same day. How come you to ask?"

"Just curious." Dundee glanced toward the woodpile, knowing Millie had done most of the chopping herself, unless Warren had left her a supply. Likely he hadn't. That's what Ollie was supposed to be for.

Back in the cabin, Ollie stretched on the cot and began to talk about the old days, when the world had been freer and fresher and the air keener and men more honest and life had been a joy to live. Dundee only half listened, nodding when he thought he ought to, agreeing now and again with a quiet "Unh-hunh." Mostly he watched Millie McCown kneading dough for supper biscuits, cutting the dough and putting it out in a flat pan. He watched her roll steak in flour and never even wondered what brand was on the hide it came from under.

Uncle Ollie came completely unwound at the supper table, and Dundee noticed that even though the old man's legs were stiff and sore, his jaw swiveled quite easily, both for eating and for talking. Ollie had known every famous cowman from the Rio Grande to the Canadian River, seemed like. He had known every gunfighter and had personally witnessed every gunfight of any notoriety since the fall of the Alamo, and Dundee wondered how come he had missed that one.

Millie finished washing the dishes, put away the wet drying towel, looked at Dundee a moment, then walked to the door. "It's nice out tonight. I think I'll get some air," she said.

Ollie leaned on his elbow, nursing his pipe, eyes focused on something far beyond the room, far back in time. "Them was the days, Dundee. I tell you, it ain't nothing like that no more. People don't enjoy theirselves the way they used to."

Dundee looked outside at Millie. "Maybe they do. Maybe it's just a new bunch doing it now."

Ollie clicked his pipe against his teeth, listening to no one but himself. "No, sir, it ain't the same. I mind the time—before the war, it was—me and my brother was out on the Keechi . . ." The old man talked on, immersed in his story-telling, his mind lost in ancient memories . . . or maybe it was ancient dreams . . . it would be hard to separate one from the other. Dundee eased out the door and left him there, still talking to himself.

Millie leaned against one of the heavy cedar posts that held up the brush arbor. She stared down the valley into the gathering dusk. Dundee knew she heard him, but she didn't look around. She said: "Expecting Warren back any day now. He's been gone an awfully long time."

"Just six days, you said. Give him time. Cattle move slow."

"So do the hours, when you're out here so far from anybody, just by yourself. Oh, I don't mean that Warren and Uncle Ollie aren't good company. But I mean, you go so terribly long here sometimes and never see a soul except family. Then, when even one of the family leaves for awhile, it's like somebody had died."

"This isn't good for a woman. You shouldn't be out here."

"I belong. It's the only real home I ever had. When Dad was living, we just drifted around from ranch to ranch. Never owned anything, never stayed anywhere long enough to gather from the gardens we planted, even. Warren said we were gypsies, always on the move, never leaving anything behind us but wagon tracks. He said someday he was going to find him a place and put down roots so deep they couldn't be pulled up by anything or anybody. And I guess this is the place."

"For a woman, it ain't much."

"It's home. When you've wandered most of your life, it means something to stand on a piece of ground and call it your own. It gives you a feeling . . . I couldn't tell you what it's like . . . to look across that valley yonder and know it's yours . . . to know that come tomorrow you'll still be here . . . and next month . . . and next year."

"It's lonesome, just the same."

"Nothing is ever perfect. This is a lot better than we *used* to have. And it'll be even better yet. Warren will see to that."

Warren. Dundee realized that her brother had taken on the aspect of a father to her. The sun rose and set with Warren McCown, and would, until some other man came along to establish a new and different relationship that would displace him.

He said: "You won't always depend on Warren. One of these days some cowboy will take a good look at you and carry you off."

She turned, and he saw in her eyes a want so deep that it startled him. She said: "He wouldn't have to go anywhere. He could stay right here."

Dundee looked away, somehow off balance. "Maybe, if he was thataway inclined."

"This is a good place. A man could be happy here."

"If he was the right kind of a man for it . . . if his feet didn't keep getting the itch to move on."

"If a man found what he was looking for, he wouldn't *want* to move anymore, would he?"

"Some of us never know what we're looking for. We're just looking."

"When you do find it, do you think you'll know?"

"I couldn't rightly say. I ain't found it so far."

She took in a slow breath. "You could have, without realizing."

Dundee looked away, fishing a small sack out of his pocket and rolling himself a cigarette, spilling most of the tobacco. He stole a glance and found her frowning in thought. Finally she asked: "Why do you work for John Titus?"

"For money, I guess."

"You could as easy work for somebody else."

"He's paid me good, and there's more coming. For once in my life I'm going to have me a stake to show for my time."

"And when you get that money, what'll you do with it?"

"Been studying about that a right smart. I'd like to have more to show for the next thirty years than I've had for the last thirty. Been thinking I might set me up a business."

"Like what?"

"Oh, like maybe a saloon. An honest one, of course."

Her eyes disapproved. "A saloon?"

"Beats cowboying. One time I spent three hard months on a ranch. Never saw the bunkhouse in daylight the whole time. Worked till I didn't even sweat anymore; just oozed blood. Went to town finally, and in three days I spent every cent I'd made in three months. *He* didn't sweat. Heaviest thing he lifted in the whole three days was my money as he toted it to the bank."

"Dundee, don't you want something better in life than a saloon?"

"It's a good investment. When times are easy, everybody spends free. Times get hard, they drink to forget their troubles. Either way, the saloonkeeper walks a-jingling."

"There's more to life than money."

"That's what they say, but I never seen much evidence of it."

"There's more to you than you let on, Dundee. You could set your sights higher than that . . . a lot higher."

"What do you figure I ought to aim at?"

"You could take your money and buy cattle with it. Maybe there wouldn't be many at first, but they'd be *yours*. You could take that little start and build, the way Warren does. You wouldn't have to work for other people. You'd have cattle of your own, something that belonged to you and you could be proud of."

"It's hard work punching cows. I *know*."

"When the cows belong to you, it's not like working for the other man."

Dundee figured he was listening to a lecture from Warren McCown, second-handed. "Sure, I've thought about that. But there's something always worried me. What if I got myself all set on a place and had my roots down too deep to pull them up, and then my feet commenced itching again? What if I came to hate the sight of the place? What if it turned out to be more of a jail than a promised land?"

She touched his hand. Her fingertips were warm and startling. It was as if he had brushed his hand against a wire fence in a lightning storm. She said, "Maybe you wouldn't ever get to feeling that way . . . if you had somebody with you. . . ."

He found his lips dry. He licked them with a quick,

furtive touch of his tongue. "Millie, I might even get tired of her, too. Then she'd be miserable, and so would I." Her fingers tightened on his hand. He felt heat rising in his blood, and he drew his hand away. "Millie, some men it's best to leave alone. There's a right smart you don't know."

"But there's a lot I *do* know. You're a brave man, and you're kind."

"Kind? Maybe you ain't heard. I shot a man in Runaway."

Her lips tightened. "I heard. Somebody told Warren."

"That ought to be enough to change your mind about me."

"You didn't *want* to shoot him, did you?"

He shook his head. "But I did do it, and that's what counts."

"It doesn't count. You just did what came necessary. I don't imagine it's an easy thing to live with." Her eyes softened in sympathy. "I've heard that when a man has to kill, it haunts him, that the dead man won't let him rest."

"I've lost some sleep, all right, but it's been mostly from worrying about his live friends."

Millie laced her fingers together and squeezed them. She tried to look at him but cut her glance away when their gaze met. Dundee stared at her with hungry eyes, his pulse quickening, his hands shaking a little. He could sense a silent call reaching out to him, a cry of loneliness she didn't know how to express.

And there was a want in *him*, too, deep as a canyon. It was that want which had brought him back here.

Hoarsely she said, "Dundee, I don't think I ever knew a man quite like you."

He had been about to reach for her, to grasp her arms and pull her to him. Now her words fell on him like a sudden dash of cold water. She'd never really known *any* man, he was sure. She waited, trembling in expectation of something she didn't even understand. She was untouched, unprepared.

Times, he'd thought how pleasant it would be to walk into a situation like this, like stumbling across an unclaimed gold mine where all you had to do was reach and take.

Now he drew away, suddenly grave. "Millie, go in the house."

"What . . . ?"

Sternly he said: "You better go see after Uncle Ollie. He may be needing something."

He sensed the disappointment that folded in around her like a dark cloud. "Did I do something wrong?"

"No, but if you stay out here, *I* might."

Face coloring, she spoke almost in a whisper: "I don't guess you'd do anything I didn't want you to."

"There'd come a time you'd wish I hadn't. You'd hate me then, and likely I'd have a contempt for myself. You got a lot to learn yet, Millie. I don't want it on my conscience that I was the one taught you."

7

Although Uncle Ollie lapped up sympathy like an old dog takes to gravy, Dundee decided it wasn't all put-on with him. The fall had really hurt the old man, and at his age repairs came slow and painfully. Dundee wanted to stay, and warm himself in the glow that came upon him whenever Millie was close. But times, the temptation to reach out and take her was almost more than he could push aside. He found that he feared himself more than he had ever feared any man.

He would have left had it not been for Uncle Ollie. The old man would be a burden to the girl if she had to take care of him alone. Dundee chewed and fretted. Once he made up his mind to leave and went so far as to catch his horses. Then he went in from the woodpile with a fresh-cut armload of stovewood and saw Millie struggling to help her hungry uncle to the table. Dundee knew he had to stay till Warren got home. But he wouldn't stay an hour longer than that. Millie being the way she was, it was just too damned dangerous.

He purposely spent most of his time away from the house, chopping enough wood to carry halfway through next winter, stacking rocks for Warren's stone corrals, hoeing weeds out of the garden patch, anything to keep him mind-changing distance from temptation. Being close to her all the time—studying about her so much— kept him fighting against himself.

Maybe what he ought to do was slip off for a quick,

quiet little ride into Runaway, where he might find a bit of diversion down toward the end of the street.

Uncle Ollie was aware, too. Once when Dundee helped him take a walk out back, Ollie said, "Millie's kind of hit you between the eyes, ain't she?"

"What do you mean by that?"

"I been noticing the way you watch her. If I was of a violent nature, being her uncle and all, I could shoot you for the things you been thinking."

Dundee's face went warm. "You got an awful imagination."

"I see what I see." Ollie's eyes narrowed with a hint of craftiness. "You know, Dundee, half of everything here belongs to her. If you was to marry her, you'd have as much to say around here as Warren does."

Dundee held his silence, knowing Ollie was fishing.

Ollie continued: "Warren expects too much out of an old man. He's working me into my grave, I tell you. But you, Dundee, you could put a stop to that. You got a feeling for an old man."

"You're a dirty-minded, shameless schemer."

"And old man has got to scheme. He can't fight."

Dundee was wondering how much longer he would be able to stand it here when he saw the spring wagon laboring its way up the valley, the team straining in the afternoon sun, bouncing the wagon across the ford and up out of the streambed. Dundee dropped a heavy rock he had been about to place on the fence. He straightened his aching shoulders and squinted. Warren? *He* was supposed to come in with a herd of cattle. In any case, Warren hadn't taken the McCown wagon with him. It stood by the saddleshed. Dundee dusted his hands on his trousers, wiped sweat from his face onto his sleeve and started toward the house, watching the wagon.

He could make out two horses being led behind it, and two people sitting on the seat. One was a woman.

"Millie," he called, "you got company coming."

Millie stepped out of the house, wiping flour from her hands onto an apron, lifting one hand to shade his eyes. "I can't make them out."

Dundee stepped into the house and came back with a pistol strapped on his hip. He said, "The man is Roan Hardesty."

Blue Roan slouched on the wagonseat like a huge sack of oats, the reins in his big hands. Beside him, the saloon woman Katy Long sat with her back straight as a ramrod. If he hadn't known better, Dundee might have mistaken her for a schoolteacher.

Bet she could teach me some things, though, he thought. *Katy Long. Bet that ain't her real name. Bet she ain't used her right name in so long she'd have to study to remember what it is.*

Roan wheeled the wagon into the yard. Dundee saw two men in the back of it, one sitting up, one lying atop a stack of blankets. His gaze fell first upon the bandage. He remembered John Titus' contrary boy, the one he'd had that scrap with in Titusville.

This was Son Titus!

The old renegade reined the team to a stop. He took a careful look around, like a coyote surveying a chicken-house, then tipped his shapeless hat to the girl by the arbor. "Evening, Miss Warren." He shifted his gaze to

Dundee, and his eyes seemed to laugh. "Howdy, Dundee. Figured this was where I'd find you at. I got me a couple of problems here I want to dump in your lap."

Dundee glanced at the woman. Katy Long wasn't looking at him; she was staring at Millie McCown.

Dundee walked up to the wagonbed and peered into one defiant eye of the Titus heir. The other eye was swollen shut. "Son Titus, what the hell do you think you're doing here?" Dundee said.

"I come a-hunting cowthieves. I come to do the job *you* was hired for."

Roan Hardesty shifted his great bulk in the wagonseat to look back. "He's the old bear's cub, all right; ain't no doubt about that. Got the looks of old John, and the temper. I *would* say he lacks the brains. Must've took after some other branch of the family."

A bunch of questions were rattling around in Dundee's head, but he figured he'd get them all answered in due course if he would keep his mouth shut.

Roan said: "He come into Runaway proud and loud. Except for a couple of saloon girls, he didn't make no friends."

Dundee asked, "What did you do, run a bunch of horses over him?"

The old thief shook his head. "Soon's I got the word who he was, I give an order: nobody was to kill him. Guess I ought to've said nobody was supposed to *hurt* him, because they tried to see how far they could go *without* killing him." He glanced down at the sullen Son Titus. "He asked for it. Felt kind of like stomping him a little myself, but I always been too good-natured for that kind of thing."

Dundee snorted to himself. *I'll bet.* He looked at the cowboy who lay on the blankets. "Who is this?"

Roan replied regretfully: "Compadre of young Titus. He done what he could to get the boy out of trouble. He's got a bullet in his shoulder. Or *did* have. Katy took it out."

Dundee glanced at the saloon woman. "Playing nurse again. Maybe you missed your calling."

Her eyes flashed. "What makes you think you know what my calling *is?*"

Old Roan growled: "Now look, I already seen enough fighting to do me awhile. I'm turning these two boys over to you, Dundee."

"Why me?"

"They're T Bar property. I want you to get them back to old John. One more thing: make damn sure this cub don't turn up in Runaway again. Next time I might not be there to protect him. Somebody might put a permanent part in his hair."

Dundee said, "Come on, Son Titus, I'll help you out of the wagon."

Young Titus snapped: "I can get out by myself. Just you move aside and don't get in my way." He scooted his rump down the wagonbed and gingerly eased to the ground, favoring sore muscles and miscellaneous lacerations. "If you want to, though, you can help my friend Tobe. He's not in no shape to help himself."

Dundee climbed up. Carefully he lifted the cowboy, who sucked air between his teeth but didn't cry out. Katy Long quickly left the wagonseat. "Take it easy with him," she spoke sharply. "He's not a beef to be jerked around."

"I'm handling him gentle as I know how."

"Then you don't know very much." She stood at the rear of the wagon, ready to help bring the cowboy down. Son Titus waited there too, though Dundee figured he would be as much help as a split slicker in a rainstorm. Millie McCown came to stand beside Katy Long. Dundee got one arm under the cowboy's back, the other under his legs, then eased him down to the women. Sensibly, they shouldered Son Titus aside. Dundee said, "Just hold him now till I can get down out of the wagon." He glanced at Millie. "Looks like you got you another invalid."

"It's all right." She had a lot of patience, he thought.

On the ground, Dundee got the cowboy's good arm around his shoulder. Tobe had just enough strength to keep from wilting completely. "Hang on, pardner," Dundee gritted. "We'll get you inside in a minute."

"It's all right," the cowboy rasped.

Old Blue Roan had silently watched from the wagonseat. Now he laboriously climbed off, his weight pulling the wagon down heavily on one side, even turning the wheel a little as he put a foot on a spoke and shifted his bulk to it.

Dundee said, "I'm curious how you knew I'd be here."

Roan smiled. "I got eyes all over these hills. I've knowed pretty much where you been from one day to the next, ever since you rode out of Runaway. I figured once you got *here*, you'd stay awhile. *I* would, was I a mite younger."

Dundee glanced at Millie. She showed no sign that she caught Roan's implication. Katy Long did, though. She gave Dundee a glare that would kill mesquite.

Lying on his cot, Ollie McCown stared in amazement as they brought the cowboy into the room. "What the hell?" He saw Blue Roan then, and he cringed, dread clouding his eyes.

Roan said: "Lay easy, friend. I come here in a flush of generosity."

Millie pointed toward Warren's unused cot. "Put him there. If Warren comes home, he can sleep outside under the arbor, like Dundee."

Roan looked disappointed.

Katy Long stared gravely at the wounded cowboy, then at Millie. "We shouldn't have moved him this far, but Roan was afraid he'd come to harm in town. He needs to heal awhile before he's moved again."

Roan said: "I feel kind of responsible, seeing as some of my boys done this to him. I don't expect you got any too much vittles in the house. I fetched some extra."

Millie straightened in a flash of pride that reminded Dundee of Warren McCown. "We're not hungry. We can afford to feed an extra one or two."

"No offense. Dundee, you want to help me fetch them vittles in."

He phrased it like an order rather than a question. Heading for the door, Dundee heard Katy ask Millie, "You ever dressed a bullet wound before?" Millie hadn't. Katy said, "He needs fresh bandaging now, so I'll show you."

Roan had brought the goods in a couple of canvas sacks. In one were dried beans and fruit and some flour and coffee. In the other, canned goods clanked together as Dundee hoisted the heavy sack to his shoulder. He glanced suspiciously at the old brandburner. "This don't sound like what I've heard about you."

"Them stories was mostly lies."

"Maybe not. I seen you awhile back, trying to run a bluff on the McCowns here."

"It wasn't no bluff."

"Then how come you to bring these groceries?"

The old man scowled. "Not for the McCowns. Not Warren McCown, anyway." He paused, face softening. "I reckon I owe John Titus a little something for old times . . . and for all the T Bar cows that have went into my pockets. I figure it's going to be some days before you can haul that cowboy home. I want to send John his son back well-fed and in one piece . . . give or take a couple of teeth."

Dundee waited a moment to see if Roan was going to carry the other sack, but it was obvious Roan hadn't really meant for Dundee to *help* him; he had meant for Dundee to tote them all. Dundee carried the groceries in, dropped the sack on the floor and came back for the other. Roan reached under the wagonseat and brought out a couple of six-shooters with the gunbelts wrapped around them.

"Better drop these into that sack. They belong to young Titus and that cowboy. Was I you, I'd keep them hid till you get them boys back to John Titus." The blue spots on his face seemed to darken. "One thing for damn sure: don't you let that Titus button go back to Runaway. Sit on him if you have to, or tie him to a cedar tree. I can't watch all the time."

"He must've ripped things up a little."

"He's a brassy little devil; I'll give him that. Rode into town like he was somebody come. Scattered the news that he was thief-hunting, and he wasn't leaving without some scalps. I told the boys to let him alone, so they all just turned their backs on him. Then's when he found the women. I tell you, between loud talk and raw whisky and warm women, he was having hisself a high old time. That cowboy, he done his best to get him out of there, but I reckon young Titus had saved up too much of an appetite. I swear, Dundee, it's a mortal shame how that boy has been deprived.

"He tried to provoke them boys of mine by calling them cowthieves, but they all knew they was anyway, and they had my orders. When the fight finally *did* start, it was over one of the girls. Son got to poaching on private territory. If it hadn't been for the cowboy, Titus would've got killed. The cowboy took the bullet for him. Next time, it might be different. Watch him."

"I will."

"And maybe if you're busy watching *him*, you won't be coming back to Runaway yourself, either. You didn't leave no friends there that I noticed."

"I expect I'll be back."

"It'd be a pity. I can't help but like a man a little bit when I respect him. I'd hate to shovel dirt in your face."

Through the open door they could see Katy Long gesturing, telling Millie how to take care of the cowboy's wounds. The old outlaw watched, a gleam in his eyes. "I swear, Dundee, that's a good-looking filly, that McCown girl. And unbroke; a man could train her to suit hisself. Was I you, I'd a whole lot rather spend my time playing games with her than stirring up dust over in Runaway."

Dundee frowned but made no reply. Hardesty went on: "An old man ought not to have to give advice to a young man in matters like this, but I will. Opportunity don't knock often in this life. When it does, you better grab."

"You don't know a good woman when you see one."

"A *good* woman is just one that ain't been given the right opportunities."

Katy Long came outside and beckoned silently with a quick jerk of her chin. Her eyes were sharp, her words clipped. "Dundee, I've told the girl what to do, but she's never had any experience with this kind of thing. You may have to help her."

Sensing her distaste, Dundee stiffened in resentment. "I will."

"There's something else you could do to help her, too. You could leave her alone."

"What do you mean by that?"

"I mean the girl is young, and she's green. She's like a wild flower way out on the prairie. She's never met your kind of man before, and she doesn't know how to defend herself."

"Who told you she's had to?"

"I saw the way she looked at you. You've got her eating out of your hand."

Heat rose in Dundee's face. It was bad enough having to answer for the things he *did* do.

She said: "I'm used to gunfighters. I've even gotten accustomed to thieves. But I'll be damned if I can find any excuse for a man who would take advantage of innocence."

"What would *you* know about innocence?"

Her eyes flashed like lightning against a dark sky. "Enough that I respect it when I see it. It's a sad thing when you lose it; I can remember."

In spite of his resentment, Dundee sensed sincerity in this woman. "If it's any satisfaction to you, I ain't touched her."

She stared hard, and he knew it would be difficult to hide a lie from those sharp eyes. Her gaze lost its edge. "I'd like to believe that."

"Take it or leave it. It's the truth."

Her back lost its rigidity. "Don't tell me you haven't been tempted."

"Hell yes, I been tempted. You think I'm made out of wood?"

For a moment he thought she came close to a relieved smile. "Well then, remember this: the test of a man isn't whether he's ever tempted or not. It's whether he resists temptation."

He glanced at the wagon. "It'll be easier now. You've brought two extra pairs of eyes to watch me."

Now she *did* smile, though it was a fleeting thing and touched with malice. "If the temptation gets too strong, there are women in Runaway."

"Including you?"

"*My* business is whisky."

Roan hollered: "Come on, Katy. It's a long ways back to town."

Dundee suggested to Katy, "If you're worried about Millie, you could stay here and protect her."

Katy shook her head. "I might have to protect myself."

Dundee watched the wagon slowly drop down into the ford and climb out on the far side of the stream. He turned then toward the cabin, bracing himself a little. His eyes found Son Titus as he walked through the door.

"You damnfool button, what do you think you was doing in Runaway?"

Defiantly Titus said, "You'd know, if you'd been doing the job my dad hired you for, instead of laying up here passing the time with some nester girl."

Dundee glanced at Millie and saw the color rise. He clenched his fist. "Watch out what you say, boy."

"If you'd been out doing what you was supposed to, you'd of knowed they made a big raid on the T Bar and run off enough cattle to make a whole herd for some greasy-sack outfit like *this* one."

"So you decided to try to make the old man see you've growed up. You decided to go and wipe out the cowthieves all by yourself."

"I ain't finished yet."

"Yes, you are. You've all but got your friend here killed. If it wasn't for old Roan, you'd be laying out yonder someplace now, feeding buzzards."

Son Titus' right eye was dark and swollen, but his left one shone with anger. "You act mighty thick with that splotchy-faced old scoundrel. I've had a notion all along you'd fall in cahoots with that wild bunch."

It was on Dundee's tongue to tell Son Titus that Roan had once been a friend of his father. But anger had a tendency to make words come hard for him. It was easier to ball up a fist and hit something. "Son Titus, if a man just worked at it a little bit, he could get to where he didn't like you atall."

"I got friends enough. I don't need *you*."

Dundee pointed his chin at the cowboy who lay in silence on Warren McCown's cot. "You like to've lost one of them. Till he gets in shape to move, you'll stay here and behave yourself. I'm not going to take any foolishness off of you, Son Titus. Cross me and I'll slap you down."

Titus' open eye glowered. "You're forgetting, Dundee; I don't take orders off of you. You're working for us."

Dundee corrected him. "I'm working for your old daddy. And you *will* take orders or I'll pack you home tied up like a long-eared maverick."

Son's swollen eye and his stiff joints hadn't left him unable to walk. He limped painfully out of the cabin, trying to stomp but hurting too badly to make it effective.

I'll likely have to clean his plow again before he makes up his mind to wear the bridle, Dundee thought. *And I believe I could do it smiling.*

Dundee turned toward the cot where the cowboy lay. "What did they say his name was?"

Millie's hands were clasped nervously, as if she had expected a fight. "Tobe, I think they said."

The cowboy spoke, barely above a whisper. "Yes, it's Tobe. Tobe Crane."

Surprised, Dundee said: "I thought you was out like a dry lamp. By rights you could just as well've been dead. Didn't you have better sense?"

"Son was bound and bedamned. I had to try and help him."

Dundee frowned. "How old are you?"

"Twenty-one."

"If you want to reach twenty-two, you got some things to learn. One of them is to pick better friends. I'd as soon carry dynamite in my hip pocket as to ride with Son Titus."

"Son's all right. He's just trying to show his old

daddy . . . to be the old man all over again . . . and he don't know how."

"I hope he lives long enough to learn." Dundee's forehead furrowed. Underneath those bandages and that bruised skin, he thought there was something familiar about the face. "Wasn't you trying to help Son Titus bob my horse's tail in Titusville?"

"We didn't mean you no harm. I'm glad we didn't finish the job."

Dundee turned as if to go. The cowboy weakly lifted his hand. "Dundee, Son has got his faults, but he's got the makings. The old man knows it, but he don't know how to show it. He's afraid of making Son's head swell, I reckon. So he treats Son like a little boy, and Son keeps on trying to prove he's not. That's all that's the matter with him. You got to understand that about Son."

"Does the old man know Son went to Runaway?"

"No. He give Son orders to go north after a string of horses. Far as old John knows, there's where he went."

Dundee glanced at the girl, whose eyes warmed with sympathy as she looked down on the cowboy. "Millie'll take good care of you. Soon's you can stand the trip, I'll take you and Son home."

"That's decent of you, Dundee."

"I'm being paid for it."

Outdoors, he found Son Titus slumped in a rawhide chair beneath the brush arbor. Son gave Dundee a quick look with his good eye and cut his face away. "I ain't in no shape to fight you right now, Dundee. But I'll heal," he said.

8

The distant bawling of cattle drifted across the long valley and fell on Dundee's ears as welcome as the jingle of coin to a broke cowpuncher. Warren McCown was back. Dundee saddled his horse and rode south toward the sound, whistling.

Tobe Crane wasn't ready to be moved yet, but Dundee seriously considered taking Son Titus home anyway. He could come back for Tobe later, or send after him. The days of sitting here waiting had not improved Son's disposition much; he still prowled suspiciously, growled when spoken to and walked around like a crown prince waiting for the coronation.

It'll be worth half my wages to dump him in the old man's lap and then kiss him goodbye with the toe of my boot, Dundee thought.

He could see two riders slowly stringing the cattle along the creek. He could pick out Warren McCown by the way he sat his horse. The other man was a stranger, evidently a cowboy Warren had picked up to help him drive the herd. Dundee splashed the horse across the creek and rode up to Warren, his hand raised in the peace sign.

The bearded Warren nodded, eyes friendly. "Howdy, Dundee. If you want to check the brands, just help yourself."

"I don't reckon that'll be necessary."

"Do it anyway. Then you can tell old John Titus that I got none of his cattle here, and you can vouch for me."

Dundee rough-counted about a hundred mother cows. They carried two brands he had never seen before.

Warren said, "I can show you the bills of sale."

"You don't have to."

"I will anyway." Warren pulled them out of his pocket and extended them at arm's length. "Just in case anybody asks you."

Dundee nodded. Then he shoved his hand forward. "Pleased to see you back, Warren."

Suspicion crept into Warren's eyes. "How come you to know I'd been gone?"

"I been at your place several days."

Warren tried not to show it, but Dundee could see the sudden worry. "How's Millie?" Dundee could tell there was more Warren wanted to ask, but he wouldn't do it, not in words.

"She's fine."

"I don't like to go off and leave her there, just her and Uncle Ollie."

"Nobody's bothered her, Warren. I'll vouch for that."

Dundee could feel the keen probing of Warren's eyes, until Warren at last appeared satisfied. Dundee said: "I found her needing help, so I stayed. Uncle Ollie got himself hurt." He remembered the story the girl and the old man had made up for Warren. "Fell off of a horse. Was too shook up to do much for himself. He's better now, though."

Warren's eyes narrowed. "More than likely fell out of a rocking chair, if the truth was known. He's like my old daddy used to be, a gypsy. He'd starve to death if he didn't have somebody to lean on." Warren paused, embarrassed. "Sorry, Dundee. I know you got no interest in our family problems. I think the world of Uncle Ollie, but I know where his weakness is. I been fighting it all my life, in him, in my old daddy . . . even in myself."

Dundee shrugged. "Anyway, I can afford to leave now that you're home."

Warren stared at him a minute, silent. "Thanks for helping Millie. You didn't have to do it."

"I couldn't of left."

Warren frowned. "And I expect I know why. I could see it, the way you looked at her, the way she looked back at you. You're not for her, Dundee. She needs a man, and she'll get herself one. But you're not the kind, and I think you know it."

"You figure I got some gypsy in me, too?"

"You're not lazy, the way Uncle Ollie is. But you got a restlessness about you. You'll never stay put. Millie needs a man who'll make a home for her and stay there."

"I been wondering if maybe I could change."

"A colt may change color, but a grown horse never does."

They loose-herded the cattle along the creek awhile until the animals settled down and began to graze. Finally satisfied they would stay, Warren signaled the cowboy and pointed toward the house. The rider crossed the creek and waited on the other side. Warren introduced Dundee to him. "We'll treat him to a woman-cooked meal before he heads for home. He's been a lot of help."

The cowboy had nothing much to say. Dundee measured him with his eyes and decided the cowboy would probably take his wages and head for the nearest town to blow them in. That, in all likelihood, would be Runaway. He would ride out of there broke, sadder, but probably not wiser. Dundee knew. *He* had done the same thing more times than he cared to remember.

On the way in, Dundee recounted old Roan's bringing Son Titus.

Warren jerked his head around in surprise. "Son Titus, in *my* house?"

"I hope you don't mind."

Warren frowned deeply. "He's there, so I guess it don't make any difference. But old John Titus looks on all of us as cowthieves. I sure never expected to see any of his kin staying in my house."

"I'm figuring on getting him out pretty quick." Dundee paused. "I better warn you: he ain't the most likable sort you ever met. Chances are he'll insult you before you get out of the saddle."

"Then I'll probably hit him."

"Probably. I want you to know there won't be no hard feelings on my part."

"Wouldn't change things none if there was."

Dundee guessed that was why he had come to like Warren McCown. Warren had a way of saying what he thought, whether it crawled under your hide or not. Maybe sometime Dundee could bring John Titus around to meet him. The old ranchman appreciated a man who could stand flat-footed and tell him to go to hell.

Millie McCown threw her arms around her brother, paying no attention to two weeks' ragged growth of beard. Warren tolerated her tears for a smiling moment, then reminded her how hungry he and the cowboy were. She begged him to tell her about his trip.

"Nothing to tell," he said. "We come a long ways. No

excitement. Now we're mighty lank and looking for something to eat."

Son Titus had been poking around somewhere back of the house. He came up now as if the place belonged to him. He stopped at the corner and stared distrustfully at Warren McCown and the cowboy.

Warren's eyes narrowed a little. "Hello, Son Titus."

Son appeared puzzled. "I don't know you. How come you know me?"

"It don't matter. I know you."

Neither made a move to shake hands. Dundee said, "Son, this is Warren McCown."

Son said: "I figured that. He's got a little of the same looks as the girl, only not a bit pretty. Did you get a good look at the brands on them cattle?"

Warren answered for Dundee, his voice tight. "He did. And I also showed him the bills of sale. You want to see them too, Son? If you do, all you got to do is come and take them away from me."

Dundee guessed he ought to stop this before it went any farther, but he didn't make a move. It would be pleasureful to see Son Titus take a stomping.

Millie was the one who headed it off. "Warren, there's hot coffee on the stove. I expect it'd taste pretty good while you wait for me to cook some dinner."

Warren gave Son Titus a hard glance. "All right, Millie. I expect it would." He walked on into the cabin, the cowboy following. Dundee strode angrily toward Son Titus.

"Son, I wisht I knew what it is that ails you. That's a hell of a way to talk to a man after you've enjoyed the hospitality of his house."

"I ain't enjoyed it very much. You're keeping me prisoner."

"You're not a prisoner. You were wondering about them cattle. Why don't you saddle up and go look at them for yourself? You're free to ride."

"You're a slick one, ain't you? You know I ain't fixing to ride very far from here without a gun, and I know you got mine hid someplace."

"You'll get it back when I turn you over to your old daddy."

"I want it now."

"Fiddle with me very much and I'll give you something you *don't* want."

"You'll have to have a heap of help." Son turned on his heel and stalked toward the saddleshed. After several paces he stopped and looked back over his shoulder. "I *will* go see them cattle. Don't hold your breath waiting for me to come back. I'll be awhile."

"Take all the time you want to." The longer he was gone, Dundee figured, the quieter it would be around here.

Son didn't come in for dinner. Warren's cowboy collected his pay, burped happily and left in the general direction of Runaway, as Dundee had expected. A good deal later Son Titus came in. Dundee should have been warned by the triumph in his eyes. But Dundee was enjoying a minor triumph of his own. "You see them cattle all right?"

"I seen them."

"Satisfied they ain't from the T Bar?"

"I reckon."

"Next time maybe you won't be so hell-bent to accuse everybody."

"Maybe not."

Dundee stared in puzzlement as Son walked on by him toward the kitchen. It had been too easy. Up to now Dundee hadn't really won a single argument with Son, except that one in Titusville, and even there it had been a victory of muscle rather than will. In the days they had been here at the McCown place, Son had contested Dundee on almost everything he talked about except the weather. The only thing that had held Son here had been the knowledge that Dundee could clean his plow. As it was, Son stayed around on the edge of things, watching suspiciously from afar, coming in to eat or visit a little with the recuperating Tobe Crane, then drifting off by himself to simmer like a pot of beans at the back of the stove. He even kept his blankets out at the saddleshed and slept apart from the others.

Mostly Dundee had watched his eyes.

The whole time we been here, he's been dreaming up ways to even the score with me, Dundee thought. *Maybe now he thinks he's got something that'll work. He'll bear watching.*

And Dundee watched him, till at dusk Son strayed off toward the corrals as he always did, to sleep alone. To reassure himself, Dundee dug down through the wood in the big box behind the stove, till he found the six-shooters where he had put them. That eased his mind somewhat, for he had begun to suspect that Son might have found his gun.

Next morning Son didn't come in for breakfast. Dundee walked out to the corrals to fetch him and came hurrying back, breath short from running. "Anybody hear a horse leave last night?"

Warren McCown shook his head. "Son Titus run out on you, Dundee?"

"He's gone . . . horse, saddle and all."

McCown smiled thinly. "Can't say it grieves me much."

"It grieves the hell out of *me*. I can't figure him going off without a gun. . . ." A sudden thought struck him like he had been kicked by a yearling. "Warren, that cowboy with you yesterday . . . he was wearing a gun. . . ."

McCown nodded. "A .45, I think it was."

"Son didn't come in till an hour or so after your cowboy left here. I bet he waited out yonder someplace, stopped that feller and bought the gun off of him." Dundee choked down some words he thought Millie was too young to hear.

"Whichaway do you reckon he went?"

"I'll hunt for his tracks, but I think I already know."

He didn't bother trying to follow the trail. The destination was plain enough: Runaway. Dundee put the bay horse into a steady trot, his mind running wild with all manner of notions about the trouble Son Titus could have gotten himself into by now. He saw him being shot, knifed, stomped, clubbed and dragged at the end of a rope. It wouldn't displease Dundee to see any of these things happen to the fool kid, except that most of them were inclined to be so damned permanent.

He stopped at the crest of the hill and looked down over the motley stretch of the town, wondering which picket shack or rock saloon he would find Son Titus in . . . if any of them. By now the button might be lying dead on that riverbank someplace, cast out there like the empty bottles and rusting cans and bleaching cartridge boxes which littered the place, giving mute testimony to many a day and night of revelry and devilment in times past. Though he didn't want to, Dundee gazed a moment at the mercantile across from the Llano River Saloon, coldness touching him as he remembered Bunch Karnes slumping in a lifeless heap on the dirt street in front of it.

He reined up at the wagonyard, stood in his stirrups and peered over the picket fence, studying the horses penned there. He picked out the sorrel that Son Titus had ridden. Son was still here, then. At least, he hadn't left here horseback.

The liveryman was forking hay into a bunk made of cedar pickets. He stood the fork against a fence and came walking, taking his time. "Howdy." From the man's eyes Dundee knew he was recognized. "Something I can do for you, friend?"

Dundee pointed with his chin. "That sorrel yonder . . . what do you know about him?"

"Just that he's a horse." The man shrugged. "He's got a T Bar brand on him. Boy come in here last night, said he was old John Titus' son. I figured if he was telling the truth, fine. If he wasn't, stolen horses ain't no lookout of mine. Either way, *my* nose don't get skinned."

"You seen that boy this morning?"

"Nope."

"You know where he went?"

"I keep horses, that's all."

Dundee frowned. "Did you hear any shooting last night?"

"There's shooting most *every* night. Most times it's just in fun. Long's it don't hurt me none, I don't pay it any mind."

Dryly Dundee said, "Thanks, friend, you been real helpful." He headed the bay down the crooked street in a walk, gazing suspiciously at every shack as he passed it. He didn't know just what he was looking for. Whatever it was, he didn't find it. When he reached the far end of town he had seen nothing that would help him locate Son Titus. He started back.

His gaze fell upon Katy Long's Llano River Saloon and, inevitably, upon the place in the dirt where Bunch Karnes had fallen. A dun horse had stood hitched there quite a while, evidently, and he had left the sign of time's slow passage on the spot where Karnes' blood had soaked into the earth.

They don't honor death here much more than they honor life, Dundee thought.

He dismounted at the saloon and looked around a moment, warily gauging the prospect of a reception. There was none that he could see. But a tingling along his spine told him he wasn't being overlooked. He stretched to get the saddle-stiffness out of his muscles, then stepped into the saloon.

Katy Long sat at a table riffling a deck of cards. She gazed up at Dundee with the faintest suggestion of a smile. He would swear she was laughing at him. "What kept you?" she asked. "Son Titus got to town before midnight."

"I sleep late." He looked beyond her to the hallway. "I don't reckon he'd be in here someplace?"

She shook her head. "How'd he get out of his cage?"

"I forgot the lock. If he's not in here, where you reckon he's at?"

She continued to smile. "You were his age once. Where would you have gone?" When he didn't answer, she added, "You'll find them down the street, *way* down the street."

"How'll I know them?"

"You're old enough. You'll know them."

Dundee stared at this woman who seemed to enjoy sticking needles in him. "Last time I implied some things about *you*, you got awful mad," he said.

"I got mad because they weren't true. But you're not mad; you're smiling."

Dundee realized that he was, and he tried to put a stop to it. "You've made a big point about how all you sell is whisky. Will you sell me a drink?"

She said: "I sure hadn't figured on *giving* you one. Cricket, fetch Dundee some of our best. I figure he can afford it."

Dundee said: "I'll drink whatever old Roan Hardesty does. He ought to know his liquor."

She shook her head. "Don't take him for a model. He'll drink anything but coal oil. Sit down, Dundee."

"I figured one drink, then I'd go hunt for Son Titus."

"He's all right. If anything had happened to him, I'd have heard. You can take time to sit down and enjoy the whisky."

Dundee looked at the layout of the windows and moved to the other side of the table where the bar and a solid wall would be to his back.

Katy Long's smile faded. "You act like you've been in towns like this before."

"Not many, I'm glad to say. Mostly I've just cowboyed. It don't pay too good, but a man's back is safe." He seated himself, took the drink the bartender had put on the table in front of him and downed it. He frowned darkly. "If this is your good whisky, I'm glad I didn't ask for nothing cheap."

"We don't get a very choosy clientele here."

"Maybe you would, if you'd handle a better line of goods."

"You want to try it? I'd sell you the place cheap."

"It wouldn't be a good long-range investment, not here in Runaway."

"You don't think Runaway has a bright future?"

"And not very *long*, either. I figure old John Titus has got some plans for Runaway, and they ain't likely to be good for the whisky business. If somebody comes along and wants to buy this place, you sell it to him."

Her eyebrows went up a little. "How come you interested in my welfare, Dundee?"

He shrugged. "I don't put no burrs under my blanket, either way. But seeing how you patched up that Crane boy and Son Titus, I don't see no harm in trying to help you out of the gully before the flood comes down."

"You know how hard it is to kill a snake. Runaway won't die easy."

"John Titus has got it wrote down at the top of his list."

She was silent a time. "Well, I came by the place awfully cheap. I don't have a lot to lose." Her eyes narrowed. "Besides, John Titus may not be as tough as you think he is."

"Don't bet on it. If you get yourself an offer, sell." He pushed his chair back. "Enjoyed the hospitality, Miss

Long." He realized it was the first time he had called her that—or anything, really—in a respectful manner. "I'd best go find the cub and fetch him home."

"You be careful, Dundee. There's people here who would be tickled to death to pitch in and help pay for your funeral."

"I'll try to save them their money."

He stopped outside the door and took a long look up the street, then down. Again, he wasn't quite sure what he was looking for, but he figured he'd know when he saw it. The death of Bunch Karnes across the street was still on his mind, and he knew it hadn't been forgotten by the people around here, either. He swung into the saddle and started back down the street. He tried not to give the appearance of looking for trouble, but his eyes kept moving. He didn't intend to miss anything.

Down at the far end of town he'd seen a couple of long, narrow frame buildings that had not known the luxury of paint, though he'd seen a woman staring out a window who *had*. He could remember when such a place would have held fascination for him, and he reasoned it might be so for Son Titus. He swung down at the first house, tied the horse and walked in. The odor of cheap perfume and whisky and greasy cooking struck him across the face like a wet saddleblanket. A woman stood at an ironing board, pressing a dress with a heated flat-iron. She was perhaps thirty or so, dressed in nothing but a shift, sweat trickling down her surprised face, her blondish hair hanging in untended strings. Plainly, this wasn't during business hours.

"Mister," she said irritably, "don't you know what time it is? It's the middle of the day."

"I'm looking for a man."

"Most people come in here, they ain't looking for no *man*. There's none here."

Dundee looked past her at a long hallway that had small rooms leading off to one side. "I think I'll go and see for myself."

Face clouding, the woman raised her hand. "Not unless you want a faceful of hot iron, you don't."

She had *somebody* back there she didn't want seen, he figured. "You put that iron down or I'm liable to lay it against your broad rump and brand you like a white-faced heifer!"

She placed the iron back on the board. He started down the hall, opening doors, the woman following along cursing him. There were four doors, altogether. Inside the last room he found a man, but not Son Titus. Old Roan Hardesty was caught with his dignity down. He bawled, "Dammit, Dundee, didn't nobody ever teach you how to knock on a door?"

Dundee said, "Didn't go to bother you."

The woman was still cursing when he walked back to the front room. Dundee laid a few pieces of silver on the ironing board. "Buy yourself a bottle."

He was glad to get into fresh air again, but he knew the next house wouldn't be any better than this one. He stopped at the front door a moment, wishing he had another drink to fortify himself. These places were hell in the daylight.

Son Titus sat in the small parlor in a settee, his bare feet propped up on a soft chair, a bottle in his right hand, his left arm hugging a small blond girl tightly against him. Son grinned with triumph. "Come in this house,

Dundee. You're later than I figured you'd be. Old age must be slowing you down."

"I'm not too old, button."

"Well, then, I bet Lutie here can find you a friend."

"All I came for was *you*, and I ain't calling you friend."

"You sound mad, Dundee. You'd of done the same in my place."

"Get up and put your boots on, Son Titus. I'm taking you back."

Son Titus squeezed the girl. "I ain't going back. I like it fine right here with Lutie." The girl smiled at Son and pouted at Dundee. He could tell she had looked into that bottle a good many times.

Dundee pointed down the hall. He noticed this house was built just like the other one. "Girl, you go back yonder and find yourself something to do. I got business with Son."

Son Titus said: "I got no business with you, Dundee. I like it fine, right where I'm at."

Dundee spoke severely to the blonde, "I told you once already, get yourself out of here!"

Eyes wide, the girl got up, tightened her wrapper and weaved down the hall, anxiously looking backward, bumping her shoulder.

Son Titus brought his bare feet to the hooked rug. "Dundee, I'm getting awful tired of you."

"I ain't having much fun with you, either. Put your boots on."

Glaring, Son Titus set the nearly-empty bottle on a small table. His fists knotted. "What if I don't?"

"Then you'll go barefooted."

"I mean, what if I tell you I ain't going atall?"

Dundee took a long breath and let it out slowly in exasperation. "Son, you're too drunk to put up a good fight. But I will fight you if I have to. I'll whip you like I whipped you that night in Titusville, and I'll enjoy myself every minute of it."

Son pushed to his feet. "You want to start now?"

The blond girl hurried back down the hall, bringing with her a large, raw-boned woman with red hair who looked like a sister of the woman in the other house. The woman shouted: "No you don't! I ain't putting up with no fighting in my house. It cost me a wagonload of money for the furniture in here, and I won't allow no brawling drunks to go busting it up."

Must have been an awful little wagon, Dundee thought, looking at the old settee, the old painted table, the kerosene lamps.

Dundee nodded. "All right, Son, if you got to have it, we'll go outside and settle things."

Son's boots lay where he had kicked them off, in a corner. To put them on without sitting down, he had to stand on first one leg, then the other. Watching him, Dundee decided the button wasn't really very drunk, for he managed the job handily.

Dundee had known the time when he enjoyed a fistfight; it limbered him up, roused his blood into good circulation, quickened his heart like a big shot of whisky. Now he felt no relish for it. Not even getting to whip Son Titus seemed worth the effort. But if the job was to be done, he'd best be getting on with it, so he could put this infernal town behind him. He walked out the door and into the street. He glanced at his horse and moved well away from the bay. A horse could be a fool over something like a fistfight. Dundee chose a place and stood waiting for Son Titus to come out.

Son took his time. When he moved through the door, his step was steady, his eyes alert. Dundee wondered if he'd been drinking anything out of that bottle or if he'd just pretended and had been trying only to get the girl drunk.

Maybe he's shrewder than I figured him out to be.

Son's gaze touched Dundee, then darted away. He was reaching for his pistol as he shouted, "Look out, Dundee!"

Instinctively Dundee jumped aside, not sure whether Son Titus was about to shoot him or was going for someone else. A bullet smashed into the frame house even as he heard the crash of a rifle behind him. Dundee whirled, hand darting down and coming up with his six-shooter. Son Titus fired at someone across the street before Dundee got turned. Dundee caught a glimpse of a man at the corner of a picket-and-sod shack, feverishly levering another cartridge into the breech of his smoking rifle. Dundee fired once, knowing he was moving too fast and the distance was too much. He saw the slug kick dust from the shack's wall. Son Titus fired again, chipping wood from a picket just over the man's head. The bushwhacker brought the rifle up again, but he was flustered now with two men shooting at him. Dundee ran, zigzagging. The rifle flashed, but the bullet missed. The man turned and fled, limping badly.

Son Titus hollered, "Let's get him, Dundee!"

Dundee shouted back: "You stay right where you're at! I ain't packing you home dead!"

Dundee raced toward the shack. He could see the man ahead of him, running stiff-legged toward a horse, a lit-

tle too far for Dundee to hit him. The man swung into
the saddle and spurred hard, the rifle still in his hand.
Dundee took one more shot at him, knowing he was
throwing lead away but figuring he would feel better
about it if he at least made the try.

He stopped then to catch his breath, letting the smoking pistol hang at arm's length. He cursed a little because
he was angrier than he was scared. He knew who had
shot at him: Jason Karnes, brother of Bunch Karnes;
Jason Karnes, who had caught Dundee's bullet in his leg
in a cowthief camp.

*Looks like I'll be forced to put another bullet in him
before this is over with,* Dundee told himself regretfully.
I'll have to place that next one a mite higher up.

Son Titus said proudly, "Well, we run him off, didn't
we, Dundee?"

Dundee nodded, sober. "I reckon we did. Thanks,
Son. If you hadn't hollered, he'd of probably taken me
with that first shot."

Son said, "Then I reckon you owe me something."

"I reckon. What?"

"Go off and leave me alone. I ain't finished all my
business with Lutie, and you're sure putting a crimp in
things."

Dundee frowned. "Son, I'd do anything I rightly could
to pay you back. But if I was to leave you here, I wouldn't
be doing you no favor. No sir, you're coming on with me
the way we started."

Son's voice flattened. "You mean after what I done for
you . . ."

"After what you done for me, you're still going back
to your old daddy. Now get your horse."

"Like hell I will!"

He stood there within easy reach, and Dundee didn't feel like a prolonged argument. He put his pistol back into the holster, balled his right hand into a fist and brought it up with all his strength behind it. It caught Son flat-footed, but it didn't leave him that way. He lay on his back in the street, shaking his head and blinking.

Son rubbed his jaw, flinching from the unexpected pain. "I swear, Dundee, you sure hit a man hard."

"It helps shorten an argument."

Son's eyes were glazed a little. "If I hadn't saved your life, you'd of been mad at me. I *did* save it, and you won't do me a favor."

"I *am* doing you a favor. I'm getting you out of Runaway while your health is good."

9

As they topped the hill, Son Titus looked back over his shoulder at Runaway below. "I wasn't finished down there."

"Yes, you was," Dundee said.

That was the last Son Titus spoke for many miles. He rode along with his head down, sleeping on horseback. It suited Dundee all right, for so long as Son was asleep he wasn't belly-aching.

I ought to charge old John Titus double for this job, he thought. *Hunting cowthieves is what I hired for. I didn't come here to wetnurse a chuckleheaded button.*

But now and again he would glance at the relaxed face of Son Titus and feel something vaguely akin to liking. Son could have stood there and let Karnes shoot him, but he hadn't. He had pitched in. Maybe it wasn't because he felt any desire to help Dundee; maybe he just wanted the excitement. No matter; if it hadn't been for Son Titus, Dundee knew he'd probably be the cause of somebody having to do a job of digging in the rocky ground that was Runaway's Boothill.

Son Titus stirred finally. He blinked, shut his eyes a while, blinked some more and came awake. His face twisted as he worked up spittle and tried to clear his mouth of a bad taste. "How far we come?"

"A ways. You ought to swear off of whisky."

"Truth is, *she* done most of the drinking. I didn't really drink much. Just a few little snorts."

Dundee had sort of guessed that.

Son said: "I figured a girl like her would hear lots of things. Figured if she got to drinking it'd loosen her tongue up, and then maybe I'd find out something."

"Did it work thataway?"

"Some. Mostly it made her affectionate. Of course, there wasn't nothing wrong with *that*, neither."

"What did you find out, when she wasn't being affectionate?"

"Found out a little about you, Dundee. Found out they're scared of you in Runaway."

"Did that convince you I ain't no cowthief?"

"Why else you reckon I'd've bothered to holler at you when that feller was fixing to let air through your brisket?"

"I sort of wondered."

"Well, it wasn't on account of your good looks and disposition."

At length they came to a creek, its clear water gurgling over the big polished stones that lay in its shallow bed. Son Titus licked his lips. "Last night I wouldn't of give you a nickel for all the water in Kingdom Come. Now it's worth ten dollars a gallon. I'm going to step down and drink up about a hundred dollars worth."

Son dropped on his belly and stretched out over the creek's bank, cupping the palm of his right hand to bring water up so he didn't have to dip his face under. He drank long and thirstily, pausing only to catch his breath.

"Ain't you afraid that stuff'll rust your gut?" Dundee asked.

"Not with the coating I put on it last night."

Dundee watered the horses. Son Titus finally seemed satisfied. He pushed to his feet, wiping his sleeve across his mouth. "Nectar of the gods. You ought to try it, Dundee."

Dundee hadn't noticed being thirsty, but he guessed it was the power of suggestion, watching Son Titus, "It's a ways yet to the next water. I reckon maybe I will."

He stretched out on the bank, a little above where Titus had lain. He was drinking when he heard Son's saddle creak and felt the reins jerked from his left hand. He rolled over and jumped to one knee. Son Titus was riding his own horse and leading Dundee's up the creekbank. Out of reach, Son paused to look back. "Go on and drink your fill, Dundee. You got lots of time."

"You bring my horse back here, Son Titus!"

"I hope you're a good walker, Dundee. It's a far piece

back to Runaway, or out to McCown's, whichever way you decide to go. Me, *I* could tell you where to go."

"Son Titus. . . ."

"Like I said, Dundee, I ain't finished all my business in Runaway yet. That's where you'll find your horse." He swung his sorrel around and led the bay. "Adios, Dundee. Enjoy yourself."

"You crazy button, I'll. . . ." Dundee broke off as he watched Son ride away laughing, into the lengthening shadows. He hurled his hat to the ground. He wanted to stomp it, but that wouldn't have been enough. One of these days he'd stomp Son Titus instead. Times, he wished he'd never strayed through Titusville, had never seen old John Titus or Son. He ought to turn his back on the whole damned mess and let them steal the T Bar blind.

But he knew he was in it too far to pull out now. He'd follow on through. But one of these days, when it was over. . . .

He clenched his fists and recited Son Titus' ancestry for several generations back.

Dundee was a cowboy, and cowboys seldom walked. It was contrary to their religion. A cowboy would descend into many types of sin before he would risk blisters on his feet. Dundee considered the distance. It might be a little shorter to the McCown place than to Runaway, but not enough to offset the time it would take to get a horse at McCown's and ride all the way back. Another thing, the trail back to Runaway was easier followed in the dark.

Muttering, he climbed the creekbank. He slipped,

caught himself, hurled a rock as far as he could throw it and started the long walk.

The night was far gone when he finally got to Runaway. Legs aching, feet blistered and sore, his anger simmering like bitter roots being boiled for backwoods medicine, he dragged himself up to the front gate of the wagonyard. Down the street he could see most of the buildings standing dark. A lantern still flickered in front of the Llano River Saloon, one at another bar farther along. Way down at the end of the street he saw a dim red glow.

The small barn was dark. Well, by George, if *he* was awake, everybody else had just as well be. "Hey!" he shouted. "Where's the man that runs this place?"

He heard a grumbling from a blanket spread on hay in the corner. He struck a match and held it down close. The drunken face he saw there, the eyes blinking in confusion, did not belong to the man he was looking for. "Hey! Stableman, wake up!"

From another corner he heard the squeak of steel cot-springs as a man turned over on his blankets. "You damned drunks . . . you won't let a sober man get no sleep. Go find your own horse and leave me be."

In the reflected moonlight Dundee made out a lantern. He lighted it and turned up the wick. "I ain't drunk."

The yardman swung his bare feet off to the ground. He was wearing long underwear, only half buttoned. He yawned, then peered irritably at Dundee. "Oh, it's you. You'll find your horse in the corral and your saddle on the fence. That button left them here."

"How long ago?"

"I don't know. I been asleep."

"Is his horse here too?"

"He kept his. Just left yours."

"Whichaway did he go this time?"

"Like I told you before, I don't notice nothing that ain't my business. That way my health stays good. Now, take your horse and get out of here so I can go back to bed."

Dundee saddled, swung up and started to ride down the street. The yardman met him, still barefoot and in the long-handles. "Wait, cowboy, you owe me a hay bill."

"How much?"

"Two bits. I ought to charge you extra for waking me up."

Dundee dug for it. A thought struck him. "You heard any shooting in town since that boy came in?"

The stableman held the coin into the moonlight and fingered it suspiciously. "Since you ask me, I heard a couple shots down the street."

"Do you know what happened?"

"Yep. I turned over and went back to sleep."

Dundee rode down the dark street, glad to be off of his sore feet and glad most of the town was asleep. He hoped Jason Karnes was, too. To be on the safe side, he reached down and drew the carbine from its scabbard.

Keeping out of the lantern's glow, he peered inside the Llano River Saloon. He saw the bulky figure of Roan Hardesty hunched over a table studying a hand of cards. Opposite him, Katy Long sat waiting for him to make his play. Best Dundee could tell, most of the chips were on her side.

Dundee rode to the house where he had found Son Titus the last time. He didn't see Son's horse tied anywhere. The house was dark now, except for the glow of a lantern in one of the rooms in the far back. Dundee walked partway back for a look-see, but a curtain was drawn across the window. He returned to the front, pushed the door open and walked in.

"Son Titus! You in here?" No reply. "Son Titus, I come to get you!"

He heard movement down the hall. He brought the carbine up, just in case. A door opened and lamplight came floating toward him, a long shadow preceding a woman. She stopped, the lamp in her hand, her eyes blinking in sleepiness. "What's going on in here? Don't you know what time it is? Decent folks are all asleep."

It was the same red-haired, raw-boned woman he had crossed before. Her stringy hair and the pouches under her eyes didn't help her looks any. Dundee said: "Son Titus came back in here tonight. I want him."

The woman scowled. "He ain't here."

Dundee saw no reason to accept her word. "Where's that girl he was with, the one called Lutie?"

"Lutie's asleep. You ain't going to bother her."

"I asked where she's at." Dundee took two long steps toward the woman. She began to retreat. "Now, mister. . . ."

"I'll find her if I have to tear this place apart. Her and him both. Now, where's she at?"

Grumbling, the woman turned down the hallway, still carrying the lamp. "She's back thisaway. But you ain't going to find out much talking to her."

She opened a door and pointed. The girl lay across a brass bed, her loose gown pulled halfway up her legs, the blanket thrown off.

"Lutie," Dundee demanded, "Where's Son Titus?"

The girl stirred but never opened her eyes. Dundee noticed a bottle lying by the bed. It was empty.

The woman said: "That friend of yours, he brought that bottle with him. Must of let her drink most of it by herself. Time he left here, she was so drunk you'd of thought he'd hit her with a sledge. She won't be worth nothing for two days. It's a sin the way that girl likes whisky. It'll be the ruin of her one of these times."

Dundee grasped the girl's shoulder and shook her. "Lutie, I want to find Son Titus."

The girl moaned, but that was all.

The woman said: "Like I told you, you ain't going to get nothing out of her. She's too drunk."

Dundee stepped back, hand tight on the carbine. Where would he go from here?

"How long's Son been gone?"

"Must've been midnight . . . one o'clock. After he left, I came to see about Lutie. This is the way I found her." She glared. "When you find that Titus, you tell him I don't want him back in here again, ever. He's a bad influence on my girls."

Dundee turned to go. "One more thing. Feller told me he heard some shooting tonight. Was that before Son left, or after?"

The red-haired woman rubbed a hand across her face, trying to remember. "There's always some drunk shooting a pistol around here. I expect it was Titus done it. He left here looking awful satisfied with himself."

Dundee glanced once more at Lutie. *I'll bet.*

Frustrated, uncertain, Dundee walked outside. At the house next door, a woman stepped to the little porch and blew out a red lantern, then retreated inside. That was the house Dundee had searched yesterday, looking for Son Titus. He considered looking again, but he figured Son wouldn't have left Lutie's place to go to another just like it. Dundee looked up the street. The only light he could see now was the single lantern in front of Katy Long's saloon. The rest of the town was in its blankets.

Dundee swung onto the bay and rode back up there. He tied the horse in the darkness and walked around to the rear of the place. He found a rear door and tried it. It was unlocked. He entered the dark hall and carefully made his way along it, guided by the moonlight through the windows. At the door leading into the main room of the saloon, he stopped to look for a moment before stepping into the lamplight. He saw only two people: Katy Long and old Blue Roan. Roan was gulping a shot of whisky and watching Katy rake in another pile of chips.

Dundee said, "You ought to know better than to gamble with a good-looking woman."

Roan turned quickly, surprised. His hand dropped toward his pistol, then stopped as his blinking eyes recognized Dundee. Katy Long was startled, but she never moved.

Roan recovered his composure. "How come, Dundee? I'd rather play cards with a good-looking woman than with any of the ugly men I've gambled with."

"Hard to keep your mind on the cards."

Katy Long said evenly: "I believe that's the first compliment you've paid me, Dundee. You must want something."

"I want Son Titus. Where's he at?"

She smiled thinly. "You'd make a mighty poor jailer,

Dundee. Can't even keep one tight-britches kid under control."

"He was in here, wasn't he?"

She nodded. "Bought another bottle, early in the evening. Said you'd probably come in sometime during the night. Enjoy your walk, Dundee?"

He ignored the barb. "My feet are sore and my patience is run out. I want to know if you saw Son Titus any more after he bought that bottle?"

"Nope. You'll probably find him where you found him yesterday."

"I already looked. He left."

"Then there's not much telling. Maybe he went home."

"Shots were fired somewhere on the street a while ago. What were they?"

Katy glanced at Old Roan, and both of them shrugged. Roan said: "Some drunk, most likely. I didn't hear any more commotion, so I didn't go look." He added ruefully, "I was winning at the time."

Dundee glanced at the pile of chips in front of the woman. "That must've been a *long* while ago."

Katy said seriously: "Dundee, he probably went home. You look like you need sleep. I can fix you up with a cot back yonder. You can go find him in the morning."

"I'll sleep after I've found him. I think I'll tie him to a wagonwheel with wet rawhide and then sleep while the hide dries."

Roan said: "I still got orders out, Dundee. Nobody hurts him."

"Does everybody obey your orders?"

"Not always."

"That's why I got to find him before some of your boys do. If they haven't already."

Dundee turned to go. His tired legs betrayed him, and he almost fell. Roan Hardesty's big mouth turned downward sourly. "He just thinks he's going someplace. You better bed him down, Katy. Next time I'll get them chips on *my* side of the table again."

She smiled. "Glad to give you the chance. Bring lots of money."

"I always do. But I seldom leave here with any." He looked at Dundee. "Wherever that boy's at, he'll keep till daylight. You rest yourself. Where's your horse?"

"Out back."

"I'll drop him off at the wagonyard. Good night, Katy."

"Good night, Roan."

Dundee slumped in a chair and watched Katy Long rake the poker chips into a small leather bag. "You always beat him like that?"

"I let him win now and again, so he doesn't lose hope."

"Crafty, ain't you?"

"I've been taking care of myself in a man's world for a good many years now. I think I know how." She counted and sacked more chips, glancing up occasionally at Dundee. She had poker player's eyes; he couldn't tell what she was thinking. Finally she said: "You're really worried about that thick-headed kid, aren't you?"

"I'm mad enough to chew up nails and spit them in his face."

"But worried, just the same?"

He nodded.

She said: "You know, Dundee, the first time I saw you I figured you were just another tough drifter with a cartridge case where your heart ought to be. But I believe I misjudged you. Times, you're damn near human."

She arose, walked to the front and blew out the lantern that hung on the porch. She shut the door and came back, lighting a lamp that sat on the end of the bar. "Blow out that overhead lamp for me. Then come on back and I'll show you a bed."

He followed her out of the dark saloon and into the hall. She opened the door to the room where she had treated Jason Karnes' wound so many weeks ago. He said: "I'll sleep a while, then slip out. I'll try not to make any fuss when I go."

She stood in the doorway, holding the lamp. Dundee stared at her a moment, a strong urge building in him. He reached up and took her chin and kissed her. She backed off a step, surprised.

"What was that for?"

"I just wanted to do it."

Her eyes studied him unflinchingly. "Comparing me to that country girl?"

"That's not it. . . ."

"Well, do I measure up?"

He shook his head, not knowing what to say. "It's like I told you out yonder that day . . . I haven't touched her. I. . . ."

"You've wanted to."

"Sure I've wanted to. I just ain't done it."

"So you come to me, figuring anything you do to me is all right."

Angering, he said: "I didn't mean to get your hackles

up. I don't have to sleep here if you don't want me to. I'll just go on like I'd figured to in the first place."

She stared at him awhile longer, and he thought he saw the laughter come back into her eyes. She blew out the lamp and set it on a table. She said: "Empty talk, Dundee. You're not a man to start something and not finish it. You'll stay right here."

10

He was up at daylight, dressing quietly to try to keep from awakening Katy Long. But the tinkle of a spur rowel brought her eyes open. She reached out and caught his hand. Her sleepy eyes smiled. "No goodbyes?"

"Hadn't figured on it. I got to find Son Titus."

"You'll be back."

"Better not count on it."

She repeated confidently, "You'll be back."

He walked to the livery barn, where the yardman wanted to charge him another hay bill for the bay horse.

"I paid you once. He ain't been back here long enough to eat any more hay."

"I put it out, and it gets eaten up. I don't know which ones eat it and which ones don't. So they all pay or they don't leave this corral."

"You're a thief."

"Who here ain't? Two bits, friend."

Dundee paid him. The carbine across his lap, he rode down the street for another look by daylight. He saw nothing of Son Titus' sorrel. He rode around back and followed the alleyway, thinking he might find the horse tied somewhere there. That proved to be a waste of time. He scouted the riverbank, but still he found nothing.

Katy and Roan could have been right, he knew. Son could have gotten his fill of town and gone back to the McCown place. It might have been that he wanted to postpone facing up to Dundee for setting him afoot.

Those shots that had been fired during the night still nagged at him a little. True, the chances were it had been some cowboy sharing his celebration with the whole town. But there was always a chance. . . .

Dundee stopped and had breakfast in a saloon that doubled as a restaurant of sorts. He wondered if their whisky was as bad as their cooking and decided it probably was. He rode up the hill looking back over his shoulder, the carbine still across his lap as the sun started to climb. Then he lined out toward the McCown ranch, setting the bay into a steady trot.

It was late morning when he arrived. He rode straight for the saddleshed, looking for sign of Son's sorrel. The horse wasn't there. Well, he thought, maybe Son turned him loose to graze. After all, he'd put in an awful lot of miles. Dundee turned his bay out. He could borrow something from Warren if he had to ride again.

Millie McCown stood in the door, apron tied around her slender waist. Her eyes were wide as she watched him approach, but he could see relief in them. She stepped out to meet him, her hands forward to grasp him. "We were worried about you."

Her fingers were warm, but he pulled his hands away. He tried not to look at her. Remembering Katy Long, he found it hard to meet this girl's eyes. "I'm all right. Did Son Titus come back?"

"You mean you didn't find him?"

"I found him, then I lost him. He hasn't been here?"

She shook her head. "We haven't seen him."

The worry that had nagged him all the way out here descended on him like a dark and gloomy cloud. Of a sudden he was certain something had happened to Son Titus, something a lot worse than Dundee himself had planned to do to him.

In the cabin he found Tobe Crane sitting up on the edge of his cot, his sock feet on a small rug Millie had made. Tobe's arm and shoulder were still tightly bound with clean white cloth. His face was pale, but it seemed to have more color in it than Dundee had seen before. "Dundee, you didn't find Son?"

Briefly Dundee told what had happened, though he left out those parts which might have brought a blush to Millie.

Tobe said: "Could be he was afraid to answer to you, Dundee. Could be he went straight back to his old daddy at the T Bar."

"Do you believe that, Tobe?"

Tobe shook his head. "Nope."

Dundee chewed the inside of his lip, his eyes narrowing. "I got a bad feeling about it. I can't put my finger on it, but I know. Harm's come to him."

Tobe pushed himself to his feet. "I'll help you find him." Tobe swayed, and for a moment it looked as if he would fall. Dundee rushed toward him, but Millie was closer. She grabbed Tobe and eased him back onto the cot, her face drained with sudden anxiety. "Tobe. . . ."

Dundee saw how Tobe clung to the girl's hand for a minute after he was on the cot. "You're not ready to go anywhere yet, Tobe."

Across the room, old Ollie McCown stiffly got up from a chair and hobbled a few steps toward Dundee. "I'll go with you. If somebody can help me get *on* a horse, I can ride him."

Dundee watched the old man till he was sure Ollie could do it. "Much obliged, Ollie. I'll be needing help. Where's Warren?"

Millie said: "He went out this morning to check on the new cattle and be sure they're not trying to drift south again. They do that, you know, till they get used to new range."

"You looking for him to come in to dinner?"

She nodded.

Dundee said: "Then we'll wait. Maybe three of us can locate Son."

They split at the creek, the three of them, each to scout a strip of the land that lay between there and Runaway. Dundee himself took the middle one, where the trail ran, for he felt that was the most likely place. Possibly somebody had followed Son Titus out of town and waylaid him. Dundee crisscrossed back and forth, slowly working toward town. In the back of his mind those shots kept ringing, the ones he had heard about in Runaway.

If they'd killed Son, they perhaps had buried him by now. Old John Titus' boy might never be found. But then, there was Son's horse. Somewhere, somebody had to have that sorrel, and it would be a giveaway.

The sun was low when Dundee sat on the hill looking down upon Runaway. He had searched out its streets and alleys this morning, and the riverbank. But he hauled the carbine out of the scabbard and laid it across his lap, knowing he had to look again. He touched spurs to the dun horse he had borrowed from McCown.

Old Roan Hardesty sat on his big gray horse in the middle of the street and watched Dundee ride in. He glanced at the carbine, then shifted his gaze to Dundee's face. "Back again? You been here enough lately that you'd almost qualify to vote."

"I'm still looking for Son Titus. Do you know something you ought to tell me, Roan?"

The old outlaw appeared surprised. "You know as much as I do. I told you I give orders. . . ."

"And you told me not everybody obeys them orders."

"Son Titus ain't in Runaway, Dundee. If he was, I'd know it."

"But he *was* in Runaway, and he ain't showed up anyplace else. Don't that make you wonder, Roan?"

The old man looked genuinely regretful. "I wish I knowed something to tell you." His gaze lifted. Dundee saw the blue spots seem to darken in the aging face as Roan stared past him. Dundee turned in the saddle. His blood went cold.

Two horsemen were coming down the hill, leading a third horse. It was a sorrel. And it had something tied across it.

Dundee turned his dun slowly around, his throat knotting. He didn't have to see any more. He knew.

Warren and Ollie McCown had found Son Titus, and they were bringing him in.

Dundee sat slumped in the saddle, numb, as the two riders came slowly down the street to meet him. At length they reined in, their horses almost touching noses with his dun. Dundee's gaze fastened on the slicker-wrapped bundle tied across the trailing sorrel. He tried to speak, but his throat was too full.

Warren McCown said quietly: "I found him out yonder, a ways from town."

Old Roan Hardesty rode up closer, his face gray in shock, the blue splotches standing out like tar spots. "Dundee, I swear to you. . . ."

Dundee found his voice, and it was bitter. "Any swearing you want to do, Roan, you better do it to old John Titus. I expect you'll get the chance."

He turned his back on the big outlaw. "Warren, it's too far to take him home to his old daddy. I'd like to bury him on your place somewhere. It's sort of friendly ground."

Warren nodded soberly. "It's a long ways. We better get started."

11

Dundee had seen men die, but old John Titus was the first he ever saw die and yet live. The ranchman scarcely moved as Dundee told him, but the blood slowly drained from his face, leaving it the color of ashes. The bright fire of life seemed to die away and go to nothing more than coals. The strong old hands knotted, the leaders standing out like strands of rope. Dundee thought he heard a single sobbing sound escape from John Titus' throat, but there was no other, and he was never sure. For a long time the old man sat there, blank eyes staring past Dundee into the infinity that only the mind can see.

Dundee wasn't sure the rancher was hearing him, but he went on and told the whole thing from beginning to end—most of it, anyway. At last he brought out the tally book and the map and laid them on the rolltop desk. Quietly he said: "I done what I set out to do, sir. I got it all here on paper, the just and the unjust alike."

The voice that spoke was not the same one which had welcomed Dundee at the door. It was a broken voice now, barely above a whisper. "Would you show me where you buried him, Dundee?"

"I'd want to, sir."

"There'll be more to do after that, Dundee. Will you stay with me?"

"I'd figured on it."

"You done real good." The old man's chin dropped a little. "Who was it you said owned the land you buried him on?"

"McCown, sir. The name's McCown."

"McCown." Titus seemed to test the word like he'd test a pot of beans.

"Maybe you've met them sometime."

"Maybe so." John Titus' eyes closed for a minute. "Dundee, go fetch my foreman, Strother James. We got plans to make."

* * *

Millie McCown had fashioned a wooden cross and placed it at the grave. The minister John Titus had brought read words from the Bible. A pale Tobe Crane stood bare-headed in the sun, his good hand clasped with Millie's. Dundee noticed, and regret touched him, but it was covered over by the regret he felt as he watched old John Titus crush his hat in his hands, looking down at the mound of earth which was all he would ever again see of his son.

Around the grave stood some thirty men, each wearing a pistol, each holding a horse that carried a full supply of ammunition in bulging saddlebags. Some wore badges that John Titus had browbeaten the sheriff into passing out as he deputized the lot of them. There hadn't been nearly enough badges to go around. Dundee had not chosen to wear one, for somehow he felt ill at ease that close to a star. The legal authority was vested in the badges. The practical authority they all carried in their holsters, and in the saddle scabbards that bristled with carbines and shotguns.

The minister finished his prayer. The cowboys waited awkwardly for John Titus to put his hat on, then they followed suit, their attention focused on the old man. John Titus shook hands with the minister. "Thanks, preacher. Now I reckon you better be heading back, for the Lord's work here is done. What comes next is the devil's own."

The minister was a thin old man of about Titus' age, badly used up by the rigors of the range country. He said: "I'd rather stand by you, John. I think you'll have need of me before it's done."

But John Titus wouldn't let him.

Tobe Crane took his good hand from Millie's grasp and held it out toward John Titus. "I'll be going with you."

The old man glanced at the bound arm. "Much obliged, boy, but you'd best stay here and mend. I won't forget that you got them wounds helping Son."

"He was my friend. That's why I'm going with you."

Dundee broke in. "You won't be able to keep up, Tobe."

"I'll keep up. You won't have to slow down none for me."

Dundee was about to tell Tobe again that he couldn't go, but John Titus cut him off. "Then, boy, you come on along." The old man turned his attention to the girl. "Much obliged to you and your family, miss, for everything you done. I won't forget it."

Warren McCown stood to one side, watching but not quite a part of it. Titus said to him: "What I told your sister, I meant. If ever there's something I can do for you. . . ."

Warren shook his head. "We'll do all right."

Titus turned to Dundee and his thirty or so men. "Boys, we got us a job to do."

Ahead of them, atop a gentle slope that led down toward a narrow creek, sat a cabin of liveoak logs, with a rude lean-to of cedar and a set of brush corrals rambling away lazily toward the hill. Three horses were staked on green grass, their ropes long enough to allow them to go down to the creek for water. In front of the cabin three saddles lay dumped on the ground, blankets flopped across them.

Three saddles, three men, Dundee thought.

When they had left the McCown place, John Titus had said, "Lead out, Dundee." Dundee hadn't realized the old man meant for him to take command. Now as they looked down on the cabin, old Titus said, "What you planning to do, Dundee?"

"I was planning on taking orders."

"I was planning on you giving them."

Dundee's jaw dropped. "I'm no Ranger or general or nothing like that. I been a cowboy all my life."

"You're drawing a right smart more than cowboy pay. I'm counting on you to earn it." With that, the old man just pulled back and checked it to him.

Dundee chewed a little, though there was nothing in his mouth for him to chew on. What smattering of knowledge he had about gunfighting was of a personal nature, man to man. It didn't cover military tactics. What's more, the men with him were cowboys for the most part, not gunhands, though Titus' foreman Strother James had managed to round up a few men who had had experience either packing a star or avoiding one; it would be hard to tell which.

Dundee figured he would have to put most of his hope in those, and in the caprices of Lady Luck, who on occasion had been known to spit in his eye.

He made a sweeping motion with his arm, signaling for a surround. He sat on the bay horse and watched while the men spread out and around the cabin, shutting off any chance for escape by the men inside. Right away he saw his first mistake. The way the posse had tightened the ring, there was no way for anyone to shoot without taking a chance of hitting one of his own men. Dundee signaled for the riders on the opposite side to move up the hill, out of the line of fire.

This was a soldiering job, and for a moment he wished he were old enough to have been in the war, so he would be sure what he was up to. But hell, he would be old and gray now, and fighting off the rheumatism.

The cabin door opened. A bareheaded man stepped out in red underwear, denim britches and long-eared boots. He walked along with head down, whistling. At the woodpile he picked up a chunk of mesquite and placed it across the chopping block. When the ax fell, Dundee started his bay forward, wondering how long it would be before the posse was seen. The woodchopper was so preoccupied, Dundee got close enough that he could chunk a rock at him. These renegades had stolen cattle here so long with absolute impunity there was no reason to suspect the puckerstring was about to draw shut.

The ax stopped its swing above the chopper's head. He gasped at Dundee, then let his gaze drift slowly to the other riders spread out across the flat. He stood that way for long seconds, the ax raised, his mouth and eyes wide. Of a sudden he flung the ax behind him and turned to run for the shack.

"Stop!" Dundee called. The man halted in midstride. Dundee let his voice drop a little. "You'd never make the door. If you don't want some new holes opened up in you, better turn around here and see how high you can raise them hands."

The rustler turned slowly, shaking. Dundee stepped down and handed the reins to the angular old brushpopper Strother James. He slapped the palms of his hands against the outlaw's pockets and down against his boottops.

"No gun. Wouldn't of been no use to you anyway. I take it there's still two men in the shack."

The outlaw swallowed, his stubbled neck quivering. He tried to speak, but nothing came out. He nodded instead, his eyes darting from one rider to another, frightened as a rabbit's. Dundee guessed he was looking at the ropes on their saddles.

"Do what I tell you and maybe you won't have to try one of them on for size," Dundee said. "You call to your friends in there and tell them to come on out. Tell them we got them hemmed in tighter than Maggie's britches."

For a minute he was afraid the outlaw was going to be of no use to him, for the man was so scared that his voice wouldn't function. "Give her another try," Dundee said firmly.

The outlaw cupped his hands around his mouth. "Jake! Hawk! They got us! You better come out!"

Dundee kept the outlaw between him and the cabin. He drew his pistol and stood waiting, his heart quickening. He saw motion at a window. A man stepped out of the door, crouching warily, rifle in his hand. He looked at the ring of horsemen and realized he had made a mistake. "Arnie, what's going on out here?"

Dundee said, "Drop the rifle and walk this way."

The outlaw still crouched, his head turning slowly as he counted the men who waited for his decision.

He made the wrong one. He decided to try for the cabin. Dundee leveled his pistol but never squeezed the trigger. A rifle roared in old John Titus' hands, and half a dozen more shots exploded in the space of a second or two. Dundee could see the puffs of dust as the bullets struck, twisting the outlaw, one way, slamming him another. The rifle flew out of the man's grasp. He fell without a whimper, cut to pieces.

Dundee heard the outlaw in front of him whisper "God!" and sink to his knees. The horses danced in fear at the sudden fusillade, smoke rising from half a dozen guns. He heard excited shouts from men who hadn't been able to see, wanting to know what was going on.

Dundee caught his breath. "You still got one friend in there. If he's any friend atall, you better tell him to come out with his hands up."

Arnie found his voice this time. "Jake, Hawk's dead. They got him. You come on out while you still can."

The door opened cautiously. Dundee saw the barrel of a rifle and leveled his pistol on it. The rifle was thrown onto the ground. The door opened wider and a man swayed out, his arms held straight up. "Don't shoot! Don't nobody shoot!"

Dundee motioned him forward. The men rode in closer, covering the outlaws with their rifles and shot-guns and six-shooters. Dundee turned and stared a moment at all the hardware, and he felt almost as nervous as these cowthieves. That much artillery in the hands of a bunch of cowboys was enough to make a man break out into a cold sweat. "You boys be careful with them guns. We want to be damn choosy who we kill."

John Titus edged his horse forward. He leaned on his saddlehorn and stared down at the two cowthieves, his eyes hard as steel. "Dundee, you reckon these two could've done it? You reckon they killed Son?"

Dundee knew he had to be careful how he answered, for the old man's fingers inched down to touch his rope. "These two ain't no more likely than anybody else."

Dundee could see the temper in the eyes of the men around him. If old Titus said the word, they'd hang these two from the nearest liveoak. Dundee held his breath. That kind of a show wasn't what he had come for.

Titus stared a long time before he said: "Tie them on their horses. We'll take them with us to the next place."

Strother James fingered his gray-laced beard, then pointed to the dead man. "What about him?"

"What *about* him? Leave him there."

Pistol in hand, Dundee approached the shack. He was reasonably sure the three men were all who had been here, but in a situation like this the man who took things for granted might not be around to celebrate next Christmas. He kicked the door open and leaped inside. A quick glance told him he was by himself. He slipped the pistol back into its holster. Seeing a lantern hanging from the ceiling, he took it and emptied the kerosene along the walls. In a corner he found a coal oil can that felt as if it were half full. He poured fuel onto the outside walls, then stepped back and struck a match on the sole of his boot. He flipped it into a patch of dry grass at the base of the wall. The flame grabbed the kerosene and raced up toward the roof, crackling. Dundee heard the horses snort in fear of the fire.

The outlaw named Arnie said plaintively, "I got a little money hid in there."

Dundee watched the flames lick across the wall and find their way into the cabin, the dark smoke aboil. "You *had* a little money in there," he corrected.

* * *

They moved fast and struck hard, over the hills, up the valleys, following Dundee's map, picking up one thief's camp and then another, leaving behind them smoke and flame. During that blazing afternoon one more outlaw showed the poor judgment to come out with rifle firing, and he stayed there on the spot where he had fallen, dead before his dropped weapon ever struck the ground.

Through it all, old John Titus never let age cause him to falter or drop behind. He moved in silence, his gaunt face like darkened rawhide dried on a stretching frame. He watched the gradually-increasing string of prisoners brought along on their own horses, hands thong-tied to saddlehorns. Titus had nothing to say until after the fourth camp had been taken. He edged his horse against Dundee's.

"These are little fish," he said solemnly. "I want the big one."

"Old Roan? He'll be harder to take. While we're trying, a lot of the others will slip out of the country."

"Let them. It's Roan I want. Wherever we find Roan, we'll likely find the man who killed Son."

Dundee shrugged. He had rather have concentrated on the easy ones, as much to sharpen up this inexperienced posse as anything else. It was one thing to ride into a two-bit rustler camp and flush out one, two or three miserable cowthieves. It might be entirely something else to beard the lion in his own den.

Titus said: "You know where Roan has his headquarters, don't you? You showed it on your map."

"I know where it is. I just wasn't too anxious to see it yet."

"*I'm* anxious."

So they rode. Sundown caught them still many miles from Runaway, but Dundee figured that might be a good thing. The darkness would help hide their movements.

He didn't know how much surprise there might still be. They had moved swiftly today, and so far as he knew, nobody had gone through the net. But it would be hard to know for sure. Somebody might have come over a hilltop and spotted them without himself being seen. If so, he probably wouldn't let his shirttail touch him till he reached Roan Hardesty.

"Pull them prisoners in tight," he ordered. "We can't let a one of them get away. Tie all their horses onto one rope and lead them."

Far into the night they rode, Dundee always a little ahead, feeling out of the way in the near darkness. There was a trail, but he chose not to follow it. They cut across the hills, climbing wherever he could find a way through, easing down the off slopes, splashing through the moon-trapping creeks that shimmered in the lazy valleys.

He had never been down to Roan Hardesty's headquarters, but he had sat on top of a hill and watched it through the glass most of one afternoon, getting the hang of it. Roan's taste in a ranch layout was much the same as his taste in whisky: rawness was no detriment so long as the thing fitted its purpose. The old reprobate lived in a small log house just far enough up from the creek-bank that he wouldn't have to flee the floodwater. He evidently didn't want to tote water any farther than absolutely necessary. His barn—such as it was—had been built close to the house, too. Sanitation wasn't as much worry to him as the length of the walk from where he had to turn his horse loose.

Roan's men—the ones he kept around him all the time—stayed in a long, low rock structure with a brush-and-mud roof. Far as Dundee had been able to tell, Roan lived in the log house all by himself, though he had had some female company there the afternoon Dundee had spied from afar. Plain house, raw whisky and a painted woman. A man should never get so rich but what he still enjoyed the simple pleasures, Dundee had told himself.

For a while he feared he was lost in the night, but at last he found the hill where he had sat that time before. The men came up around him and let their horses rest. The dim moonlight barely showed the outlines of the buildings down there.

John Titus said, "Is that where he's at?"

"Well, it's where he lives. He spends a lot of time in Runaway. The only light I can see is a lamp in the bunkhouse. Roan's place is dark."

"You reckon he found out about us and ran?"

"Maybe. Or he could be in town playing poker. Or, he could be laying in there asleep. I expect he sleeps a right smart, his age and all." Dundee frowned. "You need some rest yourself, Mister Titus. You been going awful strong."

"I'll rest when the job is done. There won't be much left for me to work for, when this is over. Son is gone."

Dundee didn't know how to answer that, so he didn't try. He had a notion that when the old man's initial grief passed, he'd be back in harness as strong as ever. Work was what kept a man like him going. Dundee said: "We'll *all* get some rest. If they *have* heard we're in the country, they could be waiting there somewhere trying to catch us in the dark. We'd best wait till daylight. But we'll move down closer and put a surround on them. That way there can't nobody slip in, or nobody slip out."

Since he seemed to be the one giving orders, Dundee told the men not to light any cigarettes through the night. That would be a giveaway.

Later a weary Tobe Crane sat beside Dundee where they could look down on the dark shape of the buildings. Crane had kept his word. Weak though he was, he hadn't fallen behind a single time.

Before long Dundee started seeing matches flare in the night, one, two . . . then five and six. He swore. "Looky there. Them matches can be seen for miles. I told them boy. . . ."

"A nervous man is bound and bedamned to smoke. And this is a nervous bunch."

Dundee grunted. "Ever so often I think about all them shooting irons in the hands of cowpunchers, and I get a mite nervous myself."

"You got a plan how we're going to take that place?"

"I ain't no general. All I know to do is just ride down there and take over."

"Looks awful risky."

"Everything we've done has been risky."

Dundee didn't intend to, but he dropped off to sleep. The first thing he heard was a rooster crowing somewhere down at the ranch headquarters. He yawned and glanced eastward, where dawn was sending up the first faint promise of color.

Tobe's eyes flickered in surprise when the rooster crowed again. "Is that what it sounds like?"

Dundee nodded. Tobe said: "I wouldn't picture Roan

Hardesty as being the type to keep a bunch of chickens around."

Dundee smiled. There *was* something awfully domestic about a set of clucking hens.

Tobe said: "Maybe he enjoys wringing necks."

"More likely he just favors eggs. Old men get contrary about what they eat, and *tough* old men can get *awful* contrary."

Dundee could see the cowboys stirring around, and he knew they hadn't slept much, most of them. From the dark pockets under Tobe's eyes, Dundee could tell *he* hadn't. Tobe said: "I could sure stand a cup of hot coffee."

"We'll cook breakfast on old Roan's stove."

He sent a cowboy to carry word to all the men who encircled Blue Roan's layout: they would move in fifteen minutes. Everybody was to watch Dundee. When he broke into the open, they were all to ride fast and try to get as close as they could. He took out his watch and marked the time. He had gone without a cigarette all night. He had followed his own orders, even if nobody else had. Now in the coming daylight he guessed it wouldn't hurt to light one. He turned his back to the houses, though, and hid the flare with his body till he shook the match out. Most of the fifteen minutes were up when the cowboy came back.

Dundee dropped his cigarette on the ground, saddled his horse and checked his saddlegun. "Everybody here ready?"

Old John Titus sat waiting. Dundee couldn't tell whether he had slept or not; he doubted it. In fact, he doubted that Titus had really known sound sleep since

Dundee had brought him word about Son. Dark shadows framed the eyes that seemed drawn back into the stony face. But there was an incandescence to those eyes, a fire that Dundee feared it might take a lot of blood to quench.

"I seen everybody," he said. "They'll be looking for you."

The saddlegun in his hand, ready for use, Dundee swung up. He glanced around to be sure the others were mounted, then said, "Let's go amongst them."

He touched the bay's ribs firmly with the spurs and brought the horse into a long trot down the slope. When he hit the flat terrain, he spurred into a hard lope. Around him he could see the other riders closing in, following his lead. A few shouted like Comanches, and he thought that was a foolish thing to do.

The horse's long stride reached out and gathered in the yards. The outbuildings seemed to rush headlong toward him, and he expected any second the puffs of smoke, the crackle of gunfire.

He could see the windows now, and count the panes; they were getting that close, the horses running full tilt, the hoofs drumming, the dust lifting in plumes as they crossed the grassless roundup grounds near the corrals. *Any second now they'll commence shooting at us.*

He watched the windows, for that was where the firing would come from, most likely.

It didn't start.

Maybe they're waiting for us to get so close they can't miss. They'll wait for us to poke our faces in those windows and then they'll blow our heads off. This is a

*damnfool way to do it anyhow. A smart man would've
sneaked us in there like a bunch of Indians.*

He was into the yard now, not a hundred feet from
Blue Roan's log house. Dundee realized he was holding
his breath, his lungs afire. The last few feet his heart was
beating so hard he thought he could hear it, but it was
only the hoofs.

Then he was at the house itself. He swung his leg over
the bay's hips before the horse slid to a stop. Dundee
jumped free and lit running, expecting a blast from the
nearest window. He flattened against rough logs, breathing hard. He realized that not a shot had been fired.

He didn't wait to puzzle it out. He ran for the door,
kicked it open with one hard thrust of his foot and leaped
inside, hands tight on the carbine, ready to fire at the first
thing that moved.

Nothing did. Dundee crouched, his chest heaving,
his confused gaze sweeping the room.

Not a soul here. Just empty tin cans and dirty dishes,
a whisky bottle on the floor; an unmade bed in a corner,
a single dark stocking lying on the blankets, the kind the
wheeligo girls wore in the saloons. Dundee examined
the messed-up plates and found the food had dried. Nobody had eaten here since sometime yesterday.

He whirled at the sound of a footstep on the board
floor. He lowered the carbine as he saw Tobe Crane.
Crane's voice was heavy with disappointment. "There's
nobody here."

"Maybe the bunkhouse."

Tobe shook his head. "Boys already been there. There
was a lamp on the table, the coal oil all used up and
the chimney burned black as pitch. They fooled us,

Dundee. They must of knowed we was coming. Looks like they slipped away and left that lamp to fool us."

Stepping outside, Dundee watched the cowboys search the barn, the corrals. He let his gaze drift to the hill from which they had started.

Tobe Crane was looking the same way. "Maybe it's a good thing there wasn't anybody here. We'd of made perfect targets."

"I never claimed to be no West Point wonder. Leading green cowpunchers into a gunfight ain't my bowl of *chili* in the first place."

Tobe said: "Maybe we ought to've known we couldn't fool an old fox like Roan. He's got eyes in the back of his head, and maybe in his rump." He paused, studying. "Maybe old Roan took to the tulies."

"It'd take more than this bunch of cow nurses to scare Roan Hardesty out of a place like this, and away from a fortune in burnt cattle. I expect he took out for Runaway, where he'd have extra men, and maybe a better place to fight."

Old John Titus silently stared at Dundee, the disappointment keen in his pinched eyes.

Dundee said: "Mister Titus, we better send for more help. If Roan has holed up in Runaway—and I figure he has—there ain't enough of us to root him out. These cowboys of yours have got their hearts in the right place, but very little else."

The old man nodded slowly. "That's already took care of. Before we left, I got word out to other ranches around us . . . told them what we was fixing to do. I told them to send men to Runaway. This is *their* fight, too."

"More cowboys? What we need is Rangers."

"I waited till the very last to send word to the Rangers. I didn't want them getting in our way. They get kind of sticky about rules." The old man made a sweep with his arm. "Let's burn it all. Then we'll get on down to Runaway."

12

Dundee had been on this hill overlooking Runaway so many times that he had just about all of the town memorized. He thought by now he knew the position of every building, every outdoor convenience, every rainbarrel. Looking down, he decided everything was in its proper place. Nothing moved, not even a jackrabbit.

He sensed Tobe Crane sitting on his horse beside him. Dundee said, "Well, they're down there all right, just waiting for us."

"How do you know? I don't see a thing."

"That's how you can tell."

John Titus halted beside Dundee, taking his first real look at Runaway. Dundee could see the old man's jaw harden. "So that's the place. That's the rattlesnake den that killed my boy."

Dundee nodded. "That's Runaway."

Titus' voice was like two strands of barbed wire rubbed together. "It won't be there when we leave."

"They're ready for us," Dundee said. "We ain't got the manpower just to ride in and take over. They'd cut us down like weeds. Maybe we ought to leave Runaway alone. There's a heap of little rustler camps we could handle instead. With them gone, Runaway would wither anyhow."

"We didn't come to catch a handful of rats. We come to wipe out the nest," Titus said.

Dundee rubbed his jaw. "It's a hell of a big nest."

"We come to take it."

Dundee turned in the saddle and looked back over the cowboys. Thirty of them he had, plus a wounded Tobe Crane and a bitter old man whose hatred was far steadier than his gnarled hand. "It won't come cheap."

"I'll pay the price. You afraid, Dundee?"

Dundee frowned. "It ain't like being in church."

"They can be taken. We got enough men to surround the town and keep anybody from getting out. Sooner or later they'll have to give up."

"They probably got enough food to carry them awhile. I know they got lots of whisky."

"You'll see, Dundee. They'll break down. They'll get nervous waiting, and sooner or later they'll try to bust out. We'll be here, and we'll be ready."

"It'll scatter us pretty thin, trying to surround the whole town."

"When the will is strong enough. . . ."

Dundee would admit that the will of these cowboys was plenty strong. If only they had the aim to go with it. . . . "We'll try it your way, Mister Titus."

"You're damn right you will."

Along the way Dundee had tried to make a study of the men and pick out the best fighting prospects. Two or three of them, he judged, could as well be down there in Runaway as up here waiting to lay siege to it. But so long as they were in on it, he was glad they were on his side instead of against him. He started down off the hill and began a wide circle of the town, dropping off a man here, a man there, at fairly regular intervals where there was cover. About every third or fourth place he dropped one of the men he thought might be better than average with a gun. He placed the men in a wide semi-circle, for the bluff itself effectively sealed off that side of the town.

"If they decide to try a break," he told the men, "they'll go for what they figure is the weakest spot in our line. One man won't be much hindrance to them. If you see trouble, burn leather getting there. The man on that spot will need all the help he can get."

He didn't really expect any such break. The outlaws probably felt a strong confidence in their superiority over a little bunch of green cowboys. If they'd wanted to leave Runaway, they would have done it before this posse got here.

The men all placed, he paused at the foot of the hill and looked at the town. Curiosity began to nettle him. How close *could* they get in there? The wagonyard caught his eye. It struck him that if the wind blew hard enough, and if a man could get to that barn and drop a match into dry hay, fire might spread down the street, touching off first one building, then the next. It was a narrow-odds bet, but he'd taken risks ever since he'd left home as a kid, gambling that he wouldn't starve to death. He'd almost lost *that* bet.

He touched a spur to the horse's ribs and decided to see just how far he could get.

He quickly found out. Dundee saw the flash of a rifle and heard a bullet ricochet off the rocks with a vicious whine. He whirled and spurred for the hill. His curiosity was satisfied.

John Titus and Tobe Crane waited on top of the hill. Tobe was not physically able to contribute much; it amazed Dundee that he'd gotten this far without dropping from exhaustion. And he knew he couldn't count on the old man for much action. He said, "Well, sir, I reckon you can see that they've dug into there like lice in a buffalo robe."

Titus' expression never altered. "They can't stay forever."

Presently Dundee's eye was caught by movement in the street, then at the wagonyard. A man rode out of the corral with a rifle in his hand, waving a white cloth tied to the end of it. He moved toward the hill.

John Titus' eyes went wide as spur rowels. "They're giving up."

Dundee said: "Not hardly, not when they got most of the chips on their end of the table. I expect thay want to palaver. I'll go down and see what it's all about."

Tobe Crane warned: "You watch them, Dundee. It'd tickle them to see you dead."

"I'll watch. That idea don't appeal to me."

He took his time, his gaze never straying far from the horseman who held the rifle and the white cloth. It occurred to Dundee that the rifle was probably loaded, just in case. His lips dry, his nerves wound tight as a watchspring, he strongly considered drawing his carbine and making sure it was loaded too. But he resisted.

He recognized Jason Karnes. Now he *knew* that rifle was loaded.

He stopped and let the be-stubbled Karnes travel the

last few lengths to meet him. Dundee noticed how the
man's leg was held out stiffly away from the saddle. *A
little souvenir I gave him.* They stared cold-eyed at each
other a minute before Dundee said, "I bet that was *you*
who shot at me a little while ago."

Karnes nodded. "It was."

"I'm pleased to find your aim ain't improved much."

"It'll get better. I got me a crippled leg now. They say
when a man loses one thing, he gains someplace else.
I'm counting on a better shooting eye."

"You ought to've counted on your horse-picking eye
and cut you out a fast one to get you away from here.
There's an old man up yonder on that hill who's come to
see blood."

"He's still on the hill, though. And that's as far as he's
going to get. Except under a flag of truce. That's what
Roan sent me for. He wants to parley with old man
Titus."

"I'll ask him."

"Roan says tell the old man not to bring a gun, and
Roan won't bring his either."

Dundee's eyes narrowed. "And maybe ride into a trap?
No thanks. The old man may come without a gun, but *I*
won't. I'll come along to be sure there don't nothing happen to him."

"Fair enough. And I'll be here to take care of old Roan
case one of your bunch gets a foolish notion."

Karnes slowly turned his horse around and started
back toward town. He shifted his body in the saddle so
he could watch Dundee over his shoulder.

Dundee wasn't even that trustful. He waited until the
distance between them had stretched to a good fifty

yards before he brought his bay around. He carried the message back up the hill.

John Titus clenched tough fists. "I got nothing to talk to Roan about."

"You say you figure on staying here and starving them out if you have to. Maybe you could convince him of that."

"I won't make him no promises I don't intend to keep. And I know what I plan to do with Roan when I get my hands on him."

So did Dundee. The thought had gnawed on him for a long time. "It won't hurt to go down and talk."

He prevailed on John Titus to leave his pistol and his saddlegun with Tobe at the top of the hill. They started down together. In town, a long way off, Dundee could see two horsemen leave the corral and start toward them. Jason Karnes was still riding the same stocking-legged black he had been on a little while ago. The other figure was the unmistakably blocky one of Roan Hardesty, riding that dappled gray he favored so much.

Dundee asked John Titus, "How long since you've seen Blue Roan?"

Titus thoughtfully shook his head. "Many and many a year."

"You may not know him, then."

"I'll know him. I'd know his hide in a tanyard."

A tiny group of liveoaks clustered below the hill. There Dundee and John Titus stopped to wait, for it was about the halfway point. Dundee had brought his saddlegun across his lap now, ready. He noted that Jason Karnes had done the same.

Roan Hardesty didn't rein up until his horse was

touching necks with that of John Titus. The blue splotches on his face stood out like the dapple marks on his horse. His eyes were soft with an offering of friendship. "It's been a long time, John." He held out his right hand.

John Titus let his own hands remain at his sides. His eyes were cold as December and seemed to freeze onto Roan Hardesty. He made no effort to reply.

Roan slowly drew back his hand and rubbed it nervously on his huge leg. He looked down a moment, framing his words as if each might fall back and crush him. "John, I felt real bad about your boy. Maybe Dundee has told you: I give orders there wasn't nobody to kill him. I've turned this town upside down, trying to find out who it was went against my orders. Nobody'll own up to it." He paused, waiting for a reaction that didn't come. "I swear to you, John, if I knowed who it was, I'd kill him myself."

John Titus' throat showed a tremor. "I come to see you die, Roan."

The aging outlaw slumped in the saddle. "We was friends for a long time, John. We warred together, remember? We rode the brush together. We seen the elephant and heard the owl hoot."

"I got a boy dead now, Roan."

"John, I've took a lot of your cows; Lord, I wouldn't deny that. But I never took your son. I never had no intention for harm to come to him."

Titus repeated, quieter this time, "I come to see you die."

The silence between them then was long and heavy. They stared at each other, the outlaw's eyes regretful, Titus' eyes cold and grim. It was Roan who finally spoke. "Well, John, I've said all I can. I'm sorry the way it all happened. We was friends a long time. But if this is where friendship has to end, so be it. You can't take our town, not with what you got here. You'd never even get into the street."

"We got you all bottled up. All we got to do now is outlast you. I'll stay all summer if I have to, and into the fall."

Roan Hardesty looked around him, trying to pick out the places where Dundee had stationed the men. "What you got, John? Twenty-five men? Thirty? And just cowboys at that." His eyes narrowed. "I'll tell you something you didn't know. I got friends scattered all over them hills. I sent word last night to the forks of the creek. When they all get here, it'll look like the Confederate army. They'll run over your bunch like wild studs over pet ponies."

Dundee stiffened. He hoped it wouldn't show. This was one thing he hadn't considered, that Hardesty might get reinforcements in substantial numbers.

Titus said tightly: "We'll take care of ourselves, Roan. Tell your men that every time one of them sticks his head out, somebody's going to take a shot at him. They'll get almighty tired of dodging every time they need a bucket of water or a sack of beans."

Roan's splotchy face was clouded now with trouble. "I'll tell them, John." He started to turn away but paused. "There's some women down in town, and a few men that got no part in this. Ain't fair to risk getting them hurt. I'd like to send them out, John."

"Send them, then. We got no war on against women."

Dundee watched John Titus' face as Roan Hardesty

slowly rode back toward town. If a momentary soft-
ness showed here, it was quickly covered by a steely
determination.

Dundee offered: "I think he's telling you the truth,
Mister Titus. I don't think he knows who killed Son."

Titus was silent.

In a little while a horseman appeared outside the barn,
a white cloth tied to a long stick. He rode into the clear,
stopped and waved the cloth from side to side so everyone
could see it. Then he turned in the saddle. Out from the
corrals came two buckboards and a wagon, trailed by a
second horseman. Even at the distance Dundee could
see the ribbons and streamers and colored dresses.

"The women," he said. "They're coming out."

Titus' brow furrowed. "No children?"

"This ain't exactly a family town."

The front rider, carrying the white cloth, was the wagonyard operator. Behind him, in the buckboard, Dundee
could recognize Katy Long. Driving was the little bartender Cricket. As they came up even with Dundee, Katy
motioned for Cricket to stop. She looked Dundee straight
in the eye, and he thought she might be laughing a little.
"See, Dundee? I told you you'd be back."

"And I told you to sell that saloon. Did you?"

"Nobody made me an offer."

"A pity."

Any smile she might have had was suddenly gone.
"You don't really think you can take that town, do you?
With *that* bunch of men?"

"Titus says we'll take it. So, we'll take it."

"Roan Hardesty says you won't. He doesn't make
many mistakes."

"He's made one."

The wagonyard operator got as close to Dundee as he could. "Friend, I got a valuable piece of property down there. I've always tried to treat you square."

"Like double-charging me for hay?"

"I'm sorry we had a misunderstanding over that." He reached in his pocket and came up with a silver coin. "Here, I'd like to pay you back."

"Keep it. When this is over, that may be all you got left."

Some of the women were protesting angrily, while others just sat and looked frightened. A couple tried to flirt with Dundee. He waved them on. The horseman who came along behind the wagons was a middle-aged, portly gent Dundee hadn't seen before. "Mister Dundee, my name is Smith, and I'm a legitimate businessman. I own the mercantile down there." He offered his hand, but Dundee ignored it. Smith went on: "I have a considerable investment. What you're doing here is jeopardizing my property. I'd like to see it stopped, immediately."

"Oh, you would?"

"I would dislike having to protest to the state authorities, but I will if I must. You have no right to stand in the way of an honest businessman and disrupt his trade."

Dundee turned in the saddle and pointed east. "Well, now, you just go right ahead and protest if you want to. About two days' hard ride in that direction will get you to Austin. Three days if that saddle makes your rump sore."

He hoped the women would go on, but they didn't. They moved a little way down the road and proceeded to set up camp. Dundee thought about all those women, and all those cowboys. You couldn't keep up much of a siege when half your men weren't on duty. He said a few choice words under his breath, swung onto the bay and trotted down to where the women were struggling to set up a couple of big tents. He noted that Katy Long was not among them, a point which brought him considerable satisfaction.

"You can just take that thing down and put it back in the wagon," he hollered. "You're not going to use it here."

The big red-headed woman he had had a run-in with before came stalking forward like an angry she-bear, her hands on her hips. Dundee wouldn't have been much surprised if she had breathed fire at him. She didn't, but her breath was bad enough. "Who the hell says so?"

"Me."

She looked back over her shoulder. The women had the tent just about set up. "Now, Mister Tall, Dark and Ugly, what do you intend to do about it? Are you low-down enough to shoot a woman? You'd have to, you know, before we'd take that tent down."

Dundee tried to hold his rising temper. "I'd ask you real polite."

"Well, we won't take it down. So what do you do now?"

Dundee said, "Then *I'll* take it down."

He lifted his hornstring and freed his rope. He shook out a loop and spurred the bay into a brisk trot, nearly bumping the redhead before she could jump aside, cursing. He swung the loop while the women ran screaming. He dropped it over the top of the tent, jerked out the slack, dallied the rope around the horn and squalled a cowboy yell as he spurred the bay into a run. The tent stakes flipped out of the ground, and the tent came sailing after him. The horses took a wild-eyed look at the flying apparition and stampeded. The wagon bounced behind them, scattering clothes and camp goods for two hundred yards up the trail.

Dundee stopped and freed his rope. Recoiling it, he rode back into a circle of shaken, angry women. His gaze fastened on the redhead. "Like I was saying, you ain't stopping here. I'll go fetch your team back, and you'll be going on your way."

He rode up the trail to where the team had finally stopped. At the side of the road, Katy Long had halted her buckboard and had witnessed the excitement from afar. Now she watched grinning as Dundee approached. "You play rough, Dundee."

"Them women got no business here. They'd just be a temptation to the men."

"Am I included?"

"You're not like them others. But you'd be a temptation to *me*."

"Well, thanks for that."

The bartender Cricket helped him take the wagon back. Dundee didn't leave till he saw the women on their way. Even then he knew they wouldn't travel far. He had seen cows that would move only so long as a horseman pushed them. When he stopped pushing, they would stop moving. Dundee knew the women would move on a mile or two, then stop again, confident Roan's bunch would win and they could go back to Runaway.

At least they would be out from under foot.

At the hill, he watched with John Titus and Tobe Crane as a man started across the street from one saloon toward another. Half a dozen rifles rattled from vantage points around town, including a couple on top of the cliff. Dust kicked up in half a dozen places. The man turned and trotted briskly back where he had come from.

"Not very good shots, are they?" Dundee said.

"They try," Titus replied defensively.

"Trying ain't going to be enough."

In retaliation, rifles set up a racket down in town, Hardesty's men trying to find the places where the cowboys were spotted. So far as Dundee could tell, their aim wasn't a lot better. "Looks to me like a Mexican standoff. We can't go in, and they can't go out."

"We can wait," said Titus. "Time is on our side."

Dundee frowned. "I don't know. I got the feeling old Roan didn't lie about having more men on the way. I tell you, Mister Titus, if there's many of them they can circle our outfit and pick off them boys one at a time. It'd be like shooting ducks in a tank."

"I told you, Dundee, I sent for more help too."

"You didn't get no promises, did you?"

Titus didn't answer.

Through the long afternoon they sat impatiently watching, waiting, Dundee trying a little mumblepeg, then whittling sticks down to a pile of white shavings, whistling some half-forgotten tune till it felt as if his lips would crack. The old man huddled most of the time like some wounded eagle, his gaze fastened on the town. Tobe Crane paced till he got tired, sat awhile, arose and paced some more. It finally got on Dundee's nerves.

"You're supposed to be recuperating. Sit down and get still."

"Walking don't bother me."

"It bothers *me*. Sit down."

Tobe Crane did as he was told, but he took his time, as if to show that if the idea didn't suit him he wouldn't have done it. Dundee softened a little. "I didn't much cotton to you coming along in the first place. You don't take care of yourself, Millie's liable to blame me. She's invested a lot of work in getting you on your feet."

Tobe Crane stared at the ground. "Yes, she has."

Dundee studied the cowboy, his eyes narrowed in speculation. "She's a real pretty girl. A man could lose his head over her," he said.

Crane said, "She seemed to think a great deal of you, Dundee."

Dundee winced. From somewhere came a touch of pain. "I'll admit, I've done a heap of thinking . . . wonder if ever I could make myself settle down and try to build a home for a girl like that."

Crane glanced at him a second and looked away. "You still thinking about it?"

"Some."

"Made up your mind?"

"Not yet. I'm afraid I know other people better than I know myself."

"Are you sure you know Millie?"

"I think so."

Tobe Crane pushed to his feet again and stared wistful-eyed down the valley. "I hope you don't figure her wrong."

13

They had salvaged a chuckwagon from Roan Hardesty's place before they put it to the torch. Now a couple of the men cooked supper, and the cowboys rode in a few at a time to eat. Dundee tried, but he couldn't stir up much appetite, looking down upon that town. They weren't any closer to it now than they had been this morning. He couldn't help thinking that Roan's reinforcements might show up, and then it would be hell among the yearlings.

The breeze came up with twilight, a breeze out of the south. Dundee got to mulling again the idea that had occurred to him during the day . . . setting fire to the town and forcing the renegades out. He hadn't gotten past the turnrow the first time, but that had been daylight. With luck a man might sneak through in the dark.

He told the old man about the notion, and Titus seemed receptive. He would accept anything right now except retreat. Tobe Crane said, "I'll go down there with you, Dundee."

"You stay here. You ain't got the strength," Dundee said.

"That's what you thought before. I'll go with you."

Dundee didn't argue any further. Tobe Crane was a grown man and able to make his own mind up . . . even if now and then he did seem to have more guts than sense. They circled southward, visiting all the posts to tell the men what they were up to.

"I wouldn't want to get the job done and then be shot

by our own bunch," Dundee said. "That'd be a real joke on us."

From the south Dundee remembered a clump of liveoaks about halfway between their outposts and the first outbuildings of the town. Saddlegun across his lap, he slow-walked the bay in that direction, hoping to get done before the moon came up. Dundee could sense Tobe Crane's nervousness. Tobe had punched cows all his life. He'd probably never been shot at till the first time he came to Runaway.

"Easy, boy," Dundee whispered. "If they spot us, be ready to leave here like a Jeff Davis cannonball."

They made the trees, somewhat to Dundee's surprise. He tied the bay. "If we get in a jam, Tobe, you run like the devil. Don't wait on me. It's every man for himself."

Dundee moved out from the trees in a crouch, saddlegun cradled in his arm. Because of his wound, Tobe carried only a six-shooter, and Dundee doubted he could hit his own hat with it. But it was reassuring to have company.

The first building they reached was a cowshed, with lots of dry hay in it. That, Dundee figured, would burn easily. The breeze was still out of the south, and it stood a good chance of carrying the fire through the summer-dried grass on into the rest of town. But the closer he could get to start his fire, the better the odds. He decided to try next for an empty-looking log shack. He bent low and sprinted across a short clearing. Flattening himself against the logs, he waited for any sign that he had been seen. When none came, he motioned for Tobe.

They'd made it this far. Maybe they could do even better. The next building was the frame house where he had found Son Titus whiling time away with the girl Lutie. He thought it ought to burn with a jolly blaze. He eased out to make a try for it. He had gone three long strides when a voice came from one of the open windows. "What you doing out there?"

Dundee's heart leaped, but he decided to brazen it on through. "Looking for a bottle. You got an extra one?"

"No. You go find your own."

Dundee let out a long-held breath. Well, he'd found out how far he could go. He retreated to the shack and Tobe Crane. "If we try to go any farther somebody'll chop us off at the knees."

He tested the door and found it open, the shack deserted. "Stay outside and keep your eyes peeled," he said. Finding a kerosene lamp, he spread kerosene on the floor and up the walls. He saved some and spilled it in a line out into the dry grass, as far as it would go. Then he fished in his pocket for the matches. "The boys ain't going to appreciate this much, so get ready to run."

He pulled up a handful of dry grass, twisted it, then used his body to shield it from the breeze until the match's tiny flame took hold and the grass blazed up. He dropped it into the heavy grass around the cowshed. In moments the flames were racing through the grass, found the kerosene, followed it across the clearing and up into the shack.

"It's pretty," Dundee said, "but let's don't wait for the whole show." They struck out in a hard run for the clump of liveoaks. A shout went up, and another and another. Dogs barked. In a moment men were running in the street, hollering, everybody trying to give orders. A few wild shots were fired. Dundee mounted the bay. "Let's go back up on the hill where the view is better."

They were halfway there when Tobe Crane said, "Dundee, you notice something?"

"What?"

"The breeze has stopped."

Dundee reined up and looked back. He saw the shack collapse in a shower of sparks, the flames leaping high, then dying down. But Tobe was right. The breeze had quit. There was nothing to carry the flames any farther up the street.

"One cowshed and one flea-ridden shack," Dundee gritted. "But at least we got our exercise."

Dundee got more exercise that night, pacing, worrying, thinking about Hardesty's outside men coming to stop the siege, and maybe laying out a bunch of well-intentioned cowboys in the grass to stay. By daylight he was up, sleepy-eyed and irritable. He hadn't slept much. He went down and pulled four men out of the line and put them off on horseback to patrol as outriders, to watch for anyone who might be coming to give aid to the town. One by one he gave the message to the other men: "If trouble comes, the signal will be three shots, fired as quick as a man can pull the trigger. You get on your horse and get there as fast as you can ride. Scattered, we may not put up much fight. Together, we'll give them their money's worth."

Later Dundee sipped coffee and watched John Titus through narrowed eyes. *Crazy old man. Wants revenge worse than he wants to stop the cattle thieving. He could've cleaned this country up, hitting a camp at a time. But he's got to take on the whole town. Crazy old man.*

The mood passed, for Dundee thought he could understand John Titus. Once, the cattle had been important. But that had been while he still had a son.

Dundee turned his attention to Tobe Crane. He thought of Millie McCown. The last thing in his mind as he dozed off to sleep was a mental picture of Tobe holding Millie's hand as they all stood at Son Titus' grave.

Three quick-paced shots brought him out of the nap and onto his feet, grabbing at his carbine. He blinked away the sleep and saw one of the Titus cowboys spurring toward him on the trail that led in from the northeast. The cowboy shouted, "They're coming! They're coming!"

He slid his horse to a stop. Dundee glanced down the hill and saw the scattered Titus cowboys beginning to get into their saddles. It would take a while before they could all get here.

"Who's coming?" he demanded.

"I don't know," the rider blurted, face flushed with excitement. "I didn't let them get close enough to tell. But Dundee . . . Mister Titus . . . there's a hell of a bunch of them. Must be forty . . . maybe fifty."

Dundee swallowed, his fists going tight. This was what he had been afraid of. He glanced back down the hill again, mentally calculating how long it would take all the Titus cowboys to get here.

"How much time we got?"

"They're right on us."

Dundee could see the dust now, and he knew the cowboys wouldn't get here in time, not enough of them. At this moment there were only five: himself, John Titus, Tobe, the outrider and a man who had stayed at the chuckwagon to cook. "Let's get to cover," he shouted. "Maybe we can give them something to chew on till the rest of the boys reach here."

He threw himself down behind a heavy liveoak, the saddlegun ready. Old John Titus knelt behind another, rifle resting against the trunk. Tobe Crane lay on his belly, favoring the wounded arm, holding a pistol in his hand.

Dundee took a deep breath, then drew a bead on the lead rider. He would wait until he knew he couldn't miss.

John Titus shouted. Dundee tried not to be distracted, but he lost his head. The old man shouted again. "It's *our* bunch, Dundee! It's ours!"

Dundee lowered the carbine. "What'd you say?"

"It's my neighbors, Dundee, the ones I sent for. That's old Charlie Moore there in the lead. I'd know his dun horse anywhere. And that man on the *grulla*, he's Walter Matthews of the Half Circle M. They've come to help us."

Dundee pushed to his feet and took off his hat, wiping cold sweat from his forehead onto his sleeve.

In town, a commotion began in the streets as the new riders showed on the hill. Horses stirred dust. Men ran to and fro. Though the sound didn't carry, there was visible sign of violent argument. Some of the Titus cowboys started dropping slugs down there, adding to the melee. Then there came the muffled rumble of hoofs, the sharp shouts of excited men. Twenty or more horsemen spurred toward the south end of town, toward the river and the span of open country that stretched beyond.

"They're trying a break!" Dundee shouted. "Let's get them!"

He swung onto the bay and took the lead, moving headlong down the hill, angling southwestward, running over brush, scattering rocks. He didn't look back, but he could hear other horses running behind him. Dundee took an oblique course that he hoped would intercept the fleeing outlaws. He could see desperation in the way they spurred, flaying horses with their quirts. Some began snapping wild shots toward the Titus posse. None struck Dundee, and he didn't have time right now to see if they hit anyone else. He just kept spurring.

Now he could begin to make out faces. He looked for the bulky shape of Roan Hardesty but couldn't pick him out from the crowd. It occurred to him that the dappled gray wasn't in the bunch. Roan was still in town.

They've run out on him, he realized. *They seen they was whipped and they run out on him.*

He saw one face he knew too well. Jason Karnes, on the stocking-legged black. Dundee couldn't hear the words, but he could almost read them on the twisting lips of the black-whiskered outlaw. Karnes raised a six-shooter and snapped a shot at Dundee. His horse almost stumbled, and Karnes was busy a few seconds getting his balance. Then the pistol came up again.

Dundee swung his saddlegun into line. It was hard enough, making a shot from a running horse. It was almost impossible, making one to the right. Dundee tried to compensate by twisting his body as far as he could.

He squeezed the trigger and knew he had missed. Karnes pulled closer, within pistol range. The pistol cracked again, and Dundee felt a tug at his sleeve, a searing pain as the bullet raked him.

Now the range was almost point blank. Dundee squeezed the trigger again. Karnes jerked backward, slipped over the horse's right hip and tumbled to the ground. Dundee lost sight of him in the dust as horses went over and past him.

Other shots were being fired. He saw the outlaws begin reining to a stop, trying to raise their hands. Some still spurred, attempting to outrun the cowboys.

Dundee's bay was slowing, tiring. Dundee let him bring himself slowly to a stop, for he knew the horse had about done its do. Around him, possemen were gathering in those fugitives who had quit. Others kept up the run.

They'll catch the most of them, he told himself. *I better get down yonder and see about Roan.*

Moving back toward town in a slow trot, he passed the still form of Jason Karnes. One look was enough. He took no pleasure in the sight, no satisfaction from bringing the outlaw down.

That's two I've took out of the family, he thought. *It ain't a thing to make a man proud.*

John Titus angled down to meet him, trailed by Tobe Crane. The old man knew before Dundee told him. "Roan's still in town."

Dundee nodded. "He wasn't with that bunch. They deserted him. Not many of them will get away."

Titus said severely: "I don't care so much about them. I want Roan."

"I'll go down there and see if I can find him."

"Roan's mine. I'm going with you."

Dundee wanted to argue, but he knew it would be useless. He glanced at the young cowboy. "You coming, Tobe?" When the cowboy answered yes, Dundee said: "Keep a sharp eye out, then. A cornered bear is apt to bite."

They rode slowly up the street, three abreast. Dundee's sweeping gaze probed the open doors, the windows, the alleyways.

Titus called: "Roan! Roan, you come on out here. I want you."

No reply.

Ahead of them lay the Llano River Saloon. Instinctively Dundee felt drawn toward it. He'd seen Roan there before. He pointed and said quietly, "Mister Titus, I think yonder's the place."

He rode as close as he dared, then started to swing out of the saddle. Halfway down, he caught a glimpse of movement, saw the big man step out through the open doors, shotgun in his huge hands.

"Hold it right where you're at, Dundee! Don't move another inch."

Dundee halted, half in and half out of the saddle, the saddlegun in his right hand but not where he could swing it into play. Tobe Crane held a six-shooter uncertainly. John Titus just sat there staring down into the awesome bore of that shotgun, both hands resting easily on the saddlehorn. If he felt any fear, his face did not betray it.

Roan said in a heavy voice that was a mixture of anger and desperation: "John, I told you not to come down here. I told you I didn't kill that boy."

Titus was steady as an ancient liveoak. "If you're figuring on pulling that trigger, Roan, do it now. It's going to be you or me."

"John, we was friends once. I don't want to have to kill you."

"I come to hang you, Roan. I'll do it, unless you shoot me."

It came to Dundee with the force of a mule-kick what John Titus was attempting to do. He was trying to force Roan into shooting him, knowing Roan wouldn't live to get ten steps down the street. He was willing to throw himself away to see Roan Hardesty brought to the ground. "Mister Titus. . . ."

Titus ignored Dundee. He said: "Go on, Roan. Do it if you're going to. I'm fixing to draw my gun." The old man's hand slowly went down to his hip, closed over the pistol there and came up again. It seemed it took him all day.

Roan Hardesty's face whitened, and the blue blotches seemed to go almost black. For a moment it was in his eyes to pull the trigger. But then his chin fell. Slowly he let the muzzle of the shotgun sink toward the ground. He leaned on a tiepost for strength.

"I couldn't do it, John."

Titus said, "Get him, Dundee."

Dundee hesitated. "What you going to do?"

"Just what I said I was. I'm going to hang him."

"You can't do that. You got to wait for the Rangers."

"My boy'll sleep easy tonight. The man responsible for killing him will be dead."

"Mister Titus. . . ."

"Your work is finished, Dundee. I'm taking over now.

We'll wait till the men get back. Then we'll take Roan to a fit place out yonder on the river. Runaway is fixing to die. We'll let him die with it."

Dundee glanced sadly at the aging outlaw, his eyes trying to tell Roan he was sorry now that he hadn't gotten away. Roan seemed to understand. "Don't worry yourself, Dundee. I already lived beyond my time. I wouldn't lie to you; I don't want to die. But I reckon I've had my day."

Dundee walked into the saloon, sick at heart. He rummaged around behind the bar and came up with part of a bottle of whisky. He stood in the door, leaning his shoulder against the jamb, drinking straight out of the bottle and watching the cowboys slowly drift in, bringing their prisoners with them—one here, two there, three in another bunch. Roan Hardesty sat slumped in a chair that had been dragged out into the street, the cowboys ringed around him. John Titus still sat on his horse, his leathery old face dark and grim.

A buckboard came down the street. Leaning out the door, Dundee saw Katy Long, a thin girl riding beside her. The girl was Lutie. The cowboys turned to stare. Katy pulled her team to a halt and took a long, apprehensive look at Roan Hardesty. Then her eyes went to Dundee. She jumped down from the buckboard and motioned for Lutie to follow. The girl moved slowly, reluctantly. Katy rushed to Dundee's side.

"What're they going to do to Roan?"

"John Titus says he's fixing to hang him."

"He can't."

"With all them cowboys? He can do anything he damn pleases."

"It's not right, Dundee. Roan didn't kill Son Titus."

"You know it, and I know it. I think even John Titus knows it. But we can't prove which one of his men did do it, so Roan pays."

Katy's eyes turned blue with regret. "Dundee, I've got something to tell you. I didn't want to, didn't intend to. But now it's the only way. It's got to be done."

"Tell me what?"

"I'll let Lutie." She motioned for the girl. Lutie came to her unwillingly, dragging her feet, looking at the floor. "Lutie, you tell Dundee what you told me."

When Lutie's story was over, Dundee found his left fist clenched so tightly the knuckles were white. He lifted the bottle and took a long, long swallow. He cut his eyes to the girl and demanded threateningly, "You sure you ain't lying to me?"

Frightened, Lutie shook her head. Katy said protectively: "She's telling the truth, Dundee. Added to everything else, it figures."

Dundee turned and hurled the bottle at the saloon wall. It shattered, the whisky spattering and running down to the floor. He rubbed his hand across his face, then stalked out into the street. He strode to where John Titus sat on his horse.

"Mister Titus, you've trusted me for weeks now. Do you still trust me?"

Surprised, the old ranchman said, "Sure, Dundee."

"Then trust me when I tell you old Blue Roan didn't kill your boy. It wasn't Roan, and it wasn't none of Roan's men."

"Then who was it?"

"I can't tell you yet. I know, but it's something I got to handle myself. Trust me."

"Dundee, I got to have more to go on than this. I got to. . . ."

"You got to wait. You got to let Roan live till I get back. Then you'll know the whole thing. Will you do that? Will you trust me?"

The old man stammered. "I ought not to . . . But I will, Dundee. I'll wait."

Dundee turned. "Katy, if I ain't back in a reasonable time, you tell John Titus what you told me."

Katy's voice held a tremor. "Dundee, you better take some help with you."

He shook his head. "This job I got to handle alone." He mounted the bay and rode toward the hill.

14

Ahead of him lay the creek, and beyond that the Mc-Cown headquarters. Face rigid, his jaw set square, Dundee rode toward the spring where Uncle Ollie McCown sat watching him. Ollie had his fishing pole, the hook sunk into the water below the spring.

"Howdy, Dundee," he called. "You-all do up your business in Runaway?"

Dundee stared hard at the old man, wondering how much he knew. "Ollie, I'm looking for Warren."

The tone of his voice betrayed him, for Ollie shrank back. Dundee could see realization sinking in. "Ollie, I asked you, where's Warren at?"

Ollie's voice was strained. "Big bunch of men rode by here some hours ago, on their way to help you-all. I reckon you took good care of old Roan and his bunch by now, didn't you?"

Now Dundee was convinced: Ollie knew. He might not have participated, but he knew.

"Ollie, I know the whole thing now. I'll ask you one more time, where's Warren?"

Ollie looked down at the water. "Dundee, Millie's up at the house. I bet she'll be real tickled to see you back. She baked up some cookies. They'd sure go good with a cup of coffee. I bet you and her could find a right smart to talk about." He paused, trying to gather strength. "She thinks the world of you, Dundee. If you was to ask her, she'd marry you in a minute. You could do a lot worse. She's a good girl."

"Ollie, does she know anything about this?"

Quickly the old man blurted: "She don't know nothing, Dundee. Warren didn't tell her nothing, and he'd of beat me to death if I'd ever even hinted to her. . . ." He realized he had said too much. He looked down at the fishing line again. Cold sweat broke on his forehead.

Dundee said, "Ollie, I still want to know . . ."

The old man wiped his sleeve over his face. "Sure is hot." His voice was almost gone. He was on the verge of crying. "Seems like it gets hotter every year. Things ain't what they used to be. Things has gone to hell, seems like. Time was when the world was fresh and sweet as dew. Now everything's got a bitter taste, and there's no pleasure left in being alive. It's hell to be an old man, Dundee."

Pitying him, Dundee turned away.

He rode to the house. Millie came out into the doorway, trying to brush back her long hair with her hand. She smiled, and her face was so pretty Dundee could feel his heart tearing in two. The joy that danced in her eyes brought the bite of tears to his own.

"Dundee, is it all over with? Are you all right?"

He clenched his teeth and tried not to look at her. He couldn't help it; he had to look, and he felt his throat tighten. "Millie, I've got to see Warren. Is he here?"

She caught the gravity in his eyes now, and in his voice. Her joy faded, and worry rushed in. "He's up yonder working on his rock corrals. What's the matter, Dundee?"

He looked toward the rock pens that were the symbol of a man's driving ambition, of a poverty-born obsession for acquiring land and cattle, for building a protective wall of stolen wealth around him so that never again could he slide back into the squalor that had scarred his soul.

Millie demanded: "There's something wrong, Dundee. What is it?"

"I'll have to let Warren tell you."

He pulled away from her and rode toward the pens. He didn't dare look back, but he knew she was standing there watching him, confusion and fear crowding in around her. Though she did not know it yet, her world was about to come tumbling down; her anchor of security was about to be dragged away.

Warren McCown stood behind a half-finished rock fence, sweat soaking his dirt-crusted shirt and rolling down his sun-browned face. Dundee guessed that by his own appearance and manner he was betraying himself, for he could see suspicion in Warren McCown.

"What's the trouble, Dundee?"

"Maybe you ought to tell *me*, Warren. Maybe you ought to tell me what really happened to Son Titus."

Warren tensed. They stared at each other a long time in silence. "You know as much as I do, Dundee."

"Maybe, I think I've figured out some things now. For one thing, I know why you used to have trouble with Roan Hardesty and his men. It wasn't for the reason you said, that they was driving stolen cattle across your land. It was because you was in competition with them. Old Roan wanted to run things in this country, but you was stealing for yourself and wouldn't split anything with him.

"That time you went south to buy cattle . . . you went north first. You stole T Bar cattle from old Titus, drove them south and traded them for cattle that had been stole down on the border. That way you didn't have any T Bar stuff on your country."

"You got an awful imagination, Dundee."

"Not very. That cowboy that helped you . . . first thing he done when he left here was to head for Runaway to fill his belly full of liquor and wrap himself around a soft, warm town girl. He told her things he ought to've kept to himself. Then Son Titus came along, and he found that girl. He got her drunk enough that she told him things *she* ought to've kept quiet. Last time he left Runaway he was coming out here to face you with the facts. Somewhere out yonder you ran into each other, and you killed him."

Warren McCown rubbed his sweaty hands on the legs of his britches. "What you figure on doing, Dundee?"

"I figure on taking you to the Rangers. If old John Titus gets hold of you, he'll hang you."

Warren's face twisted in bitterness. "Titus. It's always been a Titus. I told you my daddy died on a ranch, didn't I, Dundee? But I didn't tell you which one. It was the

Titus ranch. Daddy had dragged us there just the week before, the way he dragged us everywhere, hungry and broke and wearing castoff clothes that nobody else wanted. Old man John Titus was so big he didn't know the names of half his men. I doubt he ever even seen my daddy. Son Titus was just a button then but spoiled rotten as a barrelful of bad apples. He was playing around the herd instead of tending to his job, and he let a big steer get out. Daddy spurred off after him, and his horse fell. Daddy never knew what hit him. They buried him right there on the Titus ranch, gave us kids a couple of months' wages and told us how bad they felt. Well, John Titus has owed us something for that, something a lot more than a little handful of money."

"He didn't owe you his boy's life."

"I didn't want to kill him. He forced it on me. Said he'd take away everything we had and burn our place to the ground. I'd put in too many years of sweat. I couldn't let him wreck us."

"I got to take you in, Warren. Maybe a jury will see your side and go easy."

"And what happens to Millie? What happens to this place? No, Dundee. You're not taking me anywhere."

Dundee reached for his pistol. Warren moved suddenly, crouching behind the rock fence and coming up with a rifle.

Dundee shouted: "Don't be a fool, Warren. Kill me and there'll be others. There'll be no end to it."

But he saw the intention in Warren's eyes as the rifle came up into line. Dundee threw himself off the bay as the first shot exploded. He went down on his hands and knees. For a couple of seconds he was shielded by the frightened horse. He used that time to get moving toward another section of rock fence. He vaulted over and dropped behind it as the rifle cracked again.

At the house he heard Millie screaming. He glanced in that direction and saw Uncle Ollie hobbling up as fast as he could from the spring. Millie ran toward the corral, crying: "Warren! Dundee!"

Dundee raised up enough to see over the fence. He leveled the pistol where he thought Warren would come up. He saw the top of Warren's head, then the rifle. Warren arose, drawing a bead. This time, Dundee knew with a sickening certainty, Warren wasn't going to miss. Not if Dundee let him fire.

Dundee squeezed the trigger. He saw Warren lurch back, heard the rifle clatter against the stone. He jumped up and ran around the fence. Under his breath he was praying.

He stopped abruptly, his blood cold. He turned, and then Millie came running, crying, "Warren! What did you do to Warren?"

Dundee grabbed her. "Millie, don't go back there!"

She beat at him with her fists. Hysterically she screamed: "Let me go! Let me go!" She twisted away from him and ran on. At the fence she stopped, her voice lifting in agony.

The bay had tangled in the reins a little way toward the house. Walking in that direction, Dundee met the struggling Ollie McCown. The old man looked at him, his eyes begging. "God, Dundee, how am I going to tell her?"

Dundee shook his head, his eyes afire so that he could

barely see. "I don't know, Ollie. I don't know if you ever can."

The ride to town was one of the longest Dundee had ever made, seemed like. It was full dark long before he got there. He found the cowboys scattered in the buildings up and down the long, crooked street. The Rangers had arrived to take charge and collect any prisoners on whom they had claims. Katy Long was back in her saloon, serving liquor to John Titus.

The old man looked up as Dundee walked through the door into the lamplight. His eyes seemed to have softened now. Maybe it was Katy's whisky.

"Dundee, where's McCown?"

Tightly Dundee said, "He's dead."

The old man nodded gravely. "This girl here, she told me the whole thing, once you was a long ways down the road. I reckon it was tough on you."

"Life's always been tough on me."

John Titus pushed the bottle at Dundee. Dundee took it, though he absently rolled it in his hands instead of drinking from it. "Where's Tobe Crane?"

Somebody went out and fetched the cowboy. Dundee looked up painfully. "Tobe, Warren McCown is dead. I killed him." He took a long drink then, and followed it with another. "Millie's the one who'll suffer the most. She needs somebody right now. I think she needs *you*."

The cowboy just stood and stared at him.

Impatiently Dundee demanded: "You love her, don't you? You as much as told me so."

"I love her, Dundee."

"Then go to her. She'll never need you more than she needs you now."

Tobe turned to go. Dundee said: "And Tobe . . . you be real good to that girl, you hear me?"

"I will."

Dundee turned back to the bottle. He didn't quit drinking till his head was starting to spin. It occurred to him suddenly that he hadn't seen Roan Hardesty. He half-shouted: "Where's Roan? John Titus, you promised me. . . ."

Titus shook his head. "Don't worry. Roan has took to the tulies." He pointed his stubbled chin toward Katy Long "After this girl here told me what she did, I got to thinking. When the Rangers got here, they'd take old Roan and lock him up, and he'd never see sunlight again the rest of his days. He's an old man, Roan is. He ain't got many years left."

"You mean you just let him go?"

"We was friends once. *He* remembered it. He couldn't bring himself to shoot me. After I found out the truth of what happened to Son, I couldn't bring myself to see him rot away in a cell the few years he's got left. So I told him to head south for Mexico."

"He's liable to take some of your cattle with him as he goes."

Titus looked surprised, as if that thought hadn't occurred to him. Then he shrugged. "You can't expect an old man to go hungry."

Next morning the Rangers had picked out the men they intended to take to jail. The rest of the prisoners were turned loose and advised to see how far they could get without stopping to rest their horses.

Titus' foreman, Strother James, looked down the emptying street. "It'll be a funny-looking town, nobody living in it."

Titus said: "It won't be no town atall. We're going to burn it."

"All of it?"

"Every stick. Get the men started at the job."

They began at the far end, setting the buildings afire one at a time. Some had rock walls that wouldn't burn, but the roofs would go, and the floors if they had any.

Dundee said: "Mister Titus, I got money coming. I'd like to collect it now and be on my way."

Disappointed, Titus said: "We need you here, Dundee. I was hoping you'd stay."

Dundee shook his head. "I studied on it awhile, but I'm afraid this part of the country is spoiled for me now. It's best I go on."

"Any idea where?"

"West someplace. Don't make much difference."

"I ain't got much cash with me. I'll give you all I got and send the rest on to a bank where you can pick it up. How about Pecos City?"

Dundee shrugged. "Pecos City would be all right. I expect it's a good place to get drunk."

Katy Long had her team hitched to the buckboard and was carrying out what belongings she could pack into it. A couple of cowboys were helping her load a trunk. Dundee looked down the street where the plumes of smoke were rising. They'd be to the Llano River Saloon in a few minutes now, sprinkling kerosene, striking matches.

Dundee said, "Too bad about your place here."

She didn't appear upset. "It's worn itself out anyhow. There are other places down the road, fresh places."

"Got any particular one in mind?"

"Nope. Thought I might ride along with you if it's all right. A woman alone . . . no telling what might happen."

He shook his head. "You can take care of yourself; I don't worry none about that. As for me, I got some problems to think out. It's better I ride by myself. *Adios,* Katy. Maybe I'll see you someplace."

He swung up onto his horse, nodded at John Titus and took the trail that led around the bluff and west from Runaway.

John Titus disconsolately watched him go. "Dundee's a good man. I hate to lose him."

Katy said, "*I* don't intend to lose him."

"I'm sending him some money. He's supposed to pick it up in Pecos City," Titus suggested. He looked at the girl, and his eyes came as near smiling as they had in a long time. "Whichaway you headed?"

She arched her wrist as invitation for one of the cowboys to help her into the buckboard. Half a dozen rushed to do it. Seated, she smiled back at the old ranchman.

"I've been thinking I'd try Pecos City."

She flipped the lines, and the team took her west, while the dark smoke that had been Runaway rose into the blue summer skies and slowly dissipated over the rocky Llano River hills.